1741

Robert Mayer

To Nat Gertler

1741

Copyright 2015 by Robert Mayer. (WWW.ROBERTMAYERAUTHOR.COM)
All rights reserved.

This is a work of fiction. Any resemblance to living individuals is unintended.

ISBN-13: 978-1936404-51-3

Published by Combustoica, a prose project of About Comics.
WWW.Combustoica.COM

For rights inquiries, contact RIGHTS@ABOUTCOMICS.COM

Published May, 2015.

1741

Robert Mayer

Combustoica, a prose project of About Comics
Camarillo, California

The boundary between history and fiction at the time was decidedly blurred. Histories could be fancifully elaborated, and the first English novels, Defoe's Robinson Crusoe *(1719) and Swift's* Gulliver's Travels *(1726) adapted the trappings of histories. But unlike most histories, novels had, at their heart, ordinary people trying to make sense of an extraordinary world.*

–Jill Lepore
New York Burning

Perhaps I didn't live just in my self, perhaps I lived the lives of others.

–Pablo Neruda
Memoirs

Foreword:
Flesh for the Damned

The names are real.

Peggy Kerry. Mary Burton. John Hughson. Caesar (a *nom-de-slave.*)

They lived in the heart of one of the darkest episodes in American history, an astonishing sequence of events that not one in a thousand Americans is aware of – perhaps not one in a hundred thousand.

Google their names – they would have enjoyed the sound of that word, even chuckled at it – and you will find a reference to them here and there. Names and fates – but little more. Names without flesh. Fates without blood.

Writing history as a novel can bring forgotten names to life – even if not precisely the lives they lived.

Caesar, tall and charcoal-black, upon arriving enslaved from Africa, was purchased by a baker in the City of New York, and resided there, to his peril, in the year of frequent fires 1741. Peggy, a winsome, red-haired young Irish woman, had left her home in Newfoundland and sailed to the burgeoning colony in search of – what? Surely not what she found. Mary, also a child of Ireland, sent across the sea as an indentured servant, became through her own machinations as powerful, at the age of sixteen, as a god.

Who could foresee any of this? Yet it is all true.

Their three disparate lives came together – not probably, but provably – in a jaunty boarding house not far from the Hudson River – the North River then – an establishment of drink and feast and desire run by one John Hughson. All this is historic fact. Yet their disembodied names have not been burned into our histories, or into our consciences, where surely they belong. Perhaps by attaching lives to their names – even speculative lives – we can rectify this oversight. At least we can try.

Part One: 1739

1. Caesar

Iku Bursit. The most feared words in the *Muktu* language.

Literally, *A leaf floats on the water.*

Idiomatically, *A ship is approaching port.*

The lookout, naked to the waist, swimming in sweat, slim black chest glistening, white band around his dark head echoing his white muslin waist cloth, staggers, falls. His name is Beto. He has run seven miles through the forest from the thorny hillock. He struggles to his feet, falls again, gagging with dust. Falls at the feet of King James, the leader of the village, after blurting his message. The king, the boy's older brother, offers him drink from a bladder hanging from his hip.

The floor of the forest is yellow. Soon it will be red with the blood of his people. Some will die. Most will be marched away, never to see wives, husbands, children again.

The young king knows this. He has been expecting this. He must prepare the people to resist. Knowing that resistance is futile. Knowing that his people will disappear, that the village and a thousand years of ancestors will soon be nothing more than eddies of dust in the uncaring wind.

From their hut near the end of the village, mud walls covered with thatch, huts identical one to another, like green bananas, Triana comes running, waist cloth longer and stained with red berries, as is the female fashion. Tender breasts bare.

Your brother has no breath. What made him run so long? What did he say? Careful of the baby.

The baby is fine. What did he tell you, James?

Iku Bursit. A leaf floats on the water. A ship is approaching port.

You believe The Others will come!

James does not answer. He is remembering, withdrawing bloody entrails from the belly of the past. It was almost a year ago when his grandfather King John died of age. Even before his body was buried the elders sat deep in the forest on their sacred circle of fallen trees, beneath hanging green limbs, and looked one upon another, and knew that before long each of them would shrivel, too. The new king must be tall, dark, strong, young, especially young – young enough to lead the village for half a hundred years. Only James Dumo was discussed. Only he was intelligent enough, brave enough. There was no other choice.

They asked his mother how many years he had. She had shown them the scratches in the mud wall beside where he had slept as a child. She still added a new mark each summer. She could not tell them why.

His years are four and twenty, she said.

James wanted neither the honor nor the responsibility. He preferred to hunt in the forest by himself, to study the leaves on the trees and the insects that rode them like waves, to sit in the rain and ponder the reasons for life, for bloody birth, for wind, for dreams. But to the elders he could not say no.

Drums boomed the approval of the people. A feast of charred elephant was devoured. The new king, wooden spear in hand, white waist cloth exchanged for royal red, his smoothly muscled chest bare, began his ritual run around the outer reaches of the cluster of huts. In forgotten days this run was to seek a pathway in the forest through which the village, if desired, could expand. Now the run was mostly ceremonial. As he jogged in his blood-red waist cloth, James thought: a king should be a spirited leader, a beast of action. A lion. He felt like an impostor.

Half way around and far to his right as he ran he heard a woman's scream, then another. Leaping over browning brush he flew in that direction. He came upon young Triana, his cousin, lying in the dirt, her cloth ripped off, a heavy warrior pressing above her, taking her by force, while two Other waterside warriors watched, their tribal *jakmil* – their sharpened teeth – gleaming as they grinned, one with a face painted yellow. James sprung among them, pressed the sharp tip of his spear into the ear of the man above her.

Stand, or die!

A lazy wind blew a dirge through leafy trees. Feeling the point of the lance in his ear, the confused warrior unfolded, stood. The sight of his still extended member flashed lightning in the new king's eyes; his head erupted in thunder. Instantly he thrust the spear into the warrior's exposed belly – the spear was not tipped with metal, only the waterside trading tribes had metal, and kept it for themselves – but James jabbed hard, harder, until the wooden point emerged from the bloodied man's back. The stricken warrior began to dance as if his entrails were burning, all the while screaming loud enough to poison the in-rushing sea. The two Others hesitated – two being superior to one – yet reluctant to fight this man, black as a burned tree, who would kill so fiercely over a girl.

Perhaps they were stragglers lost in the forest after a distant raid. Perhaps they were scouts planning the next raid. At that moment it hardly mattered. Pulling a small red hatchet from his hip, the symbol of his new position, to be worn as long as he lived – worn always, the elders

had said, to keep him alive – King James chopped off the lower end of
the spear, grabbed the splintery wood, its tiny tentacles stinging his palm,
drawing spits of blood. As he stared at The Others the whites of his eyes
shone bright in the forest dark. He strode toward them. They turned and
ran. Yellow-face paused to shout: *Boku Mas! Boku Mas!*

We will be back.

For nearly a year the young king had lived within the echo of those
words. He heard of raids on distant tribes. For nearly a year his people
were not attacked. Now it was coming.

Triana seemed always to read his thoughts. *Do you think those same two
will come?*

*It does not matter. The Others, with their sharpened teeth, are all the same. There
will be many.*

He had lifted her nakedness back then, carried her to the village, lay
her on his mat, covered her with a blanket yellow and green.

How was it they lured you from the village? he had asked. As king he
needed to know such things. *They pretended they were ill. I brought them water.*

He had guarded her in his hut for two impatient months while she
recovered. Then, lying together, her head resting serenely on his chest, he
told her he wanted her to be his wife.

I cannot be the wife of the king. I am no longer pure.

*Be still. You are young, you are strong, you are courageous. You will give us future
kings.*

All too often thinking, *Boku Mas.* They will be back.

Now a ship is approaching port. When it docks it will deposit sheafs
of tobacco, barrels of sugar, bolts of cotton cloth, gallons of rum, from
across the accursed sea. The Makli will pay the white traders. One bolt
of cloth, he has heard, costs four strong men. Fifty gallons of rum costs a
woman. They will pay with our bodies. Our souls.

Likat likati!

The village has been here since time began. He does not know why
what is happening now is happening now.

Purple clouds drift into view high above the village. Sometimes these
are precursors of death. Sometimes not. Only the beasts of the forest
know.

Today, James, too, knows.

Triana kicks at the foot of Beto, who has fallen asleep on the sullen
leaves. The boy murmurs, does not wake. She laughs; is surprised at
herself; is horrified. Knows she will laugh again if he sleeps through
rain. At the edge of the forest the year-old skeleton lies concave, eyes
long gone, ripped out by birds, flesh stripped and stolen by hyenas, rib

cage pressing outward, upward, held off the ground by four slim inches of broken, greying spear. The teeth in the smiling skull are sharp as the pointed wood. The nettles and other flora of the forest floor have not grown back to shield the bones from view, as if the soil itself were bowing obeisance to the king. Sometimes in their play the children dance around the bones, dare one another to touch the fleshless feet. None do.

She takes the hand of her husband the king and leads him to their hut so he may rest; so he may ponder how to resist. On a barren branch of a tree high outside their hut he sees a parrot, blue, green, turquoise, watching him; cocking its head to the side as if to see him clearly. There are no such bold-looking parrots in the region; parrots in the forest are grey. They rarely enter the village. Perhaps this one fluttered onto a ship on the other side of the world and sailed across the sea with the tobacco and the sugar and the cloth, and alighted on the noisy dock and squawked its way through the forest, mating with the leaves, until it landed on this branch, watching. Of this he ponders as he awaits the dreamy thoughts that soothe right-thinking men before sleep.

It is the first time he has seen this parrot.

The white traders, he knows, have been moving down the coast for years, leaving silent villages behind, villages now abandoned to the forest and the earth and nature's dull decay. The elders have known this, too. He accepts against his will that they foresaw what was coming when they named him king. His forehead breeds sweat in the chill of the night. He asks the spirit of his grandfather what he should do. The dead king is silent as the grave in which he lies. Uprooting every blade and nettle in the forest of his brain, James cannot find the intellect of his grandfather; he knows he does not possess it – although wise King John never faced obliteration by such an enemy, and if he had, he might have stumbled on the same sad question. How to resist.

Likat likatu!

Why is what is happening happening *now?*

Exhausted, rolling onto his side, he gently rests his palm on Triana's tender breast. Foreboding fingers of fog invade his brain. There is no good way to resist.

2. PEGGY

~~Marguerite.~~ Margaret. Peggy.

She no longer knows who she is.

Every person in the village calls her Peggy. So she must be Peggy. But she feels that she is not. She is one of the other two. She does not know which.

Because everyone on the island smells of fish does not mean that is the true smell of people. Even Father Mallory in his black blouse and white collar, whom one would think would smell of God, does not smell of God; he, too, smells of fish. The priest does not work with the fish, not like her father and Auntie Dottie and the haulers and the trawlers and the fish cleaners like herself – everyone on the island, including Billy Reilly, before he sailed for New York – Billy smelled sweat-sweet, once you sniffed past the cod – everyone except the smallest children. Once when she was one of those children she asked Father Mallory in the cold Sunday-school room why he did not work with the fish, like everyone else.

Because I gather souls. I am a fisher of men.

She did not know exactly what souls were or if they smelled like cod but she smiled her slightly crooked smile when she pictured in her mind the priest on the deck of a trawler, the wind scrambling his thin grey hair, awkwardly wrestling a huge rope net into the sea. Pulling it up later dripping with waterlogged men. The fishermen sold the cod that were trapped in their nets. She did not know what Father Mallory did with his men.

Hundreds of fishermen from home in Ireland and homes in other places have battled the waves to reach this place called Newfoundland, her father, Travis Kerry, had told her, and built cottages on the rocky cliffs overlooking the sea, not seeking God, who was hard to find, but to catch the cod, which wasn't hard at all, her father said, except for the work.

Peggy rolled her sleeves to her elbows, opened the cold pantry, pulled out two *bakal* – two large, dried cod. One of life's circular mockeries, she thought. Last summer when her half-drunk father brought in the family's portion of the cod she had to cut off their heads, drain their blood, remove their entrails, salt them, lay them on the rocks outside to be dried by the sun and the wind. That was the only way they would last through the winter. Now in the spring, when her father wanted to eat the last of them before the new schools of cod arrived, she had to place them in water to remove the salt and soak their liquid back in. Strange roundabout. She was glad she did not have to sew their heads back on, but even so she seemed always to smell of fish.

She was not sure if Margaret or ~~Marguerite~~ smelled of fish, because she had learned of their hidden existence not long before. It was on the day she received her first letter from Billy, a few weeks after he left. Wearing her white mob cap and her beige muslin dress in the warm spring weather, she had walked quickly, almost run, to Neal's Pub-Cafe, where the mail was left when there was mail and an Irish flag was hung outside to signify so. After many disappointments, this time there was a letter for her.

> Dear Peg O My Heart,
>
>   The ship ride was mostly smooth. I found a room in a boarding house near the sea called Hughson's. Tomorrow I start looking for work so I can earn enough money to send for you. Will rite more later as there is a boat leaving soon that is taking on postal letters and I want to get there rite away. Mr. H says you never know when the next postal boat will come.
>
> Your loving boy friend William Charles Reilly III.

When she paused outside the pub to read again the too-short note, she overheard two fishermen who were drinking beer at the bar.

Did you see that Kerry girl? Prettiest face and finest arse this side of Pouch Cove. Maybe this side of County Cork.

Them dark green eyes, that mess o' wild red hair. I wonder if it's red ... you know. I'd divorce my wife, kids and all, for a juicy taste of that every night.

Divorce? I'd drown mine in the bay. What's she see in the cobbler's boy, anyway? He's a bit of a sod, with that blonde curly hair and them schoolboy looks. He's twenty-three if he's a day.

Love is blind they say.

Ya think he's gettin' any?

From Peggy Kerry? Nah. She was raised real strict by that Auntie of hers. She's a good girl, people say.

Her cheeks had reddened, looked like two small cherry pies.

As she walked home she read the note four times. Showed it to Auntie Dottie, though not to her father, he was still out on the boat with a growler of beer. He would not have cared anyway; get her out of the house, she's seventeen, almost eighteen, high time someone else paid her keep.

Kneeling on the worn heels of her boots, which Billy's father had made for her as an engagement gift, she pulled her wooden box from under her bed, lifted the lid, placed the letter on top of her other valuables – and saw a folded yellow paper in the box, which she had never noticed before. When she pulled it out it felt old, almost crumbly. Later she would remember that touching the paper felt like being bitten by a cat, but that probably was not the case then. Unfolding the paper she stepped to the window, where the late afternoon sun strained to filter in through dark clouds over the roiling seas, and she read what seemed to be a notice from the government far away. Sentences of small printed words, with *whereases* and *caused to be born this* 17th *day of* June, *anno domini 1721* – just the day and then names written large in blue ink by her father, or perhaps by Auntie Dottie. The names said ~~Marguerite~~ Margaret (Kerry.) Just like that, an ink line drawn through ~~Marguerite.~~

That's your birth paper. I put it in your box so you won't forget it when Billy sends for you. Auntie Dottie in her extra wide rocking chair made special by her late husband Roald was darning socks near the open door. *Sometimes when you move to a big colony like New York they want a paper.*

But what does it mean, these names?

Auntie Dottie, still sitting, took the form from her, examined it.

Lord Almighty! Papa never told you about your sister?

Sister? I don't have a sister.

Once upon a time you did, honey. Or did not. It was hard to tell back then.

Auntie, you're not making sense.

And so she told her. The birth had come early, when her mother Betsy-Ann started to bleed before her time. The midwife Mrs. Brogan who was just about retired perched beside her bed. There was a lot of blood. A whole lot of blood. Mrs. Brogan shook her greying head, found the head of the baby coming out, helped it into the air.

What's her name? Auntie Dottie, watching from the foot of the bed, holding warm damp towels, called this out to Travis Kerry in the kitchen. *Patrick,* he called back.

It's a girl, Dottie shouted.

Well, dang. A girl is Marguerite. That's what Betsy picked. After her French grandmother.

My goodness, the midwife said, *here comes another. Wipe the blood off Marguerite!* she ordered Dottie, while she assisted the second head to emerge. *I don't know why there is so much blood.*

Dottie said, *Lord help us, the cord is twisted around baby Marguerite's neck. She may be … I'm not sure.* She yelled to Travis that it was twin girls.

Two girls? I don't know. Margaret, he said.

Marguerite and Margaret?

That's what I said, didn't I. One will wind up Peggy, what do I care which?

Travis swallowed a long pull of spirits. It was not his first that afternoon. Nor his second.

The second baby was healthy, but the first was dead. The midwife could not tell if the infant has been born dead or if it had strangled on the cord in the air. As for the bleeding river, she could not stop it.

That's when my mother went to Heaven?

And your twin sister. When we cleaned you up and lay you side by side on a blanket, with that same red hair you both had, what you still have, we couldn't tell you apart. Except that Marguerite was dead, of course. That's why there's a line through her name.

Why didn't anyone tell me before?

Peggy thought she should be crying for her sister. She was too confused.

Your father said you had no need to know. I figure you're old enough now.

So it was that the next afternoon, when she had finished her daily chores – cleaning fish, dusting, sweeping the sand out the door – she met her best friend Nora Neal at the pub-cafe that Nora's father owned, where Nora worked as a barmaid, and together they walked away from the cabins toward the sharply up-sloping cliff set back from the sea.

I don't understand why you want to go to the church. It's not Sunday.

Not to the church. The cemetery.

Same thing. Why do you want to climb up that rocky path? It could be slippery with the sun going down.

To see my sister's grave.

You don't have a sister.

That's why I need to see her grave. Aunt Dottie told me about it yesterday. But sometimes she gets things wrong. Or makes things up.

Nora blinked her pale blue eyes several times, as was her habit, shrugged, said no more. Peggy could be ornery, would explain in due course. They held one another's hand, and wearing their white mob caps and dark brown muslin dresses they might have been two nuns climbing to pray in the steepled white church, which looked out over the sea from atop the slope, or visiting the cemetery beside it, where the best waterfront views on the island were reserved for the dead.

How will you know where to look?

It must be near my mother's grave. I've never even seen that.

How come?

Papa forbid it. Says he hates Betsy-Ann, for leaving him alone when she was only eighteen. And with a girl to raise, instead of five strapping boys to help with the fish.

You help with the fish.

Cleaning and salting doesn't count. That's women's work. Like having babies. She could have lived to have ten more babes, he says, and most of them boys. Lazy is all that girl was, he says.

Seems to me it was your aunt who raised you, not him. So he thinks if he drinks enough it will turn you into a boy?

He'd love that miracle.

Then he might love you, too.

I wouldn't count on it.

The iron gate to the cemetery was never locked. As if the church was saying anyone wanting to rob a grave this far up on the cliff was welcome to it, there were easier ways to acquire fish bait. Entering through the rusty swivel, Peggy and Nora twisted separately among the weeds and bushes that had grown up among the stones. Some grave sites had been weeded neatly and the stones were easy to read. Boylan. Hutchins. Curtis. Others were mostly hidden by gnarled branches and broken twigs. Peggy was beginning to despair when Nora called out that she had found her mother's. She was standing near a rear corner fence strung with timidly greening vines. Peggy hurried over, stumbling over a fallen tree as if she, not her father, had been drinking.

Betsy-Ann Kerry. That was your mama, right?

Approaching, hesitating, Peggy looked about fearfully. She saw no other stone nearby. She knelt on a patch of gravel to honor the mother she never knew. Made the sign of the cross across her breasts, as they had been taught in Sunday school long ago. Her armpits were wet with sweat. She realized that for an infant the stone would be small. Dropping to her knees, she parted the weeds and grass that grew where her mother's head would be. Her fingers touched something hard. She scrambled closer, pushed away clumps of green. A small stone lay flat, cringing from the greying sky. A person would not have seen it if they weren't looking for it. She leaned closer to read the small letters, tracing them with her fingers. With no warning she pitched over, turned her head to the side, tried to vomit. Nothing came up as she coughed, choked on damp dryness.

Peggy, what is it?

Nora knelt beside her. Peggy recaptured her breath.

You're a better speller than me. Read what it says.

It says Margaret.

Letter by letter. Read it to me letter by letter.

M A R G A R E T.

Peggy's nose was cold. She sniffled. Her back was hurting. With difficulty she sat up, looked at her friend. Put her hand on Nora's knee.

That's me buried under there. Not ~~Marguerite~~.

Don't be silly.
That's what it says.
Peggy, it's just a mistake. The stonecutter spelled it wrong.
If he spelled it wrong they could have had him fix it.
If they had noticed. I mean …
You're right. If they had noticed.

A white sea bird circled in from the water, high above the church, swooped down toward the cemetery, touched the fence for a moment, then as if changing its mind pinged away, around the church and out over the sea again. The two girls sat silently among the graves, holding hands. Nora, though reluctant, was the first to speak.

We'd better go back, Peg. We don't want to climb down that rocky excuse for a path in the dark. A person could twist an ankle and get killed.

Maybe it's time for me to get killed. My mother was eighteen when she died.

Don't talk like that. My plan is that we both live to sixty. We'll have no teeth, but we could still gab away.

Here or in New York colony?

Whichever.

Helping each other stand, they hugged close, as if warding off danger. They pressed their lips to one another's cheeks. Then lips to lips, lightly. Brushed sandy soil from their skirts. Wended their way slowly through the brambles toward the top of the path. The sun was half an orange sinking into the sea, shooting fiery waterlogged flames toward the beach. Nora straightened Peggy's cap, which had twisted askew when she leaned beside the grave. Tucked in a flaming red curl that rarely stayed put.

So, what were you thinking about back there? If you want to talk.

The truth? I was thinking about Billy. About which is the me he'll want.

3. MARY

Denture. I never heard that word. Or how to say it. Or what it meant. Until the day the captain come.

Sister Beatrice, the headmistress, said that me being at fourteen years of age the oldest ward, and still not adopted, she loved me like a mother but it was time now for us to part ways. That is what she said. *Part Ways.* They had too many other mouths to feed, she said, *maybe if I had been prettier … or taller …but under church law they had to move me out to make room for infants.* One day a ship's captain came from the Donegal harbor with a round face red from the sun and twinkly pale blue eyes. He had me turn around in my best petticoats and took off his black sea-going cap and said, *She'll Do.* I was glad that I would *Do*, I hated the orphanage. The ship's captain gave her money and he and Sister Beatrice both signed a yellow paper which he tore jaggedly in half and they each kept half. With her pinched face and sharp nose that sniffed a lot the headmistress smiled, which she hardly ever did. I wanted to hug her goodbye, but she turned away, she didn't want to hug her oldest child – her oldest ward. Suddenly I was afraid. I did not want to leave. Maybe as she looked away she was smiling about that torn paper; maybe she was crying about it. Maybe both at the same time, as people can. I thought the other kids or at least some of them would come out to yell and wave goodbye, but none of them did. I guess they was locked inside, so as not to be jealous.

I hugged Sister Beatrice. She surprised me by handing me a box that felt heavy and also rattled when I shook it. It sounded like candy.

Something to remember us by, she said.

I said I would remember the Orphanage with every bite.

She looked at me funny. *While practicing your ABCs.*

I was confused. I was about to run from her. But with my first step she grabbed my wrist with her strong skinny fingers and held on. I knew I could pull away from her but the orphanage was surrounded by a tall wooden fence. When last year on my third try to escape I almost reached the top, Higgins, the handyman and driver, pulled me down. And they made it harder. Higgins spent two whole days digging a deep ditch all along the inside of the fence, so I couldn't get nowhere near the top anymore.

Why did you tear that paper in half? I asked, making believe I had no thought in the world of running away. Where could I go and hide, anyway?

So we can prove it was the same paper.

But it was the same paper before you tore it.

The captain put his sea-going black cap back on. I figured I had said something smart.

These torn places are called indentures. I'll explain when we're on board.

Can I say goodbye to my horse?

You have a horse?

Gweebarra. That's where she was borned. She's not really mine, but I ride her more than anyone. Sometimes if I can't sleep I cuddle up and sleep in the barn with her.

And get whipped for it afterward. Well, Mary, it's not up to me anymore. It's the captain who owns you now.

Who owns me? Anger shivered down my body, my legs. *You make it sound like I'm a new pair of boots.*

Not really, Mary. I'll just be in charge of you while we're at sea. Like Sister Beatrice has been in charge of you here. You'll meet your new family when we get to New York.

What's their name?

I can't rightly say. But listen, Miss Mary Burton, I love horses. Nothing I like to do better when I'm home from the sea than watch the horses run. So sure, let's go say goodbye to Gweebarra. Be a damn shame not to.

The Sister looked at him as if he was the devil for saying damn. I kind of liked him for it.

I led the way down to the barn. It was painted red. Once I drew a barn that was blue. The headmistress got upset. She made me sit in a corner of the room with the little kids for a whole day. Barns are red, she said. The next day I drew a yellow barn. She went upstairs to her room. She said her head hurt.

When I opened the barn door, Gweebarra began prancing in her stall. I swung over the half door, red with a white X on it, and went in to where the floor was covered with straw, and rubbed my hand on her face and on her nose. She nuzzled her head, light grey, almost white – with black spots, just like the rest of her – into my shoulder. I stood still for awhile. Then I filled her water bucket from the well and made sure she had plenty of hay and oats in her trough. I told her I hoped somebody takes good care of her when I'm gone. But who will take care of my spiders? I call them my spiders but I don't really own them either, I just play with them, especially when I sleep in the barn with Gweebara. The spiders crawl all over me and tickle my neck or my feet. They is my friends. The only thing I don't like is if they walk in my curly hair. Because being brown like my hair they might die in there and no one will see or know. When I tell the other kids I play with spiders they go eeeeeww! and don't believe me. Until one day a spider made a mistake and bit me on the neck and a big blister came up. When I showed it to the other kids they went eeeeeww! again, but that time they believed me.

The captain, whose name was Captain Padraic Anders, was watching me and Gweebara, saying nothing. I thought of asking if I could take one last ride. Gallop far from the orphanage, make him think I was running away. That would serve him right for owning me! But I was not in the mood. They would only catch me and bring me back.

The captain knew what I was thinking. *You can take her for a quick ride, if you want. But don't try to jump that fence. It's too high, the horse could break a leg. Have to be shot. You wouldn't want to kill Gweebarra, would you?*

I decided to stay with the captain and see what happened. He seemed nice enough. He would never hurt me.

After I closed the stall and said goodbye to my spiders, who was hiding somewhere, and locked the barn, he led me away. My belongings and my new box was stuffed in a blue cotton sack with a picture of a brown spotted owl on it, like the owl that lives under the roof of the barn. *Whooo. Whooo.* I heard Gweebarra whinnying goodbye, as if she knew I wasn't coming back. But maybe not – horses might not care, just like people.

We walked from the Belfry Catholic Orphanage, which is the biggest building in Belfry, to the Donegal harbor, about a pint and a half away, as the men say. There was lots of little boats and also bigger ones with sails on them. The captain led me to the biggest boat and we climbed on board up a wooden ramp. The dark water was slurping below like a dog drinking. He introduced me like a proper gentleman. *This sailing ship is The Catherine. Cathy, meet Miss Mary Burton.* I curtsied, the way the headmistress had taught us to do in case we was adopted. Though it was hard to curtsy with me wearing both of my coats, one being way too tight. I said, *Pleased ta meetcha, Miss Cathy.* And I giggled.

She don't answer, I said, joking around like I do. The Captain joked back. *The water is cold, I think she's got herself a sore throat.* He put his arm lightly around my shoulder – I think he had took a shine to me – and led me below decks. To myself I said *Thank You* to God for freeing me from the orphanage. What a grand adventure this was going to be! Then I got angry again. Where was they taking me, without even asking if I wanted to go?

He asked me a strange question.

Sister Beatrice never told you you were being indentured?

No, sir. What does that mean?

Well, I suppose she knows her business.

I shrugged. I had an important thing to ask him.

That lady in the front of the boat. Carved in the wood, ya know? She don't got no shirt on. That ain't right.

That's called a mermaid. You've never seen a mermaid? She's half fish and half lady.

C'mon. You're spoofin' me. Without a shirt on? There's no such thing. Jesus wouldn't allow it.

The captain scratched his head under his cap. He sort of half
smiled, as if I had caught him at something.

*If you're gonna bring Jesus into it, I guess I better tell the truth. You're right,
Mary, there's no such thing, not really. But people have made up lots of stories about
mermaids, and lots of other folks believe them.*

That's pretty dumb folks, you ask me.

He showed me to a cabin below the deck and went back up. I sat
on the edge of a narrow bed. I could hear the water slurping against the
sides of the boat, this time sounding like little Johnny Byrnes sobbing and
sniffling when he got locked out at supper time. It weren't me who done
it, except that once. Three other beds was empty. I figured three more of
them dentures would be coming aboard soon.

Quickly I opened my present, which I might share with them or
maybe not. It wasn't candy at all. It was just some pencils and a lot of
empty paper.

I began to cry. I was 14 years old and still couldn't help myself.

Before long one of the crew – he was young, and kind of handsome
– brought me cabbage soup with shreds of ham in it. At the orphanage
we had lots of cabbage soup, but bits of ham was only on Sundays. Then
the captain come back. He knocked on the door of the cabin and came
in and sat beside me on the bed. He said he needed to tell me about them
dentures.

*What it means is that when we get to New York, some family, maybe that has
children, will take you in. They'll give you a room in their house to live in, and plenty
of food, and you won't have to pay them. In return, they'll expect you to clean the
house, maybe help with the cooking, maybe help take care of the children. Does that
sound terrible?*

What's New York?

A big city in the colonies. It might be lots of fun.

It sounds better than the orphanage.

*The catch is that you have to stay with that family for seven years. Unless they
sell your contract to someone else.*

*Seven years! I'll be twenty-one by then. An old maid! Do they let us dentures get
married, at least?*

I imagine that would be up to your owner.

There was that word sneaking in again. Only dumb things have
owners. Tractors and mules and cows and dinner plates. I won't like
having an owner.

I didn't say that to the captain. When he left my cabin I was angry.
I was scared. I ran after him and found him on the deck. I did not
remember his name.

Captain Captain? I want to go home. Please take me home.

He looked at me, kind of hard. Or kind of sad. It was hard to tell.

I can't do that, Mary. Where is your home?

The Belfry Catholic Orphanage, of course.

I'm afraid not. You saw us exchange papers and money. The Catherine is your home now. *At least for a few weeks.*

It's not! That's a lot of rot!

Mary Burton, watch your language. The word is rotten.

Fine. That's a lot of rotten!

You'll learn as you get older, Mary. In this life a lot of things are rotten.

That doesn't make me happy.

No, it wouldn't.

A batch of tears flooded my eyes, my nose, my mouth. I was drowning. I broke from the captain and ran to the ramp where we had come aboard and I starting running down. My shoe caught. I stumbled and fell. Two long arms around my waist lifted me up. The crew man said, *Where do you think you're going, little girl?*

I'm not a little girl. I'm fourteen.

Then why are you acting like one?

He half carried, half dragged me back to my cabin, me kicking and sniffling. I slammed the door, which I was not allowed to do at the orphanage. I screamed bad words as loud as I could, and threw myself onto the bed and wiped my nose on the pillow and chewed on one of the pencils and curled up like a caterpillar. I cried until my throat got sore.

4. CAESAR

Musket. *Say it in Muktu, King James.*

There is no such word in Muktu.

The villagers were seated on the leaves around him in a wide half-circle, in front the strong young men, then the strong young women, behind them the naked children and the wrinkled elderly. Laughter emerged from several directions. One man spoke what many were thinking.

Nothing can exist for which there is no word.

Very well. We now have a new word in Muktu: musket.

Small giggles, stern faces.

What does it mean?

They are killing sticks. They have been given by the whites to the seacoast tribes to capture us. They can kill from five times further then we can hurl a spear.

A buzz droned across the crowd like an attack of mosquitos

So how do we defeat them?

My father used to say: Laurels with your heroes lay, but live to fight another day.

Your father was not made king!

But today he would be wise. Our enemies want to seize us. No one knows for certain why. If we try to resist they will kill us with these musket guns – the old and the children first, and some of the strong. Then they will march the living away. It is best not to resist. To live to fight another day.

When we have these musket sticks as well?

Exactly.

At first there were petty arguments. The proud vowed to fight, if only with their knives. But soon the rebel voices died. Uneasy silence settled over the village like a shroud.

James instructs them how to behave when the sharp-teethed warriors return. He tells them to lay their spears on the leaves beside them, a sure sign of not resisting. Beto builds a platform high in the crown of a tree overlooking the forest path that leads from the distant sea.

When the day dawns his alarm is not needed. The forest itself shudders with the advance of a hundred warriors carrying spears and ropes and muskets and machetes and the intent of treating their fellow men like beasts.

James kisses Triana, touches lightly her rounded belly, notes with satisfaction the other men lining up in formation, spears on the ground, wives and older children beside them, the elderly, men and women both, at the rear, wearing their ankle-length robes, so the pointy-teeth do not drag them away. Several older boys and girls have slipped into similar robes and disappeared.

James is standing, unarmed, in front of his village when the head of the snaking band rounds a curve in the forest path and halts. The leader, wearing a blue waist cloth, a blue cloth wrapped around his forehead, bracelets dangling from both wrists, speaks across a space of two jumps. Their tribal languages, descended from the same mother tongue, are similar.

I am Vatok, chief of the Makli. I see we are expected. Do you surrender your people willingly?

No.

A mistake. Then we shall take you by force. Some will be injured. Some will die.

Our spears lie mute.

Then tell your people to step forward willingly, to be bound and shackled.

Each man shall do as he chooses.

This is folly. You are their leader, you can order them.

A second man, wearing a yellow waist cloth, his face smeared with yellow paint, steps beside the speaker. James recalls his features. He is one of the two who watched, laughing, a year ago while Triana was attacked.

Baku Mas!

The parrot, blue, green, turquoise, is perched atop the thatch of James's nearby hut. He squawks in a wild screech. As if he remembers.

Baku Mas! Baku Mas!

His croaking seems to mock the invaders. Another warrior shouts at the bird to be still.

Baku Mas!

The warrior lifts his spear to his shoulder, pulls back his right arm, hurls the spear at the noisy bird. The parrot sees it coming or hears it coming and with a flapping of wings jumps into the air. The whispering spear lodges harmlessly in the thatch. The bird through his curved beak is cackling now.

Baku Mas! Baku Mas!

Chief Vatok grows impatient. The return walk to the sea will be days long, days hot, days dry.

Enough. King James, as I hear they call you, order your people to surrender, or we will charge.

Then you will wound and kill your booty.

The yellow-faced invader lifts his musket to his shoulder, points it directly at James. The king has never seen one fired.

Surrender now, or I will kill you!

Myriad insects buzz. A child among the elders cries. A robed one carries it into the forest. Seeing the two go unmolested, an adolescent boy and girl, Dohi and Kara, dash into the forest behind them.

We'll get them later, the chief says.

The warriors crunch their sharp teeth in anger and disgust. More children, separated from their parents, cry.

Speak or I fire, the yellow man warns.

James say nothing.

The chief pushes the man's musket aside.

Don't be stupid. He's the tallest, the best specimen. The chief. The whites will pay well for him.

The yellow man turns away, seeming abject for his stupidity. But quickly he reverses himself, raises his musket to his shoulder, fires. The iron ball whirs inches beside the king's thigh, tears into the belly of Triana. She falls to the earth, dead before she can whimper. Sparkling blood erupts as the musket ball rips through her flesh and out her back, carrying with it bones from her spine, half of her womb, pieces of unborn child. James drops to the ground beside her, lifts her head, her shoulders, to his chest. She has been cut almost in half. He kisses her dark hair, clears it from her face. Fiercely he presses his mouth to hers, holds her, knowing it is the last time.

She does not smell pretty, as she used to. That may be the worst of it.

Awash with rage, he sets her wet flesh down. He draws a breath, another, gathers himself within himself. With two half steps he springs like a wounded lion at the yellow man. His forehead plows into the killer's chest. They tumble as one. James smashes his fist into the yellow face, crushing the man's flattened nose. Drives his fist into a bobbing throat. Lifts him by the ears, pounds his head into the ground – again, again, again, again – not noticing that his own head is trickling blood. No one attempts to stop him; yellow man apparently is hated even by his friends. When James feels the man go limp he releases the ears. He rejects the impulse to slice them off with his knife.

A curious thought washes through his bloody skull: perhaps the elders had seen in him something he himself had not.

Rolling from the body, he lies gasping on the earth, breathing, breathing, refusing to show tears for Triana. Two of the warriors approach him, twist his arms behind him, bind them with rope. Two others bind his feet. James does not resist. He seems conscious without being so.

He imagines that the parrot is the eyes and soul of his grandfather, watching what he does. Judging him. King John would not have succumbed to stupid pride, would have surrendered without the forlorn defense of idle spears laying useless on the ground. Would have surrendered quietly, as the situation demanded, and left the future of the tribe to the fates. Would not have lost his wife, his child, to a childish absurdity.

The villagers shuffle forward, offer their hands to be bound. A few are turned away as too scrawny; the whites will not pay for scrawny. This has created rumors that sting like jellyfish, rumors that the whites are cannibals, that during the long ocean crossing they will feast on their prisoners.

The villagers are strung together with ropes, chains, ankle and wrist cuffs. Two of the warriors stride toward the rear of the village, where the elderly and the children huddle. One by one they pull off the hoods of the adults, make sure they all are elderly. Two turn out to be adolescent boys. They are shoved roughly across the village compound, to be trussed with the others. One invader, noting slim feet, touches the chest of a robe, shifts his hand, squeezes, hard. The young woman shrieks in pain, is taken away. The elderly and the children sink to the forest earth, some stoically withholding tears, others moaning, weeping.

Beto has remained perched high in the dense crown of his tree, watching. Now he is torn. He can stay behind in what remains of the village, with the old people and the children, or he can climb down and follow his brother toward whatever fate awaits.

From atop the king's hut, the parrot flaps its wings, drops to the ground, struts awkwardly to Triana's torn body

Whitespaywell! Whitespaywell!

Screeching, trying to awaken her.

Ten yards away lies the body of the yellow man.

When the invaders herding their shackled and terrified captives – 70 males by the contented leader's count, 44 females, seven visibly with child – have left the village, the boy and girl who had fled into the forest emerge and peer about. Satisfied that the enemy has gone, they kneel beside the remains of Triana. As best they can they will prepare her body for burial.

A shadow falls across them. It is Beto, down from his tree.

So much blood! We have to bury her quickly. The hyenas are circling.

We have no coffin. No planks to make one. We can't just dig a hole.

No, the animals would pull her out. We'll build a fire. Go to the children, have them gather branches, twigs. I'll fetch water for safety.

The two, in their 14th year, run off. Beto, two years older, lets his stifled tears drown his cheeks. He, too, was in love with his brother's wife.

The village comes alive, children and the elderly prowling for fallen limbs. The two messengers return. Kara, breathless, reports, *The elders say they hear the wishes of King Beto.*

No! I am no kind of king! James is still king, no matter where they have taken him.

When the flaming, smoking fire has finished its work, Dohi points to the body of the yellow man, lying not far away. *What should we do with him?*

Him the hyenas can have, Beto says.

He moves toward the dead warrior, stomps with his calloused feet on the chest, the bruised neck. Walks off to be alone.

Beto would make a good king, Kara says.

There is no village left that needs a king.

She lifts Dohi's hand to her face, kisses his ash-covered palm.

Perhaps it is our task to start one.

5. Peggy

Capelin! Huddled on the narrow, gravel beach in the grey dawn, Peggy shouted to the sea, where dozens of water birds had flown far out from land and were dipping and diving into the silver waves. It happened every June, when the capelin ran not in the thousands or the tens of thousands but in the millions, and the sea birds feasted on them.

There's a whale!

A small one, the size of a large shark, parted its huge jaws, half submerged, as if to swallow Jonah, and inhaled dark water thick with the delicate fish, each no more than six inches long, the whale swallowing a hundred at a time, perhaps a thousand. No one has ever counted.

Peggy was overjoyed, as she was every year, by the running of the capelin. Though her father, standing beside her in his fishing boots, was not.

On'y good thing about them is they lure the cod. That's where the money is.

Every trawler could bring in masses of capelin with its nets but the fish factory bought only one load from each fisherman, and paid little. There were so many capelin they were almost worthless.

With traps you can catch thirty thousand pounds. You can't sell most of it, the packers can't handle them.

She knew all this, but was enthralled. The only thing he talked to her about was fish, unless it was seal season; she was happy to listen when he did; it was the only time he seemed like her father. He's more like a player playing Jesus in the Passion Play, she thought, but at least he was trying. She had learned to collect these moments like pearls, without assessing their quality.

For three days the sea birds and the whales sated themselves with capelin. Then the fisherman set their undersea nets, and following some natural rhythm vast schools of cod moved in. The whales disappeared out to sea; the cod were too big and heavy for the land birds to snatch from the waves. The cod swallowed the capelin until the nets of the men swallowed them. This was what the fishermen lived for. The fish factory paid better for boatloads of cod, which would be shipped around the world; there was a premium for Newfoundland cod. The men could feed their families through the summer and the autumn before in winter they trekked out to hunt for the pups of seals. Those capelin that survived the birds and the whales and the cod began to swim with the incoming tides onto the beach, where they would spawn next year's generation. There still were millions of them as they covered the beach like a wriggling silver blanket.

The first day the soft and leaking fish covered Peggy's ankles as she sloshed among them beside Nora, both barefoot, their shoes removed, each girl carrying an empty wooden basket that once had been filled with oranges purchased from the arriving supply boat by the villagers, who craved a juicy change from fried fish. The girls bent and began filling their baskets with the capelin, which they would clean and dry for months of winter meals.

So, who are you today?

Margaret.

Something I never asked you. How do you decide?

I don't decide.

Both stooping, their slime-covered fingers wrestling more fish into the baskets.

What do you mean, you don't decide?

When I wake up in the morning I stare at the ceiling, first light outlining the windows. Too often I remember the little grave up there. I throw the blankets off and watch to see which one gets out of bed.

I know this is serious for you, Peg. But it's also a little silly, don't you think?

Peggy flushed, swallowed an upchuck of anger.

Do you decide when to be happy, when to be sad, when to be lonely?

It's not the same thing. Those don't have names. Those are all me.

I'm not crazy, Nora. These are all me. It's just – which me?

Did you ever tell your Aunt Dottie about the cemetery?

Peggy shook her head, tried to stay calm. This was her best friend. They used to get naked together, explore each other, when the adults were at village meetings. Nora had freckles on her breasts that she hated; Peggy used to tell her they were cute, that one day the older boys would count them. Would compare notes.

Peggy!

Just teasing.

And smiled the smile that bared a crooked tooth, which despite her beauty made her seem vulnerable.

So, did you tell your Aunt Dottie or not?

Why upset her? Her truth is her truth. Everyone has their own. If she told me a different story now, I still wouldn't know what was true.

Why are you so smart?

Maybe because there's three of me.

But buried anguish choked her voice, frustration over her uprooted babyhood, over not receiving a second letter from Billy. Her feet were getting cold. Silent, they continued to squish their way along the beach, hearing only the tide sneaking onto the sand, depositing more capelin. Water swirled among their toes. Tomorrow the fish would be up to her knees. The next day up to her waist. She liked that day the best. The squirming fish pressing into her apron felt like Billy's naughty fingers had that first time, when hidden by a large rock on the cliff she let him explore her like a blind man, touch her for almost a minute before she slapped his hand away. A girl had to protect her reputation. After he asked her to marry him it was different. Fingers don't count then; not his, not hers. They were the only sin she had never told Nora about.

I wonder why there are so many capelin every year, Nora said.

Maybe Jesus is feeding multitudes with two tiny fish. I wish he'd send loaves as well.

That's blasphemy, Peg, even if you're only joking.

Who's joking? I'm hungry.

The priest says we're supposed to love every living creature. But it's true, capelin are hard to love.

Does Father Mallory drink at the pub?

Only when we're closed.

That's what I thought. Does he have a woman hidden somewhere?

There's a rumor. Some woman in St. John's. But at his age? Who would want to be with him?

Some poor soul who's trying to love God, but can't. So she settles for the priest. But listen. Father Mallory is a priest, a drunk, a sinner. Does that make him three people?

He's a liar, too. He promised he would take over teaching school after your Aunt Dottie got sick. That's been a year, and he still hasn't taught a thing.

You should do that, Nora.

Because I don't know anything? The men would rather I stayed at the pub. The women, too. They know their men won't paw me so long as Papa owns the place. But back to the priest. Do you believe in God, Peg?

She fingered that crooked tooth.

I'm waiting on further evidence.

A wash of heat lightning, the gentle kind, with no crackling arrow at the center, illuminated the innocent past crowding Peggy's brain.

Do you remember what we used to do when we were kids?

Of course. I guess at eighteen we're much too seemly for that.

I'm not seemly, Peggy said.

She reached into her basket, grabbed a fish off the top, tossed it with her left hand. That was the only rule. It landed in Nora's hair.

Oh, you!

What's yours is mine, what's mine is yours. Their mutual mantra since they were seven.

Nora reached down. Instead of a single fish she tossed her entire basket load at Peggy. Capelin swept onto Peggy's windblown hair, her shoulders, her neck. Wiping slimy fish deposit from her face, Peggy tossed her own basketful at Nora, who tried to duck away, half-heartedly. Stepping together as if they were about to exchange blows, they began picking fish off one another, giggling. Peggy pushed Nora to the wriggling mattress and fell on top of her. She kissed Nora's lips, gently. Then more firmly, as they used to do at ten years old when they were teaching one another how to kiss. Breathless and laughing they rolled apart and lay on their backs, gazing at the clouded sky until the sun broke through and they closed their eyes and lay quietly, chests rapidly rising and falling under their damp white blouses.

Nora took Peggy's hand in hers. *I love you like a sister,* she said.

And me you.

Do you know what I'm going to do for you tonight? I'm going to pray that your number one wish comes true tomorrow.

What wish is that?

That the postal boat brings you a letter from Billy. Inviting you to come to New York colony and be his bride.

One little note in two months, Nora. Something bad has happened. I may never see Billy again.

Don't say a thing like that!

That's what I think. Maybe I'll try praying, too. It won't help, but I guess it won't hurt.

The wriggling beach reflected the sun like a thousand mirrors, was shinier even than the sea. They rose and picked fish off one another like chimps picking fleas.

That was stupid, they said simultaneously, peering at their empty baskets. They stooped and began to fill them again.

I guess seemly has its place, Peggy murmured.

I hope no one was watching, Nora said.

Smiling with secret pleasure, lifting her dripping basket, her body shuddering from chill, Nora sashayed along the beach toward the warped wooden stairs, balanced her way up like a trapeze artist at the circus in St. John's, and headed toward the pub. Peggy climbed the steps behind her, paused alone at the summit. She peered out to sea, motionless, watching a gentle, lace-edged tide piddling in. She raised her gaze to the silent dark waves further out – a sea widow staring at this unforgiving enemy. She saw a tiny boat on the horizon. With no boy to hold you, she thought, with no boy for you to hug, a girl was no different than a thousand capelin washed up on the beach, small and helpless. No matter what bloody name she called herself. Or no name at all.

6. MARY

How you make babies is not a question that comes up in Belfry Catholic Orphanage. Me being the oldest girl, at 14, the answer was not considered necessary, according to Sister Beatrice. Anyone who asked a question that was not necessary would go straight to hell. So we all avoided that question, along with others a person could think of. The Belfry Catholic Orphanage was as close to hell as we wanted to get. What I'm saying is the things that happened later might not have happened at all if I had known how babies are made.

Or maybe they would have happened anyway.

It's mostly Gulliver's fault. He's the man in the book the captain brings from his cabin and hands to me as we sit in Donegal harbor the second day, waiting for wind to sail us away. I ain't never seen a book before that was not the Holy Bible. The captain says this is a funny book about a man who has lots of adventures. The man's name is Gulliver, he says. I agree that is a funny name. He 'splains it comes from the word gullible, which word I do not know. He says it means … then he stops. He can't seem to figure how to 'splain it. Then he says it means a person who will believe anything you tell him, even if it ain't true.

Like with them mermaid ladies?

Exactly.

He says there are good stories in this book. In one adventure Gulliver comes to a land full of giants. They are all much bigger and stronger than him. In another story he comes to a land where all the people are tiny, smaller than elves. He is the biggest and strongest person there. I never seen an elf, but I guess they are pretty small, from what people say.

I like that one better. I would rather be the biggest and the strongest.

You read the book before you decide, Mary. It's a long journey to New York. I lend the book to all my young passengers, to help them pass the time.

He don't say dentures, he says passengers. I never been a passenger before. I never been on a boat before. I never been away from Belfry before. It's amazing what God can do, like they tell us at church. Today I'm a *passenger*, going on a *journey*. And it's not even Sunday.

If you finish reading the book before we get to New York, I will be real proud of you.

I like the captain. I want him to be proud of me. I don't tell him I don't know how to read. Well, I can read a little bit, but not big words. I like to write better than I like to read. The nuns say I have a gift for writing, which sounds strange. To me a gift is a new dress or new shoes. Which I get only when I outgrows the old ones. Why I like to write better than I like to read is simple. When I write I write just what I want to say. When I read I am reading what someone else wanted to say. Who cares about that?

Anyhow, the next day the captain goes ashore to wait for some wind to come up. I'm sitting in the sun on the deck looking at the drawings in the book. There are only a few, but whoever drawed them is a good drawer. I especially like the one where Gulliver is lying on the beach and all these little elf-men have him tied up so he can't move. That must have been pretty hard for them to do.

Is that a good book?

A shadow falls across my page and a Hand called Arthur asks me this question. I'm not sure why they are called Hands, they got feet and shoes and all, but Hands is what they call the members of the crew what help the captain sail the boat. I don't know what to tell Arthur Hand.

Can you keep a secret, Arthur Hand? Even from the captain?

Of course.

So I tell him the deal we got going, me and the captain. I tell him I can't read much. The reason I can't read much is that Sister Beatrice is the reading teacher. But every morning it is not her but Sister Celia what reads to us from the Bible. Which I figure means Sister Beatrice can't read much neither. So how can she teach us proper? Also, the only book in the orphanage is the Bible, so who needs to read much anyhow?

Arthur offers to help me. How about he says if while the captain is not aboard he Arthur reads the stories to me. So we can fool the captain. It will be our secret. Well, that sounds pretty fun. We climb down to my cabin and close the door so none of the other Hands can see, and he reads me a story. Then we stretch and stuff and he reads another. But we also need to have a deal he says, and it has to be a secret. That after he reads me stories, we play a game what he likes.

What game is that? I like games.

So he shows me. We lie down on the bunk together and he begins to touch me here and there, and I learn why they call him Hands. He lifts my petticoat and shows me more stuff. At first it hurts a bit but then it feels good. I tell him I will play that game with him any time. But it has to be our secret, he says. Which I swear on the head of Mother Mary, whose statue with chipped blue paint and a broken nose stands in front of the Belfry Catholic Orphanage. It will be our secret.

Before he leaves he says, touching my head, *Where did you get all this curly brown hair?*

I guess it come with the rest of me, I say.

Two days later a breeze waltzes across the deck like a visiting cousin from County Cork. The crew whispers about, unsure whether to raise the sails. The captain's assistant, who they call the First Mate, shouts out loud and clear: *Captain coming aboard. All Hands on Deck.* Which makes me giggle.

The sails go up pretty and clean, like giant fresh-washed handkerchiefs. Gulliver size. My tummy starts to flutter the way it does when Gweebarra nuzzles her cold nose in my neck. Before long we will be in New York colony, and I will start my job as a denture.

I try to smile with courage. Instead I shake with fright.

7. CAESAR

What the parrot sees as he conceals his bright feathers in the thick crown of a karite tree, watching, unobserved:

He sees the invaders in their blue waist cloths line both sides of the downward sloping path through the forest, spears with metal points in their hands.

He sees the village men in their white waist cloths forced to stand between the rows.

He sees wooden boards with holes the size of a neck placed on the prisoners' shoulders, each board linking two men.

Twisting his head to search for lice under a turquoise wing with his thick curved beak, the silent parrot pauses, sees the ropes that bind the legs of the men removed, replaced by black iron ankle cuffs connected with iron chains.

He sees the ropes that bind their wrists behind their backs replaced by wrist cuffs linked by iron chains.

He hears a clanking cacophony. The men say nothing.

Preening his blue tail feathers under the whispering cover of a breeze in the trees, the parrot notices a man try to twist away from the shackles being affixed to him. The piercing point of a spear is jabbed into his thigh. The shackled man screams.

The parrot, standing on one leg, sees the men arranged two by two. He sees the women, still tied by ropes of grass, lined up behind them, neck boards binding them, also two by two. He sees a woman stumble while walking with ankles bound, the force of her fall wrenching the neck of the woman to whom she is attached. He sees the older children shackled among the women.

He does not know what he is watching. He feels an urge to scream a parrot scream but his strong tough beak remains clenched. In the small space between the men and the women the parrot sees King James surrounded by four of the invaders. His ropes, too, have been replaced by chains.

The warrior chief, called Vatok, with his blue head scarf, approaches, barks an order. The parrot uses the moment to release a blob of white parrot waste to the forest floor. The humans do not notice. He releases another. An extra chain is fastened around the knees of the king. An iron collar is locked around his neck. Attached to the collar is a chain. The other end of the chain is linked to a log.

Switching feet for comfort, the parrot sees one end of the white log chained to the neck of the man in front of the king. The log is affixed to the king's neck, then to the man behind him.

He is the one who may try to escape, Vatok explains to the nearest of his tribe.

The undersides of the parrot's feathers have grown damp. In his 77 years he has never perspired. He has not known that he could. He is not an advocate. He is merely observing.

The face of King James is opaque to the parrot, like dried mud. The king, it appears, is trying to figure what is happening to himself and his people. But the thought must be unthinkable, like imagining a forest without any trees that remains a forest. This the bird himself has tried to imagine.

What James sees in the feathers of the parrot is Triana. Who went from child to woman under the leering eyes of the yellow man. Triana, who would still be alive if he had not taken her as his bride.

Straining against the chains, James wills himself to shred this clanking image, to accept as real what cannot possibly be real. He knows he has not been imbibing, any more than the parrot watching from a tree. He remembers that his young wife has been murdered. And that after that he killed her killer. But why the one? And why the other? *Avonacon?*

Trying to clear his foggy head, he asks the passing chief if he will answer a question. Vatok grunts. The king speaks as if from ancient memory. His voice is not his own.

Why are you doing this? Long ago we were one tribe. There was a dispute. No one today recalls what it was. One third of the tribe moved into the forest. But we still speak the same language, Muktu. We are your brothers.

You are wrong, Vatok replies. *We remember well what happened. Your people defied a holy edict, and were exiled to the forest.*

What was this edict?

To file our teeth sharpened to a point.

From whom did this 'holy' edict come?

Vatok kicks at the ground.

That we do not recall.

The parrot clenches his beak again, determined not to cluck.

This does not explain why you are doing this to us.

Because we are stronger than you.

James discovers it is difficult to argue coherently when you are triple-bound.

I have heard that the whites, with all their weapons, are stronger even than you.

This is so. If we did not sell you to the whites, the whites would capture us.

The king spits on the ground, on the fallen leaves. A splinter of sunlight streaking through the trees, past the hidden parrot, glints off his wet spittle.

You are a tribe of cowards! James intones, so the trees and the forest and the broken village will hear.

Toc! Nic!

A rushing warrior brings Vatok an iron headpiece. The chief requires both hands to hold it; even then it almost falls.

Another insult, and I shall fasten this over your head. We reserve it for troublemakers. This nose piece cuts down your breathing. This mouth piece prevents you from eating. Or drinking. So be careful with your tongue.

You won't use that. I might sicken, or die. Or break my neck. I am too valuable. You said so yourself.

You are very clever. You are correct, I will not use it on you. The next time you show your arrogance, I will use it on your brother.

You do not have my brother!

Incorrect. The lad trailed us, assuming we would not see him. Assuming no doubt that if we did, he could outrun us all. Very likely he could. But my warriors are circling him even now. He will not escape.

James tries to whirl, to look behind him. The iron collar prevents him from turning his head.

Beto, you fool! You could have been free! What did you hope to accomplish?

The king slumps, his energy draining into the earth. His shackles do not permit him to collapse. Dangling from the log on the shoulders of his villagers, he crumples, defeated. Yet he remains upright, half bent, like a puppet at the children's show.

All this the parrot hears. In shades of blue, green, turquoise. All this the parrot sees. Later, in the bleak moaning of the night, he drops to the ground to eat the seeds he needs to repeat his vigil during the coming day.

8. Peggy

The letter might be considered Nora's answered prayer, arriving as it did on the supply boat the very next day, except that it had been placed into the black leather postal bag in New York colony more than a week before. When the boat docked, laden with baskets of oranges, potatoes, tomatoes, other fruits and vegetables, Nora rang the bell outside the pub-cafe, rang it until it echoed off the cliff below the church, a bell with many voices that reached the furthest end of the village. Women of many ages pulled coats over their long dresses against the morning air and hurried down the village's one dirt road toward the pub-cafe, wanting to grab prime pick of the fruit. Watching impatiently from the cabin door, Peggy saw Nora hang the Irish flag outside the pub. Coatless, she ran down the road, in her haste forgetting to don her white cap, her loose radiant hair trailing like desperate windblown flames that she could not outrun. She passed the older women, earning grumbles and angry looks from those who saw this girl flying past on her strong young legs to greedily grab the best of the fruit. Other women waved to her and smiled as she went by, remembering how impatient they themselves had been at her age when awaiting a letter from a beau. No men were visible, they were already out on the boats, hoping for a catch of early cod; cartons of off-loaded Irish whiskey would be held safely at the pub in their names.

Peggy burst first into the pub, grabbing the polished edge of the bar to brake herself. Nora was stacking periodicals, letters on a ledge. One letter had been set aside. Peggy had to arrest her breath before speaking.

Is that one for me?

Nora turned and smiled at her, or at her wind-rattled curls.

Let's just say that God answered my prayer.

Let's just say that yesterday you spotted the supply boat anchored far out in the bay, waiting for a proper wind. Give it to me!

Her hands were trembling as Nora offered the letter. She fumbled
with the grey envelope before she could tear it open. As she held it under
a hanging kerosene lamp to read it, her hands shook even more. The
paper buckled noisily. Some of the ladies entered the pub to cut through
to the produce dock. Embarrassed, Peggy pressed the letter flat on the
bar, held it down, leaned over to read Billy's words. From behind the bar,
Nora watched.

Dear Peg,

*I am sorry I have not ritten sooner, but to
tell the truth I have been too upset to rite ☐
until today. The ship ride over was fine and
I found a room in a boarding house named
Hughson's. It is not fancy but not too bad I
guess. I started looking for work rite away
so I could send for you. But I was shocked to
discover that there are no jobs available in
all of New York town, which is not what I
had heard. Most of the good jobs are held by
colored men, which surprised me much.*

*These colored men are slaves, which you know
what that means. I thought that only colonies
in the southern parts had slaves, helping their
masters to pick cotton, which I could see
would be necessary. This is not so. Here they
help build houses and carry water and do all
sorts of jobs. What's strangest, in the evening
when their chores are done they are allowed
to gather in bars and cafes like the one at
Hughson's, and drink whisky. This is strange to
witness because as you know there is not a black
man in all of Newfoundland as far as I have
ever seen. Maybe not in all of Ireland as far
as I have heard.*

*But now the good news why I am riten,
before I run out of paper and ink. I am not
riten this letter from Hughson's, but from the
home of the Widow Williams. That is my home
now as well, until such time in the future as I
can send for you. The Widow Williams is an Angel*

from Heaven. I had just about run out of money
to pay Mister H. for my room when she showed
up asking about me. She said she had a big house
with lots of empty rooms ever since her husband
Mister Williams died last year. She is needing
someone to help her around the house, she said
- she did not want one of these Negroes in her
house - and if I would help her with whatever
she needed done then I could stay in one of the
rooms for free. And free dinner as well, if I
helped to cook. When I said I don't know how
to cook she said there was plenty of things she
could teach me.

An even better part is that her husband
Mister Williams was a partner in a big company
here, the N.Y. Mercantile Co. When he died
she inherited his part of the business. She said
if I work out she could get me a job as soon as
they need another hand. Which they will when
the next big schooner, called Bluebell, comes in
from across the sea. They will need help with
unloading and selling the merchandise and I
could be the all around bookkeeper's helper
as well. When I told her I dont know nothing
about bookkeeping she said there was plenty
of things she could teach me. I would stay hired
and make good pay so long as I did whatever
she said. I moved in here last week. So far the
chores is fine. So that is my good news.

They expect this big schooner to arrive in six
weeks, depending on the winds and any storms
at sea. Then after six months of pay I should
have enough saved up to send you passage to
New York, like I promised.

Oops, the Widow Williams is coming home from
church. I better end.

Your best friend ever,

William Charles Reilly III

Peggy's face fell to the bar as if her neck could not support her head.
One hand held her forehead, the other held the letter.

What is it? What's wrong?

Without lifting her head, Peggy held the letter out to Nora, who took
it and read it through.

This is wonderful, Peg! He's going to send for you. I knew he was all right.

Did you read it?

Her mouth was muffled by the bar.

He's got himself a rich widow.

Come on, Peg. Billy's not the type to take up with some old lady.

Peggy lifted her head. Her eyes were red. The bar was damp where
her forehead had rested.

*Show me. Show me where it says she's old. She's not too old to teach him
things. Sewing? Cooking? And what else do you suppose, him living right in her house.
Dear Peg, he says. No more Peg-o-my Heart. Your best friend, he says. Doesn't that
excite your blood? He'll send for me in eight months or something. When the Widow
Williams is bored with him.*

Peggy noticed that the tables in the pub had begun to fill with men
too old to fish coming in for lunch and beer and laughter. She snatched
the letter from Nora, crushed it in her hand and ran out the door, crying.
Nora yelled something to her father, who was frying fish, and hurried into
the road.

Peg? You might be mistaken. You might be reading this all wrong.

*I'm not mistaken. You know those snakes St. Patrick drove from Ireland? They're
twisting in my belly right now. Every last one of them.*

That's the spirit, Peg. Laugh it off.

I'm not laughing. I want to die.

*Even assuming you're right – that he's been snared by this rich widow – you
really want to die over Billy Reilly? There are plenty of other fish …*

Peggy stopped walking, turned. They are at the bottom of the steep
steps leading up to the church and the cemetery. She wants to smash
Nora in the face with the clenched fist that is holding the balled-up letter.
At the same time she is swallowing laughter.

I'm sorry, Nora says.

You think this is a joke? You've never been jilted, have you?

I haven't had the pleasure. Unless, of course, you count my father.

What? Peggy stared at her. *You're joking again.*

Am I? Ask my mother. Ask her how Papa got that scar down his back.

He fell off a trawler.

Right. The trawler was the Nora Neal. Me.

Oh, God. Peggy hugged Nora close. *You never told me. How could you live with that?*

He said he would kill me if I told anyone. You can live with most anything, I think.

What did your mother do?

She scorched his back with a hot frying pan to get him off of me. Then she said, in case I was thinking of telling anyone, that it never happened.

How could she say that?

Practice. It was the fourth time it never happened.

They broke apart, still holding hands, as had been their habit for fifteen years. High above them the church bell screamed noon. A stray brown dog asleep in the middle of the road raised its head, as if annoyed by the disturbance, quickly went to sleep again.

Forgive me, Nora. But at least your father likes you.

Oh, you! As long as you can make jokes, you'll get over Billy.

I don't know. If they find my broken body on the beach, at the bottom of the cliff, tell them it was an accident.

Okay. But you'll have to wait until the capilon are gone.

Why is that?

You'll bounce.

Peggy punched her friend in the shoulder.

I have a better idea. I could fall from outside the church. The cemetery. See what God has to say. Or Father Mallory. See who they decide to bury.

If it was me who got that letter, it's Billy I would want to kill.

Don't think I haven't thought of that. But he's in New York colony.

Nora grinned. *There's boats.*

Peggy nodded absently, said nothing, looked quietly toward the sea, where white and grey gulls whirled in wide circles high above the dock.

I wonder why those stupid birds want to live.

I have to get back to the pub, Peggy. Stop already. The hurt over Billy will pass. It always does. Even with my father. Mostly. You're not going to kill anyone.

You don't think so? Maybe Margaret will do it. Or ~~Marguerite~~.

I thought they all were you.

They are.

They hugged on parting, as they had been doing since they were eight years old. Each said *I love you like a sister,* as they had been doing since they were nine.

9. Mary

The forme of binding a servant.

This indenture made the 7th day of May, the year of our Soveraigne Lord King George II being 1739, between Belfry Catholic Orphanage (Sister Beatrice, (aka Hette Greene,) director, lawful guardian for the minor Mary Burton, 14 years of age), of the one party, and Captain Pedraic Anders of the other party, Witnesseth, that the said Mary Burton doth hereby covenant promise, and grant to and with the said Padraic Anders, his Executors and Assignes, to serve him from the day of the date hereof for the terme of 7 years, in such service and imployment as the said Padraic Anders or his assignes shall there imploy him her, accordng to the custom of the Country in the like kind. In consideration whereof, the said Pedraic Anders doth promise and grant to and with the said Mary Burton, to pay for his her passing and to find him her with Meat, Drinke, Apparell and Lodging, with other necessaries during the said terme; and at the end of the said terme, to give him her one whole yeeres provsion of Corne, and fifty acres of Land, according to the order of the countrey. In witness whereof, the said Pedraic Anders hath put his hand and seale, the day and yeere above written.

Signed and sealed.: Sister Beatrice, (aka Hetta Greene,) Pedraic Anders.

10. Caesar

The walk to the sea without fetters took three days. With the villagers shackled around their ankles it took seven.

The first afternoon one of the pregnant women gave birth too early. None of the chattering women was freed to help her. King James could not even turn in his shackles to see whom it was. Mother and child lay covered with blood. The warriors halted the procession just long enough to remove her rope shackles and leave her and the bloody baby curled on the ground. They would not be carried along. None of the men could see whom it was, but her husband knew her voice.

Keenect, he shouted.

She will die!

Left alone, she would die of thirst, or starvation, or the teeth of animals.

Keenect! Keenect!

The husband was ordered to be still. He continued to scream. A warrior approached to tighten his iron collar. The man bit fiercely into the warrior's wrist. The warrior screamed. A moment later two others carried over the heavy head piece. The man was held still while the iron mask was slipped over his head. The mouthpiece was locked. Now the man still could squirm, but he could not yell. James knew whom it was. He could not help.

In late afternoon the villagers each were given a cup of water, and in the evening, a fistful of bread. They were told to sleep on the ground, still fastened to the man or woman beside them. They had to release their wastes while fastened to the man or woman beside them. Few could fall asleep that way. James slept fitfully, refusing to eliminate his wastes.

On the second day some villagers stumbled from exhaustion. They were whipped, and ordered to quicken their pace. Some fell. Their neck mates strained to drag them.

On the third day James heard women pass out. They were revived with water, and whipped again.

On the fourth day three women and two men died – the weight, the sleeplessness, too much for them; the water, the bread too little. Their shackles were removed. They were not buried but left beside the road. James's legs began to ache from the strain.

On the fifth day a heavy rain poured into the forest. Trees cringed under the deluge, dripping noisily. The prisoners were made to continue walking. With their wrists tied behind them they could not wipe the rain from their eyes, their noses. Some cursed this added burden that fell from the sky. Others felt revived by it. That night the king could not help but relieve himself. He hoped the running rainwater would carry away the wastes, the stench.

On the sixth day the rain passed. But the path through the forest was a bog. The effort required to slog chains through the sloppy puddles was intense. Five more villagers could no longer force their legs to move, the pain of cramped muscles was too great. They collapsed in tears. Only to be whipped. They were too close to the sea, too close to the sale, for their captors to abandon them. James felt that he himself would not go on if as their king he would not dishonor the village.

He saw the pain and the deaths in front of him, heard if they were behind. He attempted to keep track of the loss of men and women and babies, to bury them in the coffin of his brain alongside his shame and his rage and his despair. But even that mental activity became too much. He needed to focus on placing one foot ahead of the other in the mud.

On the seventh day, God rested.

As they came around a bend in the path, the smell of the sea of a sudden surrounded them. James tried to absorb a glimmer of relief. The forced march was over. The warriors had not brought Beto. No doubt his brother had outrun them through the forest, until they had given up, panting, wheezing, cursing. Perhaps after wandering a few days Beto had come across another tribe deep in the woods. He would tell them what had happened. Surely they would take him in.

A tribe that had not been captured yet.

11. Peggy

The Seal Killer is what the village called Billy Reilly. It was a term of honor. Four times in the past six years, from the time he was 16 years of age, the seal puppy championship of the village had been won by William Charles Reilly III. When autumn came and the fish were gone the villagers lived on dried capelin and dried cod and waited impatiently until spring when the seals far out on the ice floes would give birth to their pups, thousands of them, tens of thousands, and the able bodied men of the village would go after them, clubs in hand, to harvest the white fur of the baby harp seals, which could be sold at good prices to merchants in St. John's, who would take the furs across the ocean to dandify the collars and cuffs and cloaks of royal or just plain wealthy men and women. With his tall, thin frame and light feet Billy seemed to fly across the surface of the snow and ice like an egret, finding a still groggy pup and bashing in its head with a single swift strike, careful not to spill too much blood that would ruin a perfect pelt. Not pausing to admire his trophy, he would fly off to another pup, leaving his younger brother Ned behind to haul a sled filled with baby carcasses back to the ship anchored at the edge of the floe several miles away, where they would be stripped naked so as not to ruin the pelts with stains. The entrails and all the rest were dumped into the sea or left to rot on the pink-stained ice for the scavenging birds. This champion, who each successful year was awarded a warm woolen cap, was the young man Peggy Kerry had fallen for – and

he for her, it seemed – to the envy of the village girls and many of the
women as well. He would be a good catch for any wife. She and their
children would never go hungry.

All this ~~Marguerite~~ thought as she lay on her bed the first day after
the letter, the second, the third, blankets pulled up to her neck, facing
the wall, not changing clothes between day and night as far as Auntie
Dottie saw. Her stomach still roiled, she thinking again and again of the
ice floes. What better place do die? What better place to kill herself?
Not falling off a cliff on either side of the village, that would be messy
and might cause a broken but not dead body. She would not want to live
that way. But out there on the floes, so white, so pristine, she could be a
sleeping princess on ice. Until just two years before, women and girls had
not been permitted aboard the seal boats; the weather was too dangerous,
hunters had been known to get lost in fog and never return to the boat,
never be heard from again. The rule had been changed last year so long
as when the boats anchored at the edge of the jutting floe and the men
in hip boots set out to slog for miles to find the pups, women or girls
would have to stay aboard. The rule change was approved only after it
was pointed out how much work the women and girls could do skinning
the bleeding pups, time when the tired men could settle in with a brew or
two.

This ran through her mind while she lay on her back on the narrow
bed, sometimes turning, one hand warming the painful knot in her
stomach, the other slung across her forehead, her closed eyes. Another
day passed, and another. What I could do this year, ~~Marguerite~~ thought,
is go out on the boat with them, wait until all the men and boys had
strode off with their clubs. Then I could climb down the rope ladder to
the snowy floe and walk away – away from the boat, away from the sea,
miles and miles into icy white nothingness where no humans could be
seen and no sound heard. I would walk in circles and then spin in circles
until when I fell to the snow I had no remembrance of the direction from
whence I had come. Nothing visible but pure cold, pure white in every
direction, and then an empty white fog growing like certain death out of
the unseen sea. Lying stiff and straight on the ice, buried by next winter's
snow. I could lie there for years undiscovered, as if waiting for a kiss on
my ice-blue lips. That would be a death worth enjoying. Would I be cold?
Yes, I would be cold. I don't imagine any death is warm.

She wondered – if she died unseen on the ice – whether they
would they change the black and white wooden sign at the side of the
road from: Village of Carey, Pop. 139, to Village of Carey, Pop. 138. It

occurred to her that they had not lowered the number when Billy left the village four months ago. She wondered what the rules were for that.

In her mind she saw Father Mallory holding a service for her at the population sign, as the number was lowered by one. The entire village would be invited. The priest would pray that her Christian soul had now been added to the number of hosts of Heaven. It was a comforting image, the entire village missing her smile, her good spirits. But soon people on the edge of the crowd began to move away, to drift to their homes and shops, until the only one still standing there alongside Father Mallory as he prayed for her departed soul was Nora. With the priest still preaching, Nora seemed to hesitate, to shuffle her feet. Then even she turned her back and left, leaving Father Mallory alone preaching to the wooden sign, to the vast emptiness of cliffs and sea and sky, to an occasional gull dropping by to listen to what was going on.

She fed to the gull the scene of her ensuing burial. She wondered what this shriven image could portend.

Peggy?

Aunt Dottie approached the bed. Her wide rocker swept and creaked behind her, then slowed to silence like a dying metronome.

What? You woke up my dream, Auntie.

You were not sleeping. I could tell.

My daydream.

Oh. What was that about?

Ice.

Doesn't sound very exciting.

Well, it was.

Listen, about Billy's letter. She waved it gently. Bent and wrinkled, it resembled an ancient treasure map. *It fell off the bed, so I read it. I wish I could say something that made you feel better, Sweet Pea. But I have to agree with you. It sounds as if this Widow Williams person has got her claws stuck pretty deep into Billy.*

So what am I to do, Auntie?

Dottie settled her 300 pounds on the edge of the bed, like a resting whale. Peggy shifted toward the wall to keep from falling off.

Only two things I can think of. One is to put that two-timing cad out of your mind. Puff, he's gone. Then look around you. There are plenty of fish in …

Don't say it! I don't plan to marry a capelin. Not even two. I'd just hang around, become an old maid who everyone pities. That might be ~~Marguerite~~*, but it won't be me.*

You're confusing me, child. The other thing you can do is go to New York colony and look for him. Make sure this is not a misunderstanding. Maybe Billy does want to marry you, he's just accepting room and board, and then a job, from this nice widow. She might be a good sort.

For a moment Peggy's heart took precarious flight, like a baby bird jumping from the nest. But quickly it fell to earth.

Do you think that's possible?

I would say it's possible. But not very likely. Not from this letter. It's cold as the ice you were dreaming about.

I do have a third choice. I can go out on the floes, and in the cold I could lie on the ice until my fingers begin to freeze, then my ears, then my toes. Then my everything. Before long I would be dead, hidden by the fog. That would be appropriate, don't you think? As if Billy Charles Reilly came onto the ice with his club and bashed my skull. He's very good at that.

Lord, how you talk, Peggy Kerry. Get yourself out of bed. What are we going do with you?

12. MARY

I can't spell, no better than I can read. But sometimes I want to write things anyways, so I can remember. Like now, when we are going away. I got my pencils and a piece of paper what Sister Beatrice give me for leaving. I showed it to Arthur Hand.

You're not going to write about us! he says.

What about us? I says.

What we, you know, did.

We didn't do nothing what I remember, I say. He touches my cheek and says good girl, which I like. So then on the first page I start to write a Dairy, like I have heard people do.

> *Dear Denture Dairy—*
> *The captin is yelling Ankers A Way. Ankers A Way. Arthur Hand jumps down from the dek to the dok and unroles this long fat rope like a long fat snake. He unroles and unroles till it comes off this iron hook thing on the dok. He throws the rope up to the dek and then he jumps a big jump up from the dok to the dek. Which can be confusin, if you see what I mean.*
> *Wind is puffin out sales like fat mens bellies. The land starts spearin behine us. There be ony one place this bote be taken us. AWay. An I be cryin. I doan wan go AWay.*

Maybe I fraid the fat mens sales gonna turn this Cathrin bote overside down in the see an I be drownd. If you think I doan read too good an I doan write too good you should sea me swim. I caint. Cause there aint no water ponds near Belfree Cathlic Orfinage in witch for us to learn. Ony sometimes after a rain theres a big mud puddle. I tried to swim there one time but it didn work too good. When I come back my dress was all covered with brown an wet dirt. Sister Beetrice say, Mary Burton, that is absolutely the dumbest thing you ever done did. Which it aint, but I aint gonna tell her that.

Or maybe I is cryin cause of my frens. Leavin all my frens behine. My orfin frens. Also my hoarse Gweebarra. Doan no who will feed her. Oar if they gonna chop her up for food sumtime, like the other kids say.

Now there is nuthin but see all aroun. Blu sky an blac see. Cathrin cuts through the waves like they be blac mash taters. The oceans plate be clean. Sun show that as far as I kin sea. Wonner if that smart owl kin still sea us from that barn. Wise ole owl. Whooo whooo.

Fudge, I dropped my pencil. It rolled across the deck and into the sea. I got me another one. The first pencil disappeared under the water. Gone away. Like me.

I like having a friend to talk to when I am lonely. I turn to the second page of paper and I write at the top:

Mary's Denture Dairy
—more tomorrah

It would be silly to write more today because without wanting to I am crying again.

I want my mother.

I never had a mother, if you don't count them nuns.

I go to my cabin and hide my new dairy friend in the box far back in my sack. I don't know why I do that, I just do.

13. Caesar

Ktanga Katin. The words sear the skin of King James as if with a branding iron.

They had reached the end of the desperate walk and collapsed onto a chalky white beach between the silent forest and the simpering sea. Only a large white stone building at the water's edge interrupted the flat horizon. The enemy warriors let them lay where they fell, many gasping, others moaning, but did not remove their bindings, their chains. James was partially unshackled and dragged to the front and flung to the sand at the head of his villagers. His chains were locked again. A warrior who had been counting how many prisoners had survived the walk reported to Chief Vatok, who stood not far from James, gazing at the sea as if to spot a ship on the horizon.

Nineteen dead, the warrior said. *Twenty if you count that baby.*

James felt compelled to speak, to be part of a conversation, however useless. He thinks: *a musket ball has taken the life of Triana, has taken with it her gentle love for me.* But he would not speak like a woman to the enemy. Instead he says, *Twenty-one, if you count my wife!*

The chief turned from the sea and stepped nearer.

Your wife was an accident of combat. I am sorry for that.

We were not in combat!

I permitted you revenge.

Revenge will not warm my bed at night.

In your new country, I have heard, you might be grateful that she remains here.

With the sisters of his village sprawled behind him, he dares not ask Vatok to paint a picture. He shuts his eyes against the sight of what the morbid kites might already have done to her in the bastard night.

The other nineteen of my village, are you sorry about them as well?

That I cannot claim.

Because?

Ktanga Katin.

It is the cost of doing business.

James feels his flesh catch fire. He can smell the human smoke sizzling. He tries to keep from shouting

Your people's business! My people's cost!

It is the way of the world. When you kill an elephant for meat, you survive – but the elephant pays.

James's head drooped. He was too weary to win this argument. Vatok waved his hand. A warrior removed the neck cuff from the king.

James raised his head again.

That building by the sea. What is that?

The merchants call it Cape Coast Castle.

And you? What do you call it?

I do not speak of it. If you are curious, prisoners before you gave it their own name.

Which is?

Vatok looked to the sea again. He scooped a handful of sand. Standing, he let it drain through his fingers.

The Door of No Return.

James breathed sharply, as if with his last breath. For no apparent reason he wondered where the mystic parrot had gone. He thought he found it inside his head, where a sharp pain like a curved and pointed beak had asserted itself. The pain of frustration he could not assuage. Of fear he could not reveal. Of shame that was all too obvious. Of despair he was trying to deny.

What happens inside the Castle?

There you wait. Until there are enough of you to fill a ship.

How many is that?

Should be 400. Sometimes 600. Already 200 are in there, waiting.

Dying.

Dying?

Of fever. Of disease. Perhaps of the foul smell itself. It is not pleasant in there.

Behind the white castle James could see a mostly hidden sloop, its sails tightly furled, rocking gently, silent and ghostly, like a malignant mirage.

14. Peggy

Population: 2 *That story is the one you want? The town's first liar?*

I love that story.

I told it to you a dozen times when you were in school.

I need to hear it now. Please, Auntie?

Very well. Come sit by my feet. I'm not going to shout.

Peggy sank to her knees in front of the extra-wide rocking chair, rested her crossed arms in Dottie's extra-wide lap.

This was a hundred years ago, right? she said.

Maybe more. Nobody knows for sure. What we know for sure is that jobs were getting hard to find in Ireland, so lots of folks were pushing onto boats to try their luck here in Newfoundland. They docked at St. John's, but that was a busy town, so most of them rented wagons for their belongings and started walking west. One of the first of these was a man named Seamus W. Clapper.

I love that name, Peggy said, smiling into her aunt's plump knee.

Seamus, who was thirty years old and already mostly bald, was a carpenter and a boot maker. He brought with him from the old country his carpenter tools in one satchel and his boot making tools in another, and he started down the road. Every mile he had to sit and rest his arms. After ten miles or so, while he was sitting by the road, a family of five pulling a loaded wagon had to stop. An axle on their cart had snapped. They were grateful to find a carpenter who could fix it sitting right there, as if sent by the angels. This happened again and again. It seems there was an underground stream coming down from the cliff and causing a fissure, which was hidden by a mess of mud. Seamus, no fool, decided to set up camp there. From logs in the cliff-side forest he built a lean-to to protect himself from wind off the sea. It was June, so the weather was mild. Each day he had more axles to fix. He also talked some of the men into ordering new pairs of boots they could pay for later on. Soon people started asking him what this place was called. He put up a sign on a post across from his lean-to, and bought paint in St. John's, and decided on a name for the coming town. Since he had been born and raised up in County Kerry, he decided he would honor his home town. But he was not a very good speller, so he painted in red letters on the white sign: Village of Carey.

Didn't they have teachers in Ireland?

In those days perhaps not so many. Or maybe Seamus W. Clapper was just a bad student. Anyway, he looked proudly at the new sign, but felt that something was missing. Such signs usually told the population, he realized. So he painted with red paint, Pop: 1. But right away he became embarrassed. He didn't want people to pity him for living alone. So he changed the 1 to 2. Now the sign said, Village of Carey, Pop: 2.

With the weather turning colder, he built himself a small log cabin behind his lean-to. One day a widow woman called Mrs. Loory came by, a hefty lady leading a large dog, and stopped to rest, and listened to the waves hitting the rocks far below, and smelled the sea, and asked Seamus where his Missus was. He was going to lie, but knew he would be caught, so he explained about Pop. 2.

Watching still more axles break, Mrs. Loory told him, You know what you should do? You should open a pub here, so folks could enjoy a good Irish beer while waiting for you to fix their carts. And maybe a cafe, so they could eat while waiting.

Seamus saw that Mrs. Loory had a good head for business. He asked if she would stay and run the place. She said she would, but she would need a place to live. I'll build you your own house, Seamus told her, but first I would need to build the pub. Would you stay in my place until then? Mrs. Loory hesitated, then said, for a short time. Seamus wondered if he had made a mistake, having been a bachelor all his 30 years, but when he heard that the name of the dog, a brown and white collie, was

Lucky, that clinched the deal. Seamus had only one bed in his one-room cabin, and building a pub took time, and before long he had to cross the road to his sign and change the lettering to Pop. 3. And then 4. And then 5.

As more and more people suffered broken axles, on the way to and from St. John's, they demanded from what little government there was in the capitol city that the road needed to be fixed if they were to continue paying taxes. The government sent out men with shovels, who dug down to the fissure and filled it with rocks and covered it over with gravel. But a few days later, axles were breaking again. Men saw dog prints on the road, and decided that Lucky must have been digging up the fissure at night. They demanded that she be chained behind the house. Seamus told them the dog had not come sailing all across the ocean to live at the end of a chain. And he refused.

Some people say the dog was probably not at fault at all, that Seamus had been going out in the dark of night and re-opening the fissure himself. Who can say? Other people claim the fissure was never an act of nature at all, that Seamus W. Clapper had arrived before any of them, and dug the fissure, and covered it with mud, and waited for axles to break. But no one ever established this, one way or the other.

I'll bet that's what he did, Peggy said, raising her head from Dottie's lap.

Well, today it hardly matters. The carpenter shop and the pub-cafe are running nicely, under different owners of course, and Seamus W. Clapper lies at rest up in the churchyard, beside Mrs. Loory and her dog Periwinkle, whose name never was Lucky at all, beneath a stone that says he was born in County Carey – of which of course there is no such thing. The thinking is that he carved the stone himself before he died.

There are lots of mistakes in the churchyard, Peggy said, rising to her knees.

Are there? I wouldn't know about that. But the old sign across from the pub, as you know, now says in red letters, Village of Carey: Pop. 171. You can't hardly argue with that.

What's strange to me, Peggy said, straightening her wrinkled muslin skirt, pushing layers of crushed auburn hair back behind her ears, *is why I wanted so much to hear that story today, after so many years.*

That's easy. It's because you're thinking of leaving. When we leave the place where we were born, where we grew up, it's natural to want to take something with us. In your case it must be that history of the village.

How do you know I'm thinking of leaving?

Sweet Pea, you are not invisible. Those tears running down your face the past few weeks when you think nobody is watching, those drops hanging onto your lashes, quivering, fighting not to fall? They don't mean you're trolling for other fish …

You're right. I want to go to New York. Find out what happened with Billy. Whether he still wants to marry me.

Or you want to marry him.

But the passage costs money I don't have. I can't save enough skinning fish for Father. And cooking and cleaning the house. He doesn't pay me.

Except for room and board, he would say.

I know all that. It doesn't help.

Peggy, reach up to the top of that shelf over there. The top one. Towards the back.

It's dusty. I'm sorry. I haven't been working too good lately. Been too busy feeling sorry for myself.

Never mind dust. There's a small box up there. Bring it down.

Peggy stood on her toes and with the tips of her straining fingers found a box deep against the wall. It was small, of plain dark wood, light in weight. She had never seen it before.

When my Roald was alive, Dottie said, taking the box, *he brought in plenty of cod and seal while I was teaching. They didn't pay me much, but I managed to put some away for a rainy day. And your face these weeks has been rainy as it can get.*

I'm sorry.

Don't be sorry. What's in this box is your passage to New York colony. And a little extra for a few months' room and board.

Auntie, I can't take your money. I should be paying you for raising me.

You hush. You've been the pleasure of my life, little girl. You CAN take the money, and you WILL take the money. There is one dark side, however. I have only enough for passage one way. If you're not happy in the colonies, I don't have enough to bring you back.

Peggy's body was pulsing with excitement, like a baby seal ready to explore the world.

I think I'll be happy there. Knowing the truth, one way or another. If not, I can always get a job cooking or cleaning house, maybe as a governess watching children. I could save up my own money if I want to come home. Enough to pay you back, too.

That won't be necessary, Sweetie. The money now is yours.

Shakily, Peggy took the box, pressed it with both hands to her breast. Melting ice floes trickled down her cheeks.

15. MARY

You are a lucky girl. *I hear you've been crying because you're lonely. Let me show you something.*

I'm standing on the deck looking out at the waves doing their same old wave thing when the captain come up to me. He reaches into the pocket of his blue shirt and pulls out a yellow paper, all folded.

Do you know what this is?

I seen that before. That's my denture paper you signed with Sister Beatrice.

Right. Now, how many more of these do you see sticking out from my pocket?
I don't see no more.

Right again. Have you ever been to Dublin, Mary? Dublin has a great big port,
bigger than Donegal. In that harbor are big ships, much bigger than the Catherine here.
And you know what is on those ships? Lots of people – men and women, and boys and
girls like yourself. Maybe two hundred people on one ship. All going to the colonies, like
you.

That's what I would like. I wouldn't be lonely then.

Wait, let me finish. The captain of one of those ships would have maybe two
hundred indenture papers. Because all those people have traded their freedom in return
for passage to the new world. Just like you.

I ain't …

Well, Sister Beatrice has. The problem is, those boats don't have room for enough
food to feed all those people for the entire voyage. So during the second half they get very
hungry. The ships don't have enough beds, so the people sleep on the deck or in the hold,
which is not very comfortable. They don't have enough washrooms, so the people soil
their clothes. By the time they reach the colonies they are all smelly, and some of them
are sick. And they can't leave the ship until they have recovered. You wouldn't want to
be crowded in like that.

Why ain't I?

Because I'm not in the business of selling people. Do you know what's in the
hold down below? Half of it is Irish linens, which the ladies in New York like. The
other half is good Irish whiskey. I'm only bringing you along this trip because I know a
family in New York that is looking for a maid, and I've known Hetta – Sister Beatrice
– for a long time, and it seemed to be a good match.

So what? I'm still lonely,

Girl, don't be stupid. You have to look on the bright side.

I feel hurt when he says that. I thought he liked me.

Now I have to go up top. You see those black clouds way out there?

It looks like a big black splotch on the side of a cow.

Well, it's a great big storm, and it's much more dangerous than a cow. It's still
a few days away. If I swing around the storm, we lose two days, maybe three. If I
plow right through it – well, the Catherine is a sturdy vessel, but there's no place to pull
in for repairs until Newfoundland, and that's a long ways off. She's survived storms
before, but this trip we have special cargo aboard that I would not want to lose.

You mean that Irish whiskey?

No, Mary. I mean you.

What a silly thing for him to say.

I ain't special, captain.

Sure you are. And that's how you should start thinking of yourself.

I have an idea about that storm, though.

What is that?

We could pray to Jesus to move it out of the way.

That's what some folks would recommend. Sister Beatrice would hate to hear me say this, but them folks is just gullible. The only thing that gets things done in the real world is money. Filthy lucre. I ain't never heard tell of Jesus taking cash on the barrelhead.

I want to laugh, but it's true, I never heard of Jesus taking cash money neither.

The captain tousles my hair and turns and hurries up them metal stairs to what they call the helm station. I look out at the dark clouds far away.

Soon I go down to my cabin.

Dear Denture Dairy—

The captin thinks I am dum. I hate it when people think I am dum. Even if I be. Maybe tonite Arthur Hand will make me feel good again. Maybe down among them linen stacks.

And sure enough.

16. CAESAR

Of what the sharks do James knows little. Of history and literature, of the dethroning of kings and the fall of gods, of mythology and symbols that exist beyond the forest, he knows nothing. Of his own self he knows only the pain and the shame of a failed leader, a failed man, who never should have left his mother's womb.

Disconsolate, he seeks permission to move among his people sprawled and helpless on the beach, silent now, stunned now, tears and moans dried up like the sand. For three days they have been treated differently – given enough water to drink, enough food to eat to help them recover their strength. Each has been given a bucket of water with which to wash. Each has been given a clean waist cloth to dissipate the stench. Under watchful eyes the wives of the warriors have anointed the skin of each with aromatic oils that make them gleam with health. That make them fit to be sold.

Still shackled, as are they all, James kneels beside them in the sand, one by one. No one says a word. What is there to say? They speak only eye to eye. Some look firmly into his, as if to absolve him of blame, as if to acknowledge that they know that there was nothing he could have done. Others bitterly turn their heads away, thinking what they dare not say to their king: Why did you allow this? We trusted you. The fault is yours.

Only some of the children have the courage to speak their thoughts. *Why is this happening, King James? Where are they taking us, King James? Where is my little brother, King James?* He rubs the heads of the boys. More gently he touches the cheeks of the girls. He has no answers for them. He has no comfort to give.

One unspoken sentiment offers him tenuous balm: they still think of him as their king. Still, he can do nothing.

Slowly – his chained ankles permit nothing more – he shuffles through the sand to his place at the head of them. He hears the white-rimmed waves wrinkling onto the beach repeat again and again that final question: *Where is my little brother?*

Vatok has walked down to a wooden fence at the edge of the water, a fence between two worlds. James knows he will not be shot if he follows. From behind the fence he can see the masts of the waiting ship anchored off shore, huge sails furled. On its broad side he can read black lettering: N.Y. Mercantile Company///Bluebell. Cutting the water nearby he can see the grey fins of fish.

What are those? he asks.

Sharks. The white man's helper.

The white man has trained them to be here, so close to the ship?

No one can train them. They are here because they feed on death. Just as the freest birds in the sky are the kites, who feed on death. There is never a shortage.

Are you saying the sharks prevent the prisoners from trying to escape?

The sharks prevent them from succeeding.

James studies the ship, estimating the drop from the deck to the sea. A muscle in his chest has speared him like a lance. As if a huge snake has crushed his ribs. As if they have just slain Triana – again.

That is a large ship.

Not as large as some.

It will carry us far away. That is why they hide it behind the Castle.

For many that is the worst moment. Stepping onto the ship. When they understand they shall not return – not to their children, not to their elders, never. That is when they are most desperate. That is when some of them jump into the sea, chains and all.

Chains and sharks and all.

Yes.

And you, Vatok, the chief of your tribe, can do nothing

No.

Perhaps I should warn my people.

They will despair soon enough. But let me ask you something, James. If you were in my position, what would you do differently?

James wanted to scoff at the absurd question. But before he could answer, his face seemed to explode like a fire burning in a village hut. He had no breath with which to speak.

Vatok answered for him.

You would do just as I do. To save your own people.

The white-washed sky and the sun-washed Cape Coast Castle contrast so sharply with the black flesh of captives and captors alike that a half-mad sorcerer may have created it all. The blackness and the whiteness meet only at the cold iron greyness of the chains and the metal cuffs.

He turns away in disgust. As he does he intakes his breath, is stabbed by a puzzling pain in his chest. With his keen eyes he has noticed something difficult to believe. Atop the tallest of the three masts in the harbor is perched the multi-colored parrot from the forest, curled beak tucked under a wing, as if it is asleep. Blue as the sky, green as the forest, turquoise as the sea. James feels that it is watching nonetheless.

A voice loud and timbered as an elephant's bray slams through the air like a musket shot. A large man in front of the Castle is shouting at him in English.

You! Down by the fence! Over here! Now!

Vatok begins to translate, stops as James walks away, walks as best he can in his ankle chains to where the man is shouting. The man is almost as tall as James, has a large chest, sweat under his arms, a cutlass in his belt, a deep red scar on his cheek. James stops in front of him.

I am Cree. First Mate. You speak English?

Some.

Where did you learn?

James does not answer. He thinks: You have imprisoned my body. My mind I reserve for myself.

Did you hear me?

James remains silent. Cree raises the cutlass, presses the point into James's neck.

Speak!

James looks unwavering into the man's blue eyes. He does not speak. Behind the First Mate he sees another man watching from the Castle wall.

They told us about you. Your Majesty, the King! We had a good laugh.

James says nothing.

The First Mate lowers his weapon. *One day soon you may find yourself swimming with the sharks.* He grins, four front teeth missing. *You blackheads seem to enjoy swimming, judging by your screams.*

James shows his sweating back to Cree and shuffles toward his villagers, who are sprawled at the boundary between the beach and the trees, several musket-carrying guards standing in the shade in case of trouble. Some of his people have been lulled to sleep by the wretched heat, others cannot sleep because of it. Those who are awake are silent, careful not to scar themselves on the blistering hot chains. Beyond howls of pain or despair, what is there to say?

He vowed silently not to speak to their captors. The vow of defiance did not last. He would show his contempt that way, he thought, but changed his mind when the captain approached and bid him stand; speaking with them might gain nothing, but not speaking could lead to worse. The captain, dressed in white, with only a slight paunch, with a black three-cornered hat on his head, a kind James had never seen before, did not seem menacing. James unfolded himself from the sand. This, he knew, was the man from the Castle wall.

I am Captain Enoch Williams, commander of this voyage. A gentleman would add, At your service, but clearly I am not at your service.

Nor are you a gentleman.

You have spunk, King James, I like that. What I have come to tell you is that if First Mate Cree should again point his weapon at you, or even touch you, he will lose his right arm at the shoulder. You will get to keep it. Eat it if you want.

With all respect, I do not need that man's arm. What I need is my own two legs.

Ah, that I cannot give.

You are the Master.

I am a businessman.

Like my new friend Vatok over there? It is Satan's business.

Are you saying I am the devil?

Perhaps just his right arm.

The captain grinned. *I see that you have wit as well.*

James kicked one leg through the sand. *I also have chains.*

That perhaps I could fix, once we are on board. If you give me your word of honor that you will not try to escape.

You believe that I have honor?

Honor does not reside in the skin.

Nor in the sharks.

I will wear my chains on the ship if my people do. I am no better than they.

Free of chains, you could protect your people from the nasty crew. From First Mate Cree.

James look down, kicked at the sand again. *I will have to think on it.*

I already know your decision, the captain said. *Even if you do not.*

And how do you know that?

I am a student of humanity.

You concede that we of dark skin are human?

I do not speak for my company.

Then why do you sail for your company?

I have seven mouths to feed. Selling my soul pays well. You know, King, I have half a mind to buy you for myself, and make you my first mate.

Bought mates, I think, are not loyal mates.

That is probably true. If you were in charge, what would you do?

Me? First I would free my people. Then I would kill your crew.

Thieves, brigands, cut-throats, drunks. No loss there.

I would burn your ship. Then return to our village.

And me? What of me?

You would be free to live with us.

That's very kind of you.

In chains.

The captain laughed, his small belly shaking under his shirt.

You're as cheeky as I have heard.

I do not know this word. I thought I knew all English words.

It is hard to translate. Ornery. Irascible.

Those are big words.

There are many. Where did you learn English? It is more than Vatok.

When I was a boy, missionaries came. Promoting their dead leader. When they saw how smart King John, my grandfather, was, they made a plan. They would teach him English as well as their Jesus. Then he could spread this Jesus throughout the forest. They gave him books to learn English, and many Bibles. After they left, we studied English every day, just the two of us. I asked him why. He said, Learning does not need a reason. Though sometimes it finds one.

Did he become a good missionary?

The Bibles we used to start fires. And wipe asses.

He was a smart man, your grandfather.

Smarter than me.

Why do you say that?

When he was king my people did not wear chains.

You shouldn't blame yourself. There was nothing you could do.

Who shall I blame then? God? You have already told me you are not the Devil.

Sometimes I wonder, Enoch Williams muttered. James did not hear, had already moved toward his people. From the sand a pure white bone was sticking upward, a bone the captain did not recognize, picked clean by a creature he could not name.

Tomorrow we begin processing, the captain called over his shoulder as he strode toward the Castle. Another long English word that James did not understand.

He tried to think but the floating sun untethered by forest shade made him feel as if reason itself was being burned away in the sweat along his brow. Vatok was right, once the schooner left the harbor there would be no escaping their fate, whatever that might be. Images of gliding shark fins dizzied him. He wondered if the sharks, too, would be his friends even as they devoured his flesh. He had an idea of why Vatok and the captain were acting kinder, but it hovered just out of reach, perhaps in the spirit world.

17. Peggy

A farewell party is not what Peggy expected when Nora, taking her hand, suggested they climb the slippery steps of the cemetery for one last look at the beautiful sea that all their lives had been a nourishing mother. Peggy agreed; perhaps the stone monument to her own death would be gone, perhaps she had only imagined it that time months ago. But she knew that was not so, Nora had seen it as well. And there it still was, fringed with dry grass. M A R G A R E T. Granite does not fly away with the gulls. She knelt, touched the stone, with no more understanding than when she first had seen it, first had burrowed into its horror, a horror she still carried within her in a slimy mental pouch. She felt too young to be carrying within her her own death.

I'm frightened, she said.

Of what? Not the stone.

Of the voyage to New York.

Of the sea?

Nora, be serious. How could the daughter of a fisherman, the daughter of a fishing village, be afraid of the sea? It's the other passengers. I hear them every night before I sleep. Such a lovely young woman, what glorious red hair, are you traveling alone, where are your parents, or your husband, I bet I know, your finance' went to the colonies to make money so he can send for you, and now you will soon be married, such a lucky young man he is, what a lovely couple you will make. Nora, I won't just stand there and nod, I refuse to lie, they'd find out anyway when nobody meets the boat. But I don't want to tell the truth, either, they'd just start pitying me, like the people in the village. I could not stand that.

What do you mean, like the people in the village?

Come on, Nora, I'm not blind. People used to like me. Be happy to be around me. The men would flirt with me, and their wives would pretend to be upset, and laugh.

I'm not sure the wives were pretending. Or laughing.

But now, ever since Billy jilted me in that letter – and didn't that gossip get around Carey fast! – people look away when I'm coming. They don't know what to say, so they say nothing. I make them uncomfortable. You'd think I had sinned or something. Do you know how that makes me feel?

You're wrong, Peg. Let's go back down, and I'll prove it to you.

So it was that after they had climbed down the uneven rock steps carefully and approached Peggy's house they heard noises from out back. They circled the small dwelling and on top of the cliff overlooking the ocean they found three wooden tables that had been dragged from the homes of neighbors, laden now with all manner of cakes and cookies, tea, coffee, milk. All of the women from within a quarter mile were there, and the children; the men were all out on their boats, by choice or necessity. The only man present was Father Mallory. They all yelled *surprise*, some hugged Peggy, some shook her hand. She knew Nora was responsible for this surprise and muttered that she would get her later.

Peggy tried to judge if the good wishes were sincere. She decided that they were, but also subdued because of the circumstances of her departure. This was not a pre-marital celebration, it was ... she was not sure what is was. The impatient children were permitted to grab cookies and milk and warned not to play too near the top of the cliff.

We told everyone not to bring gifts, because you would have only one luggage to take on the boat, Aunt Dottie said from her uncertain perch on the edge of a bench – her huge rocker being too heavy to be carried out here – *but all the ladies made these divine sweets for you, Peggy* – and the divine child who was no longer a child curtsied in both directions and bit into a strawberry scone, careful not to drip red goo onto her blue blouse.

We do have one gift, Father Mallory said, and from a paper bag took out a thick book. *This is a Bible, a gift from the Carey Church of Christ,* he intoned as he handed it to Peggy. It said King James Bible on the white and gilt cover. *This is actually the Bible the Protestants use,* the Priest said, *but the general store in St. John's was sent the wrong one from the home country after I ordered it. No matter, it's all one God. The main thing, Peggy Kerry, is that during your travels, you be sure you read one verse every morning and one verse every night. That will keep you out of trouble – financial trouble, romantic trouble, and most important of all, moral trouble.* He glanced about to make sure none of the children could hear him. *Alone by yourself, you must keep your morals pure and your body chaste, until God, be he Catholic or Protestant, shows you the way he wants your life be lived.*

Amen! said the ladies, and lifted their coffee cups, many of which had had spoonfuls of Irish whiskey added to them.

Aunt Dottie told the others to stay put as she guided her huge body into the house and came out carrying a flat white box that once had held a warm coat. From the box she lifted and held up for all to see a new beige skirt.

For your trip, Dottie said. *It's from your father.*

Peggy tried to stifle a giggle. She said, *Father couldn't make a handkerchief from a square of muslin.*

Two women gasped at this impudence, but when Dottie erupted in half a ton of cliff- shaking laughter the tension dissipated.

I made it of course, she said, *but he's going to pay me for it. And then I figured, with a new skirt you ought to have a new blouse as well. So I made this.* She held up a white muslin shirt. *Also, to complete the outfit, a cap. But on the boat be sure to tie the ribbons, so the ocean winds don't carry it off.*

And your hair with it, Nora said.

Amid general merriment that might not have been expected, Dottie pulled a coin from her pocket. *One more thing before you top off your coffees*, she said. *This is also a gift from Travis.*

I can't believe it, Peggy said, taking the coin, rubbing it.

It's a shilling. A bright shiny shilling.

I doubt that will last long in the colonies, one of the women said as she emptied the whiskey bottle into her coffee. *Even if it is bright and shiny.*

It's not to spend. It's for Peggy to have good luck, Travis said to tell you. You know where it's from? The day Peggy was born, he was gutting a cod, and he found this shilling inside. He's been carrying it with him for eighteen years. Now it belongs to Margaret, he said.

Nora leaned close to Peggy's ear. *Isn't that the day ...*

Yes.

What does that mean?

You tell me.

Odd thoughts flashed through Peggy's head: *The Last Supper. Thirty Pieces of Silver.*

Much later she would remember them as premonitions.

Where is Travis today? the whiskey pourer asked.

Oh, he's out on his boat with his beer.

Even during her farewell party?

We're happy he's here in spirit. Right, Peggy? We can't expect too much.

Peggy slept that night with the coin under her pillow. Whether her father's luck would now become her own, whether that would be a good thing, she did not choose to consider.

The next morning, awakening early, donning her new outfit, hugging Dottie goodbye – her father was already gone – she lugged her carrying bag to the pub-cafe, where Nora was waiting with a hired coach that would take them to St. John's Bay.

18. MARY

Dear Denture Dairy

Will my mother come visit today? Maybe come take me away? That is what I thought first thing every morning in Belfree Orphinage. She never come. Not for 14 years.

The storm is still ahead of us. The captin is swinging south to avoid it. But on dec the sky is dark and the wind is cold, so I am staying in my cabin writing in my Dairy. Thinking about my mother again, since we are going far away. I ast Sister Beetrice many times where my mother was. She always said she didnt know. But last year she went to a wooden box in her offace and pulled out a yellow paper note. Sort of like that denture paper they toar. Sister said one morning long ago they found a box near the orphin gate, and in it wrapped in a muslin blanket was baby me. She showed me the note. I memrised what it said. It said

I'm sorry. I have no money to raise my child. I am leaving Donegal today forever. Please take good care of my little girl. Her name is Mary Burton.

Sister Beetrice said this was not unusual, two or three babies are left at the gate every year. What was different, she said, was that most mothers dont sign their name. Anyway, she said, the first thing we had t do was get you baptized into the cathlic faith. Father Robertson at the Belfree church down the road was in hospital, so Higgins drove us in the wagon to the church on the other side of Donegal. Father, I am Sister Beetrice of the Belfree Catholic Orphinage, she told the priest there. We

have a new little girl to be baptized. Thats wonderful the
Preist said, and led us to the fountain. In the name of
the Lord, he said . .. somethin like that ... we baptize this
child ... what name are you giving her? Mary. Mary Burton.
The Priest, who was holding me, stumbled and nearly
dropped me, Sister Beetrice said, but he caught hisself
in time. May I ask why you chose that name, he ast, his
face red, and she showed him the note. You caught me
by surprise, the preist said, only because ...I should have
introduced myself sooner ... I am FatherMichael Burton.
What a coincidence, the Sister said. You dont imagine
people will think-of course not, everyone knows preists
cannot marry or have children, the Sister said. Besides,
Father Burton said, there must be five or six Burtons in
Donegal. It could even be the mothers name. Eggzactly, the
Sister said. Father Burton finished the baptism, submerging
you completely under water. Like a fish I asked. Sort of,
and he sprinkled holy water on your little head, and home
we went. The odd thing is, just what Father Burton was
afraid of came true. Rumors spread through the city
that this Father Burton had a sinful baby and stashed
her in the orphinage. Thats all we know, because as soon
as Father Roberton came out of hospital, we heard that
Father Burton across town had ast for and received a
transfer to a church in Dublin. Which only increased the
rumors.

The day last year after Sister Beetrice told me all this,
I was riding into town with Higgins to buy food for the
week, and I said, If my father was really a priest, that
would make me special, wouldnt it. Could be, Higgins said,
but we dont know the mind of God. It could make you
special. It also could make you dammed.

Dammed is a very bad thing, according to Sister
Beetrice.

Now, dont you mind what an old man babbles, Higgins
said. I should just shut my dam mouth. My darn mouth.

I was afraid to ask Sister Beetrice. So I still dont
know if I am special or dammed. Or neither one. Mostly I
am sure now that my mother aint gonna visit me. She might
even never heard of New York colony.

My hand is startin to hurt from writin too much. I think I'll go on deck and see what is happenin up there. See if we have passed that storm yet.

19. CAESAR

Comparing abominations is difficult. This James discovered inside the teeming, steaming, stultifying Cape Coast Castle, where he squatted on the cement floor near a mocha-skinned man who was holding over his head a round red hat such as James had never seen. The rest of the man was naked, except for a short grey beard. The notion of ranking cruelties had never occurred to him before, but James needed to occupy his mind or go insane, as the red hat man apparently had. Unable to hold the hat high any longer, the man lowered it to cover his genitals. Almost instantly the whip of a guard cracked on the floor. The man, biting his lip against certain pain in his shoulders, again raised the hat above his head. James turned away in embarrassment.

So. Which had beens the day's worst abomination? The surgeon examining them? The selling of them like cattle? The painful branding? The march into the Castle? The suffocating stench?

Just now he would say the stench. The basement of the Castle was divided into several dark dungeons. Each could hold hundreds of prisoners. There were no windows in the thick brick walls. About 200 members of another tribe, the Kasu, lay sprawled on the concrete floor, men and women both, some naked, some wearing wet and soiled waist cloths. The floor was muddy with feces, with yellow-green urine. James did not know how long they had been there – only that already the fetid air was difficult to breathe. If you tried to light a fire in there, he thought, it might not flame .

This last day they had been awakened by the surgeon, who came at dawn, accompanied by First Mate Cree. He was a small man with thinning grey hair, dressed in white. Like the prisoners, he was not wearing shoes. Did the crew fear that he, too, might try to escape? He moved among them on the night-damp sand, examining men, women, children. Mouths, ears, genitals.

This is a healthy tribe, he told Cree. *Tell the captain he can buy them all. Except for those two quite pregnant women. The rocking of the ship is likely to induce premature birth. The infants will die amid the filth. The mothers might bleed to death. He is better off leaving them here.*

Cree shook his head, smiled. *I will overrule you to the captain, surgeon. There is no finer entertainment than watching mothers hurl their newborns into the sea.*

Rage erupted like fire in the chest of the king. His hands, bound in iron cuffs behind his back, he clenched into fists. What could he do against such scurrilous words? He tried to calm himself. They were only words.

He watched, furious, as the First Mate moved carelessly among the women, touching the cheek of one, the breasts of another. Pausing in front of Rena, the younger sister of Triana, leering into her frightened eyes, Cree hitched the groin of his trousers. *This one shall be mine,* he said.

James shuffled two short steps nearer to Cree and flung himself head first at Cree's shoulder. Off guard, Cree toppled to the sand. The tribe could not follow the argument in English, but violence speaks all languages. They cheered and whooped wildly as the first mate went down.

When he stood his cutlass was drawn.

You shall pay for that, he said.

Then you shall forfeit an arm.

I don't think so. In our legal contracts, signed by our puny captain and his rich brother, each officer has the right to one woman on the journey. It's the law.

I respect no such law. If you touch any of my people – woman or man or child – I shall throw you overboard. That is my law.

You have muscles, king. But not enough to throw me over the rail.

My plan is not to throw you over the rail. It is to drop you over, piece by piece.

Cree's face reddened. He stammered for a reply. He could not find one. Finally he muttered, *We shall see!*

Not if I take your eyes first, James said.

Cree stepped back, whipped his cutlass through the air, near James's face, but taking care not to slash him. Only the rising, sparkling sun, as it glanced off the flashing blade, seemed lethal.

The tribe members whooped and shouted Muktu epithets as Cree, rare defeat resting like a wet log on his shoulders, followed the surgeon across the sand toward the Castle.

James should have remained silent at that moment. He knew this now, but not then. He told the tribe of the offer by the captain: that he, James, could roam unchained on the boat; and that he, James, had said no, that he was no different from the other men, and insisted on being treated so. The people began to shout in Muktu: *No! Look what you have just done. You must roam free to protect us! Perhaps to free us!* The shouting did not subside until he bowed his head, accepting their desire. The shouts metamorphosed into cheers of relief.

Now, hours later, inside the stinking Castle, beside the naked man with the red hat, his nerves were writhing with debilitating guilt. Chains or no, he could not protect them; he certainly could not free them. Had he misled his own people? He had not meant to. The snakes of guilt braiding his nerves were their own abomination.

Movement beside his left eye. The red hat was coming closer. James slid to his right. The man lay his head on the ground, using the small red hat for a pillow. Almost at once he was asleep, snoring lightly. What abomination had he suffered?

The disposition of the Muktu went quickly. His people – the men still in chains, the women not – were ordered to stand in front of the bleached Castle. Captain Williams was there in his tricorner hat, along with Vatok in a fresh waist cloth. Each held a pad and pencil. They spoke in English, he could make out some of the words above the ripple of the sea. The black man was selling the black tribe to the white man. James could not believe this was happening, even as he watched.

The two men seemed to agree on a price. A discount was given because the captain was buying the entire tribe. The only dispute arose when Vatok pointed at James. He seemed to be arguing that James, as the king, who could speak English, was not part of the bargain; the captain would have to pay separately for the king. A lump in his dry throat, James heard the numbers. Four times normal. The white man refused, offered to pay twice the normal rate. They argued over the king as if he were a prize elephant. Finally they agreed, James would cost the captain three times an ordinary man. James did not feel honored. He felt sick. The going price, he had heard from Vatok earlier, was 115 gallons of rum for a man, 50 gallons for a woman, or the equivalent in sugar, cloth, tobacco, gold.

The captain acted as if he had been cheated. *I don't care how strong or smart he is, how much cotton can one man pick?*

Is that why you are taking them to New York? Vatok asked. *To pick cotton?*

The captain waved his arm toward the right corner of the Castle. Several of his crew walked in that direction. The captain handed First Mate Cree a piece of paper. Cree led the others inside. He watched and counted at the exit as the men carried out the agreed-upon merchandise and set it on the beach.

Those products, James thought, is what our lives and loves and children and ceremonies, and those of our forefathers going back through all eternity, have amounted to. Surely this was the ultimate disgrace.

Until the branding, which came next.

You speak English?

James thought he was dreaming. He traced lightly the raw scab on his chest. NY. For New York Mercantile Company. Burned into his skin with a red hot iron just hours ago. The pain still lingered. The white men had built two fires on the beach. Had lined up the men and boys at one, the women and girls at the other. The surgeon held an iron in one fire, First Mate Cree held one in the other. James as king had been branded first. He had clenched his teeth until he was afraid they might break, in order not to scream, not to frighten the others. The captain had ordered Cree to go easy on the women. He did not obey. Each was branded on the breast. Rena was pulled from the line to go first. Cree pressed the hot iron to her breast longer than seemed necessary. She screamed as her flesh burned. This set the others crying out in desperate anticipation. Several fainted, men and women both. They were branded as they lay on the ground. Three boys tried to run away. They were quickly caught by crewmen and yanked back into line. The scent of burning flesh perfumed the beach.

I asked, do you speak English?

James opened his eyes. He must have dozed for a moment. The voice came from the naked man with the red hat, who now sat on the concrete floor beside him.

How do you know? James asked.

You slept. You spoke in your sleep. I think you were being branded again.

James looked closer at the man. Scarred into his chest were the letters RI. James pointed.

What does that mean?

Rhode Island. It is another British colony, farther north than New York. They buy many slaves. No cotton, no sugar. I do not know why.

Slaves? I do not know this word.

The naked man appeared stricken. He placed his red hat on his head.

You don't know it? How can this be? A slave is what you are now. And I. And all those poor people over there. That is what the whites bought you for. To pick their cotton, their tobacco, their sugar.

Why then not call us workers?

You will be workers. But they will own your life. They will not pay you, except with meals. They will control all that you do. They can buy you and sell you as they please. Separate you from your wife, your children, as if you were dogs.

For how long will we be such slaves?

Until you die. Then they will own your children, should you have any. Until they die.

That is why they keep us in chains? Not to eat us?

No. But to work us to the bone.

James dropped his face into his hands, his forehead wet, trying to understand.

Why are you here alone? he muttered. *With a red hat.*

The hat is called a fez. They think it makes me look foolish. Like a clown. It is a long story.

It appears that we shall have time. What was I saying in my sleep?

You were talking to a person called Beto. I did not understand much. I know a Beto. That is why I tried to hear.

James grew excited, pressed the shoulders of the other man.

Beto is my baby brother!

Then it is a different Beto. The one I know — I met him just yesterday, or the day before, already it is hard to remember — he was not a baby. He was a strong boy, perhaps of 16 or 17 years. Very clever. Very fleet of foot. He killed two men while trying to save me.

James took the man's hand in his.

That is him! That is my brother. Where did you meet him? Was he not taken prisoner? I thought I would never see him again! Tell me about your hat — no one else in this stinking place has a hat. Tell me everything!

Calm down. You are ...

James. King James of the Muktu.

Mortz. Professor Hali Mortz of the Zenkor. That is the only title I can claim. Professor. And you a king!

And they will make slaves of us both?

So it appears.

But tell me about Beto. Please.

And so he did. But first he had to tell about himself.

The Zenkor were a dying tribe deep in the inland forest. Their method of survival was surviving, as is true in most of the known world. The men hunted small game, but Hali did not like to hunt. The women and children gathered twigs and berries. Hali timorously joined them. A gatherer in a hunting tribe, he was an outcast among the other boys. When passing missionaries spoke of different lands north of the forest, Hali, at age 16, told his parents he was going off to explore these northern lands. As he trekked north he came upon six villages of other tribes. Welcomed at each, he discovered that more than anything he loved collecting words; each tribe had its own language, but they shared similar roots, and he learned to speak and understand in each. With all these new words, happiness fluttered in his brain like pretty butterflies. Upon reaching the Arab lands he learned English, and became a valuable aide to traders dealing in spices, linens, other merchandise.

He was offered a job with a Portuguese Trading Company – but the day he started he discovered that the Portuguese were trading not in merchandise but in humans, his own African people, selling entire tribes to be slaves in the west; the Portuguese, he learned, had in fact originated the enslavement of the forest tribes more than a hundred years ago.

Instead of reporting for work, the next day Hali hired a fisherman to sail him down the coast. When the small boat took on water, the fisherman left him at the beach a few miles north of where an old trail entered the forest *like the sweet entry into a woman.* As Hali walked along the beach, wearing the loose white trousers and shirt and red fez he had adopted in the Arab lands, he was joined by a young man carrying a musket and a cutlass, who emerged almost unseen from the forest and asked if he could walk along. Hali was pleased by the company, horrified by the story the boy – who said his name was Beto – told about the abduction of his Muktu tribe. They slept peacefully on the beach, but at dawn were attacked by four men emerging from the forest. One carried a musket. Beto recognized them by their sharpened teeth. Without hesitating, he killed the first man with a musket ball through his chest. *For Triana,* he said. A man wielding a cutlass charged next. Beto dispatched him easily. But when the last two rushed them from opposite sides, Beto knew he could not hold them off. He grabbed Hali's money belt from his waist, yelled *for your family,* and slipped into the forest like the wind.

Hali was no fighter. The warriors made him strip naked except for the fez on his head, which made them laugh. After three hours of walking they arrived here at the Cape Coast Castle, where the warriors proudly displayed their catch. *What I am to do with him?* Chief Vatok asked angrily. *Who will buy a slave with no muscles, a paunch for a belly and grey in his beard.* The chief rebuked the two warriors, ordered Hali chained to a tree. When Captain Williams noticed Hali later, and spoke with him, he bought him from Vatok for one gallon of rum. The usual price for a male slave was four gallons, even six.

And my Beto?

The last I saw him, as I said, was when he blew into the forest like the wind.

A gate opened near the front, allowing in a narrow glow of light and air. A crew member, looking warily at the sprawled and moaning tribe, summoned both men up the long ramp to the surface. Merely stretching their legs felt for a moment like freedom. After the dark dungeon the bright sun was blinding. The captain awaited them.

What sonofabitch put you two in there? Disease is running amok in that filthy tribe. Dysentery. That's the last thing we want for you.

They watched as across the plaza First Mate Cree led the Muktus in single file toward the dungeon to their left. The men were still in chains. Some dug their heels in the sand and tried to resist, fearful of what awaited in the dungeons; they were prodded with spears until they moved. James stood tall beside the gate, hoping this would allay their fears. He was still alive. He was still with them.

Cree waved the two men inside this fresher dungeon, Hali still wearing his red fez. The heavy gate crashed down behind them.

Let's speak more on the boat, James said.

If they permit us.

Almost at once the gate was raised again, and red hat was ordered outside. In the world of slavery, one man talking was demented; two men talking was a conspiracy.

20. PEGGY

The Life and Strange Surprising Adventures of Robinson Crusoe, written by one Daniel Defoe, was the book that Nora, huddled beside Peggy in the coach as it rattled to St. John's Bay, gave her as a farewell present.

It's a new kind of book, Nora said. *The men in the pub were saying it's the talk of Dublin. Because this Defoe fellow doesn't just tell his real adventures sailing the world, as others have done. He makes up fake and scary ones. That's how it's different from any book in English that has come before. It was put out twenty years ago, and nobody has copied the idea, so maybe it isn't any good. I don't know. I had the Everything Store order it for your birthday, but it arrived from London four months late.*

I know I'll love it, Peggy said, and kissed Nora hard on the cheek.

You can read it instead of talking with the other passengers, like you're afraid of. What upset me, though, was when Father Mallory gave you that Bible yesterday. Together they'll be very heavy to carry.

Ooops!

Ooops what?

I forgot to bring the Bible. I put it somewhere and left it.

Where did you put it and leave it?

Under Dottie's bed. Back near the wall.

I had a feeling that might happen, Nora said, and hugged her arm around Peggy's neck.

From deck to dock they waved wildly at one another. *I love you like a sister,* they shouted in unison, and laughed. The boat receded from the

land. They watched across the widening gap until each was no bigger
than a capelin. As they were disappearing, the eyes of each glistened.

I was born in the year 1632, in the city of York ...

Thus began Peggy's reading. The waves under the boat were
smoother than under a trawler, she was glad to discover. She read
through dinner – and paused, stunned, at a sequence a quarter way
through the book. Father Mallory had never said anything like this. She
read the passage a second time:

After I had eaten I tried to walk, but found myself so weak that I could hardly
carry the gun (for I never went out without that); so I went but a little way, and sat down
upon the ground, looking out upon the sea, which was just before me, and very calm
and smooth. As I sat here, some such thoughts as these occurred to me:

What is this earth and sea, of which I have seen so much? Whence is it produced,
and what am I, and all the other creatures, wild and tame, human and brutal, whence
are we?

Sure we are all made by some secret Power who formed the earth and sea, the air
and sky; and who is that?

Then it followed most naturally, it is God that has made it all. Well, but then it
came on strangely; if God has made all these things, He guides and governs them all,
and all things that concern them; for the Power that could make all things must certainly
have power to guide and direct them.

If so, nothing can happen in the great circuit of His works, either without His
knowledge or appointment.

And if nothing happens without His knowledge, He knows that I am here and
am in this dreadful condition; and if nothing happens without His appointment, He has
appointed all this to befall me.

Nothing occurred to my thoughts to contradict any of these conclusions; and
therefore it rested on me with the greater force that it must needs be, that God had
appointed all this to befall me; that I was brought to this miserable circumstance by His
direction, He having the sole power, not of me only, but of everything that happened in
the world. Immediately it followed:

Why has God done this to me? What have I done to be thus used?

A few lines later Crusoe switched the blame from God to himself.
He wrote that he had led a wretched life, and that God was right to
punish him again and again. But Peggy did not relate to that. Her mother
had died just minutes after Peggy was born, her sister had died even a few
minutes before (if that was her sister and not herself) so she hardly was

being punished back then for wretched acts. It was true that she was not much of a church-goer, nor was her father or Aunt Dottie, but she could not accept that lack as appropriate reason to lose the affection of Billy to the Widow Williams in New York. Nora, one of the finest friends in the world, did go to church every week (even if dragged by her mother) yet her own father behaved horribly, brutally with her. How did God explain that? Why did He permit that to happen? It would be a good question to ask such a God, if she ever was to meet such a God.

Also in the story, she was startled to discover that in this very first book of its kind, as Nora had pointed out, the second principal person was a Negro. Never having seen one, she found this hard to imagine. Billy had said in his first letter that there were black people in New York colony, but how did you deal with them? Her father had wondered aloud before she left: Do they bite? Do they growl? Do you feed them like a dog? Do you beat them like a seal?

She thought: *I hope there will be instructions before we leave the boat.*

She thought: *I wonder if Nora would think that was funny.*

21. MARY

Fookin North Atlantic in winter the captain bellowed as the vicious rain ripped his unshaved face and the wind whipped the tiller in his hands and together they tried to sink the Catherine and all us souls aboard. Including me. He meant to go around the storm even at the cost of several days but Nature turned the storm south unexpectedly and it was chasing us across the boiling ocean like a dog chasing a duck. The sky was black with yellow flashes and along with wild wind and grasping waves the boat was bouncing us around like a mommy bounces a baby on her knee. A fake not a real mommy, thinks I.

The crew was running about the deck shouting and doing important things while hanging on. When Arthur Hands noticed I had ventured from my cabin he warned me to go back. Just then I got dizzy and was sick all over the corridor. Arthur shooed me away and found a bucket and set it beside my bed and told me to lie down and if I got sick again that's what the bucket was for. And a good thing. He said not to worry about the mess in the corridor he would clean it up. I guess he did, I never got punished for it.

As I lay on my bed the room began spinning around me like a top we played with at the orphanage. I tried lying on my stomach, my back,

my side. None of it helped, the room spun around and around and the
more it spun the sicker I felt. I don't know how long it lasted I think it
spun for days. Behind the spinning I heard the rain pounding the deck
and the waves crashing the side of the Catherine and with each day
I wanted to die more. Anything to get off that boat. I didn't care if I
was buried in a box in the earth or tossed by the captain into the sea.
Anything to stop the spinning and the nausea. I knew this denture was
a bad idea. It was even worse than I could imagine. I wondered if there
was anything I could do to help, when I heard the crew yelling about
the main sail that had got stuck and torn out in the wind and I thought
if only I wasn't sick I could rush to the deck and ask for a needle and
thread because sewing I had learned pretty good at the orphanage, and
I would climb up the mast and sew up the slit that had ripped. If only I
wasn't sick. I must have slept some, my head still spinning, until I heard
a cracking and heard the crew yelling again and figured if I went up
on deck I could grab a broomstick and rope and climb up the mast –
broke as it was it could not hold a crew member – and I would place the
broomstick along the crack and wrap the rope around it tight. As tight as
could be. If only I wasn't sick, that's what I would do. Later when I heard
the crashing of glass as the boat half rose out of the water on a huge
wave and then slammed down again there was only one thing it could
be. The bottles of Irish whisky in the hold had crashed over in a heap,
breaking and spewing whiskey every which way. Including on the fine
white Irish linen, which was not white anymore but brown. I would grab
the soiled linens and jump off the boat into the water and wash them in
the blue sea, which somehow made them white again, and carry them
back to the deck and hang them over the rail to dry as soon as the storm
passed and the sun shone again. If only I wasn't sick. Then I heard the
crew yelling *Man Overboard, Man Overboard,* and I just knew it was Arthur
Hands, and if I could swim I would have jumped into the ocean and
saved him. If only I could swim. If I wasn't sick.

   Then it stopped. The room stopped spinning. It slowed at first like
Gweebarra when I pull hard on the reins, then it stopped altogether.
The Catherine was not leaping out of the water any more like a spoiled
brat but bouncing along like a kitten, still shaking, breathing hard like
Gweebarra after a run, but slowly calming down. I tried to stand, and I
could, and to leave the cabin, and I could, and to ease down the corridor
holding on to the wall like I could, and all of a sudden I felt hungry. Like
I had not eaten food or anything for maybe a year. But just as I come out
on deck and look up and see that no sail seems to be torn or mended,
and no mast is held together by a broom, a crew man from high up in

what they call the Crow's Nest shouted, *Land Ho! Land Ho!* And from all over the boat the Hands come running to the front, slipping and sliding on the wet sloppy deck, cheering and yelling and waving their arms in the wet salty air. I crowded near the rail with them but didn't see nothing except the empty grey and wobbling sea, as far as the eye could see. Just the endless sea. Then all of a sudden there it was, so far away you could hardly see it at all, but the captain put his spyglass to his eye and shouted, *There she is, boys. We made it through. That's Newfoundland, all right.* The crew cheered. *We'll just tuck in at St. John's for repairs for a day or two, and some decent grub, on me,* the captain said, *and with clear sailing ahead we should reach New York by the start of the new year.* The Hands cheered again. Cookie rolled out a barrel of Irish beer and cartons of crackers. Arthur Hands held out a box to me. *Take a handful,* he said. But suddenly, so near to New York, I wasn't all that hungry any more.

22. CAESAR

Sequestered from his people by his ratcheting thoughts, James saw things get worse. The boarding of the ship, with its attendant outrages, had led to multiple suicides. As he stood on the slightly swaying deck of the Bluebelle, multiple sails being raised by the crew, the orange sun sinking into the sea far out on the western horizon, the events of the day, some of which he had witnessed, some of which had been described to him by Professor Moritz with the red fez, curdled in his mind like spoiled stew. The surgeon walking among the Kasu tribe amid the stench, leaning his face close to the mouths of sprawled captives, pointing to one and then another, indicating to crewmen that these prisoners, after three weeks of confinement, were already dead. The crewmen, wearing wraps over their noses and mouths, lifted the dead by stiff arms and legs, placed each none too gently on a heavy sheet, carried them out through a wide doorway that faced the ocean, hurled them over a rail into the sea. The patient sharks swarmed to the meals they had known would come. Of the 210 Kasu tribesmen and women who had been cooped up in the Castle dungeon like animals, waiting for a ship to arrive to carry them to a new world, 19 already were dead. The surgeon made his rounds a second time. Peering carefully, he selected for death prisoners who were still alive but whom, he judged, would stop breathing in a day or two, and therefore should not be brought aboard the ship. The crewmen carried these out as well – there were 15 of them.

These men and women, still conscious, realized what was happening to
them, screamed loud enough that their cries could be heard faintly even
through the dungeon walls. One by one, flailing their lives away, they
were dumped over the rail. The lucky ones drowned before the insatiable
sharks attacked. Shallow boats were used to carry the remaining prisoners
to the mother ship anchored offshore. The captives were chained to one
another so they could not escape. For some this was the worst moment
of their ordeal; they would be taken far away from their homes and
families, never to return. Some decided they would rather take their
chances out-swimming the sharks the few feet to the beach, although,
ripped from forest life, none of them could swim. When the first small
boat was pushed off from the Castle, with a crew member aboard for
further security, four of the ten chained slaves enacted a quick conspiracy.
Leaning to one side, they all at the same moment lunged forward. This
capsized the boat, plunged them into the water, alongside those with
no knowledge of the plan, as well as the crewman, who was caught
by surprise. The chained men flailed about on the surface in different
directions until the chains began pulling them under. They screamed as
the teeth of the sharks found their legs. For the rest, next came the ship,
The Bluebelle. Built years before to carry inanimate merchandise, it had
been converted into a slave ship. That meant the hold, about seven feet
high, had been divided by yoked boards horizontally, creating two equal
holds each about three feet high. James had to watch as his villagers
were lifted off the low boats and shoved into the lower hold and made
to sit, their bowed heads touching the upper boards. They would not be
able to stand. They had to spread their legs; the next man had to slide in
backwards, his rear between the thighs of the first man. Four across, thigh
to thigh, sitting that way, their limbs reached more than half way to the
front of the hold, where the women were packed into similar positions.
Some villagers were wearing waist cloths, others were naked. Crewmen
distributed buckets that would be the only repository for wastes, to be
emptied overboard when full. When the Muktus were thus settled skin
to sweating skin like spoons, the foul and perhaps diseased Kasus were
shoved in similar positions in the upper half of the hold. This because if
they died they could more easily be fed to the sea.

     James, his blood draining from his brain, felt faint at the thought of
his people spending five weeks in that position, though he had heard they
would be let up on the deck once or twice a day for exercise. He took
hold of the deck rail to avoid falling, hung on, bent over the rail like a
doll.

     Are you feeling alright, James?

The naked professor with the red hat was asking. James partially straightened up.

Of course. Who could ask for finer accommodations?

Another, huskier voice asked almost the same question.

Not feeling very well, king?

The words seemed to drip yellow and black, matching the teeth of the speaker. First Mate Cree did not end his jibes there. *Wait until you taste the slop you'll get to eat. And are forced to dance on deck while the crew watches. And see new mothers feeding their babies to the sharks. Those should lift your black-skinned mood. Also the adult dead and sick thrown overboard. Your friends losing their minds and jumping over the rail rather than face what lies ahead.*

All this is fun to you? James asked.

No. It's business. But a person might as well enjoy his work.

In the water James could see the sloughing sharks. They would follow the ship across the sea like death itself.

As if to end all conversation, the captain chose that moment to bellow from the helm station, *Anchors Aweigh!* Cree turned as smartly as a slovenly man can turn and half-jogged aft, as if he had important work to do. A screeching, curling sound from atop the tallest mast mimicked the captain: *Ankers Away!* Barely managing to raise his head, James saw the stowaway parrot, the late sun gleaming off its feathers. *Avast Ye Fuggin Maties, Ankers Away!*

It seems the bird has been to sea before, the naked professor said.

That's strange.

Legend has it that a bird on board is good luck; if it leaves, it's bad luck.

What would be counted good luck, in this situation?

Not sinking to the bottom, I suppose.

You might get an argument on that. So. What does a parrot eat on a ship?

According to legend, someone or something appears in the night and feeds it kiwano seeds.

And that someone or something is ...?

The naked professor pulled his red fez low over his ears. *As in all powerful legends,* he said, *that is a mystery.*

James stared hard at the bird. In the shape of its colors he saw his unborn son.

End of Part One

Part Two:
1740

23. PEGGY

His name was Hughson, first name John. He was judged a wimp by some because of an odd quirk, not quite an affectation – or was it? – in the way he talked. Through some grinning conspiracy of god or the devil it was Hughson who would become the glue – better still, the rope – which soon would bind our three strangers together. John Hughson was quite content with being thought a wimp. It served his purpose.

Now, now, there's a comely lass, he whispered to the freezing air as he watched the few passengers debark from the St. John's Bay. *I wonder. I wonder if that red-headed beauty is available.* His words hung in the frost like icicles of smoke, ready to be read by his dear wife Sarah, who was quarter of a mile away at the moment, preparing supper in the kitchen of the lodging house. Not that John was a rover, Sarah would batter him with a rolling pin if she found out he had strayed. *Yes, yes she would,* he acknowledged to no one in particular as he stood with his dray horse and splintery cart at the end the frigid pier. All fantasies and no action, Hughson nonetheless found himself imagining the redhead taking a room at the Inn. *Sure, sure would be fine for business, if for nothing else.*

Peggy Kerry, too, was raked by the cold and blustery wind as she stepped on to the wooden pier, canvas valise in one hand, *Robinson Crusoe* in the other. As she watched in the cloudy afternoon a pair of her fellow passengers climbed into a private coach with the aid of a footman, another pair slid into the only public carriage visible. Now she felt stupid that she had spent the entire voyage in the company of Crusoe and Friday while ignoring the blood-and-skin passengers. If she had been just the least bit more forthcoming, one or the other couple might be offering her a ride. She would already have friends here. Instead she felt cold and lonely as a mama seal. Her gloveless hands were stinging. She could not remember being this cold in Newfoundland; maybe on the northern ice floes, but not in Carey.

She saw at the end of the pier a man dressed in grey standing beside a horse and cart, a woolen cap pulled over his ears. She did not know how to act, a woman alone in the city. Would it be wrong to approach him? She decided it would, he might take it as an overture. Instead she began to walk down the center of the pier, which was slippery from ice that had formed underneath. The man seemed to sense her need and began walking to meet her halfway. When they came together he said in a soft voice that seemed gentle enough, *Can I, Miss, I mean may I be of some help as to your destination?*

I need to find an inn. A room in which to sleep. Is it always this cold in New York?

No, no, he said, *and then, yes, yes, I can help you find a place to sleep. Quite. Quite. My name is Hughson, John. John Hughson. I own an inn not five hundred yards from here. Which is to say Sarah, Sarah being my wife, and I own it. She is at home cooking the evening meal. At least I hope so. May I offer you a ride in my wagon? It is not fancy-fancy, but Dobbin, my horse, who is also not fancy-fancy, has never failed to get me there. And which inn just happens to have rooms to let, which is why I met the St. John's Bay — the boat that is — in the first place. In case there should be needy passengers such as yourself in need of a room— not so pretty of course, nor so rosy-cheeked as you.*

Mr. Hughson struck Peggy by his angularity — a pointy nose, pointy chin, perhaps pointy ears below the grey woolen cap that was pulled down almost to his eyes against the nipping frost. Beneath his long coat she imagined pointy elbows and perhaps pointy knees. Yet for all that there was a kind of jollity about him, which did not seem to fit.

I am not needy, Peggy said, *I'm just in want of a room. I can certainly pay. My name is Peggy Kerry and I will take you up on your kind offer, assuming your wife approves.*

Sarah, Sarah definitely will approve, being that boarders is what supports the bunch of us — my wife Sarah and my daughter Sarah — we being in the inn business.

Your wife and your daughter are both named Sarah? Is not that inconvenient?

She thought of the gravestone spelled Margaret back home, and suddenly wished she was back there, with Aunt Dottie and Nora. The people here were strange.

Inn-convenient, yes, I get the joke, very good, Peggy Kerry. As for Sarah and Sarah, that is a long story, my dear, if I may call you that on such short acquaintance, a story that I shall let Sarah tell you. Or Sarah, as the case may be.

Speaking of the case, let me take your bag — to which she tightly clung. *Don't worry my dear, do I look like a thief to you? The kind of man who would leave you cold and caseless? I'd cut the throat of any man or boy who dares to say so. But enough chatter.*

She released the valise to him, which he set carefully in the back of the cart and then — Peggy could not help smiling at the chatter of this Hughson, John, and she had the strangest thought — *perhaps I have found my spiritual father at last* — as she crushed her skirt and petticoats together and let him help her onto a seat behind the horse. *It's not so much of a seat as a plain board in need of planing,* Hughson allowed. She wondered if this nonstop patter was rehearsed or came to him naturally like a dog's whimper or a cat's meow. He circled the cart and, slipping, sliding and grunting, climbed onto the other side of the seat. He tapped Dobbin gently with a whip, and the horse or mare, as the case may be, itself struggling to find traction on the ice, began to move forward, although no road was visible. Hughson found a blanket somewhere in the cart and spread it over them both. It happened to be white, although splattered with dried mud.

Which is when the miracle occurred. Or what Peggy thought for a moment was a miracle.

The miracle was whiteness. A break in the clouds allowed the sun to flood the world – a world of ice and snow and frost and white smoke in every direction except the river behind her. Dobbin was following not a road but hoof prints in the snow. Straight ahead a white building was visible because of the movement of white smoke issuing from two white chimneys – one surely from a wood cooking stove, the other from a large fireplace. Beyond the house falling snow formed a curtain made visible only by its movement, hiding whatever lay in the distance – mountains or plains or buildings or another sea – as if New York colony existed in ghostly privacy. Peggy felt she had been here before. She realized when it had been – when she had lain on her bed for three days and imagined the whiteness of the ice floes and how she wanted to walk as far out on the ice as she could walk and lie down and slowly die, finger by frozen finger, toe by frozen toe. Oddly, this sudden New York whiteness exhilarated her. It seemed to clear her spirit of the uncertain past, of ~~Marguerite~~ and her dead mother, her drunk father and the Widow Williams; to allow her to look to a joyful and prosperous new life, any kind of life she wanted. She cuddled deeper under the white blanket wrap, images of a brave new world warming her.

The feeling lasted twenty of Dobbin's skittery strides. Perhaps thirty.

Wait! Stop the cart!

What is it, child? You want to absorb more of the beautiful world in which we live?

There was a blanket back there in the snow. A blue blanket.

What concern is that of ours?

There was something in the blanket. I couldn't see clearly, but it looked like a child.

No child could live ten minutes in this frost, Peggy dear.

That's what disturbs me. Please go back. I won't sleep tonight unless we have a look.

Hughson shrugged his narrow shoulders under the white blanket and reined the mare to a stop and yanked it to the left. Awkwardly it began to dance sideways across the unseen road.

It was back there. About fifty feet.

I understand, dear. Dobbin will do it her way. She is not very talented at backing up.

As the mare tried to turn, the right rear wheel of the cart dropped off the unseen road into a snow-filled ditch.

I'm going out there! Peggy said.

Be patient, girl. You don't know how deep the drifts might be. Dobbin will get us there soon enough.

Soon enough for what?

Ay, there's the rub. I suspect this is a case of someone being cruel in order to be kind.

Mr. Hughson, your talk is lovely, but I don't know what it means.

It's not my talk, I'm quoting Mr. Shakespeare.

And who would that be?

You don't know? I thought that, your toting Mr. Defoe all the way from Newfoundland, you might be enamored of Shakespeare as well.

I didn't just tote it, I read it. Every word.

Very good, very good. As for Shakespeare, he is our foremost playwright, though he lived more than a hundred years before Mr. Defoe. But let me tell you about the child in the blanket. My strong hunch is that it will turn out to be a mulatto – half white and half black. Many a time a white master uses force on a female slave, and the result is a mulatto baby. The master does not want evidence of his depravity growing up in his house. The mother has no resources with which to raise the child. Worst of all, if she succeeds in doing so, when he grows up he, too, or she, as the case may be, will be a slave, because the mother was. Many is the slave woman who does not want to see that happen. So she leaves the infant in the ice, where it dies a quick and, we hope, painless death. Being cruel only to be kind – do you get it now?

I think so.

Words, words, words. Shakespeare put the words in the mouth of Hamlet. Lord, I would have made a grand Prince of Denmark. That's who I wanted to play in my acting days. The greatest character ever created. But Mr. Winkle, the director of our acting troupe in Trenton, decided I was more suited to Polonius. He took on Hamlet himself. Can you imagine fat Winkle as Hamlet? It was a disaster.

Peggy, no longer interested in the perils of John Hughson, twisted her neck under the mud-spotted white blanket, trying to see the blue one in the snow as Dobbin kept struggling to free the cart from the ditch. The innkeeper, caught up in his own narration, scarcely noticed.

That gave me a brilliant idea. During our final performance, on a Saturday night, while I as Polonius lay dead under the arras, someone shouted, The strong box, it's gone! All of the players except yours truly ran behind the curtain to look. This confused the audience, of course, because no strong box had been mentioned in the play heretofore. The players came back out accusing me, which as I pointed out to them was absurd, me having been dead behind the arras at the time the strong box, containing the entire week's receipts, had gone missing. While they pondered that, I leaped up and caught them by surprise – few things in life are more surprising than a dead Polonius leaping up – by dashing out the stage door of the theater. They took off after me, shouting, After Him! Which of course was my plan. I led them a merry chase through the narrow streets of Trenton, and, it being night, found it easy to slip out of the city. A week later I met up right here with Sarah – my wife, not my daughter –well, she also had young Sarah with her, but she did not have the strong box, which she had hidden in a safe place according to my instructions. She had brought just enough cash hidden in her petticoat for our immediate purpose. Which was to purchase the decrepit and dying Pierside Inn and rename it Hughson's, which of course was not the name I had been using as an actor. All this was six years ago, in case I neglected to mention that. The inn has done well by us.

Peggy felt her eyes closing against the glare of the snow.

But getting back to Polonius. As I wended my way from Trenton to New York I was struck by an idea. I have, like yon Cassius, a lean and hungry look. Like men who think too much. More Shakespeare, words he put into the mouth of Julius Caesar. Do you know, Peggy, what is passing strange? I know of four different slaves right here in New York called Caesar. When he lived a thousand years ago, give or take, the emperor Caesar was the most powerful man in the world. So why do these slave masters name their helpless charges after him?

But I digress. Still in the mode of Polonius from the play, it occurred to me back then that if a man talks fat, like Polonius, and acts fat, like Polonius, then that is how others will perceive him, and not even notice the lean and hungry man within. I decided that even as John Hughson, which is my true given name, I would continue to hide inside a voluble Polonius, if you get my meaning. For six years now it has worked to a farthing, to the point where I could not speak lean-and- hungry even if I attempted to.

With a loud neigh of distress, Dobbin suddenly bolted forward, freeing her ankle from the snow and ice in the ditch, rattling the shaky cart back onto the road. She pulled the cart forward several feet, then stopped, shivering her roan coat against the cold, awaiting instructions from her master's whip. The sudden movement shook Peggy awake. Looking about, gathering her skirts, she jumped off the cart before Hughson could stop a her, and ran ankle deep in snow to the blue blanket and knelt beside it. Hughson had been correct – the child appeared to be a mix of black and white, what he had termed a mulatto. Its blue eyes were open and staring straight into the brilliant sun, lifeless. She wrapped her arms under the blanket and lifted the child, pressed it to her breast, tears rolling from her tired eyes, dropping from her rosy cheeks before they could freeze. She carried the infant to the cart and carefully climbed in. Hughson, who appeared to have talked himself to sleep, was shaken awake.

What are you planning to do with that?

I don't know. Take it to the police, I guess.

So flights of constables can sing him to his rest? They'll dump him in the Negro cemetery, and that will be the end of it.

What else can we do?

You can put him back where you found him, and let someone else come upon him tomorrow, or the day after, and take him to the police.

But it's so cold.

I assure you he is not feeling cold any longer. Which is what his poor mother intended.

What's the difference who takes him?

The difference is you, Peggy. You are just off the boat. A stranger young and pretty, with that flaming red hair peeking from under your cap. The police will assume the baby is yours. That you killed it yourself. Murdered it. How can you prove that is not so?

My body shows no signs of …

Exactly. Do you want to disrobe before them, show them …

I would not do that!

Of course not. Unless they force you to, in the interests of justice. The judge might even want to examine the evidence himself.

That's horrible!

Sometimes justice is. Place the baby back where it was, and the issue will not arise. In this life, the less commerce there is between us humans and the constables, the better. Take that as the wisdom of New York.

Shaken, she did as she was told. As she placed the infant on the ice she kissed its forehead. Already she felt what she thought was love for it.

They will bury you without a name, she said to the lifeless child. *No one will remember you. No, that's not true. Your mother will remember you. I'm sure I will. Because I alone know your name.* She stood and brushed snow from her coat and looked at the infant one last time. *Your name is Welcome. Welcome to New York.*

Back in the cart, pulling the white blanket around her shoulders, her cheeks still wet, she thanked Hughson for his good advice.

I promise you this, Peggy Kerry. So long as you are with us, meaning me and Sarah and Sarah, I shall never steer you wrong.

He tapped the whip on the frosty flank of Dobbin. The mare, having been turned around by Hughson, this time carried them straight down the middle of the invisible road to the large if not quite majestic veranda of Hughson's Tavern.

24. MARY

Dear Denture Dairy
The captin is a hero.
That's what the man in charge of the repair yard says. He says without the captin's C-manship we all would have been drownded. He says three ships sunk down to the bottom of the ocean in the nasti storm what we passed through. He says 38 sailors lost their lives on two of them, and with us it would have been 49 sailors and one girl from Belfree Cathlic Orfinage. Th third ship he says was a larger boat also from Ireland. It was lost to the sea he said with its crew plus 90 dentures aboard – I guess the crowded kind that Captin Anders tole me about. When we heard that, the captin come stand by me and put his arm around my shoulders. He didn't say nothing with his mouth. Just one more big wave hitting us is all it would have took, the repair yard man says, and the whole of our boat the Cathrin would have blown apart. He says it will take 2 weeks or maybe even 3 to fix.

The second thing they will have to do is raise the boat out of the water so they can repair the hull. The first thing was to empty out the cargo so the boat would not be too heavy for the winches. The Hands spent the day off-loading, they called it, the Irish whiskey and the Irish linens. I helped carry the linens. That felt good. Like I was part of the Hands. I think I will make a good off-loader some day. We put the cargo on wooden palits in a store house right in the ship yard. When we were thru the manager put a great big lock on the door. So rats couldn't get in.

We stayed every night in the Seamen's Inn which was not far away. All the crew got to stay in one big room with lots of beds, but I was stuck in a small room with only two beds. This got me angry because they could have fun together and I had to be alone. The captin said the reason was because I was a girl. I don't know why I should be punished for being a girl.

We ate breakfast in the mess hall. It looks pretty neat to me. One day Arthur Hands came down with that book Gulliver's Travels, which he must have saved from the captin's cabin. He asked the captin if while we was in port he could teach me how to read. I closed my eyes and thought, Dummy, we already tricked the captin, he thinks I already know how to read. The captin didn't say nothing about that. He just said it was okay to teach me to read, so long as he didn't teach me anything else. All the Hands laughed when he said that. I was glad they agreed with me, that learnin stuff is a waist of time.

Dear Denture Dairy
We walked all over the town today. There was nothing very inneresting to see. Then the captin met up with us and took me alone into a store and bought me all kinds of new clothes for New York. I said I saw my sack with the owl on it carried into the store house, but he said no, Im sure it sank down into the sea. So the ship company will pay for new clothes.

The next day there was no more shopping, so nothing exciting happened. I hope tomorrow will be more inneresting.

Dear Denture Dairy
Waiting around makes me bored.

Dear Denture Dairy
Waiting around again makes me bored again.

Dear Denture Dairy
Arthur Hand told me today that when you are bored you have to make up your own fun. I decided to draw a picture.
Here is a picture of a boat. That is me on the dec.

Dear Denture Dairy
Today I is going to draw two boats.

That is me on one boat and my mother on the other boat

Dear Denture Dairy
Today I tried to draw two boats crashing. It did not come out two good.

Dear Denture Dairy
Today was not boring it was worse. The ship yard master gathered us around. He said he had just got a letter from Rhode Island colony, which is closer than New York. He said the same storm we got through kept going south and struck a big slave ship coming from Africa, and the ship disappeared under the sea. People on the two nearest boats said they could tell this was a slaver ship because they could smell it from miles away. The first mate of the ship Drake said one huge wave carried five bodies from the sea onto the deck of the Drake - one white man and four colored women with hands in grass chains. No other facts is known as to where the slave ship was going the yard master said. He turned away from us as if he might cry, but then he turned back. According to those who count such things, he said, more than 400 ships have disappeared under the waters in

these parts in the past 50 years. How many people were drownded they do not know

> *Dear Denture Dairy*
> *Maybe New York colony won't be so bad after all.*
> *Dear Denture Dairy*
> *The Cathrin is fixed. That's what they say. Tomorrow we leave I think.*

25. CAESAR

For five weeks the wind had blown them in a circle.

So King James thought as he peered from the anchored ship at the long, low Cape Coast Castle.

Not really, the professor said. He was no longer naked, had been given a white waist cloth, but continued wearing his fez by choice. *They do look similar, but it's an illusion. That building is not to hold us, it's a military fort. Fort Greene, they call it. You can see the big guns from here, pointing out to sea. New York fears the Spanish fleet will try to conquer them.*

Why would they do that?

Because that is what white men do.

In fairness, black Vatok's tribe conquered us.

To save themselves, yes. Which is understandable. If not quite ethical.

What is this ethical? It was not in our English book.

The professor nodded, as if he were not surprised. He gazed over the rail to the fort a quarter mile away. The dark blue water was slapping lazily at the hull of the ship. The huge sails had been furled.

Tell me, James said. *How do you know all this? About the fort. About the Spaniards.*

This morning the captain summoned me to his cabin. He had much of interest to say.

To a slave?

It must be highly unusual. But so was the story he told. At first he stood looking out a porthole. Behind him on his desk were three gold coins and a sharp silver knife. I wanted to laugh, it was so obviously a test of my honesty. To see if I could be trusted. He may have had a crewman watching, but I saw no one. Finally he turned and said what was on his mind. I hope it will not upset you. He said there would be a change in my future. Which was odd, since I had no idea what my future was to be. Other than a slave in Rhode Island, as you know from my RI branding. It seems that Captain

Williams has made many trips there to sell slaves. Rhode Island imports more slaves than any colony except South Carolina, he said. He did not say why, they do not grow cotton or sugar or tobacco there that needs to be picked. Anyway, he said a Judge name of Ellington, a retired judge whose wife died, asked him to be on the lookout for an older slave, a gentleman who could serve as the judge's housekeeper. Not one who is young and angry. A gentleman, the captain actually said. As you know, most of the men captured for slaves are like yourself, between 15 and 35 years old. And strong. The captain said he took one look at me on the beach, with grey in my beard and in my hair and a slight paunch in my belly. When he learned I speak English plus several tribal languages, he bought me for the judge. But all that changed yesterday, he said. As soon as we dropped anchor, a small rig came out from the port with messages. One thing it brought was a letter for the captain from the judge's daughter. It said the judge had died a few weeks ago, so he would not be needing a housekeeper. She offered to pay the cost if necessary. Well, the captain said, he thought about that overnight, and had a better idea. He could make more money by keeping me for himself. How? My task would be to teach English to slaves whose masters want them to learn it. That would make him more profit than selling me, he said; nobody wants a 50-year-old slave. This made me happy, of course. I love to teach. That's what I was doing on the continent when they captured me.

Well, good for you, James replied, and clasped the professor's arm. *But why did you think this good fortune might upset me?*

Because the captain could have chosen you.

Me? I'm young and strong. Besides English I speak only Muktu. I'm happy for you professor. As for me, I will survive.

He looked toward the white castle that was not a castle. And up toward the highest mast, where the parrot still perched, and appeared to wink at him, like Beto. And, with closed eyes, to the village in the forest where Triana still lived …

Do you know when we will go ashore?

I asked the captain. Five or six days. They have to advertise the slave sale in the weekly newspaper. Meanwhile they will feed us fresh meals, to fatten us up after the voyage. They'll clip the beards and shave the heads of anyone who has grey showing. They'll oil our skin so we look healthier.

It appears they know many tricks.

They have had much practice.

James was about to ask the professor how he knew so many tribal languages, and what he knew of Beto, when they heard a female scream from the hold, then a hundred heels beating on the floor like programmed thunder. James sped to the entry and leaped down the ramp to his people. He saw First Mate Cree hunched among the seated women, shouting a command to one of them, pulling her hair while the woman screamed. It was Triana's younger sister, whom Cree had fancied on shore. The first mate dragged her to the space between the men and the women, pushed her face forward against the wall of the hold, stripped off her waist cloth. He made her bend forward, naked, hands against the wall, while most of the chained men and horrified women banged their heels against the floor. James leaped quickly behind Cree's back. The first mate knelt to loosen his trousers. As he did, the handle of his cutlass dangled loosely at his waist. James pulled it free, raised the cutlass as if to slash down with it. The blade hit the low ceiling. He lowered it slightly and with all his force swung the sword horizontally. The first mate screamed as the cutlass severed his right arm at the elbow, blood spurting. He reached with his left arm across his chest to his right arm, which was no longer there. It was hanging loose by a snippet of skin. James pulled its free, grabbed Cree by the back of his neck, said, *Come, let's watch the sharks eat your flesh.* Cree seemed stunned, shocked, unable to speak. James pulled him up the ramp onto the deck, from darkness into light, hurled the detached arm into the sea. He pulled Cree, who seemed like a wooden figure, closer to the rail. James knelt, placed the cutlass on the deck, wrapped his arm around the first mate's knees. As he stood he lifted Cree's unresisting form and shoved it over the rail. The chunky officer seemed to be vomiting in the air as he tumbled to the depths, where the sharks were waiting. James retrieved the cutlass from the deck, whirled to face three crewmen who were moving toward him. Seeing the cutlass in his hand and the fierce fire in his eyes they stopped where they were.

The thunder from the hold gave way to joyous trilling. James hoped the three crewmen would not advance on him. By killing the first mate he had been protecting his women. Shedding further blood instead of giving himself up would be harder to justify.

Don't move, anyone!

The shouting voice was that of Captain Williams as he descended from the quarter deck.

You, hand me that cutlass, he said to James, who complied at once. *You crewmen, don't touch yours. The first mate threw himself overboard. There is no need for violence.*

Sir, this slave threw him over, one of the crewmen said.

Stokes — it is Stokes, isn't it? — are you calling me a liar? I was looking down from the helm station and saw the whole thing. Cree must have come unhinged during the voyage. He tried to kill himself with his cutlass. That explains the blood. When he was too cowardly to finish the job, he climbed the rail and leaped. Isn't that what you saw, you other two men?

The crew men were silent.

Well, speak up. I have good eyes. I know what I saw. I expect my crew to be as sharp-eyed as I am, or I won't hire them again. Is that clear? Speak up, what did you others see?

The same as you captain. He jumped.

Aye aye sir. He jumped

And you, Stokes?

I must have been mistaken, sir. If three of you saw him jump, then of course he jumped.

Good. I'm glad we're in agreement. A crazed man jumping overboard, there won't even be a hearing. Slaves do it all the time. So, back to your posts. Stokes, hose down that blood. You – James? – follow me to my cabin.

The king did not know what to think. He followed the captain, passing the astonished professor on the deck. A rising wind was beginning to paint whitecaps on the incoming waves. The captain slammed the door behind them. He wrapped a white towel around the blade of the cutlass and began to pound the handle on the metal door. James did not know what that sound was supposed to represent to the crew. If he were being beaten it would not sound like that.

When he stopped, James said, *I don't know why you protected me, sir. I'm grateful, but I don't understand.*

Because you served my purpose.

Sir?

You got the bloody first mate out of my hair.

I'm still don't understand, captain. You wanted Cree killed?

I could hardly do it myself. Back on the beach by the Coast Cape Castle I saw how you stood up to the first mate. You're the first slave not to fear him. I decided right then that you were my weapon. That's why I let you roam free on the deck, unchained. So you could strike him down when the time came.

How did you know he would provoke me?

He claims in every tavern in New York that he has never made a slave voyage without raping a woman. Or three, or four. And that he never will. He must have been afraid of you, to wait so long. Then his lust overcame his fear.

What if I did not react?

I knew you would. God gave you to me as a weapon.

That is a strange god.

Aren't they all? But if you did not react I would have found another way. It was time the earth be rid of Cree.

Captain Williams sat in his chair, motioned James to the only other one.

I feel like having beer. There's a bit left in the barrel. Can I get you some?

I've never had.

Well, maybe not then.

James allowed himself a small smile at the gesture. His brain rocked gently with the ship. He thought: This man owns me. Will this killing earn my freedom? He dared not ask.

If it is not too personal, captain, sir, why did you want Cree dead?

Captain Williams stood, instead of beer went to a cabinet and pulled out a small humidor. From it he took two cigars. Sitting, he placed one between his teeth, offered the other to James.

I never saw one of those.

Don't smoke it on the ship, then. Save it for when you need a favor.

Turning the cigar between his lips, holding a match to the tip, the captain puffed several times, until the tip caught fire. James liked the sweet aroma. He thought: those would be useful to make fires in the forest. The flame lingers.

The recent popularity of cigars had made the growing of tobacco Virginia colony's largest industry. This had vastly increased the need for the importing of slaves. The captain chose not to mention this.

Why did I want Cree dead? Two reasons. First, he killed my brother.

Killed him? You have laws. Why is he walking free?

There were no witnesses.

Then how can you be sure?

Theo often could not sleep at night. He would walk in a dark field between his mansion and the river. One night Cree followed him. Stabbed him in the back, then many times in the chest. A slave couple – they were married, but owned by different families – sometimes would meet in that field after dark. They saw Cree do the stabbing. They told me privately in the morning. Theo was well liked, despite owning half the Trading Company, because he treated his own servants well.

But you said there were no witnesses.

The captain puffed on his cigar, blew the blue smoke away from James.

In a court of law, the word of a slave means nothing against the word of a white man.

If you know he is a killer, why did you hire him on as first mate?

Cree always wanted to captain his own vessel. Be in complete control. Theo knew he was a bully, and would never give him a ship. That's one reason Cree hated him. The second was Theo's wife. After his first wife died of the dysentery, Theo waited several years, then met a young woman returning from school in London. Ellie Larkin. She was from a good family, and without doubt one of the prettiest women in the city. Theo was smitten at once. She was half his age, but Ellie came around after a while. Why not? Theo was still handsome, was good to her, and had more money than King George. A woman could hardly do better.

What does this have to do with Cree?

The bastard wanted Ellie, of course. And Theo was in his way. Cree would stop at nothing. She was the Widow Williams now, had inherited much of New York Mercantile. It was only a matter of time before Cree would move in on her, one way or another. So I made him first mate, at a large salary for a sailor. That would keep Ellie safe for at least three months.

But when the voyage ended, wouldn't he just threaten her again?

What do you think, James? Do you think he will?

The captain flicked his cigar ashes on the floor, smoothed them with his boot.

Now you'd better get back to your tribe. If you haven't been royal to them the past few days, you certainly are now.

James wiped his dry mouth on his wrist. Holding the inert cigar, he moved toward the door.

And James?

Yes?

Don't do it again.

26. Peggy

John Hughson was a meticulous man. Six years earlier, bored with his stay in Trenton, he rode the weekly coach to New York, to see if he thought his wife Sarah and his daughter Sarah would enjoy living there. He stayed at the Pierside Inn, enjoyed a good night's rest, more or less. The once-white building was more or less a decrepit grey, with peeling paint and warping boards, but more clean than less, and he wondered why it was for sale, aside from the obvious negative that it had very few occupants. For sale, in fact, at a reasonable price that he might be able to afford. More or less.

The next morning, excited by a novel idea, he found his way to the office of the city recorder several blocks away. That gentleman offered him the following facts:

The population of the city was ten thousand residents, give or take.

Of that population, two thousand were Negroes, give or take.

Among the Negroes were sixteen hundred slaves and four hundred free colored, give or take.

You're not planning to start a rebellion, the recorder asked.

Hughson grinned but was taken aback. He could not tell if the man was joking.

Leaving the office, the future innkeeper wanted to thank the city recorder for his help but could not recall his name. It was long and difficult and had something to do with horses, more or less. He settled on Houyhnhnm, which he knew was not correct. Houyhnhnms were the smart horses in the fine new book by Mr. Swift of England, but it was the closest Hughson could remember, so he called the recorder Mr. Houyhnhnm. The man's actual name was Daniel Horsmanden. Which Hughson would have good reason to remember later on.

So we bought the Inn with the Polonius money, if I may call it that. I hired two men to help me paint the outside, the two Sarahs scrubbed the inside, and we changed the name to Hughson's Tavern. That was not a matter of self-aggrandizement, I might add. The Inn was named to honor my grandfather, who had passed away the year before.

Whose name just happened to be John Hughson.

Right you are, Miss Peggy.

Three weeks had passed since Peggy moved in. They were drinking tea in the corner of the main dining room, close to a fire blazing in the large stone fireplace. The weather had warmed up considerably, the melting ice and snow turning turning New York into puddle city. There was even a distant whiff of spring in the air, but indoors a fire was still required. There had been no mention in J. P. Zenger's *New-York Weekly Journal* of the frozen baby, nor any advertisements of a suitable job for Peggy. A slave auction had been announced for that afternoon, however, and at Peggy's request Hughson had agreed to take her to watch

So that's the story of how we turned a failing inn into a success, Hughson said.

Not really.

Did I leave something out? Well, gol darned. Of course. The sign. That's the heart of the matter, more or less, and I plumb forgot to tell of it. Polonius must be getting old.

What kind of sign are you talking about?

The first thing I did after painting the inn was buy a small hatchet. I told the two Sarahs to go to the market and buy enough food to make twenty mince pies. Also a big batch of lemonade. Turned out the market was out of lemons so the lemonade was just water and sugar, more or less. Nobody seemed to mind. But that's getting ahead of the story. I found a few Negro boys nearby and told them that the next day at six o'clock there would be free supper for everyone at the new Hughson's Tavern, and they should tell their parents and the whole neighborhood. I could tell they did not believe me, but who turns down even the illusion of a free meal? So the next afternoon Sarah and Sarah had the 20 mince pies, give or take, all baked and sliced, and gallons of

lemonade, more or less, and at six o'clock I went onto the veranda and the front lawn
– this was in the summer – the front lawn was mobbed with colored folks – I would
say a hundred, more or less – men and women and children – and more and more kept
coming. Including some white folks, come to see what the fuss was about. So it was
time. I didn't say what was happening, I just positioned a painter's ladder under the
large white and black sign that hung over the veranda, and I fetched my new hatchet,
and I climbed up a few steps and began chopping away at the painted letters on the
sign. I started at the end, and after a few strokes the Y wasn't there any more. Then I
chopped off the L, then the N, then the O. At first the folks watching was trying to figure
out what I was doing, then a few understood, though they held their breaths because
they could hardly believe what they were seeing, and then a few murmured, and then
more murmurs, and murmurs and whispers began to run across the lawn like puppies
as children began asking their mamas or papas what was happening. Because the only
word left on the sign, which had been hanging there a hundred years, more or less, was
the one word WHITES. I didn't stop to explain or nothing. I moved the ladder and
climbed up again and now I took big swings with the hatchet, one, two, three, and all
at once the whole word Whites as in Whites Only came crashing down. The former
Pierside Inn, now Hughson's, no longer was restricted. Well, folks, I said, come on
in for your free mince pie and lemonade, as advertised. They hesitated, no colored had
ever been inside before, but a few brave little boys shrugged their boney shoulders and
passed through the front doors, and then some older folks. And when the full impact hit
the crowd a great cheer went up, which became a wave of sound pounding the inn like
a rough ocean wave pounding the shore. Someone showed up with a banjo and started
to play, and then another fellow with a drum, and some of the women began to dance.
The music and laughter sounded the word for blocks and blocks, give or take, and before
you knew it there was a huge party going on the lawn and the street across that lasted
until dark. Some constables came by and consulted with themselves, and when they saw
the WHITES ONLY sign was gone they shook their heads but just stood in the rear
and watched. Big Sarah came out on the veranda and waved to the constables to come
in, and after a while they did, and raved about the mince pie like everyone else was
doing. I think the coloreds, who were some slaves and some free, would have preferred
that the officers remain outside. But I figured they would have to get used to mingling,
and it didn't take long before they did. The next evening we started charging for Sarah's
food, of course. That was six summers ago, and the dining room has been filled with
hungry folks, both colored and white, every night since, give or take.

That is quite a story,

Yep. And every word is true. More or less.

As if to comment on his last statement, the large old Comtoise clock in the corner of the dining room sang out a tinny solo ring. It was one in the afternoon.

What time is that auction? Hughson asked, and reached for the four-page newspaper that lay further along the table. He turned to the back page. *Two o'clock,* he said. *We have time. The*
auctions are held on Wall Street. That's not very far.

Scanning the ink smeared paper, Peggy found the small advertisement at the bottom:

SLAVE AUCTION

The Bluebelle having recently arrived from Africa, more than 200 slaves will be auctioned at 2PM Thursday, Jan. 20. Men, women, children.Top quality specimens include a village King. New York Mercantile Company, Ellie Williams. Cash Only.

27. MARY

The evil eye don't always show right away. Sometimes it is hid by a smile. But the smile got threads of tight at the corners. The corners of the eyes are afraid.

These things I learned from Mrs. Camelia Ramsey, who was my first indenturix, and barely older than me. She did not tell them to me. I learned them from watching her.

Camelia was called Goldilocks by her husband, who was Mr. Ramsey. They did not meet us at the dock as had been expected. Perhaps because the streets was all puddly and muddly. Or perhaps because we was three weeks late. So Captain Anders took my hand and my sack and said we would walk. I sure was glad I had my new boots on, there being all the pud and muddles in the streets. And I sure was glad the captain had bought them for me. While we was waiting in Newfoundland for the Catherine to be fixed, someone got a letter from New York colony saying as how this winter was the coldest it had ever been down there. The captain took one look at my worn out boots from Belfry Catholic Orphanage, which had big holes in them, and said we better get you new ones. He asked around and they said the best boot maker was a ways down the road in a village called Carey. The captain hired a wagon that took us there and we met the nicest boot maker, name of Reilly. He had nice brown leather just come in he said, and how would it be if he used that? I said it would be fine so long as he got rid of the holes. He measured my feet and started cutting leather.

You're going to New York? he asked, and we said yes and he said, *My son Bill went down there about six months ago. I haven't had a letter of late but I bet you will run into him.*

Why is that? I asked, and he said, *My boy has a golden touch, he's probably famous down there by now. Not for killing baby seals, which I doubt they have in the big city, but for one thing or another.*

Do you think it's fun being famous? I asked, and he said he wouldn't know, no one ever got famous from making boots.

While Mr. Reilly was cutting out the heels the captain took me to a market nearby that sold clothes that had already been worn by other people. He was worried that the too-small coat I was wearing would not be warm enough in New York colony, from what he had heard. In the store crowded with all kinds of old stuff that made me sneeze I found a big pink coat that looked almost new. I tried it on. It fit just fine.

That's much too big for you, the captain said, *it hangs down past your knees,* but I said it was better than the one that was much too small, and I really wanted it. *Well,* he said, *I guess in the orphanage you didn't get what you wanted very often.* So he bought the pink coat for me, and we left the too-small dark blue one there for someone else to buy. I felt like a grand lady as we walked back to the boot maker and I tried on them new boots and they was perfect. Mr. Reilly showed me what he had done on the bottom of the heels. He had carved a M in one heel and a B in the other.

That way you'll know they alway go together, he said.

I wanted to hug both these men. Why were they being so nice to me? So I did hug both of them. If people are extra nice to you, which is not very often, I figure you should hug them. I asked Captain Anders why he was buying me things. He said that as long as he held my papers, I was like a daughter to him. I said, well, if you just keep my papers, then I could be your daughter always. He said, *Things do not work that way.* He didn't say why not.

We was both hungry so we stopped in a pub-cafe to eat. We decided to walk back to St. John's after being cramped on the Catherine for so long. I felt so proud in my new pink coat and my new boots. I kept wondering about what the boot maker had said, about his son maybe being famous. Maybe in New York colony I could be famous, too.

As me and the captain walk through New York, through the splashy puds and muddles, me in my brown boots and pink coat, my

initials carved secretly in the heels of the boots, the sun shining bright,
past buildings and houses and markets and churches, to meet my new
dentures, I am nervous but somehow have the same feeling: here I could
become famous, like that Gulliver fellow in the story I pretended to read.

I realize I ain't told you much about Mrs. Cecelia Ramsey. When
Goldilocks decided she didn't like me, that was a big reason I did become
famous. If not for her being mean I might never have knowed Mr. John
Hughson and Miss Peggy Kerry and that black slave called Caesar and
all them others. Mrs. Ramsey didn't get mean until I started *showing*, as
they said, which was not until months after we come. So I guess there
ain't no harm if I tell it next time.

28. CAESAR

The innards of the slave-holding house at the base of
Wall Street were always dark. Such windows as had been included in the
original design had long since been bricked over after unruly captives
smashed the inviting glass. Horizontal slots high in the walls served
more to exhale the fetid air than to inhale the fresh. Standing beside
one another in the crowd of other men, women and children about to
be sold, James and the professor had no sense of each other's substance.
This was not a time to talk, except to your deity. Or to discover, to your
surprise, that you had one.

In the plaza outside, prospective buyers crowded close to the auction
block, where they would get the best look at the merchandise: whether
the men or women for sale had adequate muscles under their glistening
skin, whether their teeth were not so rotten as to indicate disease, mostly
to read their eyes in search of defiance. A modicum of hatred in the slave
was a good thing; those who possessed it would be the hardest workers,
as if to prove something to themselves or to their meeker fellows. But too
much defiance in the eyes might one day get your throat cut. Pressing
behind the buyers a well-dressed crowd in winter coats began to gather
as the hour of the auction approached – single men, others accompanied
by wives and even children, some of whom ran about under a cloudy
winter sky lightly whipping one another with leafless tree branches in a
game of master and slave. Auction day on Wall Street provided more
entertainment for the adults than the imported comedy shows at the New
Theater on the wide Broad Way. For the children it was the second most
anticipated day of the year, after Christmas.

When Peggy and Mr. Hughson walked up they had to stand near the rear of a crowd of several hundred. A wooden table stood to the right of the auction block. Three men were approaching it. The rowdy children were hushed. Chatter among the excited crowd drained like water from a sieve.

Looks as if we're just in time, Hughson said.

Jointed and jaunty, he was happy to be approaching the crowd with Peggy at his side. Peggy whose crooked tooth, visible only when she smiled, was the only evidence that she was a vulnerable young woman, not a red-haired Venus or a fiery Aphrodite.

Two of the men approaching the table were tall and scarred, wearing white blouses open at the neck – they seemed immune to the winter chill – brown trousers tucked into brown boots, bright red sashes from which hung naked cutlasses.

They're charged with quelling any disturbance, Hughson said, *although I don't recall there ever being one.*

As the guards stood behind the table, the third man, younger, slimmer, dressed in matching grey coat, waistcoat and breeches, white stockings, black buckled shoes, white cravat, seated himself in one of two chairs, a plain, practical wooden one. He placed in front of him a thick ledger and what appeared to be a box of cigars.

He'll record the sales, Hughson said.

From the rear of the crowd the fellow seemed familiar to Peggy – his every movement – but she did not know why. Perhaps he had been a passenger on the boat from Newfoundland. Beside this man's chair was a far plusher one, covered in burgundy velvet, the ornate carved frame tinged with gold. For the moment it remained empty.

Who is that chair for? Peggy asked. *It's fit for a king.*

A queen, more likely. The trading company was inherited last year by the owner's wife – which is somewhat irregular, but not against the law – when the owner suddenly passed away, intestate. I've heard she's the only woman slave-ship owner in the world. I know she's the only one in New York. And surely the prettiest.

Don't tell me. The Widow Williams!

How did you know that?

That fellow with the books. I can't believe it. That's my fiancee!

Is that truly so?

I hardly recognize him. He's become quite the dandy, for a brawling seal killer. He wrote me she had promised him a good job when her ship came in.

Well, the Bluebelle arrived the other day, and that's a good job all right.

Her forehead began to perspire. Her chest felt invaded by a hundred swimming capelin slamming together. She thought she was going to faint.

I have to speak to him. But I don't know what to say. I never thought to see him so soon. I thought he might be in Australia by now.

Hughson placed his hand gently on her arm.

Talk to him when you will. But this is not the time nor the place. His name is Billy, correct? Billy Reilly? He stayed at the Inn for several months before he ran out of cash and took up with the widow.

More likely she took up with him.

In the affairs of men and women it is not always clear whom is the master and whom the slave. Look, here comes the widow now. On the arm of the captain.

What captain?

Her brother-in-law, Enoch Williams. He pilots one of her ships. A fine fellow he is. Many's the interesting chat we've had as he drained a draught or two at the Inn.

A fine fellow? The captain of a slavery ship?

Well, if he's a bad fellow, there's only two kinds of men on this earth: the bad and the worse.

That's not true. You're a good man, Mr. Hughson.

Not hardly. I told you my thieving story.

You took down that Whites Only sign.

To earn a barrel of cash. Many barrels of cash. Not to mention a large bucket of hate. Some day they'll kill me for that. I asked the captain once why after his brother was foully murdered he did not take over running the business. He says to me, he says, I would rather pilot a hundred ships across the ocean than spend a single day behind a desk. It could be elephants or gold or the King of France on the ship, it would make no difference to him. It's the salty blue waves he's in love with – the constant battle with the wild, roiling sea.

It sounds as if you like him.

Admire is a better word. We're a lot alike, Enoch and I. I, too, like the excitement of a running fight.

In the dark holding house James and the professor were crowded by the others toward the slowly opening door. They wore white trousers. Their chests were bare. A guard had told them they would be the first to go on the block. The professor, given his flabby physique, believed this was a mistake. As they peered over the shoulder of another guard, their eyes blinked blindly in the light. They wished the auction would begin, if only to free their ears from the wailing of the little ones. *Children,* the professor muttered, *save your precious lungs. There will be plenty to scream about later.*

As if descending from a silver cloud in a golden chariot – or so it seemed to Peggy – the Widow Williams, dressed in a royal blue dress and a matching bonnet, appeared in her plush chair beside her young secretary. Enoch Williams, dressed all in white, doffed his tricorn cap to her, leaped onto the auction block, waved his arms for silence and introduced himself to the gathered throng, which was alternately roaring and quieting with pulsing eagerness. He himself would serve as the auctioneer, he told them. He motioned to a guard in the doorway, who took the professor's arm. Wearing his red fez, which after its damp and windy time at sea resembled a scrawny, bloodied animal, and new white trousers he'd been given by the captain, the professor felt his knees begin to tremble.

James asked him, *Do you think we can trust the white man?*

The professor choked down a guffaw, which led to a fit of coughing; he had not heard such mordant wit from James before, was surprised to discover it was part of the king's nature. He'd encountered it often in bustling Arabia, but how had it bloomed in the forest?

His thoughts were overwhelmed by laughter. It began in the front row, among the men looking up at him. It rolled outward in ripples of chuckles, then in a tide of guffaws as the crowd took note of him standing alone and droopy on the block, beside the captain. He could hear individual shouts:

You call that a slave?

Is that a rat on his head?

Look at the paunch – is that where he keeps his cash?

And the grey hair on his chest.

He has no muscles!

I'll bid one farthing – he can help my wife darn her stockings!

Captain Williams raised his arms, waited for the shouting to subside. He intoned, *Professor Fez is not for sale,*

And a good thing, too! We're wasting our time here.

You are meeting a smart man, the captain said.

Him? That blackamoor?

More laughter, a few neighborly slaps on the back.

I dare say the professor is smarter than all of you put together – with the exception of the ladies, of course. I also concede he is not nearly as pretty as them.

He doffed his hat again in the direction of the widow. A murmur of grumbles fell on the crowd like an unwelcome drizzle.

Professor Fez can speak eight African tongues. Can any of you speak even one?

Silence.

I thought not.

We're here to buy slaves, not dictionaries!

Let me explain. We are planning to build a school room, over which the professor will preside. Most of the properties today do not speak English. It would be more efficient for you if they did. The professor will teach them.

At no cost?

When you make your purchases today, for an extra 20 per cent your new properties will be given English lessons for three months.

Twenty per cent? That's robbery!

No one is forced to do this. You have three days to decide. After that, the charge will be 50 percent.

Who will get this money?

The trading company, of course. The captain grinned. *Unless the professor is smart enough to convince me he is entitled to a percentage of the profits. To be banked against the day he can buy his freedom.*

The professor nodded. That part was news to him.

At the rear of the crowd, John Hughson touched Peggy's shoulder. *Captain Williams is one clever businessman.*

Peggy did not respond. She had not heard. Her eyes remained fixed on the Widow Williams, on her arm spread across the wooden table, not quite touching the arm of Billy, not quite not touching it.

The captain led the professor down from the block. Emerging in his place through the door of the holding house, having to duck his head, was the contrasting, gleaming form of King James. No laughter greeted his appearance. Instead there were oohs and ahhs – many of them, Hughson noted, from the ladies. Even Peggy Kerry tore her gaze from her fiancee and the widow to see what the stirring was about. Men began to shout numbers. James could hardly understand them. He did not care to. He did not follow voices from face to face to learn who wanted to purchase him. His gaze was fixed above the crowd, above what little he could see of the city, toward the endless grey winter sky above the endless ocean. Towards Muktu. For a moment he saw or thought he saw the parrot pass overhead, flutter to a stop on a roof across the road. But when he looked again in that direction it was gone. He wished he could see Triana now. He was glad Triana could not see him now.

His grandfather, King John, he thought, might have been able to explain to him why his life had taken such a terrible turn. He himself could not begin to know. Not since the missionaries had disturbed the forest when he was a child and brought with them the strange tongue English had he seen humans the color of pale sand instead of the night sky – not until the seamen on the boat, and never in such large numbers. Never had he seen land not hung with trees, nor could he imagine what such land was for. Never had he seen dwellings of wood instead of thatch, pregnant with second levels that blocked the sky.

The bidding climbed higher.

Is that all? The voice of the captain, shouting at the crowd. *Are you done with this fine specimen at seven pounds?*

Scuffling boots in the still-drying road. Shoes sounding nervous, uneasy, as if they themselves were speaking with their tongues..

Eight pounds!

Ten!

Silence.

All done at ten? Let's go, gentlemen! This man was king of his village.

Fifteen, but no higher!

Sixteen!

I have sixteen pounds. According to our records, the most ever paid for a property at this auction block is twenty. And not for such a fine specimen as this! Do I hear twenty? How about nineteen?

Twenty pounds and out.

Silence again. Prolonged silence. Random coughing. *Can we go home?* a child asking, whining. James lowered his gaze from the sky to the white people in front of him. He did it slowly, had discovered that quick movement of his head up or down created a moment of discord, of dizziness, as if he were on the boat again, at war with the waves.

Very well. Going once at twenty pounds. Going twice ... This man speaks almost perfect English. You would not have to pay a surcharge. Again, going once ...

Excuse me, captain.

The recorder seated beside the Widow Williams stood from his chair.

Yes, what is it, Billy?

I have a secret bid here. Anonymous. The bidder offers two pounds over the highest bid. But not to exceed twenty-five pounds.

Well, then, a new player! Now there's a man who knows his flesh! I have twenty, plus two. Twenty-two. Any more? Any more?

A voice previously silent: *Let's milk the arrogant bastard, whoever he is. Hiding in an envelope. I bid twenty-three.*

Very good, thank you, sir. I now have twenty-three, plus two. Twenty five pounds. Going once to the secret envelope for twenty-five. Going twice ... Who will give me twenty six?

Thirty pounds!

The words lit up the auction plaza like midnight lightning.

Is that an actual bid? Who is it that bids thirty pounds? Show yourself. Ah, the baker Vaarck. Is that a true and honest bid?

My friend Captain Williams insults me. Are you implying that I would reneg?

No, no, never.

I have bank notes in my pocket, if you care to inspect them.

No, forgive me. Very well, the secret bidder is finished. Sold to Vaarck the baker for thirty pounds.

The throng burst into applause, to a series of fractured rounds of awed conversation.

James looked at the sky again, uninterested in what had transpired. As if this were happening to someone else in an ancient tribal tale.

The baker mounted the block with some difficulty; one leg seemed to have been injured, perhaps at birth. *If I might make a statement.* He was wearing a white blouse, black trousers, brown leather boots. His lean face, with deep-set brown eyes, suggested more a scholar than a baker. *When you encounter my new man in the street, or in the bakery, as of course you will, it would be awkward for you to address him as King James. And awkward for him to hear that. So I have gone back in history, to choose the name of another man of strength and courage, as I believe this man is. From this day forth, this fellow shall be known as Caesar.*

The parrot fluttered atop the auction house, squawking, as if he did not care for the name.

But can he bake a decent pie?

Amid mild laughter, a stranger's throaty voice distinguished itself: *Beware the ides of March!*

It's likely that few present besides John Hughson understood the reference. A pointless joke, Hughson thought; the baker Vaarck had no known enemies, and why threaten a new slave?

Vaarck led James—now Caesar—down from the block. The auction resumed, moved along more quickly. The other men were bought with far lower bids than King James, the slave women for less, the children for lesser still. One family of four slaves, a couple with two children, were purchased separately. The children screamed as the guards dragged them from their mother.

Now it's just mortals and courtiers and maybe some jackals, Hughson whispered. He took Peggy's elbow. *Let's have a closer look at that Caesar fellow who is worth thirty pounds.*

She held back. *He's standing right near Billy. I won't know what to say.*

How about, Hello, Billy.

I'd rather say Go to Hell.

My, my, is that how proper young ladies speak in Newfoundland?

I'm not in Newfoundland anymore. And who says I'm a proper lady?

Caesar wearing his odd new name like an ill-fitting blouse followed his slightly limping new owner slowly through the streets. The most uncomfortable sensation was the oddness of everything. He a grown man did not know what anything was. He, a king, did not know what anything

was for. Only the sight of other black slaves along the dirt road, watching
in silence as he passed, held his attention.

29. PEGGY

A box full of evil. That's what the metal box on Billy's table
became to Peggy as the auction continued, more quickly now, more and
more men placing bills or bank notes in the box and walking away with
their human purchases.

She did not speak to him, not then. He was busy. That was a
good excuse. Seeing him with the Widow Williams made her stomach
hurt. She tried to concentrate on the auction. Watching men, women
and children being sold like fish at a market made her stomach hurt
even more. Among the worst, after the screaming children, was when
a husband and wife were put on the block together. The man's hands
were shackled in front of him. The woman's were not. But she held his
shackled hands in hers, as if to proclaim they were together until death.
It did not work out that way. They were a married couple, and would
be sold that way, the auctioneer told the crowd. But no one bid on them
together. Several men bid just on the woman, who was naked above the
waist. At first Captain Williams refused those bids. Then he shrugged, as
if to say, *What can can I do?* He allowed the woman to be sold separately,
for one and a half pounds. As she was taken away her husband tried to
run after her. The guards with cutlasses blocked his way. He swung his
shackled hands at the head of one. The other poked his side with his
sword. A slight trickle of blood appeared on his waist cloth. He began
to shriek for his wife, who was hurried to the carriage of her new owner.
Perhaps because of his anger, no one bid on the man. His feet were
shackled with iron chains and he was shoved back into the holding room,
out of sight.

That's awful, Peggy said to Hughson. Her cheeks were wet. *Why
weren't they at least bought together?*

*She's a comely Negress. Whomever bought her might have plans he does not want
the husband to witness.*

He wouldn't be so considerate!

*It's not consideration. He doesn't want to wake up one fine morning with his
throat cut. Or worse.*

What could be worse?

When Hughson did not answer, Peggy's fair skin blushed crimson from her cheeks to the roots of her flaming hair. She turned away.

I think you've had enough auction for today, Hughson said. *There goes the baker with his new man. I know him, he drinks at the tavern of an evening. I'd like to find out why he paid so much for that fella.*

Up the thawing road the baker Vaarck with his limp leg was walking slowly yet confidently. Caesar by his side had adopted a similar slow pace. Soon they were out of sight. Hughson veered toward the money table and greeted the Widow Williams.

And this is Peggy Kerry, a new boarder at the Inn, just arrived from Newfoundland.

The young widow glanced at Peggy, up and down, without standing.

Ah, you must be Billy's fishing wench. Come to snatch him back.

Peggy nodded. *And you must be his New York wench, renting him your snatch.*

The widow flushed. *Well I never!*

Oh, sure you have! Many times.

Billy Reilly's ears burned red as he listened, but he never looked at either woman. He kept his eyes on the money box. As Hughson led Peggy away they heard the widow saying, *Billy Reilly, why did you not defend me from that awful person? Really!*

That's a powerful lady, Hughson said to Peggy as they trudged up the road. *You shouldn't make an enemy of her. And where did you learn such language?*

A fisherman's daughter learns every word there is. Perhaps I could teach alongside Professor Fez. Fill in the words he leaves out.

She grinned through her pain but was also ashamed. What had come over her? Was this New York's doing? Or Billy's? Or the widow's? Ashamed but also liberated. Free. Free to laugh. Free to cry. Had that been Margaret speaking? Or ~~Marguerite?~~ What would Nora think?

She did not want to look back down the road at him but like something weaker than human she could not stop herself. Twisting her neck, she could see only his broad back tight beneath his grey jacket as he bent over his cache of cash. It was Billy she would have to confront, she knew, not the widow.

Only a few yards ahead of them, Caesar and the limping baker walked ever more slowly. Hughson, always open to good gossip, strained to hear what they were saying. His ears grew large as a rabbit's.

My friend Captain Williams suggested that I purchase you. He said that more than any other slave he had encountered, you were quick on the uptake.

I do not know those words, Sir.

Quick on the uptake means that you understand what needs to be done, and you do it.

If the captain said that of me, perhaps it is so.

Good. Because I have big plans for you, Caesar. Something no one has ever done before.

30. MARY

Being a denture ain't no fun. Wash the dishes, peel potatoes, make the beds, sweep the floor. I done all that at Belfry Catholic Orphanage without having to sail across the sea. There I could also ride my horse, Gweebarra, and I could make the little children cry. Sometimes it was fun to make the children cry. Scare them with my spiders. Then I could pretend to be their mommy and hug them until their crying stopped. Here there ain't no horse and there ain't no children so there isn't any fun.

One day about three months after I become a denture, while I am sweeping the dining room, Mrs. Ramsey calls me over and says to stand near where she is sitting on one of those hard dining room chairs. She puts her hand flat against my belly and she asks me, *What do you have under there?*

Nothing, mam, just my chemise.

Mary Burton, I think you are pregnant, she says.

What does that mean, I ask.

You don't know what pregnant means? It means you are carrying a child.

No mam, just this broom, and I show her.

Have you slept with Mr. Ramsey?

She seemed to be angry when she said that.

No mam, I have the room you give me to sleep in.

So how did you get pregnant?

I do not know, mam.

What about the men on the ship?

What about them, mam?

I think you are mocking me, Mary Burton. You are old enough to know of what I am speaking.

I wouldn't mock you, mam.

Didn't they teach you anything at that orphanage?

Yes, mam, they taught us lots of things. How to spell words. Also arithmetic. One and one makes two.

Sometimes, Mary, she says, *one and one makes three.*

With all due respeck mam, that is not what the teacher said at Belfry Catholic Orphanage.

Never mind that. Was it someone on the boat that did this to you?

You mean play that fun game without no clothes?

Yes. Who did you play that with?

I'm not suppose to say.

Who told you not to say?

Arthur Hands. He told me not to tell.

One of the boat hands?

I guess.

Wonderful. He must be back in Ireland by now. I shall speak to Captain Anders about this. He cannot go around purveying damaged goods.

No mam.

I purposely asked for nice Irish help, not some Negro hussy. I won't have easy girls around my husband while I am fat and ugly. Not that you are very pretty yourself.

Yes mam. No mam.

But with men you can never tell. Even my husband. Pack your things, you will hear from Mr. Ramsey about this.

Yes, mam.

I was happy to pack my things, though I did not want to go on another boat. Not back to Belfry Catholic Orphanage.

When Mr. Ramsey came home from the bank where he works I heard yelling and shouting by Mrs. Ramsey, telling him to keep his letchrus hands off me. Soon it came to pass, as they say, that Mr. Ramsey sold my denture papers to Mr. John Hughson who owns that big Inn down by the river. Mr. Hughson took a bunch of bills from his pocket and gave it to Mr. Ramsey, and Mr Ramsey took a bunch of papers from his pocket and gave it to Mr. Hughson. So I had a new denture owner right then.

I've been needing more help serving dinners at the Inn, Mr. Hughson said to me, and he took my bundle of clothes from my hand and led me down the road, me in my good coat on top of my house-cleaning dress, and my new boots. The snow was long gone with spring coming and the road had hardened to wagon ruts.

This is my favorite time to be out walking, Mr Hughson said, *with the short day dying in the river in front of us and the long night trailing behind, and one of Sarah's joyous repasts waiting on the stove, dry logs crackling in the fire and good fellowship waiting thereafter.*

He talked funny that way. It was hard for me to understand. I think it meant he was hungry. He could've just plain spoke that.

Inside the Inn was noisy when we passed the wide doors to the dining room. He led me down a long corridor with a lot of closed doors on both sides to the last one, which had a number on it, number 12. The lady inside number 13 hearing us come opened her door across from mine and Mr. Hughson said, *Mary Burton, this is Peggy Kerry, who lives here. Peggy, this is Mary Burton who will help Sarah serving the meals and other chores. Perhaps you will become friends.*

Nice to meet you, I'm sure you'll like it here, Miss Peggy Kerry said, but I don't know if she means it so I don't say nothing back. My head is spinning with all these changes but maybe it will be for the good. Maybe Mr. Hughson has a horse like Gweebarra that I could ride. Maybe he could send for her. Though I don't know if they allow horses on boats.

He tried to push open the door to number twelve but it did not push. He kept shaking the knob. *The damn door is locked,* he said, *excuse my language, ladies. This room is vacant, it should not be locked.*

Mr. Hughson, Peggy Kerry said, *I think Mrs. Hughson transferred some travelers from up front to that room. They had a baby with them. They said the front room was too noisy last night.*

Is that so? No matter, we'll just put you in another room, Mary. Maybe number 2, right across from my office, in case you have any problems.

I wished I could of stayed across from Miss Kerry, she was so pretty. *You are so pretty,* I said to her. *I wish you were my mother.*

How sweet. You mother must be pretty, too.

I never seen her. She left me at the door of Belfry Catholic Orphanage. That's where I growed up.

I'm so sorry, Miss Peggy said, and she touched my shoulder with her hand. *You know something? I never saw my mother either She died while I was being born.*

Mr. Hughson picked up my sack of clothes. He took a step away. *Sounds as if you ladies will have plenty to talk about.*

And Mr. Hughson, Peggy Kerry said, *I know I'm late with my rent. Your wife reminded me today. But it's hard to find a job. I've walked all over the city. Most of the jobs I can do, like sewing and dressmaking and cooking, have been given to slaves. I didn't know there were so many here. I didn't think my money would run out so fast.*

Don't worry, Peggy, we'll never put you out on the street. I shall speak to Sarah with my grandest wisdom about not pressuring you.

Miss Peggy smiled a cheerful smile. *Could I ask you one more thing? The window in here has been locked shut all winter. Now that the weather is warming, perhaps you could get someone to open it?*

I'll do that myself, right after supper, Mr. Hughson said. So we left Miss Peggy and walked back down the corridor. Room number 2 was empty as if waiting just for me.

Set down your things, Mr. Hughson said, *and come to the dining room with me and help my daughter serve supper. We're just in time.*

I followed him into the noise of the dining room and he pointed to a big bowl of meat-smelling stew on a side board with a pile of white bowls next to it, and he says, *Start serving those men over there. Be careful not to spill anything.*

They was mostly black men where he pointed, I never seen the likes of them. In Ireland I never seen even one.

I won't serve no colored men, I said.

What? Mr. Hughson looked at me like I was crazy. Well, one of us was, and it weren't me.

I said, I don't serve no suppers to black men.

Everybody in the that dining room, which had a long wooden table down the middle and long wooden benches on both sides, stopped talking. Miss Peggy Kerry come into the room, and stopped, as if the sudden silence was a wall on which she banged her pretty nose. Mr. Hughson looked red as a cabbage. He took some deep breaths, his chest bumping in and out. The dining room itself was holding its breath. Mr. Hughson looked around the room. Finally he told his daughter Sarah to serve the stew to everyone before it gets cold. The black men and some white men among them gave me looks with eyebrows popping. Amid the return of the talking and joking which was even louder than before, Miss Kerry sat herself on the bench among the coloreds. I could hardly believe my eyes.

We shall talk about this tomorrow, Mary Burton, Mr. Hughson said, loud enough for them Negroes to hear. *Now go to your room and stay there. That's what I get for buying a pig in a poke.*

I didn't know he also bought a pig. I ran to my room and jumped on the lumpy bed and curled up and held myself tight not knowing whether to laugh or to cry. I was hungry for that good-smelling stew but I stayed curled and nervous and angry on the bed until I fell sleep.

The next morning Mr. Hughson called me into his office, which was room number 1, the first one past the dining room. He had a wooden desk in it with square holes above it that had keys in them and some of them had papers. He sat alongside his desk in a wooden chair and I sat on the other side. I said I was hungry for breakfast but he said we had to talk first. He said I looked like I could grow into a fine young woman after my denture ended, but first he wanted to know why I refused to serve the Negroes. I asked him who they was, eating there with some whites. He said some were free men, but most were slaves. I thought slaves got locked up at night, I told him, so they would not run away. In the southern colonies, he said, where some men had hundreds of slaves picking cotton or tobacco all day, they mostly lived on big plantations and was more or less confined there. But that was not the case here in New York, he said. Most families with slaves had only a few. The slaves did their chores during the day, working on the docks or building homes or cleaning house or fetching for drinking or tea casks of water from Comfort's well, the only source of fresh, uncontaminated water nearby, he said. It was only a block from Hughson's, and in the evening, when they were free to do as they pleased many slaves gathered indoors at the Tavern or outdoors at the well to talk and laugh and exchange the latest news and gossip. New York Colony is an island, he said, surrounded by two rivers, the East and the North, so there was no place for slaves to run. Most of them coming from inland Africa couldn't swim anyway, he said, and if they did try to swim away, guards posted on the shore would fire a musket ball that would blast their heads apart. So at night if they had made some money doing extra chores or had been given some coins by their master some of the slaves came to the Tavern to eat.

But now to the point, he said. *Why do you refuse to serve them?*

Because they smell bad, I said.

Have you ever even been near a Negro? How do you know they smell bad?

Everyone knows that. Mr. Higgins said so.

Who is everyone?

The boys and girls at Belfry Catholic Orphanage. And the nuns.

Even the nuns?

Yes, mam. I mean, yes sir.

Though I didn't know if that was exactly true.

Any other reason?

Because they is dumb like animals and must be treated as such.

How do you know that?

Same way. Also Mrs. Ramsey.

What if I told you that is all wrong? he said. *What if I told you the coloreds are human people, just like us?*

If that is true, I said, *then why are they slaves?*

He looked at me without saying nothing. He looked out the window for a time, his fingers pressed together each touching each, like a game we used to play at Belfry Catholic Orphanage, making our fingers look like a church with a steeple. He turned back to me.

I don't want to force you to do anything, Mary, he said, *even though I could. But I don't want tension here at the Inn. That's a good way to lose customers. So your job will be to make the beds of guests and wash the sheets and towels and empty the chamber pots and help Mrs. Hughson in the kitchen and wash the dishes afterward. You will not be a server, as I had planned. My daughter and my wife will do the serving. Now go to the kitchen and get your breakfast porridge and then Sarah will put you to work. One more thing. With the weather warming you will start to see spiders in the rooms. Guests don't like spiders, when you clean the rooms be sure to kill them all.*

Why don't they like spiders? I asked.

Most people are afraid of them.

Do the guests like flies?

No, they don't like flies either.

Well, spiders spin their webs to catch flies. So which is better?

Mr. Hughson sort of cocked his head to one side when I asked that and looked at me funny but he didn't say an answer he just shooed me out of his office. I figured it was best not to tell him I would never kill a spider no more than I would serve a black man.

I done the washing and all as I was told – even emptied chamber pots which was disgusting and I held my nose – so you might think that was the end of the discussion about me and them colored slaves what come to eat. But it weren't. Mr. Hughson wanted to tell the judge about my views toward the coloreds, the things I said in his office that morning. But the judge would not allow him. The judge said, *We are not here to investigate attitudes, Mr. Hughson, we are here to determine facts.* That was much later on, of course, almost a year later. At the trial.

31. Caesar

The largest man in New York colony was an illiterate slave called Zion. He, too, was owned by John Vaarck. Caesar would bunk with him in a wooden shack behind Vaarck's Bake Shop, Caesar was told. It would be close quarters, Vaarck conceded, but said *I have no plans to build a hotel for the two of you.* The slaves did not smile. Zion stood six and a half feet tall, weighed nearly three hundred pounds and beneath his cherubic face he was laden all over with sweating flab. Hidden inside the flab were sinews of iron, however; he could lift the weight of three men. Vaarck had purchased him five years earlier for only few pennies, with no one bidding against him. Who would want a slave with no tongue? Zion's tongue had been sliced out by his master in the Caribbean before he was sent north for sale. What he had done to deserve such punishment no one knew except himself. But the baker was looking for an inexpensive slave who could pull a heavy cart, and despite his size Zion's upkeep would be less than that of a horse. You did not pull a cart with your tongue.

For five years Vaarck had made good use of him. Zion easily pulled or pushed the wooden cart from the bake house each morning laden with hundreds of pounds of cakes, biscuits and pastries. Vaarck's only other slaves, three young women who did the baking before sunrise, lived upstairs in the main house. Zion pulled the cart to the bake shop's primary customers – Hughson's Tavern and the Black Horse Tavern and ships in the harbor that needed provisions for journeys of many weeks, the principal diet of the seamen being salt pork, dried fish, biscuits and bread. Unlike most men in the city Vaarck was not a rabid supporter of slavery, but if he had to pay wages to his bakery girls he could not stay in business. When Mrs. Vaarck– her name was Stephanie – heard that John had spent thirty pounds to buy Caesar she asked if he had lost his mind. *Caesar will make my plan work*, Vaarck replied, and because she approved of his plan to expand the business she did not mention the subject again, but went about her newly assigned task, in the absence of any children, of teaching the slave girls how to make tarts, croissants and other delicacies that otherwise were available no closer than Philadelphia. Once people tasted these, Vaarck believed, he would command most of the bakery business in the city.

As Caesar and Zion became comfortable with one another, which was difficult with only one able to speak, John Vaarck decided it was time to tell them of his plan. He led the two slaves to the south side of the bake house and with a walking stick drew a long large rectangle in the drying mud.

Until recently, he told them, most women in the colony baked their own bread. They baked their breads and pies for the week in one day, usually Friday, because the detritus spread into the air from burning logs in wood stoves set people to coughing and worse. The previous winter two babies had died from it, so more and more, families were inclined to purchase their bread from commercial bakeries, of which there were only three in the colony, Vaarck's being the most appreciated. This trend no doubt would continue, the baker told them. Besides that, the city is growing rapidly, is expanding its boundaries out into the countryside above Houston Street. Land was being sold along the Hudson River, where people were building homes and importing more slaves to work the land. All of them would need bread, and he, John Vaarck, intended to supply most of it. The first major chore of Caesar and Zion would

be to build a large addition to the bake house along the lines he had just
marked with his stick. He had learned of a fellow in the Pennsylvania
colony, name of Franklin, who was working on an improved version of
the cook stove. These were not yet on the market, Vaarck told them,
but he had ordered two of the prototype cast iron models to be shipped
by wagon to New Jersey. From there, Caesar and Zion would somehow
haul these heavy new stoves across the river and install them in the
expanded bake house, where two new female slaves would join the
existing crew. And that was just the beginning of his plan. Zion would
continue to pull his loaded cart through the immediate area, where he
was a well-known if silent figure, but Vaarck would purchase a horse
and a cart, and Caesar, with his good English tongue, would deliver the
day's baked goods throughout the outlying areas, and take orders for the
following week. The cash for the purchases would not be in jeopardy
from highwaymen; the purchases would be billed to weekly or monthly
accounts.

I've found the perfect horse already, the baker said. *Or rather, the perfect mare.
That's a female horse. She's owned by a fellow in the country. He calls her Spotty, but
she isn't really spotted. She's piebald. That means she has large splotches of black and
white. I'll call her Pie.*

Pie – the baker's horse. Get it?

Zion nodded. Caesar smiled wanly.

There's not another horse in town looks like her, Vaarck said. *Everywhere you
go, people will say, That's Pie, the baker's horse.*

He smiled again but for days afterward Caesar was morose. This
was the grand plan the baker had for him? He needed to talk about it
to someone. Busy repairing a dilapidated barn behind the bake shop,
the roof of which had disappeared during an ice storm, he had not seen
Professor Fez in a week. He sought out the professor at his school on
Williams Street, found him alone, reading at his desk. The walls were
pasted with simple drawings, English words hand-lettered underneath:
man, woman, boy, girl, house, horse, river.

What are you reading? Caesar asked.

The professor looked at the cover. *The Laws and Regulations of the
Colony of New York As Pertain to Negro Slaves; 1740 Edition*

Interesting?

*Enlightening. We are not permitted to carry weapons of any kind. If we ride a
horse in the city, it must be ridden slowly, gently. The one I find most interesting is that
no three of us can gather together in the street and talk, unless we are on a mission for
our masters.*

What are they afraid of? Caesar asked.

An uprising. A rebellion. They had one about thirty years ago. People died. Negroes and whites both. They don't want that to happen again.

Yet they keep importing more of us.

Yes.

Caesar shook his head, shrugged, glanced around the school room. *Door. Window. Meat.*

So, how are your pupils doing?

Some pick up the language quickly, others do not. As might be expected. So why this visit, James? I take it you've been busy at the baker's. Although I always enjoy your company, of course.

Caesar told him about Vaarck's expansion plan, about how disappointed he was. *That's why he spent thirty pounds for me? To deliver bread to lazy ladies?*

What did you expect? the professor asked, closing his book. *That he would appoint you king?*

Caesar looked down at his hands, said nothing.

Let's walk while we talk, the professor said, setting down his book, stretching his arms, standing, scratching his paunch beneath his loose white blouse, tightening a red scarf that almost matched his fez and held up his loose white trousers – the same outfitting that Caesar and most slaves wore, except for the fez– they went hatless – and the red sash, which was replaced by a rope tied around their waists to hold their trousers up. He led the way down a slight slope into Williams Street, Caesar walking beside him.

Do you know what most slaves do who are brought to these colonies? the professor said. *I have heard many tales from my students. They work under the hot sun for twelve hours picking cotton or tobacco. They are made to remove their shirts, men and women both, and they are lashed if they have not picked enough that day. Whenever the master wishes, he summons a woman to his house, right in front of her husband, who can do nothing, and he has his way with her. I doubt there is a slave anywhere who would not trade his position for yours – to ride through the countryside behind a horse, delivering bread. We've both been very lucky, you and I.*

My tribe is scattered, Caesar said. *I do not know what happened to them. I would not know where to look.*

Perhaps you will meet some while riding about. And unlike your friend Zion, you have a tongue with which to speak with them. Be thankful. Pride goeth before a fall, the white man's Bible says. So, too, does self-pity.

You think that's what this is?

You tell me, James.

They walked down Williams Street in silence. At the intersection of Wall Street they could see and hear in front of City Hall a crowd gathered, heard stinging epithets darting through the air like mosquitoes. They walked in that direction, drawn by an invisible magnet, could not see from the back of the crowd. Zion's silent head and shoulders soared above the rest in the front row. They elbowed their way beside him. The jeering grew louder, most of it coming from women. In the street, beneath the center of three arched windows in the building's second story, stood the Public Whipping Post. A woman, white, was fastened to it, her arms above her head, wrists shackled together and looped over a high hook. Her bare feet barely touched the ground. The front of her grey dress had been pulled down to her waist, baring her breasts, her back. Pale brown braids circled her head.

Mercy, I forgot this was today, the professor said. *Today is her punishment day. They're about to give that woman thirty-one lashes on her back. Artemis, her name is.*

Why? What was her crime?
Fornication.
Which means?
Making love.
That is a crime here?
White woman, black man. That is a crime.

A tall man in boots, dressed all in brown, carrying a braided rope, stepped behind the woman. He was the Common Whipper. If a slave owner wanted to punish a slave, but did not want to wield the lash himself, he could hire the Common Whipper, for an appropriate fee. He also worked for the city.

The cheers grew louder as the man – thin-faced, pointy-nosed – looped the rope behind his shoulder and lashed out with it. The snaking whip struck the woman's back with a sickening bite. She winced but did not cry out. A dark cloud covered the sun, as if that worthy did not want to watch.

Again! some in the throng shouted

The Whipper again slashed the woman's back with his whip. And again. Caesar could see the woman gritting her teeth. The lash was leaving bloody stripes across her back. Still she did not cry out.

I'm going to stop this, Caesar said, spitting into the dirt. *I'm going to stuff that whip down his throat.*

No! the professor warned.

James tried to rush forward. He could not move after half a step. Zion held his right wrist tight.

Let go!

Zion shook his head. James punched the larger man's arm. Zion did not flinch, did not loosen his grip.

Slash!

A red bandana circling the Whipper's head grew dark with sweat.

Slash!

The woman's back was red with blood.

Slash!

The sound of ripping flesh was torture to Caesar, to Zion, to the professor, to every black person watching. This was a white woman!

Slash!

Her knees buckled. Still she made no sound. More cheers rose from the crowd, only slightly more subdued. The onlookers were getting tired.

James, the professor said, *look at the arched window above. Do you see that man looking down, watching.*

With the fat white face?

His name is Horsmanden. He's the city recorder, and a judge on the Supreme Court. Somehow he's placed himself in charge of punishment,

Slash!

Slash!

Again James tried to pull away from Zion. He could not move.

If you try to interfere it will go badly for you, and maybe worse for the prisoner.

The woman Artemis had slumped against the post, blood dripping from her back to the back of her skirt.

Look at her. I think she's fainted. And still he whips her.

Again Caesar tried to pull toward her. Zion still held him fast.

One more slash, and the whipping stopped. The crowd cheered, chattered, slowly began to disperse. It was time for lunch. The Whipper approached the post, unshackled the woman's wrists. She slumped to the ground, unconscious.

What of the man? Caesar asked. *Do they know of the man?*

She refused to name him. They sentenced her to sixty lashes, then a year in the dungeon, right here beneath City Hall. That is a rotten stinking dark airless place, a playground for rats and disease. They announced that if she gave the name of the man, or if he came forward, they would reduce her lashings to thirty-one, and skip the dungeon.

Who could resist?

That brave lady did. But her lover came forward to spare her. A free Negro, not even a slave.

What did they do to him?

He's in the dungeon. He may be sold as a slave.

The beaten woman lay alone in the dirt. The squeamish sun broke through the clouds. They saw a woman move toward the post, carrying a small jar. She was younger, dressed in blue, red hair streaming from under a white mob cap. She knelt beside the victim, raised her head slightly, urged her to drink. At first she could not. Then she began to sip. She revived some, drank more water.

I've seen that woman, Caesar said. *In the dining room at Hughson's. Will she be punished for this?*

They all three looked toward the second floor window. The silent observer was gone.

Probably not. The beaten woman was not sentenced to die.

Barely able to move, the woman drained the cup. Her benefactor pulled the torn dress up over her breasts. The woman, with a shaking hand, held it there. Slowly the one helped the other to stand. She slumped, leaned against her rescuer. With small steps they began to walk away.

Zion dropped Caesar's wrist. He strode toward the women. With his powerful arms he carefully scooped up the beaten one, one arm under her knees, the other across her shoulder. The woman in the white cap pointed. Zion nodded, easily carrying the woman, whose head hung low, who may have fainted again.

I should have done that, James said.

He glanced up at the arched window, now vacant. On a ledge below it dozens of grey pigeons had gathered, cocking their heads, cooing pigeon coos as if they were glad the whipping was over. Or as if they wanted more – there was no way to tell.

Look! James said,

Pigeons. The city has thousands of them. No doubt you've noticed.

Not the pigeons. In amongst the grey. The big blue one. It's the parrot from Muktu. From the ship.

Not likely, the professor said. *I see no parrot. Although I concede your young eyes are stronger than mine.*

The colors, the markings, they're exactly the same. It's the same bird. I'm sure of it.

And what do you make of that?

I have no idea.

Walk with me back to the school, if you will. And try to forget what we've seen.

They walked. Meandered. They did not forget.

A few days later, with the ground now fully hardened by the sun, with planks and boxes of long nails stacked in the corner, which had been carried by Zion from the lumber yard two streets away, John Vaarck's two male slaves began to build the addition to the bake shop. People with nothing better to do paused to watch. Housewives from the outlying areas were delighted to hear that soon they would have fresh bread delivered to their doors every morning. The bread would cost a few pennies more than bread they could bake themselves, but the cleaner air for the children, they told their husbands, would be worth it. As the expansion of the bake shop rose, the street, which merged into Broad Way like one half of a slingshot, became officially named Varick Street, Varick being the English pronunciation of the Dutch name Vaarck.

One very hot day, presaging an early summer, his shirt hanging on a nail, sweat running down his back, reaching for another plank to nail into place, Caesar saw the red-haired woman in the mob cap among those gathered around. He sensed that she was watching him. He felt like an animal in a cage. Quickly he turned his back on her.

32. PEGGY

You remind me of Desdemona. So John Hughson said to her one afternoon as she sat by a window in the dining room, her thoughts far away. She turned to face him.

Who is Desdemona?

Do you know we have a playhouse in town?

The New Theater. I've passed it on Broad Way. What about it?

I would love to put on a play there. I would choose Othello. It's a play by Shakespeare. Desdemona is the young woman in it, about your age, a beautiful bride. You could play her, no reason she could not have red hair. I would play Iago, the villain. He's real slimy. It's fun playing a villain, I'm suited for the role. Othello, the central character, is Desdemona's husband. He's a great general. And a Moor, which means he's black. You know who would be perfect for Othello? That big slave of Vaarck's who pulls the bread cart in the mornings. Zion. He looks so strong, so proud.

Zion has no tongue. He can't talk.

Oh, right. Well, that would be a bit of a problem. I wonder who cut out his tongue. Not a theater critic, I hope.

That's terrible. It's nothing to joke about.

You're right. Well, I'm a terrible person. I thought you would have figured that out by now.

She was growing uneasy. She was afraid he was going to bring up the matter of her unpaid rent. She excused herself from his silly ideas. She could wait no longer. The money she owed the Hughsons, and her

with no job, was making her nervous, as if a fish hook had caught in
her skin and was tugging her flesh, every few seconds tugging again, an
insistent message she could no longer deny. She had to confront Billy, no
matter where it led.

Donning her best dress, pale burgundy, with stiff white petticoats
peeking from beneath, and a matching burgundy bonnet tied under her
chin, she walked from Hughson's to Wall Street. After passing it several
times, she approached a small green door marked New York Mercantile
Co. Her heart began thumping like a native drum. *It's only Billy,* she told
herself. *What can he do to me?* Knowing that what he did could determine
the rest of her life. Knowing, too, that whatever it was, he had already
done it. Breathing deeply, she turned a gold-colored door knob and
stepped into a dark hallway. At the far end she could see muted light
behind an inner door that was half dark wood, half tinted glass. On the
glass was writing that blurred before her eyes as she approached. She
stopped, waited until the writing cleared. *New York Mercantile Company.* Like
an obscenity.

Her stomach hurt. She needed a drink to relax. She had never tasted
alcohol in Newfoundland, her father drank enough for both of them. Her
first taste of liquor occurred in Hughson's Tavern her first night in New
York colony, after supper, when John Hughson toasted her arrival before
a small group of regulars who had braved the freezing cold. The alcohol
tasted terrible in her mouth – she almost choked on it – but it warmed
her innards nicely when it hit bottom. Since then she would sip a drink
in the evening now and again – never more than one – often ordered for
her by one of the male diners. They enjoyed her presence. She might be
white, but she was beautiful.

Nervous, she made her way back down the hallway and out into
the street. She had passed a saloon on the previous block. A stop there
first might embolden her assault on Billy in his lair. The sun half-blinded
her for a moment. She hurried north to the Wall Street Saloon – and
was at once disappointed. A sign in the window said *No Unescorted Ladies.*
She had not noticed that earlier. She considered pushing her way in and
demanding a drink, then almost grinned, chagrinned. A fine intrusion
that would be – even if they served her a drink, she had no money to pay
for it. Summoning her courage, she returned to the Mercantile office, and
with her gloved hand knocked on the glass part of the door. Her knock
was not very loud. She pounded.

Come in.

Even though it was muffled, she recognized Billy's voice. Opening
the door, she stepped into an office hung on two sides with large oil

paintings of sailing ships at full sail, one on each side wall, framed in dull gold. She did not know if these were ships owned by Billy's company, as she had come to think of it. Billy was sitting at a wooden desk in front of a maroon velvet wall hanging, which softened the sun trying to invade through a hidden window. The hanging ended at a wooden door in the corner on which a brass plaque said: *E. Williams, President.* Billy was wearing the same grey suit he had worn at the auction, writing in a ledger. He did not at first look up at her, as if he had visitors all the time and preferred to make them wait. Her anger rising, she said, *I see no portraits of slaves.*

Stunned by her voice, he looked up, dropped his quill on the blotter.

Peggy! Peggy Kerry! What are you doing here? Why are you not in Newfoundland?

She smiled a rueful smile. *That's progress, I suppose. At least you remember my name.*

He came around the desk as if to hug her. She stepped away.

What's wrong? You seem angry.

I suppose I have no cause to be angry.

We're engaged to be married, darling, as soon as I make my fortune. Just as we planned long ago. Didn't you get my letter?

The last letter I received, you were working for the Widow Williams. You still are, I see. Most likely night and day.

I wrote explaining everything. It must have gotten lost at sea.

Billy Reilly, your ears still blush red when you are lying.

Peggy, sit. I'll explain everything.

I would rather stand, thank you.

Fine. As you know, I was hired by the Widow Williams just as my money was running out. And a good thing that was.

So I have imagined, many times.

But you don't know how good.

Are you going to paint me a graphical picture?

Let me tell you about the slave business. It was started by the Portuguese, who sent ships to Africa and captured the natives and shipped them to their colony in South America. The Spanish soon copied them, began capturing the coloreds and sending them to the West Indies. Seeing the profits being made, our England, with more ships than anyone, jumped in. The slaves were brought to the colonies — so of course the colonies started bringing in their own. For slaves our captains purchase from tribes in Africa, we get double the price here, or more. Do you know, Peggy, that the slave trade is the biggest commerce in the world? And the city recorder, Horsmanden, estimates that New York has more slaves per capita than any city on the continent. It's a runaway

*business. It's making the colonies rich. The Widow Williams says if I'm still in her
company in a year …*

In her cunny you mean.

Peggy! I'll ignore that.

Of course. You've had a lot of practice ignoring me.

*Let me finish. In a year, she will make me the official Secretary of the company.
With my name on the door. And a big raise. In two years, she will make me Vice
President of the company. With a share of the profits. That's when I plan to build a
large house for you and me in the country, overlooking the river, and send for you, and
we will marry and have lots of kids running around. Does that sound so bad?*

The widow won't let you marry.

I hardly need her permission.

It appears that you do.

*Do you know what Ellie says about marriage? She says the man is giving charity
to the woman, in return for certain services.*

And that is what you believe?

Well, it is sort of true.

So you expect me to wait two years? Or more?

In Newfoundland that's not a long time. Helping your aunt, your father.

*Billy Reilly, you've known since the winter that I was was here. You saw me at
that auction, with Mr. Hughson. You were busy that day, I'll give you that. But never
once did you come looking for me.*

I didn't know …

*There go your ears again. I suppose Mrs. Williams did not let you. Was she
afraid I would win you back?*

We never go to Hughson's.

Because you look on the men there as trash?

Because most of them came over on our ships.

Peggy breathed deeply. She turned to leave. Billy took her sleeve.

Listen, if you need money, he said, *I have plenty to give you. I know that jobs
are hard to find.*

*Do you think that's why I came here today? For money? I don't want your charity.
I'm glad you don't come to Hughson's. I don't want to see you ever again!*

She twisted away from him, left the office, closing the door hard
behind her.

As she walked through the dark hallway, she wondered, indeed, why
she had come.

Even as her tears, which seemed to know, ran down her cheeks.

What her tears knew would take three days for her mind to decipher.

Something Billy had said about marriage. Something terrible.

Charity for services rendered.

It would take four more days for her body to assimilate the thought. The definition. To prepare. To accept as her only salvation. Her only way to pay her bills. Her only chance for self-respect. She fingered the coin in her pocket. She reached deep inside herself, as if she were filleting a cod. What she found was ~~Marguerite.~~

Within a week she had surpassed the daily expansion of Vaarck's bake shop as the primal chatter around Comfort's well, from which, as their final chore of the day, the slaves drew water and carried caskets home for the evening tea of their masters.

The window to room thirteen, the whispered chatter went from slave to slave. *You climb in, you climb out. The last window on the side. Room thirteen.*

33. MARY

Dear Denture Dairy-

Before my denture was bought by mr Hughson I never before slept in a room by myself.

In Belfree Cathlic Orphinage all the girls slept in one big room and all the boys in another. On the boat I left my door opened and Arthur Hands come in to visit most nights. At the Ramseys the Ramseys slept together in one bedroom and I was in the maid's little room but I was not alone because their dog George liked me and jumped up on my bed every night and I slept with my arm around him, all cozy. So I was scared to be in my own room at Hughsons Tavern. The night mr Hughson was mad at me about not serving the coloreds I was frightened near to death. There was so many of them and one was big as a horse with a big mouth shaped like an O but no words. I never knew what he was thinking, maybe he would crash down my door. So I tip-toed down the hall and and knocked on the door of miss Peggy Kerry. She say who is there and I say Mary Burton and she open the door in her light blue night gown and ask what I want. I tole her I was frightened to sleep alone, so she invite me in and I climb onto her bed like that dog George use to do - just for a little while, she said - and she laid down next to me under the covers and the next thing I knew there was light coming through the window curtain and the little while had become morning, me sleeping with my curly head on her chest. Same thing happened the next night. We talked about growing up without no mothers and why a mother would leave her baby at Belfree Cathlic Orphinage and she said it was not my fault. We became good frens. She were 21 years of age and me just turned 15 but she became like my new mother. So the night after that when I was on the commode in my room and all this blood come rushing out of me and I thought I was going to die I ran down the hall to get Peggy instead of Mrs Sarah Hughson and she come and looked and said she was sorry but I just lost my baby. How can you lose a baby I ast and she pointed to this thing in the bowl and put her arms aroun me and said she was sorry. It was just this bloody lump what didnt look like a baby to me, but I said that was okay I didnt want no baby anyhow. Which she said was smart, I should wait till I was a few years older and married before I had another. That sounded good to me. I still kept coming to her room most nights after that. She told me to listen to all the noise that come through the walls into my room from the dining room, there was always men in there drinking and laughing and nothing bad could happen to me so long as I heard them laughing and talking until I fell asleep. I done that but still most nights I run down to her room and sleep there in her bed with her, though sometimes she went to the dining room and I had to wait to go to her till later.

Dear Denture Dairy-
Lots of citement today over by Vaarcks Bake Shop, which is across the street from Gordons Milk and Cheese Diary where our milk and cheese come from. I saw it during lunch time with lots of other people. They was gathered by the river, even that Professor Fez with his white blouse and white pants and sandals and that red hat what always seems attached to his head, watching two slaves poling in a thick flat barge what had a big cook stove on it, the biggest I ever seen since Belfree's Cathlic Orphinage, only much shinier. In the back poling was that big fat slave with the big O mouth that makes no sound. Poling in the front was a slave I had seen around who

when he smiled it lit up his white teeth like a cerosne
lamp. He jumped off onto the beech and smiled that smile
and poled the front of the barge onto the beech with the
O-mouth slave still poling in the back. Then he jump into
the water and the two of them go on the barge and lift
that big shiny stove off of the barge and onto the beech
and set it down, and catch their breaths for a minute.
Then together hugging it to their chests they picked it up
lookin about to burst and they carried it slow step slow
step up the small hill and into the wide door of the new
room they had built at the bake shop. The people watching
and me clapped our hands. One lady said no other two
men in the whole colony could lift that cast iron thing.
Professor Fez said no four men - but maybe one strong
lady. Everybody laughed. Then the two slaves climbed back
down to the beech and got onto that barge and began poling
it back out into the river that was rippling along the shore.
They was going to haul over another stove from Jersey,
a man said, whose name was mr Vaarck so I guess he
should know. But I couldnt watch that one, I had to get
back to work ....

Dear Denture Dairy-
The day after them big stoves was brought in there
was nearly a big fire right there. But it wasnt from the
stoves it was across the street at Gordons Milk and
Cheese Diary. The nice smile slave whose name is Caesar
who is owned by mr Vaarck told about it that night after
supper. I stood in the doorway to the dining room and
listened. I saw that Peggy Kerry was in there listening too.
Caesar said that he and Zion - that is the big O-mouth
slave - was setting up the stoves when mr Gordon from
the Diary come running into the street yelling Fire, Fire and
some smoke could be seen above the roof of the Diary.
That frightened everyone because once long ago the whole
city burned down from a fire. People was yelling call the
Fire Brigade, get the buckets to the river, but before anyone
got to do anything mr Gordon com back out and shouted
there was no need. He was cursing some customer, Caesar
said, who threw a cigar out the back door of the Diary and
it caught on straw that ws near the barn out back where

they keep the cows. The cows started mooing, they was afraid they would become roasts, Caesar said, but before the barns could catch fire mrs Gordon who is a big sturdy woman, bigger than her husband, picked up a large milk can and poured the milk on the burning straw and put the fire out. So no cows was hurt, Caesar said, but there would not be much milk in the morning. I always liked beer for breakfast anyways, one man said, and everybody laughed and ordered another beer....

Dear Denture Dairy –
Peggy Kerry hates me. She is my best frend. She is my ony frend. Now she hates me, and I dont know what I done. Two nights ago I felt lonely and went down to her room and knocked on her door. Who's there? she said. She never said that before, she would just open the door. This time she ast who's there. Mary Burton, I said. After a minute she opened the door a crack, she was putting on her maroon robe, I could see she had no clothes on underneath. I need to come in, I told her. I'm sorry Mary, she said, I can't let you in tonight. Why not, I said. Because I am working she said. You can work in your room, I ast. That's right she said. That must be a nice job I said. I never heard of such a job. I was feeling bad but there was nothing to do but go back to my room

Same thing happened the next night. She said she was working. Maybe I could help you work in there I said. No I'm afraid that would not work, she said. But thank you for offering. I went back to my room and cried. Why did she hate me?

Tonight I went down there again, and the same thing happened. This time she did not even open the door, she just yelled Go Away. Now my feelings was really hurt bad. What had I done to her. She yelled out that she had company. I couldn't stand it any more. I began kicking the door. Kicking and kicking as hard as I could. Stop that I heard her yelling. But I didnt stop, I kept kicking and kicking. I needed to find out why we were not frens any more. Finally wearing her maroon robe she open the door half way. Mary Burton you stop that raket she said. You'll wake up the hole Inn. I need to talk to you, I said. I need

to know what I did wrong, I need to know why you aint
my fren no more. Why you hate me. Oh, Mary, she said.
She closed the door behind her and come out into the hall.
Of course I'm still your fren she said. She put her arm
around my shoulder like a fren. She hug me like a fren. Its
just that I have to work to pay my bills. Everyone has to
do that. You do the laundry and sweep the floors and all
that to earn your keep. I said, Because I am a denture.
Yes, and I am a free woman, but I still have to work to
pay for room and bord. I have to do my own work. But I
love you just as much as ever, Mary.

    I was trying to control my sobs. Her arm felt so nice
on my shoulder.

    I tell you what, she said. Tomorrow is Sunday. I
wont work tomorrow night. You can come by and we can
swap stories again. I'll tell you about fishes you can walk
right through up to your knees, and you can tell me again
about your horse Gweebarra that jumped over the moon.
You remember that story, I ast. Of course, she said,
how could I ever forget a horse like that? It reminds
me of you. Why is that I ast. Because when you are
finished with your indenture, you will fly over the moon
yourself. That was a pretty silly thing for her to say, the
moon being far up in the sky, as near as I could tell. But
I didn't say nothing. So, she said, do we have a deal for
tomorrow. I rubbed my teary eyes. Every Sunday, I said.
Now I didn't say that, she said. But why not, I said, why
not every Sunday, if you love me. You drive a hard bargain,
Mary Burton she said, whatever that means. All right, you
have a deal. Every Sunday night we will spend together,
telling stories. You promise, I ast, just like we used to
do. I promise, she said. Now you go back to your room
and go to sleep, and come by tomorrow night.

    I stopped crying then. I come back to my room and I
writ all this. I was not happy, but some happy. I had a
fren again. Sometimes me and Sarah, not mrs Hughes but
Sarah the girl, would play run and jump and games like that
outside. But that is not the same as a real fren, what you
can tell your heart to.

34. CAESAR

He is a slave but he has never felt so free. He is a king but he has never known such strength.

He is a spear flung far with balanced density.

He is an arrow sprung with tight intensity.

The breeze off the river rumples his short curly air as Triana's fingers used to do, eliciting a poignant smile in his chest. He is on the back of Pie, no saddle, no reins, no cart, leaning low over her bowing neck, fingers wrapped in her flowing mane, faint gurgling of the river at the edge of the shore cheering him on as the mare with its own instincts, or his, conveyed from head to arm to hands and into her wild mane, dodges boulders too high to jump, rounds fingers of forest too thick to penetrate, splashes droplets onto the narrow beach with unshod ankles, galloping, galloping as she has never done before, as he has never done before, this feeling new to her and new to him, they must do it again every sunrise if possible he thinks, every dawn if possible until the end of days.

Except – they neither of them know this yet – except they never will do it again. Never.

Six weeks have passed since Vaarck led the purchased mare into the small barn behind the bake shop. Troughs in the barn were filled with water Zion had carried in casks from Comfort's well and with hay he had carted from the edge of the city where farmers sold whatever growths they had to sell. The baker showed Caesar, who had never been close enough to touch or smell or fear a horse, how to befriend the mare by letting her lick sugar from his palm, showed him how to attach the bridle and the reigns, how to link the mare to a newly purchased cart that would carry the bread and cakes of Vaarck's bake shop far and wide across the rural miles of an expanding city. Through all this the mare stood stolidly without complaint as if she had done this all before, which she had, which was the main reason the baker had selected her, odd piebald patchy intermingled white and black coloring which he liked so much notwithstanding. Which inspired her perfect name Pie notwithstanding. The baker had financed his expansion – the new cast iron stoves, the extended shop, the piebald horse, the cart, two new slave girls imported from Providence – with a loan from Wall Street's First Mercantile Bank. So much construction was taking place in and around the city that the banks were doing almost as well as the slavers.

The first day master and slave sat side by side on the cart, boots beside sandals on the buckboard, Vaarck wielding the reins, Caesar watching wide-eyed and intent as they rode the dusty winding paths of the countryside, the baker drawing a map with graphite on a sheet of yellow paper, pausing near each white-painted house to draw a rectangle, and in it write the name of the family that resided there. Beside almost every house was a small cabin to hold one or two slaves, mostly women who cooked and cleaned and helped look after any children.

The second day they switched places. Caesar held the reins and at each home the baker climbed down careful of his bad leg and knocked on the early morning door and when someone usually a woman wearing a house dress or house coat opened the door he introduced himself and told of his new delivery system, of which many had already heard, and introduced Caesar – who smiled his disarming smile – as the boy who would be delivering the goods. As a first-day special gift, Vaarck told them, with each loaf ordered would come two free sweet pastries. With this inducement he obtained orders from almost every home. Who could refuse free manna delivered to the door?

The third day Caesar's chest was running away with itself as he and the baker loaded the cart with bags and boxes of baked goods prepared by the five slave girls under the direction of Mrs. Vaarck, on each bag or box the name of the customer writ large. Caesar vaulted up onto the driver's bench, behind the horse by himself this time, and as he flicked the reins lightly and Pie began moving slowly up Varick Street, cart wheels creaking, the baker allowed himself to puff out his chest and place his arm around the shoulders of his wife. Never had thirty pounds been better spent, he thought – alright, it was the bank's thirty pounds – but never had money been better invested than in his purchase of Caesar, formerly a king, who could read and write and speak fine English and was quick on the uptake and could smile that benign smile that put the ladies, even these white country women, at their ease. He owed Captain Williams for the tip, would bake him a special cake, or two or three, when the laden Bluebelle next returned from Africa.

When he began his deliveries out in the countryside Caesar was astonished. At the first door he knocked upon the lady of the house took in the bag of bread and pastries – *smells wonderful,* she said, and told him to *wait a moment* and disappeared into the house and came back a moment later and handed him some coins. *This is for your trouble,* she said. *That's not necessary,* he replied. *I know that, but take it anyway,* and he did, saying *Thank you mam.* For several homes in a row the same scene occurred with more or less the same words spoken. He stuffed the papers with their already written orders for the next day or the next week into the right-hand pocket of his white trousers and placed his new riches in the left. Only a few houses did not offer him such a gratuity, the ones where the doors were opened by Negro housekeepers, most likely slaves like himself.

When he had completed his rounds, his cart empty except for the warming aroma of baked dough, the day had not yet reached noon by the rising sun, and he felt joyful. His right pocket filled with new orders would make Vaarck happy. His left pocket of coins ensnared him briefly in a fantasy. He had never forgotten something Captain Williams had said as he led Professor Fez away from the auction block that impossible day. *Unless the professor is smart enough to convince me he is entitled to a percentage of the profits,* Captain Williams had said. *To be banked against the day he can buy his freedom.* Caesar had thought it was a joke at the time, still thought so. Could it be possible for a slave to buy his freedom? If these gratuities continued, would he some day have enough? He certainly could not ask Mr. Vaarck if that was possible, it was much too soon, he had cost the baker a lot. Probably it would always be too soon.

Caesar smiled at every door each day and returned home with his pocket laden. He unhitched Pie and rubbed her down and filled her troughs with hay and water and wondered what to do with the money. Spotting a sharp tool hanging on a nail in the barn, he knew. He trusted Zion completely but the first time Zion was out of the cabin Caesar used the tool to pry up a floor board beside his bed. He flattened his coins under the board and stamped it back in place. If he continued to get rich – he laughed at the notion – there were other boards he could loosen.

The seventh week he fell victim to a fantasy. He knew that if he acted on it he could be in much trouble. But it became an obsession; if he did not do it now he might never have another chance. He wanted to know what it would feel like to ride a horse. No cart, no bridle, no reins, no saddle, just he leaning forward over the black mane of Pie as if they were one beast running perhaps faster than any creature in the jungle, running perhaps faster than the wind.

He imagined the consequences. They would have to do it on the narrow beach, where there were no obstacles, where no one would be watching. First he would detach the cart from Pie. But what if sensing this freedom the mare galloped up the beach, dragging the reins, what if in the finger of forest that reached down into the water the reins Pie was trailing got caught on the limb of a tree, she running at high speed might break a leg, or two, and die from it, as horses did. The mare might stand still after he unhitched the cart, but when he removed the bridle and the reins then surely the mare would know it was free and might gallop up the beach and splash around the protruding forest and disappear, leaving Caesar stranded, alone, with no way to catch the runaway mare, stranded six or seven miles from help. He would not be able to pull the empty cart that far as Zion might be able to do, would have to slog his tired legs and sweating body all the way to Varick Street, show up there naked, as it were, no horse, no cart, nothing. What would Mr. Vaarck do to him? He had no idea. Worse than any punishment his master was likely to inflict was the taunting and laughter that would greet him at Comfort's well and at Hughson's dining room that night and the next night and perhaps forever, the expensive slave too stupid to keep a horse and cart together. How could he risk that?

On the other hand, Pie was his friend. Pie, licking sugar from his palm, might behave.

Night after night Caesar lay awake in bed, debating whether he dared indulge his fantasy.

He did not know why he was consumed by this. One evening he went to ask Professor Fez in his schoolroom. By lamplight the simple words on the walls seemed to be floating ideas.

Perhaps riding this mare as you describe represents freedom to you, the professor said.

What is this: represents?

Symbolizes. Stands for. The way that parrot once represented your wife. You know Triana was not really up in that tree. She was in the tree of your mind.

This tree is in my head? That is a very small tree.

But it casts a long shadow.

Does the red fez you always wear represent something?

I suppose it represents that I am a thinker, not a warrior.

And what am I?

That you will have to discover for yourself.

Caesar, somewhat confused, thanked the professor. As he walked home in the falling dark the small tree in his head began to hurt. It told him nothing about riding Pie. That would be an adventure, if he dared to do it, but certainly not an escape. Not freedom.

He dreamed that night of the red-haired white woman sitting on a horse. She wore a gown of gold. In his tentative new world of represents, this confused him even more. Had the dream showed him on the horse, that would have been easy to understand, a simple message from the secret tree. But what did the woman mean?

Trembling slightly, he decided to do it anyway. After his last delivery that morning he guided Pie and the cart down a narrow path they had never traversed before, a path to the river.

At the bottom, he pulled on the reins. Not far up the beach he saw
three men silhouetted against the horizon, holding long poles over the
water, fishing. The sun glinting off the river made him shiver. Dare he
walk the horse and cart past them with no problem, mount Pie when they
were out of sight? If there were a problem it would come from them,
he had no control. *What are you doing this far from town, boy?* he could hear
them asking. Frustrated, or was it relieved, he turned the horse, the cart
and his tremulous excitement back toward the city.

The next day they were gone. He glared up the river, then down.
Nobody. He jumped from the cart, let Pie lick sugar from his palm.
He unhitched the cart as he did every day outside the barn behind the
baking shop. The mare showed no more inclination to run off than she
did on Varick Street. There followed the bridle and the reins, more sugar.
Her interest seemed only in the sugar.

The next step was getting onto her back. He did not know how
she would react. Placing one hand on her, he vaulted up, but not high
enough. He stepped back and tried to jump onto her, but crashed into
her flank and fell to the ground, his shoulder bruised.

Pie stood solid, stolid. Caesar had an idea. He pulled the cart
alongside her. She nosed it, as if wondering at this new relationship.
Carefully he climbed onto the cart and crossed it. He slipped one leg
over her, holding onto the side of the cart, then let go and pulled the
other leg over. He was on her back now. She did not try to buck him off,
as he had feared. Apparently she had been ridden this way before. With
no reins to hold he leaned forward and wrapped his hands in her mane.
She shuddered, took a small step forward, then another. This was the
first moment, it seemed, that she understood she was not hauling a cart,
that nothing was holding her back, that she was free to run. He patted
lightly the side of her head. She walked a bit faster. He patted her again.
She took off, began to trot, then to gallup. Caesar was terrified and
exhilarated at once.

Faster Pie ran, faster, faster. The river rushed by on his left. He
dared not look at it, kept his eyes straight ahead. He had no control of
the mare, she had no control over him. Free – they both were free. The
notion seemed to excite her, she galloped even faster. Ahead he saw a
boulder in their path. He could only hope the horse saw it as well, knew
what to do, because he did not. As he hung onto her mane Pie did not
veer off course but ran straight ahead and leaped over the grey boulder
and continued running, flat out, as fast as her four legs could carry them.
Ahead a finger of forest blocked the narrow beach. Pie of her own
volition without slowing down veered to the edge of the water, splashed

her way around the trees, came out on dry land again, the bottoms of
his white trousers wet, and of her mottled legs. Faster and faster she ran,
the wind whistled in his ears, the world whistled away. Caesar still riding
fell to the beach like a snake sloughing its skin, he was no longer Caesar,
he was King James again. Being a slave was gone he was even more
free than a king, no decisions to make, no one to answer to. The free
wind blew harder, flew in off the river, blew through his hair, chilled his
sweating scalp. He wished the parrot could see him now, though he did
not know why. Perhaps it could. He did not know how far they had run
or how far they could run, when a spit of sand kicked up in front of them
followed instantly by the sound of a musket shot. Pie reared, slowed,
stopped running, frightened at the sound. Caesar almost lost hold of her
mane. She slowed to a walk, not wanting to go any further. Another shot
from the edge of the forest kicked up dirt directly in front of her, close to
her forelegs. She shuddered, whinnied. Caesar might have done the same
if he could. Two men stepped out of the forest, or rather a man and a
boy, the man holding a musket, the lad, about fourteen years old, cradling
a rifle, both wearing light shirts, dark trousers, boots, both with curly
hair, the man's black, the boy's brown. But if you asked Caesar what they
looked like he would not be able to say. His eyes half blinded by the sun
saw only the guns.

　　Trying to run away, are ya? the man said.

　　They had closed to within ten feet of Pie.

　　No, sir, Caesar said.

　　Well, yuz are a slave. ain't ya? Ya got that frightened look.

　　Yes, sir.

　　So who might ye be belonging to?

　　Mr. Vaarck, sir. The baker.

　　I know Vaarck. Does he know you're this far from the city.

　　I don't think so, sir.

　　*Ya don't think so. What does ya think? Ya don't think much, that's for sure. Don't
ya know this is an island, that there's more water up ahead? Ya expectin that horse to
swim ya across, with you on his back.*

　　Yes, sir. I mean, No sir. I was planning to turn back.

　　You were? So why was ya running so fast?

　　Caesar wanted to say, *It's symbolic,* but thought better of it.

　　The man turned toward the boy. *This is more fun than shooting wild
turkeys, ain't it Jed?* he said, and grinned through missing teeth. *There's
always a price on runaways, dead or alive.*

　　He raised his musket and aimed it directly at Caesar.

　　Of what use is a dead slave, Dad? the boy asked.

Plenty of use. Serves as a good example to the other slaves, for one.

Caesar felt himself shaking in his skin. He hoped his fear did not show. He swung his eyes across the nearby tree tops. The parrot was not there.

My cart, he said, desperate. *It's down the beach. That will show I belong to Mr. Vaarck. There's even a box of pastries in it. Mrs. Morton said it was the wrong order.*

I remember you now, the man said. *I was at that auction last winter. Fun things to watch, those are. Vaarck paid a ton for you. Treats you like a prince, I hear. And you runnnin away like this. That's what he gets for being weak.*

I was not running away, sir. I was just riding the horse.

Hell bent for Connecticut. Hey Jed, you feel like some pastries? I'm kinda hungry myself. Bring the horses and we'll follow him to this here cart, see if he's lyin. He tries to run, we'll give him two big holes in his back.

They rode slowly down the beach, his two captors slightly behind, one on each side. Caesar sat straight up, his back arched involuntarily, ready to receive a musket ball there, knowing that bones do not stop them.

Triana.

It was almost a year since they had murdered her. Maybe it was more than a year.

A flock of grey geese passed overhead. Caesar and Pie both flinched as the man's musket exploded. Sweat ran down Caesar's chest, inside his blouse.

Damn!

Why you shooting at birds over the water, Pop? We ain't got the dogs here to retrieve.

We got this big black dog. You'd go in the river after a bird, wouldn't you?

Caesar looked straight ahead. *Whatever you say, sir.*

The man shoved another musket ball into the barrel of his gun, pointed the muzzle at Caesar. *Jeez, I hate to go back without hitting nothin.*

It wouldn't be the first time, the boy said.

Don't get smart, lad. I could always tell your darling mother it was an accident. We'd give you the grandest funeral … Even get that fey English teacher to talk about God.

His musket exploded again, spitting up dirt beside the boy's horse.

Beto. Only Beto could save him. But Beto is in Africa, if he is still alive. Or else in chains on a slave ship coming here.

At last the cart became visible down the beach. The man and the boy chomped Mrs. Morton's rejected pastries greedily.

Caesar in his relief made a mistake. *I've got more proof,* he said. He reached into his right-hand pocket, pulled out a sheaf of papers. *These are the bakery orders I took for tomorrow, for next week. If I was running away why would I take those?*

Let me see those, the man said. Caesar handed them to him. *Very interesting,* the man said, glancing at the first few. He seemed to think for a moment. Then he thrust his hand into the air, throwing the papers. Tumbling and twisting brightly in the warming sun they scattered along the beach like crazy birds, were blown by the wind into the river. It was a wide river. Across the bleak water Caesar could barely make out the shore of Jersey Colony.

There, the man said, grinning his toothless grin. *Now you surely are a runaway.*

Better to have given the man the coins in his other pocket. Shaking his head at his stupidity, Caesar fitted Pie's bridle on and hitched the reins to the cart. The man ordered him to lie in the back face down and took the boy's belt and tied Caesar's wrists with it and looped the reins of the boy's horse to the back of the cart and told the boy to climb onto the cart and drive them into the city, the man with his musket level following. The boy climbed onto the seat and took the reins. He lay his rifle beside him. Twisting, Caesar from the corner of his eye could see the rifle gleaming. It was within reach if he could free his hands.

He managed to raise up onto his left shoulder. One eye could see above the side of the cart. Some of the homes they passed were on his route. If people were about they might recognize him. He did not know if this would be good or bad. But no one seemed to be out in the midday heat.

Entering the city they passed a small tavern. A man in work clothes was standing outside. He yelled, *Hey, Hobart, what you got there?*

A runaway, Hobart replied,

Why don't you just shoot him?

Worth too much, Hobart called out as the cart continued on.

Deeper into the city, some people took notice, others did not. In front of City Hall Hobart told Jed to pull up the cart. Three men were standing together, talking. They were wearing white wigs, and all three were dressed in the fanciest clothing Caesar had ever seen – coats, waistcoats, breeches that ended snugly at their knees, long white stockings, flat black shoes with silver buckles that glinted in the sun. Two of the outfits were solid brown, one blue with a yellow waistcoat.

Must be a trial going on, Hobart muttered, and called out, *You, Horse ...*

The man in blue turned to face the cart before Hobart concluded his insult.

...manure

The other two men placed white handkerchiefs in front of their lips to stifle chuckles. The man so addressed, his face reddening, said nothing.

You'd better shine up your Whipping Post, Hobart continued. *I've got me a runaway.*

Daniel Horsmanden ignored the insult as if he had not heard it. *Take him around to the deputies.*

Not this one. I'll be getting a nice reward for this one.

Caesar recognized the man from the window who'd been watching that woman get whipped.

You should have shot him, one of the other men said. *Next time he'll slit your throat.*

You city folks are much too afraid, Hobart said. *Don't know how you can live like that.*

He motioned to the boy, who tapped the reins and got the cart moving again. The man was riding beside the boy now, no longer afraid his captive would try to run.

How come you called him that, the boy asked.

Because I hate that man. He's a tub of fraud. He acts big because he can put men in the dungeon, have them whipped, even have them hanged. But slam one punch into his own gut and he'd be on his knees, begging for mercy. Over there. Pull up in front of the bake shop.

When John Vaarck heard the clattering of wheels come to a stop outside his shop he went outside and asked the man and the boy what he could do for them.

I've brung back yer runaway, Hobart said.

I don't have a runaway, Vaarck replied.

Well now ya do, cause I brung him back..

Vaarck peered into the cart. *That's no runaway, that's my Caesar. Untie him right now.*

Hobart nodded to the boy, who dismounted, climbed into the cart and removed his belt from Caesar's wrist. Caesar rubbed his wrists where the belt had cut into the skin and rubbed his shoulder that ached from lying on it and leaped down from the cart.

You're Vaarck, right? the man said. *If that boy wasn't running away, how come I caught him way up by Sugar Hill, running that poor horse's legs into the ground.*

He couldn't have been trying to escape. There's rivers on all sides.

I didn't say he was a smart runaway. Just a runaway.

Caesar stood sullenly, watching the two men speak.

How about it, Caesar? What were you doing way up there. Riding detached from the cart, I take it.

Yes, sir.

Well, explain yourself.

I never rode a horse before, sir. I wanted to see what it would be like. To ride as fast as Pie could run, as free as the wind. I surely was not running away. I'm sorry, sir, no man would understand who hasn't done it himself.

There, Hobart said, *he admits he wanted to be free.*

I'm going to tell a little story, the baker said, addressing Caesar as Hobart stood by with his son, waiting impatiently. *When I was about your age I owned a horse. His name was Aberdeen. A real solid black beauty, the fastest horse in all creation. We had match races throughout the colony and won every one. I amassed a nice bundle of cash betting on him. Then a fellow named Borden moved in nearby who had a roan named Jack, who he thought was the fastest in creation. He beat all the horses Aberdeen had beaten, so there was a lot of excitement when we agreed to a match race, for big stakes, winner take all. With my winnings I was going to buy a nice piece of land I had seen outside of Philadelphia and move down there. We decided we'd race on Long Island, where the beaches are real sand, no rocks or trees or whatever in the way like there is around here. So we barged the horses across the river and with us came dozens of blokes from all the taverns, making their own side bets. We laid out a course maybe five hundred yards long and drew a finish line in the sand. We got my Aberdeen and his Jack standing quietly side by side, the appointed starter fired his pistol in the air and off we went, right together. Side by side we was running, matching stride for stride, maybe one horse sticking his nose in front, then the other. Borden was whipping his horse for all get out, and I hadn't laid a stick on Aberdeen yet. Then the finish was looming up and I figured I had to move, so I tapped my horse just once on the flank and he leaped ahead. In those last twenty yards we was running away with the race. Then Aberdeen stuck his leg in a hole in the sand and went down broken and me flying head over heels over his head. I landed with my butt just past the finish and saw Jack fly by a second later. I felt awful for my horse, I had heard a bone crack when he went down. But I had won the race and a nice bundle of cash. Philadelphia here I come. Then the three judges huddled together. There was no disputing that I had crossed the finish line first, but they decided that the race was between the horses not the riders, and Aberdeen never did finish. I could hardly argue with that. I had to shoot my horse between the eyes to put him out of his pain and I was carrying plenty of pain myself for him and for my money, and some fellow claimed a man betting on Jack had kicked that hole in the sand with his boot right where we would be running. I don't know if that was true or not there was no evidence either way. We dug up a lot of sand to cover Aberdeen right there, away from the ravens, and I hobbled along on a cracked knee until we crossed the river back. My leg ain't been worth a damn ever since, as you can plainly see when I walk. Lucky for me, after a while I met a woman named Stephanie, who could bake bread and cakes like you never tasted, and we got hitched and with what little money I had left plus a loan from the bank we opened a little bake shop. Which has grown a lot since then. The point being, Caesar, that like you I know what it is like to ride a pony flat out fast like that.*

The baker turned to Hobart. *You have the advantage of me, sir,* he said, *you know who I am and I still don't know your name. If you were entertained by my tragic story, that's fine, but I'm not sure why you are still hanging about.*

I'm waiting for my reward, of course, for bringing back your runaway. If he was not running away, ask him for the bakery orders he took today.

The man threw them onto the beach and into the river, Caesar said.

Is that boy calling me a liar?

I heard no such claim, Vaarck said. *As I mentioned at the outset, I have no runaway. You heard Caesar explain what he was doing. I did not advertise any reward, because he was not missing.*

Hobart's face was reddening, growing thick with rage. *The custom is to pay a reward,* he said, and spat from atop his horse into the street. *I catch that boy in my parts again I'll put a musket ball in his belly and bring him back dead. You paid a lot for this turd, as I remember. I think a large reward is in order.*

Sir, you just told me that next time you will bring him back dead. That makes him not a very valuable property. He looked at Caesar. *I'll tell you what I will do. Do you have your day's gratuities in your pocket?*

Yes, sir.

Hand them over to me.

Caesar did as he was told, and the baker gave Hobart the money. *There, now you have been rewarded, and the boy has been appropriately punished. What I will also do, I will throw in a loaf of freshly baked bread to take home to your wife, best bread this side of Paris, everyone says.*

Damn your bread, Hobart shouted.

Hearing this ruckus in the street, Zion emerged from his cabin and joined the others. Hobart's eyes blazed as he took in the mute's huge mass, which threw a shadow almost as big as the horse. *Are you trying to intimidate me?*

Sir, the baker said, *it has been my motto for all of my 43 years never to try to intimidate a man holding a musket. I see no reason to change that motto now. But if you will move yourself and the boy off my property, I would be much obliged.*

Hobart stared at Vaarck and at Caesar and at Zion and whipped his horse's neck and moved the critter several yards. His son followed. *You haven't heard the end of this, baker,* Hobart yelled, *not you and not your Negro.*

Caesar and Zion and Vaarck watched in silence as Hobart and son moved slowly up Varick Street.

When they were out of sight, Caesar turned to the baker. *Sir, will I be getting my gratuities back?*

Certainly not. I think some punishment is in order. Pie could have broken her leg on that nasty beach, and then where would we be? Besides that, I now have to take the mare and ride the route myself and bother folks to recover the orders you lost. That is not something I am looking forward to doing.

No, sir.

Caesar felt chagrinned but also courageous after the wild ride on Pie, after learning that the baker in fact understood.

If I may, sir, word is about that they are serving pork chops at Hughson's tonight.

Zion nodded in confirmation. *I was wondering, sir, if I might borrow two coins from you. I will pay you back tomorrow.*

The baker thought for a moment, then reached into his pocket and handed Caesar the coins. *Enjoy the pork chops,* he said, *but tomorrow you will pay me back three coins.*

Three? Why is that, Sir?

When you lend a man money you always get back more than the loan. To make up for the risk he took. That's your first lesson in high finance. Think about it.

I will, Sir.

Now go on about your chores, the baker said, a hint of pique in his voice, *while I try to recover the orders that you lost.*

Vaarck climbed onto the cart with his bad leg, tapped the horse with his heel and together they moved slowly up the street. Caesar turned to Zion. It was one of the many times he wished the big man could speak, could express his thoughts on what had transpired. Zion grinned. That would have to be enough.

Later, when they walked together to Comfort's well to carry back casks of water, one for the house, the other for the bakery, word of the day's events had already reached the gossip trading post, probably spread by the baking girls who had overheard it all, and Caesar's slave name for the night became Runaway or Horseman in teasing remarks from his friends gathered at the well, Quack and Cuffee and Sambo, Fortune, Will, Quash, Ben, Galloway, two more Caesars and others. Caesar smiled at the jests and took no offense. The wind-ridden ride on Pie and his safe escape from Hobart's musket had left him soaring like a bird above any angry thoughts. When the jesting continued over grilled pork chops and fried potatoes and tankards of beer in the dining room at Hughson's he continued to grin. He had thought of a way to treat himself, to top off his extraordinary day, though he had no coins in his pocket. There were plenty safely hidden in the cabin.

The window to room thirteen was blocked by a green cloth. He could see the faint glow of an oil lamp behind it. He watched for shadows of movement, waited, saw none. Perhaps the time was right. He tapped lightly on the window. It was was opened from within, the lantern illuminating his face. He blinked.

Well, don't just stand there. I don't deliver. Climb in.

He vaulted into the room easily.

My name is Caesar, he said.

I know your name. And what you do. What took you so long? There are five Caesars hereabout. I've already tumbled four of them.

She was wearing only a blue robe. In the lamplight she was even prettier.

A shudder brushed his heart, as if he were jealous. Which is stupid, Caesar, that's her job.

He knew two of the Caesars, not the other two. He had often wondered at the logic of his name. According to Professor Fez, the Roman Caesar had been one of the most powerful men the world had ever known. He had never asked Vaarck to explain.

A pink-nippled breast was peeking at him from beneath her robe.

The truth? I haven't wanted to betray Triana, my wife.

I suppose that's sweet. Stupid, but sweet.

You sure have a mouth on you, Peggy Kerry.

That's not all I have.

So I've heard.

This wife. She controls what you do with your body?

She only controls my mind. She's dead.

I'm sorry. The disease?

A musket ball. In Africa.

She took his hand. *I'm sorry. Truly.*

Will you drop your whore's act, then? I've seen your heart. It suits you better.

When do you think you saw that?

Months ago. At the Public Whipping Post. When you brought that poor woman water.

Someone had to.

But you're the one who did.

You've been watching me, then?

As you've been watching me.

I didn't think you noticed.

Whatever happened to that woman? Do you know?

Her name was Artemis Adams. We met later on, for tea. She tried to live in peace, but her neighbors wouldn't let her forget her sin. They harassed her every day until she couldn't stand it. Finally she moved to Boston. But her sin followed her there.

How do you know?

After a few months she drowned herself.

Caesar breathed deeply, exhaled slowly. Waited before speaking again.

About her. I came here with a question. Why are you not whipped, as she was? And the men not thrown in the dungeon?

The men who come here, most of them, are owned. They can't be taken away from their masters. As for me, I give part of my earnings to Mr. Hughson. He gives some of that to the recorder.

That Horse fellow?

Horsmanden. But the real reason is larger than that. They never bother prostitutes, especially not us whores to the slaves. They think a satisfied Negro is less likely to cut their throats. They call us trash, but who we're really servicing is the whites.

As in everything else.

She pulled her robe tighter around her. The movement caught his breath.

Enough politics. I'm sorry I was rude. I've been hoping to meet you.

Why didn't you just speak to me in the street?

White woman, black man, talking? They would not like that. So. Tell me about your wife.

He did. And more. He told of watching Triana grow from a seedling in the forest into young womanhood, of the assault on her by the pointy-teeth men, how he had killed the worst offender with his spear; of how he had cared for her and made her his bride, who soon was carrying his heir. He told of the attack on the peaceful Mucktu a year later by the pointy-teeth tribe, how Triana and her baby were shot through with a musket ball, how he still blamed himself for her death. These were things he could not tell, had not told, to any slave besides Professor Fez, because all had suffered much the same. He told her of the long walk in chains to the sea, of the deaths of infants and the laughter of First Mate Cree. No slave had ever told her these things, they came to her to ease their bodies, not their hearts. He spoke of the voyage cross the ocean but omitted his murder of Cree. She was, after all, still white.

His eyes were far away as he spoke of these things, of how Triana for many months had filled his waking hours as well as his dreams. While his eyes were distant she was able to study his life in his face.

How awful, she said when he was done. *So much love destroyed.*

Yes. But I know the problem now is not between Triana and me. It is between me and me.

And you have not resolved it?

Not yet.

Peggy stood from the edge of the bed where she had been sitting transfixed. She walked about the room, gazed at herself in a mirror on the wall, and at his reflection in it, saw in him a blending of innocence and unignited flame.

Caesar, go home. Come back when your turmoil has dissolved.

That was my intent. I'll pay you for your time.

No, talk is cheap – especially for the fifth Caesar.

He took her hand, hesitated, kissed it lightly. She leaned forward, kissed him gently on the cheek.

Go now. While you are thinking of Triana, I will think of you.

For a moment their eyes locked. Neither turned away.

I knew the real you is sweet, Caesar said.

She smiled, as if in affirmation. *Don't tell your friends. It will ruin business.*

He squeezed her hand, hard, pushed the green covering aside, leaped agilely out the window. For the second time that day he was flying.

35. PEGGY

Crumple the letter and shove it into her mouth and stuff it down her throat until she gagged. That's what she ought to do because of her lies. That's what she ought to do because of her thoughts. But she did not crumple the letter because she felt compelled to read it again. And again. Darkness was falling outside the green curtain on her window as well as in her head. She turned the kerosene lamp as high as it would go and sprawled on her back on her bed and in the mute circle of yellow light she read it yet again.

Dear Marguerite

That is what I am calling you because that is how you signed your most recent letter, which is so full of good news that maybe Marguerite changed your luck. I have to admit that your first two letters did not make me very happy. The fact that you discovered that Billy Reilly had taken up with the rich widow, as you suspected, was not a surprise. Now I can tell you, which I never did before, that I always thought he was a cad, good for nothing but pumping himself up by killing baby seals. It is almost that season now and the town will miss his killing ways. Isn't that strange? You are better off without him, unless you have seals to kill down there in New York Colony, which I doubt. Your second letter, about how you could not find a job there because the Negro slaves have filled most of them, and that you were running out of money, also depressed me. The only glimmer of good I found in it was that you might decide to come home and we could be together again. Which was very selfish of me, I miss you so much. But this new letter about your sudden change of luck is exciting. Imagine, getting a job as receptionist at the Hotel New York, where all the famous people stay! That hotel I hear is the largest on the continent except for one in the city of Charleston, South Carolina Colony, where all the traders come for slave auctions.

And then for the owner of the hotel to fall in love with you! If he is as rich as you say I think it does not matter that he is old. But what a choice you have! Between him and that young baker who might not be so rich but is handsome as the devil, and fun to be with, even if his leg got shot up in the Indian Wars. I wish I had a choice like that. Here there is nothing but the same old boredom and the same stink of fish.

But I have a surprise for you! For months I have been saving as much money as I could from my pay and gratuities at the cafe. When I have enough, which could be in a few weeks, I plan to buy passage on a ship to New York and come to visit you! And maybe stay there if I like it! My parents do not know this yet, so don't breathe a word to anyone. Between your rich hotel owner and your handsome baker I think I would settle for either one. (You would get first choice, of course). That is a silly thought, but once I get down there who knows what fate might bring? I am counting the days until I see you again. I don't know how many days that will be but I am counting them anyway.

Your best friend,

Nora

This time she did crumple the letter, then tried to smooth it again as if that might erase Nora's words, or her own lies. Imagine wishing that Nora would fall off the cliff near the cemetery and die so she would not discover the truth. Imagine hoping her boat to New York will sink in a storm and all the passengers will be drowned, Nora most of all. Her best friend! She hated having these thoughts but there they were. What kind of monster had she become? She punched her pillow as hard as she could and pressed her face into the depression it made, sobbing. Her mouth found the corner of the pillow and she began to bite on it. Soon she was merely sucking, and in the circle of lamp light she fell asleep, a baby suckling at its mother's breast.

36. MARY

There is trouble in the Kerry Beans. That's all people talked about today in Vaarck's bakery shop.

Sometimes when I do extra chores Mr. Hughson gives me a coin to buy myself a treat.

He did that today and I walked over to Vaarck's to buy a blueberry tart. They also have strawberry and raspberry and prunes, but I always get the blueberry, even if it makes my lips turn blue. The shop was more crowded than usual but folks didn't seem to be buying much bread or cakes. They was talking and talking and talking, all about the same thing, something they had read in Mr. Zenger's newspaper. All about the Kerry Beans, whoever they are. It seems the slaves there did not like being slaves, so they stored up knives and guns and one day they started killing the white folks.

I wish Zenger had not published that, one man in the bake shop said, *it could give our slaves ideas.*

But the rebels were caught and executed, another man said. *More than executed. Some were just shot, but others were tortured. One man had an arm cut off, another had his leg cut off, a third lost his tongue. That should be a warning to any angry slaves here.*

All slaves are angry, a woman said.

Well, they shouldn't be, not if they are treated well.

In their own eyes they are not treated well unless they are free.

So what are you saying, we should kill all the slaves before they kill us?

Of course not. We should let them go.

That's preposterous. That would destroy our economy. Hey Vaarck, come out from behind that counter and get into this. You have how many slaves?

Seven right now. Five baking girls and Caesar and Zion. I try to treat them well.

If you didn't have those slaves, what would happen to your bakery?

I would go out of business.

And why is that?

Because if I had to pay workers to bake and deliver the breads, I would have no profits. I would have to close.

And all the rest of us would lose your wonderful confections, right?

Right.

So you see, madam, that is why we need the slaves.

Is that worth getting killed for?

Nobody is getting killed, not here. We have laws to keep the slaves in their place. Such as, they can't congregate more than three at a time in the street, so they can't plan an uprising.

We may have the laws but they are not enforced.

Perhaps we need to get the city to enforce those laws, another man chimed in.

I was almost through with the blueberry tart. It was so good, even if my lips was sticky.

Take away that freedom and the slaves will get even angrier. They could meet in secret to plan a rebellion.

As they were talking, so fast I did not know who was who, I noticed they all was white. Then a big shadow filled the doorway and in walked that huge slave Zion carrying a cask of water. All the talking stopped. Zion set the heavy cask behind the counter.

Thank you, Zion, Mr. Vaarck said.

You thank your slaves for doing their work? a man asked. *What kind of discipline is that?*

Perhaps they will spare me, Vaarck said, *comes the rebellion.*

Do you really think that will happen here, like down among the Kerry Beans?

How can it not? Mr. Vaarck said.

That fellow Zion is some piece of work, a man said. *I would hate to meet up with him with a knife in his hand.*

Has he ever told why they cut out his tongue?

He could hardly do that.

He could write it down.

Which was a silly thing for that man to say. I don't think Zion is lit'rit like me.

As Zion left he was passed in the doorway by a gentleman fancily dressed in a suit with ruffles, wearing a white wig. Some of the people shook his hand.

Hey, Mr. Recorder, someone asked. *We've been talking about the slave uprisings in the Kerry Beans. Do you think that could happen here?*

We are always on guard. At the first sign of trouble we will crush it immediately. So you think it is possible?

Anything is possible. That's why we must remain alert at all times.

Three cheers for Horsmanden, a man said. *If this were a pub I would buy you a drink.*

It ill becomes a judge to imbibe in public, Horsmanden said, *but I will take that as a sign of approval of strict measures. Above all, we must not give way to fear.*

By this time I had finished my tart and my hands were sticky and my mouth was thirsty and I was bored with all this Kerry Bean talk so I walked on home. At Hughson's I saw Peggy Kerry drinking coffee in the dining room. I asked her if she was a distant cousin to the Kerry Beans. She did not know what I was talking about. Sometimes I think she is not as smart as I think.

37. CAESAR

Black and white.

    Entwined.
An etching.
White and black.
    Entwined.
A mirror.
They sleep.
Entwine again.
Caesar is morose. Peggy senses it.
Is it not good?
It is fine. Sublime.
Then what? Triana? I cannot be Triana.
No one can. That is not the problem. I am stupid. Because I am jealous.
Of who? Of what?
I don't like being the Fifth Caesar. I don't want others having you.
That's sweet. She lays a palm gently on his cheek, looks into his eyes.
But it's my work. It's how I pay for my room, my food. You know that.
I have money, he says.

I don't understand.

I get gratuities. I've been saving them. Hiding them. Against the day I can buy my freedom.

That's wonderful!

But it is a false hope. That day will never come.

If anyone frees a slave it will be Vaarck.

Not even him. He needs me too much. So the money is doing nothing. I want to use it. For you.

I still don't understand.

I will pay Hughson for your room. Your meals. Every week. Then you won't need the others. That will make me happy.

I don't know. You're sure you want to do that?

I'm sure.

They lie in silence.

Breathing lightly.

They touch fingers. Lightly.

Entwine.

At Comfort's well, the other slaves are not happy with him for placing an off limits sign on Peggy. He is not concerned. They will go back to what they had done before, will frequent the hotbed houses near the waterfront. Lydia and Jane and the others will satisfy their needs, even if they will not set their dreams aglow.

Several weeks later, on Maiden Lane, he encounters a man who looks familiar. The man is carrying an empty cistern. They want to pass without speaking, but their eyes have met, they must pause.

Akra!

My name now is Condor.

You are the first Mucktu I have encountered here, Caesar says. *Do you know what happened to the others?*

Some died of disease on the ship. Most were bought by men who are starting farms across the river, in Jersey Colony. The men plough the fields. The women work in the houses. Cook. Clean. Service their owners.

Condor stopped in mid-sentence. He knew Triana's younger sister was there.

You had a wife, Caesar says. *Is she well?*

She is in Jersey Colony.

An embarrassed pause. *Have you news of your brother?*

Beto? No. He hesitates. *The people must hate me. For not protecting them better.*

Akra wipes sweat from his face. Caesar says, *I remember how you used to win almost all the sporting games back home.*

I must go, King James. My master wants water for his tea.

He lifts his empty cistern and moves on.

38. PEGGY

Winter has arrived early, and fiercely – just like a year ago. Peggy snuggles into her warmest coat. Wraps a blue scarf around her head. Small flakes of snow, almost invisible, whip crosswise, sting her cheeks, redden them, as hunched over she walks to the schoolroom, climbs the small hill, knocks on the door with a gloved hand. From inside she hears Professor Fez. *Who is out in this blizzard?* He opens the door and she steps into the room, shivering. He seems naked without his fez.

Peggy! What a nice surprise. Come, I was just stoking the fire.

She approaches the fireplace in a corner of the school room, warming herself, removes her wet scarf, looks around at the empty chairs. Sleet is pounding against the window at the rear of the room.

Your coat as well. Maybe it will dry a little. I just put up a kettle for tea. You will have some.

Thank you, professor. I came now because I heard you were not busy, that your classes are finished.

Only until next week.

What happens then?

A new ship arrives.

New York Mercantile?

Of course.

I'm sorry. Very sorry.

It can't be helped. Better the poor souls learn English than not.

From Africa or the Caribbean, this one?

I'm not really sure. It hardly matters.

He approached a wood stove at the head of the room, removed a black kettle from it, poured water into two ceramic tankards, stirred in tea leaves. She saw a narrow bed neatly made behind his desk, against the wall. Clearly the classroom was the professor's home.

Professor Fez, I have a question about the law. I thought you would be the best one to answer it.

Go ahead, let's see if I can.

He carried the tankards to a table, motioned to a chair and they both sat.

My question is, if a woman – a free white woman – gives birth to a child, and the father is a slave, is the child born free, or born a slave?

Professor Fez tested the heat of the tea with the tip of his tongue, took a small sip.

I believe I know the answer. But let me look in the book to be sure.

He went to a bookstand in the far corner of the room, which held only a few books, and brought one back with him, a book with a black cover. He sat and turned the pages.

Yes, here it is. I was correct. The mother determines the status of the child. If a slave woman gives birth to a child, the child is born into slavery. But if the mother is free, as in the case you cited, then the child is born free.

Peggy's hands flew to her lips like twin birds, she issued a soft sigh.

If I may be personal – from your reaction, Peggy, I am guessing the woman in question is yourself.

She nodded, tears forming in her eyes.

And the father is … ?

Caesar.

I thought as much. Please do not be offended, but how do you know he is the father?

She took several deep breaths.

It's a fair question. But I am sure. My bleeding did not stop until I was with Caesar alone. After that it stopped.

The professor nodded, seemed to be fighting back a small smile.

Drink your tea, Peggy, before it gets cold. Have you told Caesar yet?

No. I needed you to answer my question first. I would not deliver a child into slavery.

Most women would not. That's why we find so many drowned babies.

I came across a frozen one a year ago. My first day here.

He reached for her hand, squeezed it.

I think this will make Caesar happy, he said. *In Africa, his first child …*

I know. Was murdered before it was born. I'm hoping he'll be pleased to have another. Alive and free.

I'm sure he will, the professor said.

They sat in silence, contemplating, listening to the bawling of the wind outside. Peggy stood, moved about the school room. The walls were covered with pictures, and random words describing them. *Mother. Father.* She peered about, vaguely disappointed at seeing no word for child. When she asked why, he said it was a weighty word that might distract slaves who'd lost their children.

You do not have many books on your shelf, Professor. May I donate one?
Of course. All books are welcome. Would I recognize the name?
Robinson Crusoe. I've read it twice.

A wonderful book. You have a copy of that? I could read certain passages to my class. It would get then excited about stories. But you might want to save it until your own child is old enough to read.

They both grinned at the distant thought, the charming image.

At that time I'll borrow it back and read it to him, Peggy said.

Her farewell gift from Nora. The recollection struck her between her shoulder blades with the force of a falling icicle. She closed her eyes against the threat of tears. How will she ever face Nora?

The wind was dying, the snow letting up with forgotten grace. She donned her coat and scarf and after thanking the professor set out into the white streets, willing her good mood back. What news she had for Caesar!

39. MARY

It's the last day of the year and Mr. Hughson is making a party. Everyone is invited, all the slaves who come here many nights to drink beer and talk gossip, guests at the Inn though there are none here in the middle of winter unless you count Peggy Kerry, me and young Sarah is invited, although Mr. Hughson has warned us not to drink any beer we are too young and might get sick. The party will be so big that they borrowed extra tables from somewhere and set them up in the dining room and Mr. Hughson has rented three of the baker's slave girls for the evening to help with the cooking in those big new iron stoves they got over there, the baker saying therefore there will be no bread deliveries the next morning. Me and young Sarah spent the afternoon hanging streamers from all the walls, red and silver mostly so it looks like a fairyland, while Mrs. Hughson has been scurrying back and forth between her big kitchen and the baker's to supervise the cooking. The menu will be roast duck with Shepherd's pie and some vegetables and pumpkin soup to start things off and chocolate cake from the baker's for dessert. I can hardly wait. I changed clothes into my best dress, green with pink ribbons, and Sarah did too. That big Negro Zion helped Caesar unload three big barrels of beer from somewhere and set them on the veranda where they will stay cold. Soon after it got dark outside the guests, who was really slaves, began arriving. Each took a tankard from a table on the veranda and filled it with beer through a spout in the barrels

and come inside and stood around the big table and talked. They didn't
have to pay anything, the party was free for everyone who was invited,
Mr. Hughson was celebrating what a fine year he had. There was always
gossip that when things got stolen from houses in the colony which
happens a lot the robbers come to Mr. Hughson and he pays them for
what they stole and during the night he hides it in the basement of the
Inn until a ship come in to the port and then he sells stuff to the sailors.
This is against the law so I don't know if it is true. I never saw it myself
but if everyone says it is true then I guess it must be. Soon two guests
arrived carrying fiddles and they started to play and it sounded real good,
we don't hear music much in the Inn. When most of the guests had
arrived Mr. Hughson told them to sit at the long table. He told me to sit
at a small table that had been added to the end, and said Sarah his
daughter would join me there for the meal after she finished helping her
mother serve the pumpkin soup to everyone. Which she did and it was
delicious. I saw Peggy Kerry sitting along the middle of the table next to
Caesar the slave. Lately they seem always together. I never get a word in
edgewise with Peggy anymore since Caesar come on the scene. I hate it
when people do that to me and don't let me get in a word edgewise
anymore. Especially if they was my friend. I think they was holding
hands in their laps. The other slave guests I recognized some of their
faces from when they come to the Inn to drink nights and I knew some of
their names such as Fortune and Dick and Quack and Cuffee and Will
and such but I didn't know which faces belonged to which names. Then
the door opened and the big slave Zion come in carrying a big tray that
had a roast duck on it. He set it on the side board and left again and soon
came back with another roasted duck and then another, which I guess
had been roasting in the baker's big stoves. Caesar helped Mr. Hughson
cutting up the ducks and putting the pieces on a platter and the guests
lined up by the side board and put pieces of duck on their plates along
with Shepherd pie and green beans Mrs. Hughson had brought in from
the kitchen. The food smelled wonderful when I put some on my plate
and Sarah done the same beside me. The fiddle music stopped so the
fiddlers could eat too but with everyone talking happy between their
eating it sounded like music anyway. When their tankards of beer got
empty they went out to the veranda and got some more. Me and Sarah
was drinking just water and that is a good thing because as the guests
drank more beer their voices started getting louder when they was telling
jokes and I think some was arguing. I got tired but I did not want to miss
dessert which would be served at the arrival of the new year, which would
be 1741. So I did not go to my room but crossed my arms on the table

and lay my head on them and fell asleep right there no matter the noise. I
don't know how long I slept but when I woke up Mr. Hughson at the
head of the table was standing and banging his knife against his tankard,
which made a racket until it got all the guests to stop talking and look at
him. I rubbed my eyes that was sticky with sleep and listened to what he
was saying. He thanked everyone for coming to the party to celebrate the
new year. He said he had one wonderful announcement which he don't
know if everyone knows yet or not, which is that in a few months our
friends Peggy Kerry and Caesar Vaarck will be having a child – and that
child will be born free! There was hollerin' and whoopin' and I saw
Peggy's cheeks burn almost as red as her hair. Caesar was looking down
at the table as if he did not want Mr. Hughson to announce that news,
her not showing yet and all, but too late it was done and he squeezed
Peggy's hand for all to see. Then Mr. Hughson said, *Now let's everyone raise
a tankard of beer to toast the new year.* Lots of them raised their tankards
except one or two who was drunk already, their heads lying on the table,
when someone shouted, I think it might have been Quack, shouted, *Aside
from that child what will be so good in the new year? The rest of us will still be slaves.*
Mr. Hughson said unfortunately that was true, he wished he could do
something about that but he could not, and then someone else, Cuffee
maybe or was it Fortune said, *Maybe WE can do something about it.* Caesar
said, *What do you have in mind?* and one of the others said, *I am talking about
rebelling to free ourselves.* There was a bunch of cheering until Caesar said,
*That's been tried before and it never worked, people got killed, white and black both,
but nobody got freed.* Some of them grumbled and one answered, *Because it
has not been planned well in the past.* Soon the new year celebration was forgot
and this discussion kept going on about freedom or no freedom. *I would
rather die fighting to be free,* one of them said, *then live as a slave.* Which started
lots of hands clapping. *What kind of plan are you talking about?* another fellow
asked, and Cuffee or Quack said, *The key to everything is fire. We burn down
the city. When the white men rush to put out the fires, we kill them all. Their wives we
can take for ourselves, to rape or to marry.* Which led to a lot louder buzzing. *For
that we need to stockpile knives and guns,* someone said, and someone else said
Knives will be better, because they is quiet while gunshots bring everybody running. I
looked at the faces I knew around the table. Mr. Hughson had a small
smile on his face. Caesar and Peggy and Mrs. Hughson were staring
straight ahead, I could not tell what they was thinking. Through all of
this the plates of chocolate cake in front of us had been forgot. Zion the
big slave who can't talk went out and carried one of the barrels of beer
right into the dining room and people started filling up their tankards
right there while the talk went on and on. Mr. Hughson lifted his tankard

and beer sloshed over the table and people laughed and he said, *If you make this happen, I will become King of New York,* and he looked down along the table at Caesar and said, *Caesar, who has already been a king, will be Governor.* The slaves laughed some more and clapped. When I finished my cake I was feeling tired and Sarah was too because they might keep talking like this till the sun come up in the morning. We left the dining room together and in the hallway in front of my room I asked Sarah if she thought all this talk would lead to killing and stuff, like in the Kerry Beans. She said not a chance, she had heard it all before, many times, they are all drunk and will sleep it off and in the morning they won't remember anything they said. *You think?* I asked, opening the door to my room, and Sarah said, *Don't worry about it. I know.* So I closed the door to my room with them still talking out there and took off my pretty dress and put on my night shirt and went to bed and fell asleep without worrying about anything.

End of Part Two

Part Three:
1741

40. JOHN PETER ZENGER

The hues of the fire were the hues of hell – orange, yellow, red, mutant mixes of sharp-edged flames foraging the rooftop of the Governor's Mansion, just inside the north wall of the fort, in the darkling gray afternoon. The bells of the churches became pleadings from Heaven as they summoned the city to resist. By law every house contained a three-gallon leather bucket, and the bells sent every man scurrying to get his. John Vaarck beside the bakery grabbed his bucket but it was taken from him by Caesar. *With your leg I'll get to the fort way before you*, Caesar said, and leaped into the street and ran south toward Fort Greene, joining dozens of other men white and black carrying buckets. At the Fire House on Broad Way four stout horses were hooked to the city's two fire engines and driven three blocks to where the transparent flames were reaching higher on the rooftop, arching their backs like angry cats. If the flames leaped the wall of the fort the entire wooden city could burn. The men carrying buckets, more and more men each minute, formed two brigades that drew water from the river and passed the buckets hand to hand toward the engines, where the firemen dumped the river water into the cisterns of their vehicles. From these it was pumped high at the rooftop through leather hoses to drown the growling flames, but sixty gallons a minute was not enough. Driven by howling winds roaring in from the sea the flames flew over the north wall of the fort like angry sea birds and hooked onto the building just outside the wall. That building being the Secretary's Office, which contained all the important papers and archives accumulated by the city through the years, much of New York's history was about to be put out like the eyes of a man condemned to be blinded. As a journalist dependent on sources for facts I especially hated to witness this. To avoid this catastrophe men ran into that burning building, climbed stairs and began tossing files of documents out of the third floor windows. Some files fell to the ground, others fluttered apart in the wind. I imagined mother sparrows forcing their protesting offspring to fly. As soon as the men fled the engulfing flames, hoses were turned on the building. Countless files containing countless documents were reduced to soggy trash. When more men charged into the flames to save what archives they could, they were thwarted in a strange battle. The building itself began to explode. Hundreds of hand grenades came hurtling at the men, as if the archives were defending themselves. Would that they could have. The entire fort was a munitions arsenal, and hundreds of grenades has been stored in the basement of the secretariat. The men had forgotten. They had no choice but to flee as the grenades exploded around them. In the end it was not the citizens but a sudden pouring rain that saved the remainder of the fort, and the city itself.

The date of that fire was March 18, 1741.

41. CAESAR

Even the mare seemed skittish, though surely that was my imagination. But as I delivered my bread the day after the fire, the tension in the air was as real and as dark as the soot. This was north of the city, as far from Fort Greene as you could get and still consider it New York, but apparently the fire had been the sole subject of conversation that morning and the night before between husbands and wives, neighbors, even children. Women who usually greeted me warmly and were grateful for the bread seemed to hold back their feelings and establish an invisible wall between us. This was also reflected in the tips. I did not know what I had done to offend.

When I reached the home of my favorite customer, a widow lady named Lissa Grey, who often invited me into her kitchen for coffee and home-baked cookies and chatter, she seemed to hesitate. My normally contained exterior crumbled.

Is something wrong? I asked her. *People seem very upset about something.*

It's the fire, Mrs. Grey said. *It has everyone on edge.*

I can understand that. I imagine that's true throughout the city. But, if I can speak plainly, your neighbors seem to be blaming it on me.

Oh, Caesar — here, have another cookie. Butterscotch chip. It's not you personally, it's just that there's talk going around, started by some of the men who returned from the city last night, that the fire possibly had been set on purpose.

Who would do something like that?

Well, the gossip is that an angry Negro might.

Did they name a name?

Oh, it's nothing like that. It's just generalized talk, you know how people are. It's a shame they let you see their feelings, after how well we've all gotten to know you this last year.

There were as many black men — slaves! — as white men fighting the flames.

I'm sure there were. But that's being logical. Fear has nothing to do with logic.

Fear? What are they afraid of? You folks are miles from the fort.

There, now you're being logical again. Let's talk about something else, shall we?

I'm afraid I have to be on my way. People are waiting for their bread.

Of course. Here is my order for next week. My daughter and her family will be visiting from Philadelphia.

If they don't get frightened off.

Now Caesar, that's not called for. This will all be forgotten in a day or two.

What quieted things down, two days later, was when the *Weekly Journal* published the official determination of the Fire Marshall. The fire had been ignited by a careless plumber, who was using a soldering iron to fix a leaky gutter on the mansion. The red-hot iron had ignited leaves that clogged the gutter. It had been a stupid accident.

I hoped things quickly would return to normal on my route. They did, more or less. But not quite as friendly as before. Some of the warmth was missing. As if light clouds were weakening the sun.

42. PEGGY

A second fire was spotted a week after the first. It was much smaller. Flames appeared on the roof of the waterfront home of a sea captain. This one was blamed on a faulty chimney. The firemen responded quickly, and were able to save most of the house.

Its soot did not help clear the air, though. The soot was making me sick. Or so I thought. Then Mrs. Hughson told me I sounded as if I had morning sickness. Which happens to most pregnant women, she said. I did not know that. What does nature need that for?

Having been indoors for two days, I decided to walk into town. I put on an old mob cap against the swirling ashes that still were smoldering in the fort, and a worn dress, pale blue. Much talk in the streets was still of the fire, but I was bored with that. To evade a gust of blowing debris I stepped through an open side door of the New Theater. I had never been inside that place, and looked around. There was a raised wooden stage at one end, perhaps three feet high. Benches filled the rest of the space, much like the church back home. What did I expect? On the stage a tall man in work clothes was wrestling with a small boat.

May I help you, Miss? he said, turning his attention to me.

No, but I can help you, and I lifted the other end. *Where to?*

Straight back, behind that curtain he said, and thanked me when we set the boat down.

We closed the show last night, he said. *The men went out and got drunk, and are late showing up to strike the set. We're leaving for Philadelphia this afternoon.*

Are you an actor? I asked.

He mopped his sweaty brow with a large red handkerchief.

Actor, writer, producer, stage manager, carpenter, booking agent, ticket seller, paymaster – you name it. My name is Goldsmith, of the Goldsmith Traveling Players. And you are?

Peggy. Peggy Kerry.

Are you an actress, Peggy Kerry?

I smiled, pleased by the thought.

Hardly. I grew up cleaning fish. That's what I do best, I imagine.

Hmm. I imagine differently. With that flaming red hair, you are much too pretty not to be on the stage.

I could feel myself blushing.

Would you be willing to try? I'm just finishing a new play. The King's Ransom. *I'm stuck on it, because no one in our company inspires me to write the queen. You've inspired me already.*

I couldn't get up on a stage in front of people.

Nonsense. Everyone feels that way, until they say their first line. Put on the gown of a queen, the airs of a queen, and you become one. I'll tell you what. I don't have time to try you out now, but we'll be back in New York in six weeks time. Tell me where you live, I'll come get you and we'll see how it works. I can see it now, in front of the theater, a big sign: The King's Ransom, *with Leo Goldsmith and Peggy …*

~~Marguerite~~

Beg your pardon.

If I were to try this, which I won't, I would use my full name. ~~Marguerite.~~

Even better. A perfect name for a queen. Maybe she's French. Married off unhappily by her father. See, you inspire me already.

This is very nice of you Mr. Goldsmith.

Leo. Call me Leo.

But you've got the wrong person.

Leo Goldsmith knows talent. Let me take off your cap. My goodness, such hair. You emanate talent. Where do you live? I'll come knocking when we return and prove it. The pay is not much, but enough to keep body and soul together.

At Hughson's Inn, I said. *But you'll be wasting your time.*

Let me be the judge of that.

It was a nice fantasy, as I pulled my cap on tight and walked slowly back to the Inn, most of the soot having settled. Me a queen, even on a stage! I knew he was not serious, of course. Such as Leo Goldsmith live a life of fantasy. I suppose all actors do.

When Caesar returned from the bakery I told him about the conversation. I thought he would smile indulgently, laugh, make a joke, but his demeanor remained solemn.

You already are a queen, he said.
How do you mean?
I am King of the Muktu. You are my queen.
He took my hand in his.
We did not appear in the dining room that evening. We were busy.

43. MARY

Dear Denture Dairy—
    The post today got Peggy to feeling low. She was
sitting on the veranda crying when mr Hughson came
by and asked what she was crying about. She said
she was upset because she had lied to her best fren
in Newfoundland about how wonderful she is doing
in New York Colony, with a wonderful job and two
men who wanted to marry her and such, which was
all lies, and now her fren is coming to visit her and
would see it was all lies, and she would be upset
and her fren would be upset and maybe tell on her to
the people back home. She ast mr Hughson what she
should do. He raised his arms high, like he was going
to recite a pome, and he did:
    Oh what a tangled web we weave
    When first we practice to deseev.
    I ast if he wrote that hisself and he said no.
People think it's from Shakespere, he said, but it's
really from Walter Scott.
    I don't know either of those gentlemen. Either
way, it didnt make Peggy feel better.

44. CAESAR

I can hardly believe it – I'm going to be a father. Have
a baby. A boy. Of course it will be a boy. He will grow up free, to do
whatever he wants, wherever he wants. *Right, Peggy?*

He is whispering because she is asleep beside him and he does not
want to wake her. The mother-to-be.

But he cannot lie still, he needs to tell someone. He rises from the
bed, drops from the window, treads quietly through the brush to the

cabin at Vaarck's, where Zion is reading a book by the light of a kerosene lamp.

Zion! I've got something to tell you. A secret. I'm going to have a baby. That is, me and Peggy are going to have a baby. A boy.

Zion puts down the book, reaches out to Caesar, squeezes him several times on the arm, a wide smile on his burly face.

Caesar looks curious. *What are you doing with that book?*

Zion picks up a pad of paper and a pencil that lie beside his book. He writes: *I have a secret, too.*

What? Where?

The big man writes again, shows the paper to Caesar.

Professor Fez has been teaching me. Many months.

Caesar hugs Zion. *This calls for a beer. Two beers. One for your reading and writing, and one for my boy! Do we have any here?*

Zion scrawls slower this time, biting his lip. *What if they make the child a slave?*

Caesar's reply is immediate, hoarse, venomous. *I... will... not... let... them!* *It's against the law!*

The big man said nothing. Sometimes it was advantageous not to have a tongue.

45. PEGGY

Another slave auction. Peggy drawn to it like cod to capelin. Not sure why herself, perhaps to flaunt her pregnancy. But Billy was not there. Another young man sat at the table beside the Widow Williams.

What had happened to Billy? She wanted to ask, but didn't dare disturb that rich lady. Then summoned up her nerve. She had a right to know, he was supposed to marry her!

She approached their table, circled the widow's round yellow sun hat, leaned forward and put her question.

Who is this person? the widow said. *Roger, please get her away from me.*

Roger stood and took hold of Peggy's shoulder.

Let go!

Instead the young man grabbed her other shoulder, trying to lead her away. A million capelin swam through her head. To free herself she jammed her knee, hard, between his legs, into his groin. He groaned as he fell to the ground, doubled over, with both hands pressed against himself. He began to retch beneath the table.

Constable! the widow shouted, still in her velvet chair.

Don't worry, I'm leaving, Peggy said. She nodded towards Roger, who lay white-faced, twisted, speechless. Tightening the strings of her blue bonnet, she added, *You might need to find yourself another boy.*

Small waves were rippling in her brain. She could smell the bay. She felt exultant, stronger than she'd ever felt since coming to New York. Her basket was full.

She roamed through the mass of people, a lilt in her step, and found Mr. Hughson watching the auction from the rear, as he usually did. He did not come to buy slaves but to gather gossip. She commented on the size of the crowd.

It's because the slaves are Caribbeans, Hughson said.

Or as Mary Burton calls them, Kerry Beans.

She is strange sometimes, that girl.

Why do they draw more buyers?

Those from Jamaica, Antigua and such are known as seasoned slaves. They've been slaves before, so they know how to behave – how to build houses, how to cook, take care of children – most of them already speak English.

From what we read in the newspaper, they're also seasoned at rebelling, at killing white folks. I'd think people would be afraid to purchase them.

Not really. Most of those who rebelled were caught and killed. Those sent here are fairly tame.

They paused while a naked black family on the block was auctioned, the father to one new owner, the mother to another, a young boy and a girl to still another. The children had to be removed forcibly from their mothers, amid screams.

You don't come to these sordid affairs very often, Hughson said. *What brings you here?*

She did not answer, instead requested a favor. Would he ask the Widow Williams what happened to her assistant Billy, Peggy's onetime beau?

It's always a pleasure to talk to that pretty lady, Hughson said. He bowed deeply, theatrically, and left. By the time he returned three more slave families had been broken up and sold.

Turns out it's an interesting story, he said. *As gossip goes. It seems the widow was tiring of Billy's being overbearing, as she put it. He became jealous whenever she conversed with another young man. I am not your slave, she told him, and Billy sulked for days. Most likely he realized he was about to be dumped, that the widow was not going to keep all the promises she had made to him. In any case, one day a fortnight ago he absconded with 300 pounds belonging to the company. He most surely has left the colony. Your beau is on the run, my dear, and not likely to set foot again in New*

York. So it behooves you, Miss Peggy Kerry, to bid good riddance to that particular gentleman, for gentleman he is not. He has Exited Stage Right – or Stage Wrong, in this case.

Gallantly he lifted a pink handkerchief from his breast pocket, with which to dab away her tears. But there were none.

46. MARY

What in tarnation? I don't know what that means but that is what people been saying a lot lately, mostly Mr. Hughson. What in tarnation! It is because of them fires, which is making a lot of people afraid. Not just them first two fires, there's been a bunch more. The first two were on Wednesdays, and the very third Wednesday there was another. This was at a big storage house along the docks, which was partly filled with hay. The hay caught fire from a man smoking a pipe, they say. People were not too afraid yet then, except it being three straight Wednesdays, so people wondered. A man in the bakery when I was buying a blueberry tart said he did not know fires could read calendars. Which I thought was pretty funny. And he wondered out loud what would happen the next Wednesday. But the fires was not keeping calendars after all because on the very next Saturday two more fires started. I was mopping the floor of the dining room at the Inn when a man come rushing in and Mr. Hughson come out of his office and the man said, all excited, *Did you hear? Two more fires!*

What in tarnation? Mr. Hughson said.

A haystack burned at the Fly Market stable, the man said. *People came out with their buckets and put it out. But just as they was heading home there was another cry of Fire. This one was at Ben Thomas's house on the West Side.*

What in tarnation! Mr. Hughson said again.

They put that one out pretty quick too, because they already had their buckets. So no one was hurt?

No, but listen to this. The fire marshall says this fire was arson. He says it started near a straw bed where a Negro slept, and from there there was a trail of hot coals leading to the fire. And a lady says she was looking out her second floor window and saw three Negro slaves walking by, and one of them, a fellow called Quack, was singing Fire, Fire, Scorch, Scorch and threw up his hands and laughed. Until the constables came and arrested him. But he said he didn't do nothing, so they had to let him go, because there was no proof, no eye-witness. But now folks is scared and suspicious, wondering if maybe all of them was started by the Negroes.

Well, I'll be danged, Mr. Hughson said.

I expect you get danged in tarnation.

Then on Monday there was four more fires! At four rich people's houses. Now, even I know that is a lot of fires to start by themselves all in one day. Again they was put out quickly, but the slave called Cuffee was seen near one of them, and when he took off running, a whole mob of white men chased after him as he climbed over back fences, and they caught him and carried him to City Hall. That's when folks got very frightened, especially the ladies. Some people started saying, *The Negroes Are Rising! The Negroes Are Rising!* Some of them began to leave the city. Wagons were lined up to get out of New York, all the way to Little Current, kids running beside them, and dogs. They's afraid their own houses might be the next to burn, with them stuck inside like roasting pigs.

What else can a person say? *What in tarnation!*

47. JOHN PETER ZENGER

City officials, mainly Daniel Horsmanden, had to do something. But what? There was no easy answer. This was one of the rare occasions I had sympathy for them. I nodded to each, and each nodded back, as they entered the City Hall chamber, each wearing his newest suit and his freshest wig. But I had barely settled in to enjoy the discussion when they voted that the meeting would be closed to the press.

They could not stop me from publishing anything I saw fit – that had been the law for six years now, thanks to Mr. Hamilton's brilliant orations as my attorney – but neither could I stop them from closing their meetings. So I cannot report how the discussion went. It must have been lively, judging by the proclamation they passed. Quickly they had it posted throughout the city. To wit:

A Proclamation Offering a Reward
to any white person that Shall
Discover any person or persons
lately Concern'd in Setting fire to
any dwelling House or Store House
in the city (So that Such person or
persons As be Convicted thereof)

**the Sum of One hundred pounds
Current Money of this Province and
that Such person Shall be pardon'd
if Concern'd therein. And any Slave
that Shall Make Such Discovery to
be Manumitted or made free. And
the Master of Such Slave to Receive
Twenty five pounds therefor.**

People gathered on street corners to read the Proclamation, rich and poor alike, black and white alike, some solemn, some jocular. *Hey, Duke, I'm gonna turn you in and get my manu-admission,* was one comment I heard. *What you'll get is a knife in your back,* came the reply.

When two weeks passed with no response, Horsmanden tried a different tactic. He announced that every room in every house in the city would be searched for evidence linking the resident to the fires. They actually did that. It was a clear invasion of privacy by the government, but with Horsmanden waving the flag of conspiracy, who could object? When the *Weekly Journal* reported that they had found nothing suspicious in the entire city, the judge became the butt of private jokes.

That was pretty dumb, I overheard the child Mary Burton saying when I stopped for a beer at Hughson's. *They announce it ahead like that, people gonna hide their stuff.*

Soon after, I picked up frightening scuttlebutt from City Hall. Horsmanden was telling his fellow judges he is convinced the fires were part of a conspiracy by Negro slaves, to burn down the city – and he is determined to get to the bottom of it.

Such inflammatory speculation, of course, I did not print.

The coming days likely will be fraught with implications for the body politic, as it is Horsmanden's burning ambition to become governor some day.

48. Caesar

A rectangle of bright white filled the entryway to the small barn. Caesar worked deep in the darkness, forking hay into the trough of the mare. A featureless figure he could not identify framed itself in the whiteness.

That you, Caesar, in there?

That's me, Caesar replied, and kept working. *Who are you?*

Jude.

Caesar did not care for Jude. He hung too much with the two rowdies, Cuffee and Quack.

I need to talk to you

I got work to do. Come on in if you want. He sensed hesitation in the visitor. *Don't worry, the mare don't bite.*

We need to talk in private.

She don't blab, neither.

Jude entered the barn with caution and approached Caesar. Pie ignored him. Caesar kept forking hay.

I got a deal for you.

I'm not looking for a deal.

Don't be ornery. Put down that fork and listen. John Hughson told me to talk to you.

Caesar turned to the visitor, stabbed the pitchfork into the earth.

I'm listening.

Jude looked about the barn now that his eyes had adjusted, seemed to be making sure no one was lurking in a corner.

Here's the deal. You know Hogg's shop over on Broad Street? Got a side door into Jews' Alley.

I know it.

Fellow name of Wilson was in there this morning. He's a sailor off a ship docked in the harbor. He bought stuff, saw Mrs. Hogg make change from a drawer full of Spanish coins – pieces of eight. Also saw a bunch of silver plate. Wilson come to Hughson's, told us about it. We made a plan. Wilson went back to buy some rum. While Mrs. Hogg was busy, he slid back the bolt on the side door. Nobody noticed. There's silver alone worth maybe 60 pounds in there, plus the coins, just waiting to be took. I'm going in there tonight. Three in the morning. Jews' Alley will be dark and dead. I need someone to help carry the stuff. Hughson don't trust this Wilson off a ship no-how. He told me to talk to you.

You know Professor Fez? He's got a book of laws. I looked in it once. The penalty for robbery, or just for receiving stolen property, is hanging by the neck until dead.

They have to catch you first.

Who says they won't?

The side door ain't locked. No noise. Easy pickings.

Caesar shook his head. *I have a child on the way.*

I heard about that. A white one.

White, black, brown, it don't matter. I intend for him to have a daddy to help him grow. Not a thief hanging from a rope.

So your answer is no? Hughson won't like that.

What's Hughson to me? What about your buddies, Cuffee and Quack?

They's in the dungeon for settin' those fires.

They're the ones? Stupid. What did they expect to gain?

I didn't say they did it. You didn't hear that from me.

Pie nudged Caesar's shoulder with her nose, trying to get past him to the trough. Caesar did not budge, instead rubbed the mare's long face. A game they played. Finally he moved aside, let Pie get to the hay.

You like that horse? Do this deal you can buy three horses.

I don't need three horses.

Jude hitched his trousers.

The horse gives me an idea. That huge friend of yours. He could carry three times as much as you.

Zion doesn't want in neither.

He's big enough to speak for himself.

He can't speak.

All the dummy has to do is nod his head.

Caesar placed his hand tight on the fork. He hurled the tool the length of the barn, where it cracked wood on wood, fell safely to earth. The mare raised her head at the sound, waited, went back to chomping.

You involve Zion in this and you won't live out the week.

You can't threaten me.

I just did.

Jude grinned, two front teeth long gone. *If you won't do a robbery, you don't have the guts to kill a man.*

Well, you would be the fourth.

Jude squinting, assessing the truth of this. Uncertain.

You know the punishment for killing a man? Same as for robbery. Hanging by the neck until dead.

Some things are worth hanging for, Caesar said.

49. PEGGY

Alone in bed she could not sleep. Had always slept on her stomach, but not now with the baby growing inside. She was afraid of crushing it. On her back its weight pressed into her. On her sides worked best. On her left side her arms around Caesar. On her right side his arms around her. Protected sleep.

But tonight he was not there.

He would sleep at Vaarck's tonight to make sure Zion did not get into trouble, he'd said. She did not ask what kind of trouble. Better you don't know, Caesar would have said.

She turned and tossed for hours, as on a battered boat, before finally drifting off.

And was awakened by voices beneath her bed.

She listened. Not right under her bed, but somewhere down there. The basement. She had never been, but knew it extended under her room. Sounds, voices, but not words she could understand.

Off with the covers, wrapped a robe around, tied the belt, hurried barefoot down the corridor. Out the side door near Hughson's office, into the moonless night. Harsh dead grass spiked her feet as she neared a horizontal door cut flat into the earth. She knew there were stairs beneath it.

The voices were louder now, but still obscure, until she lifted the white-washed door. She knelt and placed a small stone beneath the edge to hold it open a crack.

How about in here? The voice was Mrs. Hughson's.

That's the first place they'll look. I created a new cranny. They'll never find it.

The sound of coins clinking.

Now I just slide this over. Presto, they're gone. Now let's be gone before anyone wakes.

Wait a minute, where's my share? A male voice she did not know.

After I move them, Wilson. A few weeks.

That wasn't the deal. Give me mine now.

You'll get caught if you flash them now.

He's right Wilson. Another male voice. Might be Jude.

You never told me that. Wilson speaking, louder. *How do I know I can trust you?*

Keep your voice down, damn-it.

I'm leaving. You'll be sorry for this.

A footstep on the stairs, a creaking. Removing the stone, she scurried out of sight around the corner of the Inn. The man called Wilson emerged from underground, muttering.

You'll pay for this. All of you.

He let the horizontal door clatter behind him, strode away, dissolved into the dark. Peggy retraced her run to her room. Thought Mary's door might have been open slightly. But maybe not.

Two days later, four constables came to the Inn, one wielding a rifle, three with cutlasses. They tied the arms of Hughson and his wife behind their backs.

What in tarnation? Hughson said.

You're under arrest for receiving stolen property.

Young Sarah heard the commotion, came into the dining room.

You too, miss.

What? My daughter? What did she do? Who's going to run the Inn?

You have bigger problems than that, Hughson. And you – Peggy Kerry. Where were you night before last.

In my room. Sleeping.

All night?

Of course.

She thought quickly. She had to protect Caesar and Zion.

With my husband.

You're not married, Peggy.

Caesar. Caesar was with me.

We just spoke to Caesar. He says he was home that night, at Vaarck's. One of you is lying. It's been my experience that lying usually covers a crime.

They tied Peggy's hands behind her as well.

Search the basement, you two.

The constables did not find the coins.

Until they did.

50. JOHN PETER ZENGER

Let me tell you about the dungeon, since I have personal experience with it. It is a massive windowless crypt that can make eight months enclosed there-in feel like eight years – or eight lifetimes. It's the basement of City Hall, all concrete and darkness and foul smells, yet it lingers in my mind as a somnolent beast. And poor Andrew Hamilton, I suspect he is not done with the memory either.

The foundations for City Hall had been laid in 1699. It took four years of labor by men both enslaved and free to raise the stones into place. In 1703 the building began to accommodate meetings of the Supreme Court, and the Common Council. In 1711, a few single cells in the large basement were walled off by masons. A jailer's apartment was built over the west wing in 1721. Entry and exit is down a guarded staircase from the first floor. A doorway once existed in the west wall for the convenience of the stoneworkers, but is no longer in use. With the passing years the windowless cavern has become foul with the stench and sweat and wastes of those imprisoned there.

When I was arrested in 1935 on charges of libeling the governor, I was incarcerated there. Andrew Hamilton, the best attorney in the colonies, came up from Philadelphia to see me. We met in the dungeon, where I was to await trial; that's mostly what it was for. But not three minutes had passed before the eminent attorney turned white of face, loosened his cravat, pulled out a handkerchief, and, mopping his brow, intoned, *I shall not spend another minute in this foul bastion.* Upstairs, when he had calmed, he demanded he be given a respectable place in which to meet with his client. The court agreed. A good thing. Without Hamilton, we journalists might still be laboring under the threat of prison every time we chose to criticize in print the government, or one of its corrupt members such as Governor William Cosby. But Hamilton got me off. He was brilliant before the jury. I can hear him now, words that will live in history:

It is natural, it is a privilege, I will go farther, it is a right, which all free men claim, that they are entitled to complain when they are hurt. They have a right publicly to remonstrate against the abuses of power in the strongest terms ... The loss of liberty, to a generous mind, is worse than death ...

But you remember his words as well as I do.

51. MARY

Bells were ringing. I love to hear bells ringing. They remind me of the churches in Belfry. The nuns dragged us to church every Sunday. I did not like the churches but I loved their bells.

Today is not Sunday, though. It is Tuesday. These bells are not church bells. They are City Hall bells. They are ringing, a constable told me, to announce that a new Grand Jury has been seated. I do not know what is so Grand about it. Neither did the constable. But if they really is Grand I suppose they should be allowed to sit.

I was on the veranda of the Inn taking in the warm April sun when the constable came for me. The Inn is closed and empty so I had no work to do. I found milk in the ice box so I drank that for breakfast. After people came and asked I wrote a sign on paper and nailed it to the front door. I wrote: INN CLOSED BECUASE OWNER IS IN THE DUNGEON.

The constable wanted me to come to City Hall. He said the Horseman needed to talk to me. I told him I did not want to talk to the Horseman, he does not seem very nice. The constable said I had to go

with him. I said I would not go with him. He said I had to go. I told him
us people is supposed to be free, even if I was a denture, and I did not
have to talk to nobody I did not want to talk to. He said he would go to
City Hall and get a paper from the Grand Jury saying I had to come.
Which if I did not obey I would go to the dungeon myself. I did not know
if he was lying so I told him to go get it. He wasn't lying.

City Hall is a big stone building with three big windows in the
second floor. It was scary to go into for a girl from Belfry Catholic
Orphanage. The constable led me up steps and into a room where the
Horseman was sitting. It was just me and him if you don't count the
pigeons on the window sill, which was 12. Also a bigger bird that was
green and blue.

Through the window, down in the valley, I could see men building
something. I asked the Horseman what they was doing. He said they were
building gallows. I asked him what that was. He said that's was where
they would hang the prisoners. I said, *Oh.*

He told me the Grand Jury was going to ask me questions about the
robbery at Hogg's and all them recent fires. I didn't say nothing. He took
me into a big room where the Grand Jury was. They was seated, all right.
The sheriff explained that normally there are 24 men on the Grand Jury
but for this one he could only get 17. So I thought it was not so Grand
after all.

They tried to swear me in to tell the truth. I didn't let them. They
kept telling me it was important. The Horseman took me to his private
office and then back to the too-small Grand Jury. Still I did not talk to
them. They read me that announcement they had posted everywhere a
few weeks ago, saying how if I told what I knew and it led to a conviction
I would be free of my dentures and also get 100 pounds sterling. I was
too frightened to care about any of that. I didn't know nothing.

This went on all morning. Then they got upset with me. The
Horseman said they should arrest me and take me down to the dungeon.
Maybe that would loosen my tongue. They took me down one stairs
and we started down another stairs to the dungeon, which was in the
basement. Before we got near I could smell this terrible smell and could
hear people yelling and screaming. I felt sad that Mr. Hughson was in
there, and Mrs. Hughson and even Sarah. Also Peggy who used to be
my friend. The dungeon got me so scared I changed my mind. I told the
constable to take me back up, I would talk to them. This time I let them
swear me in.

A man, whose name was Judge Philipse, talked to the Grand Jury.
Here is part of what he said:

The many frights and terrors which the good people of this city have of late been put into, by repeated and unusual fires and burning of houses give us too much room to suspect that some of them at least did not proceed from mere chance, or common accidents, but on the contrary from the premeditated malice and wicked pursuits of evil and designing persons. Therefore it greatly behooves us to use our utmost diligence by lawful ways and means, to discover the contrivers and perpetrators of such daring and flagitious undertakings, that upon conviction they may receive condign punishment.

He went on all boring like that. I didn't know big words like flagitious and condign. I figured he was saying them fires didn't start by themselves, and you got to find the bad persons who started them. So why didn't he just say that?

Finally he finished up.

This crime of arson is of so shocking a nature that if we have any in this city who have been guilty thereof, should escape, who can say he is safe, or tell where it will end?

I was nervous with all them fine gentlemen looking at me, me in my Sunday dress on Tuesday except for a hole in my white stocking down by my ankle. I started by telling them I would tell them everything I knew about the robbery, but I would not talk about the fires. I said that because I didn't know nothing about the fires. But somehow they took this to mean that I did. You would think they could understand English better than that.

I told them that the night of the Hoggs robbery I heard Mr. Hughson and Mrs. Hughson talking down in the basement, and I saw Peggy Kerry running that way, and that if Peggy was there then Caesar must have been down there too, because they was usually always together at night. But the jury people was much more interested in them fires. They said it was widely known that many a night lots of coloreds gathered at Hughson's to eat and drink and carouse, and since I lived there, did I know if that was true. I told them it was true. They said there was rumors that a big feast had been held there near the end of the last year, and what about that? I said that was true, too, I had been there myself. They asked who else was there, so I told them. Mr. Hughson, of course, since it was his party, and Mrs. Hughson, who was cooking in the kitchen and bringing food out but also sat down to eat. And their daughter Sarah, who sat right next to me when we ate. Any other white people, they asked, and I said Peggy Kerry, that was all. So they asked about the Negroes who was there and I told them Caesar and Cuffee and Quack and Jude and Fortune and a few other names I knew.

They asked what was talked about there. I was sworn to tell the truth, so I told them. There was a lot of talk about the slaves rebelling.

Somebody had a plan, that the best thing to do was to set fires, and when
the white men came to put out the fires they could kill the white men
and take the white women for their own. I told them I did not remember
exactly who said what, except for one thing. Mr. Hughson said that
when they had taken over the colony, Caesar would be Governor and he
himself, Mr. Hughson, would be King.

Well, that got the jurors buzzing like nothing else. They asked me
who else was there who heard this and I said I did not know all the names
but if I saw them I could point them out. So they sent constables out into
the streets to pick up colored men. When they brought one in I said he
was there, and the Horseman nodded and smiled. I could see he liked
that. So after that every Negro they brought in I said yes, and each time
the Horseman smiled. I guess he was beginning to like me. It feels nice
when somebody likes you.

When it was time to go home for the day I told them I was afraid
to go home because someone who did not like what I had said might
try to kill or even poison me. The Horseman said that was a good point,
that I would stay in the protection of the jailer, Mr. Mills, who had an
apartment right there in City Hall, and the constables downstairs would
make sure nobody got into the building to cause me harm. Mr. Mills
looked mean.

What happened next I especially want to talk about. When the
jurors left it got around the city that I had named who had set them
fires. The Horseman said I had uncovered a *vast conspiracy* – I did not
even know that word – a *vast conspiracy* on the part of the Negroes to
take over the city, and Mr. Hughson would be King and Caesar would
be Governor. But no slave was smart enough to come up with a plan
like that, he said, so Mr. Hughson must be behind it all, and he called it
Hughson's Plot. The thing I need to remind people is that I never said who
set them fires. I didn't know who set them fires. All I knew was what they
talked about. That is a different thing. Even at 16 years old I knew that
what you talk about and what you do is not always the same. In Belfry
Catholic Orphanage the nuns told us every day to be sure and say our
prayers before going to bed. I always said I would. I never did. Talking
and doing just ain't the same thing.

Yet them fires did happen.

52. CAESAR

The Second Door of No Return. That is how Caesar experienced the dungeon. It was much like the Cape Coast Castle – the stench and the rats and the darkness and the disease. Everyone who was marched into that place came out a slave or dead. This place felt much the same.

Now, having done nothing wrong, he knew he was doomed. He had denied the robbery. He was innocent of conspiracy, had not claimed he would be governor – that was Hughson's stupid prattling. But the dungeon proclaimed approaching death

Nor was there anything he wanted to say to anyone in the dungeon. Not even Hughson, who often could make him laugh with his theatrical oddities.

He wondered who was delivering the bread. Most likely Vaarck himself, until he could buy and train another slave.

So day by day Caesar sat alone on his thin mat and sipped his thin soup and chewed his bread and lived again in his mind the time when he was king.

53. PEGGY

Morality seemed an odd thing to find in a whore. To Daniel Horsmanden, Peggy Kerry, pregnant and now alone, seemed the most likely of the Hughsons regulars to confess. She had denied involvement in the burglary of Hogg's, denied knowing anything of the fires. Because she was with child, she had been given one of the few single cells in the basement. And he had ordered fresh food, including greens, be brought to her each day to keep her child alive. He did not want to be accused of allowing her baby to die before it was born.

Now Horsmanden, desperate for a witness to back up the statements of Mary Burton, removed his powdered wig, held his nose and descended to the dungeon to interrogate her again. He found her looking unwell, her lovely red hair stringy from the damp. Yet her breasts, swollen with milk, had outgrown her corset, which she no longer wore beneath her chemise. Horsmanden told her he would recommend that she be pardoned by the governor if she told what she knew of the conspiracy. Her reply was an unexpected statement of principle.

If I should accuse anybody of such a thing, I must accuse innocent persons, and wrong my own soul.

This coming from a prostitute! Worse, a white woman who gave herself to Negro slaves. Pretending now to morality! Horsmanden smirked. His eyes kept seeking out her inviting breasts with a will unbecoming a judge; therefore, with a will of their own. Disappointed, he climbed back to the second floor to escape both the stench and his defeat. Peggy slumped on a stone bench in her cell, her chemise soaked with the sweat of her defiance.

She had never prayed. She did not believe in any god worth believing in. Her present circumstances had not changed that. Still, alone in her cell, her belly large as a filled sandbag beneath her soiled white shift, she slid to her knees on the earthen floor, clasped her hands in front of her, and prayed. She did not pray for Caesar, she knew it was too late for that. She did not pray for herself, she would accept whatever was meant to be. But she prayed for her child. She prayed that they would allow it to be born. To be removed from this filthy dungeon where it would surely die, and be raised in the sun and the rain and the clean air that nature provided, and with the freedom the law allowed. She prayed for some being, human or divine, that would see to all this.

The next day Horsmanden returned. She had been given her own walled cell not only because she was pregnant, but also so that Horsmanden could come down and interview her whenever he wanted. He was growing impatient. His only witness so far to the planning of the fires and the rebellion was Mary Burton. He knew that the barely literate orphan, with her blue lips stained from too many blueberry tarts, might not be credible. Whereas Peggy, even if a prostitute, was 21 or 22, an adult. She had been at the same party, had heard the same talk. If she confirmed what Mary had related, the conspiracy would be broken. Convictions would be much easier.

And those breasts!

He helped Peggy up from her knees. The fact that she had been praying gave him hope. He sat beside her on the stone bench in the cell, asked if she was now ready to tell the truth about the plot.

I have been telling the truth, she said. *All that was shouted at that party was drunken nonsense, drunken joking. No one believed it, except maybe stupid Mary. That bitch has fetched me in and made me black as the rest.*

The judge replied, *Those fires were not drunken jokes.*

He left her cell frustrated as ever. Peggy, one hand supporting her belly, eased herself to her knees and resumed her prayers.

54. Mary

Day after day they brought in more black men. Day after day I said they was involved.

I knew that's what the Horseman wanted.

I didn't much like sleeping in the jailer's apartment. But it was better than being killed, or even poisoned. He let me sleep in his bed and he slept in a chair near the door. In case anyone tried to come in.

There was about 80 slaves arrested altogether so far. Half of them told the Horseman they was innocent. They was taken down to the dungeon. The other half said they was guilty, and they named others who was guilty too and should be seized. I guess they figured if they confessed they would be freed. They was taken to the dungeon, too.

Next day a funny thing happened. The Horseman had to go out of the city, and while he was gone half of those who had confessed came upstairs and unconfessed. I guess they was even more frightened of the Horseman than I was.

55. John Peter Zenger

Daniel Horsmanden pondered his next move. If the alleged conspiracy was first called *Hughson's Plot*, then *The Negro Plot*, and finally *The Priest's Plot* – we'll get to that – the investigation was all Horsmanden's. He would question every person arrested – there would be more than a hundred – before they appeared before the grand jury. Singlehandedly he planned to save the city, to reign as a hero in the history books, to rise perhaps from the positions of recorder and judge to the governorship itself.

Although there had been no fires for several weeks, he wanted a scapegoat quickly to use as an example, to frighten the conspirators. He selected Caesar Vaarck. He knew that Caesar was intelligent and proud and was looked up to by many of the slaves. He knew that Caesar was considered handsome. If Caesar could be brought down swiftly, he believed, the others would crumble and confess. The problem was that Caesar had been charged only in the robbery. There was not enough evidence yet to convict him of conspiracy. Horsmanden did not want to wait. He decided that the first trial would be that of Caesar Vaarck. No matter that it would be only for robbery. The penalty if he was convicted would be the same.

56. CAESAR

The news bubbled through Caesar's skull like a death rattle. If they were going to try him first, they were planning to hang him. And probably Hughson next. There could be no doubt. He threaded his way through the crowded dungeon and found John Hughson in a rear corner, which he had claimed as his own, often spouting what he said were Shakespearean soliloquies to whomever wanted to listen.

They're going to hang me for sure, Caesar said.

Alas, my friend, Hughson replied, the jester even now, *it's curtains for us all.*

Sometimes they chatted. Today neither had anything to say. Caesar worked his way back to the position he preferred, near the bottom of the stairs, where he could survey the new prisoners skulking in. As he moved away he could hear Hughson's oration over the murmuring mass of unwashed flesh.

O what a rogue and peasant slave am I …

A rogue he surely was, Caesar thought. A slave? Perhaps here in the dungeon he was as much a slave as anyone. *Hughson's Plot.* They could hardly let him survive.

The bottom of the stairs was the source of news and gossip as new prisoners stumbled into the darkness of the dungeon. It was here he heard about John Vaarck's wife, Stephanie. She had begun teaching Julia, the brightest of the bakery's five female slaves, how to make the special cakes and fruit tarts that were the bakery's main attraction. This gossip had surfaced at Comfort's well. Coming with the news that she was not looking well, Caesar thought Mrs. Vaarck must be ill. Although they had never chatted, she seemed like a fine woman.

Each time food was brought to a line-up of the prisoners – watery soup and a small loaf of bread, twice a day – Caesar thought of the bakery. The bread was good, he knew from its buttery taste that it had come from Vaarck's. Why the Common Council would buy bread for the prisoners that was more expensive than from the other bake shops in the city was a puzzle, until he heard rumors that his master had reduced the price sharply so that the prisoners could enjoy their skimpy meals. This meant Vaarck would be losing money on each loaf, but Caesar knew, and his master knew, that the crowded dungeons would not remain crowded for long, once the hangings began.

One day six slaves were thrown into the dungeon together, accused in the alleged conspiracy. They were known in the city as the Spanish Negroes. England and Spain were at war at the time, and when the British navy captured a Spanish ship at sea and brought it into port at New York, the white sailors aboard had been held as prisoners of war. But the six black seamen were pronounced to be slaves, and were sold at auction. They were among the most bitter of the slave population, easy recruits, it was said, for rebellion

57. JOHN PETER ZENGER

Caesar's trial was held a day after Horsmanden's announcement. A petit jury was sworn. As he was led from the dungeon between two constables, his hands tied with rope, the other prisoners yelled encouragement. He could not distinguish who said what. It hardly mattered.

The jury was already seated when he entered the room. The court constables untied his arms, led him to a table near the center of the room. In the section of seats for spectators, behind a wooden railing, he saw Professor Fez and Zion seated together, but not John Vaarck, his owner, his master, his mentor. The section was filled, mostly with white women. Some he recognized from his bread route. They were looking at him without expression. He could not tell if they were there to see him freed or to see him condemned. In his pocket was a small slip of paper with six word written on it, which a constable had shown to Horsmanden, who had nodded.

Call Me In Your Defense – Vaarck

Kbunk!

Those in the courtroom were stunned momentarily by something striking the one large window. Over the years numerous small birds had been killed by flying into the glass. Whirling to look, Caesar saw the blue-green parrot drop to the sill, either dazed or dead. For some moments it did not move. Finally it lifted its head, shook its body, and settled in, as if to listen to the proceedings.

The case brought by the prosecutor, an attorney named Smith, moved quickly. The Prosecutor told the jury that the morning after the

burglary at Hogg's, a fellow named Christopher Wilson had come to City
Hall and confessed to the crime. Wilson was a seaman on a ship in port.
He said he would name the others involved in the crime if he would not
be charged. He told Daniel Horsmanden that he and a slave called Jude
had taken the stolen coins and other items to Mr. and Mrs. Hughson in
the basement of their tavern. The seaman was not available for further
questioning, Smith said, because his ship had already left port.

Mary Burton was called to the witness stand. She testified that
during the night of the robbery she had seen Peggy Kerry running to the
basement. Peggy would have no reason to be going down there, Mary
said, unless Caesar were there. Jude, on the witness stand, said definitely
that Caesar had helped with the burglary.

Caesar did not try to contradict Jude. He knew that the testimony
of slaves did not count for much, and his denial – he had already pleaded
Not Guilty – would add little. He summoned as his only witness the man
who owned him.

58. CAESAR

The door to the courtroom opened, and John Vaarck was
shown to the witness stand, limping as usual. To Caesar he looked very
tired, perhaps because he had been making the outlying bread deliveries
himself since Caesar had been imprisoned. But there was something
more. In Vaarck's face Caesar saw a rare mask of despair. He thought his
master's wife must be dying.

Vaarck was sworn in.

On the afternoon of the Hoggs burglary, he began, *Caesar was pitching hay
in my small barn. I was behind the barn, tightening a wheel on my delivery cart. I
saw the slave Jude approach the barn. When he entered it, I could hear easily through
the rear wall as Jude asked Caesar to help him that night in a burglary of Hoggs.
Caesar refused. Let me repeat that. Caesar refused to participate, and they almost came
to blows. When the perpetrators were apprehended the very next day, while Caesar
remained free, this was reason enough for Jude to implicate my man. I have owned
Caesar from the day he arrived here, and have never known him to be anything but
honest.*

Caesar breathed deeply, his chest expanding with new hope. Surely
the jurors would take the word of a respectable white merchant over that
of a slave. He had heard that they always did.

But gentlemen, Vaarck continued, *we are all adults here. We all know that this trial is not about a burglary. We would not be here today were it not for the hysteria permeating the city about an alleged conspiracy by the Negroes to burn the town. In this atmosphere, every Negro slave is viewed as a possible arsonist. Of this I will tell only what I have seen with my own eyes.*

When the alarm bells rang signaling the first and worst of the recent fires, at Fort George, I grabbed my three-gallon leather bucket, as citizens through the city were doing, in order to go join the bucket brigade. Caesar saw this. He knew that with my bad leg it would take me many minutes to walk to the region of the fort. So he took the bucket from me and flew like the wind down to the fort. When I reached a knoll overlooking the bustling scene I saw Caesar hauling water in the brigade. He worked all day, as hard as any white citizen, trying to help douse the fire, which rainfall eventually did. Personally I have seen no evidence of this alleged conspiracy. No evidence has surfaced against Caesar beyond the dubious rantings of a young girl. In this time of fear we must be careful not to tar all of our slaves with the same brush. Thank you.

Such was Caesar's defense. He felt indebted to his owner, perhaps for saving his life.

59. John Peter Zenger

The Prosecutor huddled with Judge Horsmanden,

then gave his final summation.

Gentlemen of the jury, he said. *John Vaarck has been an honest merchant in this city for many years. Far be it from me to question anything he has said here under oath. There is no doubt that he spoke the truth. But let us examine those truths more closely. The defendant is not here being tried for setting any fires. But since his witness mentioned them, let us look at what he testified. He said the defendant had virtuously fought the fire at Fort George. We must accept the truth of it. But so did many other Negroes join the bucket brigades. Is it farfetched to assume that the author of this outrageous plot, whoever that may have been, specifically ordered the Negroes to join the bucket brigades, precisely to deflect suspicion from themselves? In this court of law we dare not be so gullible. If we are, we have a city to lose.*

Now, about the burglary at Hoggs. Mr. Vaarck testified that, out of sight behind his barn, he clearly heard his slave Caesar rejecting a request to participate. No doubt that is true, or John Vaarck would not have testified to it. But consider this. Caesar knew his master might be within earshot. So he made a point of loudly repudiating this illegal plan. But by nodding his head, or making such and such motions with his hands, he could easily have agreed to join in.

Mr. Vaarck was not at Hoggs that night. The man Jude was – and he says that Caesar was with him.

Now let us look at motive. Caesar has readily admitted to cohabiting with the white woman Peggy Kerry. That in itself is against the law. But we also know that from his own funds Caesar was paying for the room and board of Peggy Kerry. If he ran out of money, his lover, if I may use that term, would be relegated to the poorhouse. We all have heard what a terrible place that is, no better than the dungeon below us. What stronger motive could any man have, slave or free, than to protect his woman from that terrible fate.

Finally, Mr. Vaarck testified that Caesar had to his knowledge always acted honorably. Yet several months ago a fellow named Hobart, who resides north of the city, while out hunting turkeys with his son, encountered the defendant riding a horse hell bent, as the saying goes, in an attempt to escape. Caesar denied that he was trying to escape, and Mr. Vaarck handled that incident in his own manner, as every slave owner may. But it hardly exemplifies a good and satisfied slave.

Oh, yes, one last point. Mr. Vaarck conceded that the defendant is his property. What he did not say is that when he purchased Caesar some fifteen months ago, he paid for him the astonishing sum of thirty pounds sterling – by far the most ever paid for a slave in this colony.

How is that relevant? Because should the defendant be convicted and condemned, Vaarck would be out a pretty sum. No master wants to lose a slave without compensation. But even if you are a friend of the witness, his loss should play no part in your deliberations.

With that, gentlemen of the jury, the prosecution rests.

The Prosecutor turned toward the judges. Horsmanden instructed that the jurors be led from the room to consider their verdict. When they were gone, the prosecutor approached the Judge. The two shook hands, warmly.

The jurors deliberated just fifteen minutes before returning with their verdict. The foreman spoke it: *The defendant has been found guilty as charged.*

Judge Horsmanden thanked the jury for their work and dismissed them. The spectators were warned to remain seated until the prisoner had been led from the courtroom. Caesar's hands were tied for the journey down two flights of stairs.

The crowded dungeon, which now contained more than a hundred Negro slaves, was a pit of silence. News of his conviction had preceded him.

60. Peggy

That night – the middle of the night it was – she heard a light tapping on the door of her cell.

Who's there?

Open the door. It's Goldsmith.

Goldsmith. She did not know any Goldsmith. Wait! That actor fellow …

What are you doing here? she asked as he entered. *How did you get past the constables?*

Shh, let me talk. I've come to rescue you. Not tonight, but two nights hence.

That's not possible

Cash makes things possible. I finished my play, inspired by you. Philadelphia loved it. The money poured in. They held us over an extra week. And that was with a local lady playing the queen. With you they would have held us longer. So this is our fortune. In two nights I'll be back, same time. The side door will not be locked. We'll escape in my waiting carriage. On to Boston, Providence.

I can't leave.

What do you mean you can't leave.

Caesar. My husband. I am carrying his child. I can't abandon him.

You heard of the verdict today. They are going to hang him.

He's innocent.

They will hang him just the same. And you, too, unless I get you out of here.

I can't.

You must. If nothing else, think of the child. His child. Wouldn't he want his child to live? From Providence we might sail to England. The theaters there are large, and celebrated. I'll teach you the part. As Queen Marguerite you'll be the toast of the continent. The child will grow up carefree as a prince. Or princess.

A light knocking on the cell door.

I have to go. Money buys only so much time. In two nights. Gather what little you have. Be silent, and ready. A good-hearted constable is risking his neck for you.

I haven't said I'm going. I have to think.

Think all you want. Then we go.

He opened the door and slunk out. As an actor he had learned to walk lightly as a mouse.

The door closed silently on her dilemma.

61. MARY

A week in City Hall ain't no fun. It might even be two weeks already. Going from the jailer's apartment to the courtroom to the jailer's apartment to the courtroom. You see what I mean? In the courtroom I tell in each trial about that party at Hughson's. The same thing again and again. I told it so many times I'm starting to wonder if it really happened or if it was a dream. But they are locking up everybody I tell it about so I guess it was really real.

Outside it is May now and the sun is shining warm on the window. I miss it shining on my face. I get this idea. If everybody I talk about is locked in the dungeon, which they is, then I don't have to be worried about going outside, because nobody will be out there to kill or even poison me. So without asking permission or telling nobody I walk down the hall to the stairs and go down to the main floor and walk out the front door, with nobody even noticing me. It feels so good outside that I skip down the street and while I am skipping I jump in the air and twirl around and I keep doing this like I am happy. Most people don't recognize who I am and those that stop and look at me has this funny look on their face that I don't know what it means, if they like me or don't like me. In City Hall I think most people like me, at least those who ain't got their hands tied, but outside it is hard to tell. On Broad Way I come to the theater called The New Theater. I look to see what is showing there. I have to spell out each letter: T-H-E B-E-A-U-X' S-T-R-A-T-E-G-E-M. The only word I know is THE. I turn and walk up Broad Way and come to Varick Street across from the bakery and keep on going past Fair Street. I come to a carpenter shop that has a beautiful wooden carriage in front of it, all polished with dark wood. For the first time I think of the money I will be getting soon, a hundred pounds. When I get that money I could buy this carriage I bet. I go in past the carriage looking for the man who made it and see lots and lots of coffins piled up, made of wood that is almost white, and sawdust on the ground that smells like sawdust. A man wearing a blue apron with the sleeves of his work shirt rolled and lots of muscles showing is making another coffin.

How come you got so many coffins, mister? I ask him.

He says, *Because there's gonna be lots of hangings, girlie.*

I say, *Oh.*

I ask him where a person might buy a horse to go with that carriage and he says to keep going about half a mile and you come to a farmer who is selling horses. So I keep going about half a mile and sure enough there is a bunch of horses in a pasture and a sign on a wooden fence that says FOR SALE. The horses is mostly brown with some black ones and then I see a grey one. She looks just like Gweebarra. For a minute I think it is Gweebarra but I know that can't be, she sure could not gallop across the ocean. This one has one white leg and the rest grey. Gweebarra was all grey. But she is pretty anyway. I call out *Hey, Gweebarra* and a few of the horses come walking to the fence to see who is there. But the Gweebarra one doesn't come. I touch one of the brown ones on the face through the fence of grey wood and he jerks his head away and kind of snorts. I figure maybe he don't like to be touched so I stop. I think of my money again. Wouldn't it be grand to have one of these horses pulling that beautiful carriage through the city and me sitting in it like one of them grand ladies, and a footman – I think that is what they call him though I don't know why – a footman in a yellow suit with gold buttons driving. Jarvis, I tell him – that is what all footmen are called, Jarvis – Jarvis I tell him, take me to the New Theater on Old Broadway, I want to see that show called THE.

I am funning about the name of the show, of course, but if you been stuck in City Hall for two weeks, or maybe it is three by now, you might be funning, too.

Clouds come up and hide the sun and it is starting to get cold. I turn to go back. On Varick Street I think I will get a blueberry tart. I don't got no coins because Mr. Hughson has stopped giving me them, but I think they will give me a tart on account of I will soon have money. But the bakery is locked. A sign on the door says, CLOSED DUE TO DEATH IN THE FAMILY. I still think I should get a tart, I didn't do no death in the family, it ain't my fault. I say this out loud but nobody is there to listen. So I walk back to City Hall and push open the door and in the hallway everybody is running around yelling *She's gone, where could she be?* and *What if she was kidnapped?* and such. I see the Horseman in his blue suit and green vest and silly white wig and I tug on his waistcoat and ask him, *What's going on?* and he starts to answer and then he touches my shoulder and he says, *It's Mary! Mary, where have you been?* I tell him I went for a walk. He says, *You didn't ask permission, or tell anybody. You must not do that again. We need you for more trials. Next time you ask first.* I tell him that I will, though maybe I won't.

I figure this is a good time to ask for my money. He says he will write to the Common Council about that, but most likely they will want to wait until the trials is over, pending convictions. I don't know what *pending* means, but I don't ask.

62. Caesar

Once again he was in the courtroom, seated alone at the center table, his white blouse and trousers dirtied from the dungeon. Though convicted only of the robbery of Hogg's, not yet formally accused in the conspiracy, he would be the first to be sentenced, as if this were an unspoken honor, or recognition, as if in an unlikely acknowledgement that once far away he had been a king. The jury box was empty. The spectator section again was full, not with the women who had come to witness his trial – not one woman was present today – but with men come to see the sentencing, all manner of men: lawyers, bankers, doctors, workmen, farmers. He recognized only four: His owner, Vaarck, looking as if his face had been stepped on by grief; Zion and the Professor; and near the rear the man called Hobart, who had claimed Caesar was trying to run away. With a rifle draped over his shoulder, Hobart was staring at him. Caesar stared back, refusing to hang his head in shame or fear.

Sitting beside Judge Horsmanden, Judge Philipse pronounced sentence.

You, Caesar, the Grand Jury having pronounced an indictment against you for feloniously stealing and taking away from Mr. Hogg sundry goods of considerable value, you pleaded Not Guilty, and for your trial put yourself upon God and the country. Which country having found you guilty, it now only remains for the court to pronounce that judgment which the law requires, and the nature of your crime deserves.

Caesar sat still, his arms on the table, his eyes on the judge reading the sentence. The courtroom was silent except for the occasional cough by a spectator.

But before I proceed to sentence, I must tell you that you have been proceeded against in the same manner as any white man guilty of your crime would have been. You had not only the liberty of sending for your witnesses; asking them such questions as you thought proper; but likewise making the best defense you could; and as you have been convicted by twelve honest men upon their oaths, so the just judgment of God has at length overtaken you.

Unable to stop himself, Caesar glanced quickly at the spectators, wondering if any of the jurors had come to watch. If they did, he did not spot them.

I have great reason to believe, the judge continued, *that the crime you now stand convicted of is not the least of those you have been concerned in; by your general character you have been a very wicked fellow, a hardened sinner, and ripe, as well as ready, for the most enormous and daring enterprise.*

Caesar began to anger, slowly. Where was this nonsense coming from?

The time you have yet to live is to be but very short.

A low murmur swept through the spectators. There was the answer they had been waiting for. Caesar breathed deeply. He was not surprised.

I earnestly advise and exhort you, the judge continued, *to employ it in the most diligent and best manner you can, by confessing your sins, repenting sincerely of them, and praying God of his infinite goodness to have mercy on your soul. And as God knows the secrets of your heart, and cannot be cheated or imposed upon, so you must shortly give an account to him, and answer for all your actions; and depend upon it, if you do not truly repent before you die, there is a hell to punish the wicked eternally.*

As if drawn by a magnet, Caesar's eyes moved from the judge reading the speech to Horsmanden, who sat aloof and expressionless, although to Caesar the man's eyes were dancing. Caesar was convinced that Horsmanden was the speech's true author.

It is not in your power, the judge went on, *to make full restitution for the many injuries you have done to the public. So I advise you to prevent further mischiefs by discovering such persons as have been concerned with you in designing or endeavoring to burn this city and to destroy its inhabitants. This I am fully persuaded is in your power to do if you will. If so, and you do not make such a discovery, be assured God Almighty will punish you for it. Therefore I advise you to consider this well, and I hope you will tell the truth.*

Now, before I pronounce sentence, do you have anything to confess, or anything to say to this court?

All during the night, during the long periods when he could not sleep, Caesar had vowed to himself not to speak a word to the court. But words he thought proper entered his mind now. He stood, and spoke a single sentence:

It is easier to kill a man, he said, *than to kill a lie.*

That was all. He sat. The judge did not respond.

Nothing further remains for me to say, the judge said, *but that you, Caesar, shall be taken hence to the place from which you came, and from thence to the place of execution, and there you are to be hanged by the neck until you be dead. And I pray the Lord have mercy on your soul.*

It is so ordered that the execution be thirty days from this date certain, between the hours of nine and one of the same day. And further ordered that after the execution of the said sentence, the body of Caesar shall be hung in chains.

With that, Judges Philipse and Horsmanden turned quickly and exited the courtroom. The spectators stood, chattering, milling about, as at the end of a play at the theater. Vaarck, Zion and the Professor

remained in their seats, silent. Caesar did not move until two armed
constables, one on each side, led him back down to the dungeon.

63. PEGGY

A different knock on the door of her cell. She heard it,
had been expecting it. She rose from the stone bench, moved to the door.

Caesar?

Yes.

I'm so sorry. I don't know what more to say.

When the constables brought him down the prisoners had parted
like the waters in the white man's Bible. He had walked to the far wall, sat
alone on the ground for a time, cross-legged, in the manner of his tribe.

They're going to hang me in a month.

I know.

Have you heard the rest?

What rest? What more can there be?

*When I'm dead they will wrap my body in chains and hang me from a high post
for all to witness.*

The bastards! What will that accomplish?

*Nothing. It's supposed to be a warning to the others. To frighten them to confess, I
suppose. Will you come watch them hang me, if they let you?*

*No. Unless you want me to. I'm afraid it might scar the baby, even inside my
body. Women have lost babies for less.*

You're right, of course. Don't come.

It's a strange God they worship. That brought you three thousand miles, for this.

She placed her palm against the inside of the solid door, as if she
would touch him, comfort him. She did not know if he was doing the
same on the other side.

How many weeks before the baby is due?

Five. Maybe six.

You remember your promise? he said.

*Of course. To raise the baby strong. Don't worry. He will always know his father
was a king. If they let me birth him. If they let me raise him.*

Day and night are indivisible in here. They try you in two days?

Three.

The three whites together. You and the Hughsons. That might be a good thing.

How can it be a good thing?

Negroes are not permitted to testify against whites. The jury might find a lack of evidence.

Don't try to raise my hopes, Caesar. Or yours. There is always Mary Burton.

I try to forget that. It would be a good motto for the City of New York.

What would?

'There is always Mary Burton.'

She managed to laugh. He chuckled. They were in the stinking dark of the dungeon but a momentary sliver of sunlight knifed through the clouds.

They're serving what they call the soup now. I don't know if I can swallow that piss, but I suppose I have to try. We'll talk again soon.

Yes.

If am still here, she thought. If I have not escaped into ~~Marguerite~~ the queen.

64. MARY

So they are going to hang Caesar – the Caesar owned by the bakery man who sells the tarts. I do not like him much. He's the one who took Peggy away from me. When I am around, he acts what the Horseman calls uppity, never noticing me, never speaking to me or saying my name. As if I was a spider under his foot. Still, I'm not sure if it is right to hang anyone, even if you do not like them. In fact, I think it is wrong. Me and the nuns at the Belfry Catholic Orphanage did not agree on many things, but I think on this they would agree with me. Hanging people is wrong. If they was not sure, they would ask the priests who they called the Church Fathers, who were not really fathers at all. And the Church Fathers who were not really fathers would say just as I say. That hanging people is wrong.

Thinking about Caesar makes me hungry. I wonder if the bake shop is open. I wonder if they have blueberry. I think I'll go and find out.

I tell the jailer I am going there. So they don't think I am lost or kidnapped or run away before the trials are finished. The jailer says I should not go to the bakery. I ask him why not. He says they might not be very friendly to me. Not tonight.

65. CAESAR

He will not count the days. That is how he will defeat them.
He will not count the days until the gallows. He will make his death
come suddenly, without time for fear, as it often does in Muktu. A bolt
of lightning. An errant spear. A berserk lion. A tribal raid. Sudden,
unexpected darkness. Instant, unexpected surcease. Unplanned. So he
will not count the passing days.

    One.

    Two …

    Hono maliki

    He bolts upright from where he has been drowsing on the dungeon
floor.

    Hono maliki

    Elephant trap.

    What brings this to his mind now?

    He pictures a wide ditch circling the entire village. Deeper than a
standing man's hand. Covered with brush, invisible. The approaching
warriors do not see it. They fall in. They can't climb out. They are
prisoners of the Muktu now.

    A glorious victory.

    It is nonsense, this image. He would have needed ten men as strong
as he to dig the trench. When the first marching warrior fell in, the others
would halt. They would not be fooled. They would laugh at this feeble
attempt. They would throw a bridge across the trench.

    Hono maliki pu. Elephant traps are for elephants.

    There was no way to resist.

66. PEGGY

She knows the virtue of loyalty. Learned not from Father
Mallon, not from her father in his drunkenness. From Aunt Dottie, most
likely.

    The demand of loyalty is clear. She must remain here with Caesar
until the end.

    What will this loyalty achieve? Her own death on the gallows, most
likely.

    So be it.

But the child then will be alone. His child. Is that the loyalty he would want? Would he not urge her to flee with the actor when she has the chance? If she has the chance. If she did not merely imagine his coming to her cell in the night, his offer of escape. A creation of her mind?

What is this loyalty? You cannot see it. You cannot taste it. How does she know there is such a thing. Because people say so? People say many things that are not true.

Go ahead, Peggy, justify what you want to do.

But I do not know what I want to do.

A faint tapping on the door. This is the time he said. Is it true?

She pulls her wrap around her, opens the door. Leo Goldsmith, she thinks. He is wearing only black, she cannot quite see him. Black for the escape through the dungeon, into the night. She has only white to wear. Dirty white.

Come on, let's go!

It is him. She knows the voice.

I'm not going.

Of course you're going. Grab your things.

I have only this. A comb.

Fine. Take off your shoes, carry them. Walk quietly.

He is whispering.

She does not move. How will Caesar feel when he learns she is gone?

He kicks. The child inside her kicks. She ducks through the doorway.

Leo takes her hand. They leave the cell, move along the wall toward the nearly forgotten door. Silently. No one in the dungeon stirs.

How will Horsmanden feel when he learns she is gone? She denies her face a small smile.

Leo Goldsmith drops her hand, struggles with a trouser pocket. Produces what must be a key. Is he an actor or an angel? For a moment she is not sure.

67. JOHN PETER ZENGER

An Open Letter to the Court: My Esteemed Sirs:

A terrible cloud hangs over our city – the cloud of fear. Few New Yorkers have been able to rest easy since Judge and City Recorder Daniel Horsmanden declared that our normally peaceful slaves are prepared

to rise up against us, to burn our homes, to kill our men, to ravish
our women. According to the last census we have a population of ten
thousand souls. Eight thousand of us are white, five hundred are free
Negroes, fifteen hundred are Negro slaves. To imagine that this large dark
minority is prepared to use violence to gain control of the city is fearsome
indeed. And there were, of course, several fires in recents months to lend
possible credence to this fear. Some of our families have already fled the
city. But no evidence has been produced in public to show that these
fires were part of a conspiracy of rebellion, as the judge has asserted.
Upwards of one hundred of our slaves crowd the city dungeon in
conditions that are barely livable. But only one man has been tried and
convicted – the popular slave Caesar, owned by the baker John Vaarck
– and he was not accused of arson, but of receiving stolen property, an
offense that deserves punishment but is hardly a threat to the common
welfare. If the court has evidence of a conspiracy of arson beyond the
unsupported word of an innocent young girl, it must be produced in
public. Trials of those in the dungeon are the proper forum, so that any
evidence may be submitted under oath, and the truth of the alleged
conspiracy be proved or dismissed. It is axiomatic that justice delayed is
justice denied. We at the *Weekly Journal* call for justice now, not only for
the accused, but for the entire city.

68. PEGGY

If it is a key he is holding it must be covered with

rust because he jiggles and jaggles it in the lock of the old door making
noise in my ears loud enough to alert the boats as sea. This seems
to go on for minutes he is cursing under his breath surely the other
prisoners will hear or the constables and will come to investigate. Boston
Providence England are behind that door, it is amazing how far the mind
can fly in a moment. My boy or my girl growing up in a different world,
Caesar's boy or Caesar's girl. I am not worried about the play, I already
am an actress, I acted in bed with every man every night, they never
knew and kept coming back for more performances. Acting the part of a
queen cannot be more difficult.

A metal clunk. Something has given way. He bends his knees and
leans a shoulder against the door then crushes his shoulder into the door.
A wisp of air and then a gush of air as he leans harder, pushes the door
open further. A wash of pale light outlines his face as he backs himself

against the door, leaning back, pressing bodily against the stubborn wood. He is a thin man, would that he were stronger. Finally it gives way, yawns wide, and we are out! A moon or half moon that I have not seen for weeks smiles down on us. Or maybe not smiles but frowns because it lights us, and it is dark we need. He grabs my hand again, my rescuer, one step, two steps, we are moving along it seems an old abandoned path littered with stones they must have dropped when they were building this place. Three steps, four steps, he in the lead squeezing my hand, me just behind. A curve in the path and he stops. I bump against him. Bright silver gleaming in the night. Cutlasses. Four cutlasses. No, five. Drawn in readiness in the hands of constables. There is no way to pass.

Bastard! Leo mutters. In a quarter of an instant he has become not Goldsmith but Leo.

A portly figure pushes between two of the swords.

My, my, taking the evening air, are we Peggy? Horsmanden, a sly grin in his words. *It is much preferable to the dungeon, is it not?*

Reading my thoughts.

You! he says. *The actor, I believe. I ought to toss you in the dungeon for safekeeping. But I've got a hundred arsonists in there, bigger fish to fry. So you are lucky. Get you and your retinue out of the city before noon this day, or I will change my mind.*

Leo looks at me. He does not want to drop my hand. The moon shines plaintive in his eyes.

Marguerite, he says.

Gently he touches my swollen belly.

Go! Now! This from Horsmanden.

Two of the constables separate to allow him egress. He steps between them, looks in the face of one. He seems about to spit. *Bastard!* he says. They are for a moment statues in the moonlight, preparing for war. But Leo moves on, one stride, two. Soon he is running, I can hear his footsteps growing more faint as he runs away from me.

I should have thanked him, the judge says, jowls fluttering, *for this gift. What clearer evidence of guilt for the jurors than for the prisoner to attempt to escape?*

69. John Peter Zenger

Here she was in court. The three whites at the center table: John Hughson, Sarah Hughson, Peggy Kerry. The trial of young Sarah had been delayed, in hopes that the deaths of her parents, if they were convicted, might break her will. The city might then have a second witness. Who was also a child, but …

For days the spectator gallery had been almost empty as dozens of Negro slaves were tried and convicted, with as many as six tried together and sentenced to die, following the testimony of Mary Burton. But today the gallery was filled, with the defendants being white, John Hughson, who was a well known character about town, being called the ringleader of the plot, and Peggy Kerry red-haired, beautiful and pregnant about to burst.

Hughson, the innkeeper, pleaded guilty to receiving stolen property. How could he not? The cache of stolen Spanish coins had been found in his basement.

All three pleaded not guilty to being part of a plot to burn, to kill.

After Mary Burton testified about the notorious New Year's party, at which all three had been present, the prosecutor said that two slaves, Quack and Cuffee, had confessed to being part of the plot. They had named Hughson as the leader, and the two white women as participants. The prosecutor did not tell the jury that the men had made these confessions at the gallows, chained to wooden poles, surrounded by piles of wood they thought were about to be set afire. They had confessed in hopes of receiving mercy. They had not been told that the actual sentences would not be carried out for a month. The state's ploy had worked. The prosecutors had obtained confessions, signed when the prisoners were brought back to the dungeon. The terrified slaves would receive no mercy – just twenty-nine more days to look ahead to being burned alive. When they were told this, both recanted their confessions. But Daniel Horsmanden asserted that surely they had been telling the truth when on the brink of death.

A Criminal Confesses himself guilty at his own Peril, Horsmanden said. *Once he confesses his Guilt it will be standing Evidence against him. These criminals might flatter themselves that they deserve a pardon, as if for their sakes, vile Wretches, the whole Town must run the risk of their Houses being fired about their Ears, and having the Inhabitants butchered. One can scarce be thoroughly satisfied when it is that they do speak the Truth.*

The signed confessions were especially useful, because living blacks could not testify against whites.

In their confessions, Quack and Cuffee named thirty other blacks they said were involved in Hughson's plot. Those men had been quickly rounded up and locked in the over-crowded dungeon.

Ending his case before the rapt jurors, the prosecutor concluded:

Gentlemen. It will appear to you in the course of the evidence for the King upon this trial, that John Hughson was the chief Contriver, Abettor and Encourager of all this Mystery of Iniquity – That it was He who advised and procured secret and frequent meetings of the Negroes and the rest of the conspirators, at his house, there to form and carry on the horrible Conspiracies. That it was He that swore the Negroes Quack and Cuffee, with many others, and himself too, into this direful Plot. That it was He who devised Firebrands, Death and Destruction to be sent among you – He – Murderous and Remorseless He! Infamous Hughson! Gentlemen, this is that Hughson! whose Name, and most detestable Conspiracies will no doubt be had in everlasting Remembrance, to his eternal Reproach, and stand recorded to Posterity. This is the Man! This, the Grand Incendiary! That arch rebel against God, his King and his Country. Gentlemen, behold the Author and Abettor of all the late conflagrations, Terrors and Devastation that have befallen this City.

The jurors filed out, silently; there was buzzing in the gallery.

The jury convicted all three on all charges.

The dungeon was becoming filled as more and more blacks were arrested. Many sought mercy by confessing and naming other blacks. Like a contagion, Hughson's Plot spread through the city.

To save time, the thirty-day delay between conviction and sentencing was eliminated.

John Hughson was sentenced to hang. On a legal technicality, he could not be sentenced to be burned, though many of the spectators would have liked to see that. But like Caesar, his body would be chained after death to a high post for all to see. One black and one white. Equality in death. But not really. Many more blacks were waiting to die.

Sarah Hughson also was sentenced to be hanged.

About the sentencing of Peggy Kerry, the prosecutor explained:

This court has never put to death a pregnant woman. There is precedent for the following decision. Marguerite Kerry is sentenced to be hanged. But the execution of said sentence shall be delayed until after the birth of her child. One week after that birth, she shall be hanged by the neck until dead.

Peggy pressed her hands to her rounded abdomen. She dared not smile.

Her child would be allowed to live!

70. MARY

I dreamed I was a giant spider. The jailer Mills – I was still hiding in his apartment – was in charge of buying food for the prisoners in the dungeon, so he was sent papers about each sentence, to know how much food to buy. The night before my dream he began reading them off:

Caesar Vaarck, to be hanged; Prince, to be hanged; Fortune, to be hanged; Cato, to be hanged; Venture, to be hanged; Galloway, to be hanged; Frank, to be hanged; Harry, to be hanged; York, to be hanged; Othello, to be hanged. Oh, here's two that won't be hanged.

Who is that?

Quack and Cuffee.

But they was two of the loudest at the party. They gonna go free?

I didn't say that. They're gonna be burned to death. They chain them to a pole and put kindling and wood all around them and set it afire and while they scream the people come and watch them burn.

Eew. That must hurt.

I think that's the idea. But it's not the worst thing the prosecutors have come up with. A few years back they built a grill as long as a man, and filled it with coals, and chained a Negro to the grill and slow-roasted him alive. His screams could be heard for three miles. It took him six hours to die. Hundreds of folks crowded around to yell and make jokes and watch the fellow get roasted.

All of a sudden I felt sick. I reached under the bed and pulled out the chamber pot just in time to vomit up everything I had ate that day, and then everything I had ate the day before. I laid on the bed sweaty and shivering while the jailer finished his count to hisself.

You've been been a busy girl, Mary Burton. They'll start off tomorrow by hanging Caesar Vaarck, and by the time they're done they'll hang seventeen Negroes, burn thirteen Negroes, hang one white man and hang two white white women. That's thirty-three dead altogether.

One more white man would be added later – a priest – but I didn't know that yet.

I still felt sick when I finally fell asleep. That's when I had the spider dream. In the dream this spider was on the roof of City Hall. It had built a great big web that stretched over the whole city. There were lots of black bugs caught in the web. Somehow I had a spyglass with me, like the one Captain Anders had on the Catherine when he was looking at the storm. I turned the spyglass to the web and saw that what I thought was bugs was really people. Some of them was dead. Others was flailing their arms and legs about, trying to get unstuck. Then I turned around and pointed the spyglass at the spider. His face looked just like the Horseman, only without his wig. You wouldn't expect a spider to wear a wig. But while I was looking the spider turned into me. That was scary. I screamed and woke up. I used to like spiders when I played with them in Belfry. But not this big a one. Dreams is the strangest things in the world. Or maybe they ain't even in the world, because we can't see them when our eyes are open.

This one made me think I should go get my money and leave this place. So I changed from my night dress to my day dress – the jailer was gone by then – and I went down the hall to see the Horseman. He was not wearing his wig this time. I don't know when he looks funnier, with his wig or without. The room was warm but he was still wearing his coat and waistcoat as he sat behind his desk. Outside the window were seventeen pigeons. On his desk, which usually had a lot of papers, there was only one. I was about to tell him that in my dream he was a spider, but I was afraid he might get angry. Some people just don't like spiders. Then I was about to ask him where is my money, when he said, *Mary, just who I want to see. I was going to send for you.*

What for?

He looked at the only paper on his desk.

Do you know a man named John Ury?

I don't think so. Who is he?

This man passes as a schoolmaster, the Horseman said, *but we have been told that secretly he is a despised Roman Catholic Priest, and an abettor of the conspiracy. I want to get to the bottom of this. At the party at Hughson's that you have often described, when the plans were laid to fire and murder, was this white man Ury present?*

This was foolish. *I told you the very first time,* I said, *that the only white people there besides me and young Sarah Hughson were the two older Hughsons and Peggy Kerry. I can't change my memory now.*

No, I suppose you cannot, the Horseman said.

I could see that he was upset. *But there was this white man,* I said, *with a very short name, who every night since Christmas slept at Hughson's, and many times he and Hughson would disappear down into the basement and talk privately.*

Did you hear what they said?

No, they was down in the basement. But what could they be talking about every day, in private, if it was not this plot?

That's a very good point, Mary.

The Horseman stood then, and come around his desk and said, *Come with me, Mary.* He led me down the stairs and then down the other stairs to the dungeon. There was a lot of Negroes there and one short white man I could see. *Is that the man you saw speaking with Hughson every day?* he asked.

That's the man, I said.

The Horseman nodded. What with one thing and another they found some Negroes who said this fellow name of Ury had been telling them to join a plot to burn the town and kill the people, and that him being a priest he could forgive them of their sins. So they held a trial in the court and asked me about the priest and here is what I said:

Why I have seen Ury very often at Hughson's about Christmas and new-year, and then he stayed away about a fortnight or three weeks, and returned again. I have often seen him in company with Hughson, his wife and Peggy, and several Negroes, talking about the plot, burning the fort first, and then the dock; and upon some of the Negroes saying they were afraid of being damned for being concerned in the plot, I heard Ury tell them they need not fear doing of it, for that he could forgive them their sins as well as God Almighty, and would forgive them. They were to burn the whole town and to kill the people: Ury was to be captain of a company of Negroes, and he was to begin the fire where he lodged; that when they were once together above stairs, Ury, Hughson, his wife and Peggy, and I went up, but when I came up stairs, Ury had a book in his hand, and bid me go away, and asked me what business I had there, and said they did not call me, and he was angry and shut the door too again, and I looked under it, and there was a black ring upon the floor, and things in it that seemed to look like rats, I don't know what they were. Another time I heard him talking with the Negroes, Quack and others, about the plot, and turned the Negroes out of the room, and asked me to swear? and I said I would swear if they would tell me what I was going to swear, but they would have me swear first; and Hughson and his wife went and fetched silks and gold rings, and offered them to me in case I would swear, but I would not, and they said I was a fool; and Ury they told me he could forgive sins as well as God, I answered I thought it was out of his power. One night, some time about new-year, I was listening at the door of the room upon the stairs, where there was Ury, Hughson, his wife, Vaarck's Caesar, Prince, Cuffee and other Negroes; and I looked through the door and saw upon the table a black thing like a child, and Ury had a book in his hand and was reading, but I did not understand the language; and having a spoon in my hand, I happened to let it drop upon the floor, and Ury came out of the room, running after me down stairs, and he fell into a tub of water which stood at the foot of the stairs, and I ran away. When they were doing any thing extraordinary at nights, they would send me to bed.

Ury did his own defense and said he had never met Hughson or Mrs. Hughson or Peggy or me. The trial took nine hours. In fifteen minutes the jury come back. They found him guilty.

The Horseman told Mr. Zenger who owns the newspaper that this priest was behind the whole plot. That probably he was a Spanish spy who wanted to destroy the city so the Spanish who was at war with us British could come in and take it over. That is why the first thing they burned was the fort. So the newspaper said how Hughson's plot and the Negro Plot had all the time been the Priest's Plot, according to the judge. They had finally gotten to the bottom of it, the Horseman said. The priest John Ury was sentenced to be hanged by the neck until he was dead, the fourth white person to get that sentence.

71. JOHN PETER ZENGER

The priest wrote a statement for the Weekly Journal:

I am soon going to suffer a death attended with ignominy and pain; but it is the cup that my heavenly father has put into my hand, and I drink it with pleasure; it is the cross of my dear redeemer, I bear it with alacrity; knowing that all that live godly in Christ Jesus, must suffer persecution; and we must be made in some degree partakers of his sufferings before we can share in the glories of his resurrection. And I am to appear before an awful and tremendous God, a being of infinite purity and unerring justice, a God who by no means will clear the guilty, that cannot be reconciled either to sin or sinners; now this is the being at whose bar I am to stand, in the presence of this God, the possessor. Never had I any knowledge or confederacy with white or black as to any plot; I protest that the witnesses are perjured.

I have not more to say by way of clearing my innocence, knowing that to a true Christian unprejudiced mind, I must appear guiltless; but however, I am not very solicitous about it. I rejoice, and it is now my comfort (and that will support me and protect me from the crowd of evil spirits that I must meet within my flight to the region of bliss assigned me) that my conscience speaks peace to me.

Indeed, it may be shocking to some serious Christians, that the holy God should suffer innocence to be slain by the hands of cruel and bloody persons; (I mean the witnesses who swore against me), indeed, there may be reasons assigned for it; but, as they may be liable to objections, I decline them; and shall only say, that this is one of the dark providences of the great God, in his wise, just and good government of this lower earth.

In fine, I shall depart this waste, this howling wilderness, with a mind serene, free from all malice, with a forgiving spirit, so far as the gospel of my dear and only redeemer obliges and enjoins me to, hoping and praying, that Jesus, who alone is the giver of repentance, will convince, conquer and enlighten my murderers' souls, that they may publicly confess their horrid wickedness before God and the world, so that their souls may be saved in the day of the Lord Jesus.

72. MARY

In the streets people was reading the newspaper and shaking their heads. I asked the Horseman if this meant that Mr. Hughson and Mrs. Hughson and Peggy Kerry and all them slaves they was planning to hang and burn in the next few days would be set free.

Why would you think that, Mary? he said. *They are all still guilty. It's just that the priest put them up to it.*

So I asked him when I would get my money. He said he would write to the Common Council about that. Which is a tune I had heard before.

73. CAESAR

The gallows were built north-east of the city limits, beside the vast acreage of the Negro burial grounds. The choice made sense. After the blacks were hanged their bodies could be buried quickly. But not so with Caesar. His remains would remain on view for many weeks.

From the dungeon he was led to a cart and climbed in, his hands trussed behind his back, constables armed with cutlasses riding in the cart on either side of him. Two others, armed with rifles, would walk behind the cart. Still others were stationed along the route that the small procession would take. A rumor had been spreading that someone or some group would attempt to rescue Caesar before the hanging. How the rumor started was not known, nor who the alleged rescuers might be. It made no sense to Horsmanden. How could he be taken? Where could he be hidden? Still, the judge was taking no chances.

A small crowd had gathered outside City Hall to watch the carriage depart. Many shouted their views, loud, contrasting.

Burn him! Hanging is too good for him! He should be drawn and quartered! Free him, free them all, there was no plot! The girl and the judge are fools!

The shouts on either side struck Caesar's ears like paper darts, unheard. His mind was riveted by fourteen words that had ruled his fitful final night. *I will be hanged as a slave. But I shall die like a king.*

His blouse and trousers were clean. A constable that morning had tossed fresh clothes onto his mat. At first he ignored them; what was the point? He could see their reasoning. When his body was hung on chains from a high pole the sun would make clean clothes more visible in the city. But soon he changed his mind. Dying clean would at least afford a semblance of dignity.

Peggy did not go to the execution. Nor were any of the other prisoners taken to the site. Why risk the unfettered rage of a horde of desperate men? Not with those rumors afoot.

I will be hanged as a slave. But I shall die like a king.

Caesar had attempted to translate that thought into the Muktu language. He could not do so. In eighteen months he had lost much of his native tongue. He was English now.

That thought bothered him as much as his impending death.

The large wooden wheels of the cart, three feet in diameter, began to turn, creaking. The cart moved slowly up Broad Way, pulled by a sleek black colt, driven by another constable. Daniel Horsmanden himself fell in line behind the cart, wearing a light blue suit, a red waistcoat with gold buttons, white blouse trimmed with lace at the cuffs and collar, white stockings, buckled black shoes, his freshly washed formal white wig. He had solved the conspiracy that had threatened the entire city. This being the first execution, he would take his figurative bows at the gallows.

Throngs did not line the entire route but rather gathered in small knots at intersections to shout their feelings. At Cortland Street: *Burn them all, like they burned the fort.* And, *Free your slaves, free your fears!* At John Street: *Hey, black man, where's your white whore?* And, *Horsmanden is a horse's ass.* At Fair Street: *Without slaves we'd starve.* And, *With them you'll get your throat cut.*

Caesar's ears were closed to the shouts. The judge heard them but looked straight ahead, impassive except for an occasional twitch of his right eye.

The morning still was young but the air was moist and already the sun was fierce. New York in August. Like the rumors of rescue, mosquitoes whined around most every head. A large one landed on a roll of fat on Horsmanden's neck. He slapped at it, drawing blood. Not for the first time he thought of leaving New York, but right now it was the best of stepping stones.

His handling of the conspiracy had made his name known from Boston to Philadelphia.

The route swung onto the High Road to Boston, the onlookers forming a ragged parade as they followed behind the prisoner and the judge, past the city limit and down a small valley between Windmill Hill and Potbakers Hill, where the landscape formed a natural amphitheater. It was filled with spectators, many hundreds, perhaps a thousand – a tenth of the city – gazing down to where the gallows stood mute and

ominous. The marchers veered off into the crowd as the cart creaked and
rattled down behind a wooden platform. The hangman, dressed all in
black, a mask hiding all but his eyes, stood at the ready, holding a thick
rope with a noose at the end.

They will hang me as a slave. But I shall die as a king.

The elders, when age had robbed them of restful sleep, used to
debate from dusk till dawn what happened after death. What came next?
It had always seemed to Caesar a useless preoccupation. Soon he would
find the answer.

Constables had formed a line about twenty feet in front of the
gallows lest anyone try to interfere. Daniel Horsmanden noticed that
almost all of the spectators were white – men, women, even children
brought to see the spectacle. But at the far end of the amphitheater he
saw at least a hundred Negroes together, watching. He approached the
captain of the guard.

What's going on over there?

Nothing so far, judge.

Are they free Negroes or slaves?

A mix of both, I would imagine.

*You would imagine! If they're slaves they're breaking the law. No three may
congregate in public.*

Would you have us disperse them?

Of course! You've heard the rumors.

*They're a hundred yards away, Judge. They can't interfere with the execution
from there. Suppose we order them to disperse, at the point of rifles. And they don't
move. What would you want then? A massacre?*

Horsmanden looked about, impatient to get on with the hanging.

Very well. Just keep a wary eye on them.

The captain stalked away shaking his head. Horsmanden
approached the grass before the gallows. Caesar had been led up three
wooden steps, the hangman was about to slip the noose over his head.

Wait! Mr. Hangman, the judge said. *Caesar Vaarck, you are about to meet
your maker. Do you have anything to confess now, to cleanse your soul? This is your
last chance.*

Caesar looked down at the judge and said nothing.

Very well. Proceed.

Horsmanden stepped to the side. The hangman slipped the noose
over Caesar's head, tightened the knot. Expectant silence enveloped the
amphitheater. The voice of a child could be heard asking, *Daddy, what
are they doing?* Just then a commotion erupted at the line of constables
guarding the gallows. Two were thrown to the ground like dolls as the

slave Zion burst between them, leaped onto the platform, raised a knife high, and as the hangman still holding tight to the rope bent out of his way, afraid for his life, Zion slashed down at the rope and severed it.

The hangman, who had been pulling the rope taut over a horizontal bar, tumbled off the platform. Hush prevailed. No one was sure what had happened. Caesar remained still in the noose, the rope dangling behind him. Zion dropped the knife. The Negroes to the side began to cheer, wave their arms in the air, shout in unison *Zi-on Zi-on Zi-on*. Whether they had seen Zion cut the rope or thought he had killed the hangman was not clear. Horsmanden looked at them, feared a rebellion brewing, turned to the captain of the guard, who was dealing with the nearer emergency. *Grab that man!* the captain shouted. The constables dared not move until they saw the knife on the ground. Then four of them leaped onto the platform and grabbed Zion, two by each arm. He did not resist. The crowd began to murmur as spectators who had blinked asked their neighbors what they had missed. The hangman, unhurt, most likely white-faced under his mask, climbed back onto the platform from the rear.

Arrest that man! Take him to the dungeon, the judge said.

John Vaarck, who had been watching from nearby, scurried to confront the judge. *Arrest him on what charge?* he asked.

Attempted murder! the judge replied.

There was no attempted murder! Vaarck shouted in his face. *A thousand witnesses will testify that Zion could easily have killed the hangman if that was his intent. All he did was sever a rope. Is that now a crime in New York colony?*

Flustered, Horsmanden said, *Interfering with justice, then!*

Vaarck shook his head. *You were about to hang my Caesar. You will do so in another five minutes. Is that interfering with justice? It's hardly a case for the courts. I will deal with Zion myself, as I am permitted under the law.*

The spectators were getting restless, some yelling *Hang him!* some yelling *Free him!*, some referring to Caesar, some to Zion.

Get him out of here, the judge said to Vaarck. *See that he behaves or the fault will be yours.*

With his bad leg Vaarck climbed with difficulty onto the platform. The constables released Zion. Vaarck took his shoulder and led him away, the black onlookers still cheering his name. The hangman removed the spent noose from Caesar's neck. Tossing it aside, he leaned under the platform and pulled up another rope, the noose already fashioned. He placed it over Caesar's head, slung the remainder over a horizontal metal bar, pulled at the slack. Walking away, Zion looked over his shoulder.

Caesar, trying not to smile, offered the slightest of nods, so slight that no one but Zion noticed. Then he looked straight ahead again.

The words kept reverberating in his head

They will hang me as a slave. But I shall die as a king.

In the stillness of the air he felt a sight breeze on his face. Seeking its source he glanced upward, and saw a large bird hovering about ten feet above him, about ten feet in front of him, treading the air like a hummingbird, large as a parrot. The parrot was turquoise and blue and green. With his last breath Caesar decided this: The parrot was a messenger of history, who when the time was appropriate would tell the world the story of a king.

A weight fell from his shoulders. His legs dropped beneath him. The noose broke his neck. He did not hear those in the crowd who were applauding his execution, or those who were shouting epithets in six tribal languages, or those who looked on silently, their faces frozen with grief, or those who quietly wept.

74. Peggy

Word from the gallows reached the dungeon quickly

by way of the constables. How Zion had slashed the rope before Caesar was hanged. How Caesar, on the gallows, still had refused to confess. How John Hughson, hanged an hour later, also did not confess. How spectators had begun to say that, if these men had not confessed in the face of imminent death, perhaps they were truly not guilty. How the bodies of both men had been wrapped in chains, as per their sentences, placed in the wooden cart and how a small boat carried them then to a small island in the nearby Collect Pond, where they were strung up on poles 33 feet high, where they would remain for weeks or even months as a warning to other criminals, close enough to the city to be clearly seen but far enough away so as not to be smelled.

Alone in her cell, Peggy was more concerned about what would become of her child. The loss of her own life in the dark damp dungeon would be not much of a loss at all. But now that she was eating fresh food every day – even more than before she was imprisoned – she was confident the infant would be born strong enough to survive. Losing her mother and her twin at birth, in a Newfoundland that seemed a thousand miles and a thousand years away, had been enough; she would not lose her child as well. But who would rescue it from the dungeon, nurse it, nurture it, love it, raise it?

She did not know any of the free blacks in the city, although it was said there were several hundred of them. The white she would have turned to was in the dungeon with her, scheduled to be hanged: Mrs. Hughson. Young Sarah had confessed to knowledge of the so-called plot, backing Mary Burton's words. Her trial had been postponed. She had recanted her confession, her trial had been postponed again. Even if she eventually were freed she was too stupid, Peggy thought, to raise a child on her own.

She choked on the next name that came to mind: Mary. Mary who almost alone had put the word conspiracy on every wagging tongue. Months before the uproar erupted Caesar had offered Mary a shilling each week if she would help Peggy in her time of pregnancy, and with the child after. Mary had said she might do so for a white baby *but not for no half-colored one.* Worse, she later told Horsmanden, and testified at Caesar's trial, that the money he had offered her had been not to help with the child but to buy her silence about the Negro plot.

One or two of the country white women to whom Caesar had delivered bread might be amenable to raising a mulatto child, but she doubted that their husbands would.

John Vaarck's wife Stephanie might take the baby, Peggy thought. Then she recalled the rumor that Stephanie Vaarck was dying, or even dead.

Her brain lit up as if a match had been struck within. That woman! What was her name? The one who months ago had been lashed near to death by the Common Whipper outside City Hall. Peggy had helped her, befriended her. Artemis, that was her name. Artemis Clay. Her only crime had been sleeping with a Negro. She might love to raise a mulatto child! But the flame quickly flickered and died. Fleeing the harassment of her neighbors, Peggy recalled, Artemis had moved to Boston – where her so-called shame had followed her like a disease. She had drowned herself in Boston Bay.

What of the Widow Williams? She certainly was wealthy enough to raise a child in fine fashion. Peggy hated her for stealing Billy away, but she could forgive that for the sake of the child. Might the widow take him, out of guilt – she who had made her fortune importing and selling slaves? It was hardly likely.

Her reverie of despair was interrupted by a knock on the cell door. A key turned in the lock, a constable whom she knew stood in the doorway.

Horsmanden said to tell you you have a visitor.
Don't tease me, Hack, we both know visitors are not allowed.
No, really. Horsmanden personally approved it.
What, the old goat is in a good mood because the hangings started? Who is it?
The old goat don't tell us young sheep nothing. I got no idea.

The door closed, clicked shut. Peggy waddled back to the bench, sat gingerly, her left arm cradling her huge belly, and pondered. She felt tired, so tired.

She recalled imagining walking out onto the ice where the seal pups were battered and lying in the snow and letting the Newfoundland cold stop her heart. The New York noose would do the same.

75. MARY

I still ain't got my money. They been hanging people every day and burning people every day and the Horseman says the trials is over, the plot has been uprooted with the hanging of that priest, so they won't be needing me any more. They has hanged seventeen coloreds and burned thirteen and hanged three whites and are waiting only on Peggy Kerry to deliver her baby and they will be done. I didn't go watch any of them hangings or burnings like lots of people did, why would I want to watch something like that? I just wanted the money they promised.

The Horseman told me it was safe to leave the jailer's apartment now, that I was a hero in the city. He said when John Hughson was convicted the city had bought my denture to keep me around for the trials. I had done good work so now they was tearing up my denture and I was a free person, free to leave. I told him I knew a place where I could stay but I didn't have money for food because I ain't got my hundred pounds yet. He reached into the pocket of his waistcoat and pulled out a leather case and from it he give me three one-pound notes.

That should keep you in victuals for a while, he said.

I didn't know what victuals was, but I figured out pretty quick that he meant vittles. Because I left his office hungry.

If I was a hero in the city like he said, the city had a odd way of showing it. When I walked through the streets the people started calling me all kinds of names. Both white folks and Negroes alike. It weren't nice names. It wasn't hero names. I wondered where he got that idea.

I won't tell the names they called me. They didn't make me feel good at all. The one that upset me most was *liar.* I sat at that New Year's

feast and heard them planning to set fires and kill white people. I told
what I heard. If I was lying, how come all them juries believed me? If
I was lying, how come they killed all those Negroes and the Hughsons?
People on the streets got no business calling me names. Maybe it was
because of the newspaper. Here is what it wrote: <u>Looking back now that
the trials are over, the city had been afraid for some time of a slave revolt
here like the ones in the Kerry Beans</u> (they spelled it wrong.) <u>Burton's
story – whether true or not – followed by the actual fires, sparked those
fears and created a blazing inferno that needed to be fed.</u>

I don't even know what that means.

Anyhow, the place I meant to stay was Hughson's Tavern. I walked
over there by the river and of course it was still closed, what with Mr.
and Mrs. Hughson both hanged and young Sarah still in the dungeon
whilst the judges decided what to do with her. I went around to the side
and found Room 2, where I had lived as a denture. At first the window
was stuck but I pushed and pulled and finally got it open. I climbed in the
way Caesar used to climb in to visit Peggy in room 13. The bed was still
there, some of my clothes was still there – the city had bought me new
clothes for the trials – and the box with my Denture Dairy was still there.
I sat on the bed and opened the box and started a new sheet of paper,
writing:

Mary Burton's No More Denture Dairy

I sat and sat but couldn't think of what to write. Maybe because
I was hungry. So I climbed back out the window. I was going to go to
Vaarck's bake shop for a blueberry tart but then I didn't feel like going
there. So I went the other way, to the Black Horse Tavern. That's at the
Corner of Smith Street and Garden Street. Them taverns usually has
food available for visitors. But while I was walking there, across Little
Queen Street, I started getting afraid. Someone was following me. He
was a white man and dressed in a nice suit but every time I turned or
stopped he turned and stopped, and when I started again he started
again. He followed me right to the door of the Black Horse Tavern. But
when I went in he kept on going. So maybe he was not following me at
all. Maybe I was just down to my last nerve. After I showed them in the
tavern a one-pound note from the Horseman to prove I could pay, I had
myself a bowl of pig stew, and a chunk of bread which was hard and
not as good as Vaarck's bread. When I went back home I climbed in the
window and wrote on the first page of my No More Denture Dairy:

*It is August already and I still aint got my Hundred
Pounds Sterling.*

Oops, I forgot something. You have to be nice to your Dairy. So I wrote above that:

Dear No Denture Dairy.

Then I fell asleep on my old bed like a tired puppy and slept until light come in through the window and woke my eyes.

I went back to that same tavern for breakfast, which was the same pig stew and tasted pretty good, with lots of salt and beans. Afterwards I wanted to sit in the sun on the veranda at Hughson's but the table was gone and all the chairs was gone. They must have been stole, which people do when you get hanged. So I climbed in and got my Dairy and climbed out and sat on the floor of the veranda with my legs crossed under me. I was still trying to think what to write when this man come walking along. He was dressed like the Horseman in a blue suit and white stockings and shoes with buckles but he was not fat like the Horseman and he wasn't wearing a wig. At first I was scared because of the way people been acting and me all alone out there with him. He looked sort of like the man who followed me. But surprise of surprises, we had this nice conversation

Are you Mary Burton, or are you not?

Since if I am not I am nobody, I guess I am.

Very good, Mary, you're just the person I want to see.

Which was nice, I ain't been told that very much at all.

And who be you?

My name is Mr. Jones, but that's not important. What is important is that I've heard you have not been paid the money you are owed by the city for all of your testimony. I am here to help you get that money.

Now he had my full attention, as they say.

What I got to do?

I see you have paper and pencils there. That's perfect.

He pulled a folded sheet of paper from the pocket of his yellow waistcoat and unfolded it.

There are five names on here. You just have to copy these names onto your paper, in your hand.

And then I will get my money?

I'm sure you will get it within forty-eight hours. Maybe sooner.

So I copied them names. Then he said I should take another sheet of paper and copy them one more time. So I did that too. Here was the names:

Alexander
Colden
Livingstone

Osborne

Clarke

Now what I got to do, I asked him.

He took his paper back and folded it into his pocket and left me the other two.

Do you know where the print shop is?

Sure. It's right across from the Black Horse Tavern.

Good. You are to go there and ask to see Mr. Zenger. He is the printer. If they say he is too busy, you tell him you are Mary Burton and you have new information about the plot. I'm sure he will see you.

Then what?.

You give him one of the papers you just wrote, and tell him these was the real bosses of the plot to burn the city. And that you are on your way to City Hall to give the names to Judge Horsmanden. I'm sure he will be interested.

What if they ask me how I know these names is true?

You ate supper last night at the Black Horse, did you not?

Yes, duck stew.

You tell him these men were there too, and they were talking about the fires, and how next time they would get the Negroes to set all the fires at the same time.

What if these men were not there last night? What if they check?

But they were, Mary, God's honest truth. You just did not see them.

But I heard them?

Right. You heard them. You tell Horsmanden that and you will get your money. Nobody will get hurt, and you will get your due. It's only right.

How would I know their names? I don't know many men in ruffles.

Good question. After they left, you asked some man who was eating there who they was. And you wrote down their names on these papers.

I guess I can do that, to get my hundred pounds sterling. I'll go to the newspaper right now.

Then you might even have your money this afternoon.

Which got me pretty excited.

So I walked back to the Black Horse and across the street to the print shop. I asked for Mr. Zenger and a boy about my age who was carrying a bundle of newspapers said he was in the composing room. *Where's that?* I asked, and he showed me. In the composing room was high tables and on the tables was flat wooden boxes divided into little compartments. When I looked into them the compartments had a bunch of tiny ABCs in them. Two men wearing dark blue aprons with dirty fingers was picking up the little letters and making them into words. I guess this was like a school for grown-ups and they was learning how to spell. One of the men looked at me and came over and asked me what

I wanted. I said I had something important for Mr. Zenger. He said he
was Mr. Zenger. So I pulled one of the papers with the five names on it
from my pocket and gave it to him. *What's this?* he asked. I told him my
name was Mary Burton and these are the men in ruffles behind the fire
plot, and I was going to City Hall right now to give the names to the
Horseman so he could arrest them. *Men in ruffles, huh?* he said and took
off his apron and asked if I would mind if he walked with me to see the
judge. Which of course I did not mind, it was nice to have company
especially with people in the street calling me a liar. Mr. Zenger seemed
like a nice man and said I had done the best thing in coming to him first,
and as we left the composing room he said to the other man, *I'll be redoing
the front page when I come back,* and he sounded all excited about that. As
we walked together to City Hall he stopped to go into a building for a
minute and then came out and we continued on our way. The sky was
cloudy and looked like rain but it didn't which I was glad about since I
did not have my coat with me. Also I remembered I had left my Dairy on
the veranda and it might get ruined if it rained.

At City Hall I ran up the stairs to the second floor. Mr. Zenger
walked slower behind me. I burst into the Horseman's office. He had his
jacket off and his wig.

Mary, what a nice surprise, he said.

I got to ask you something, I said. *This morning you said I was a hero. So how
come people in the streets is calling me a liar? That hurts my feelings.*

He stood from behind his desk and come put his arm around my
shoulder.

That's not nice of them, he said. *But you shouldn't get upset. It's not about you.*

Who else then?

*It's about money, Mary. Those people we had to execute for what they did were
slaves. That means they were property of their owners. When we hanged them or
burned them their owners were losing money. They had paid for those slaves. Now they
would have to buy new slaves. People don't like it when their property is taken away.
That's why they're angry. It's their own fault that they bought slaves who were not
loyal. But we did what we did to protect the entire city. And you helped us do that.*

I felt a little bit better, and then Mr. Zenger come into the room and
I remembered why I had come.

Zenger, what are you doing here?

It sounded like the Horseman did not like Mr. Zenger. I thought
they both was nice.

*Judge, you've given me the cold shoulder throughout the entire conspiracy
investigation,* Mr. Zenger said. *But I thought I'd give you a preview of tomorrow's
edition. Did you give him the paper, Mary?*

I pulled it from my pocket and handed it to the Horseman. He looked at it.

What's this? he said,

Them's the real people behind the plot.

His face turned red as a radish.

Mary, do you know who these people are?

They's men with ruffles, I said.

These are some of our leading citizens! Three lawyers and two bankers. They can't be involved. Why do you say they are?

So I told him about the Black Horse Tavern and how I heard them talking last night.

The Horseman started breathing heavy and blowing air out his mouth, hard.

Mr. Zenger said, *In case it is of interest, judge, I just spoke with Alexander. He confirms that the five of them had dinner at the Black Horse last night. They did not notice Mary there, but you know how big that place is, and how they keep the lanterns turned low so you can't see the gristle in the beef.*

You can't print this, Zenger!

How are you going to stop me, judge? We fought that battle six years ago.

Do you know what the people will say?

I suspect many will say that since Miss Burton is ly … is mistaken in this case, she may have been mistaken in every case since Christmas, and that thirty-three people have been put to death who were innocent.

You would love that, Zenger.

I just print the news. And this is certainly news. I won't be telling people what to think.

Who put you up to this, Mary?

I don't understand.

You and I know, Zenger, that people are using Mary who want to stop the investigations.

I am just taking Mary at her word, judge. As you have for all these months.

The Horseman began pacing his small office the way Gweebarra used to pace in the barn when she wanted to get out for fresh air. I never thought of this before, maybe that's why they call him the Horseman.

That warning to the Negroes I gave you, about more plots brewing, the judge said. *Will you still print that?*

Of course. Right next to Mary's new charges.

At least that will save some of her credibility.

And yours.

You'd better print it.

Are you threatening me, judge?

No, I'm not threatening you. Now get the hell out of my office. Mary, I think I'll have your money tomorrow. But you may have to promise to leave town right after.

I think I can do that, I said.

I skipped down the stairs and tripped near the bottom and nearly fell and broke my head.

That man who give me those names was right! I'll be getting my money tomorrow!

76. JOHN PETER ZENGER

I assumed the judge was correct this time. The girl was being used, probably by the very men on her list. But she was not smart enough to realize it. This left me briefly with an ethical dilemma. If I was certain her charges were false, which I was, would it be proper to print them? Would I not knowingly be defaming these righteous men? But Mary did accuse them before the judge, who said he would investigate. This was news, as much as the charges she had made against the Negroes. It was not my task to protect my friends. I decided I would go ahead and print the story.

I was charmed by her description of the rich white men as *men with ruffles.* I definitely would quote that. It made me wonder if there was not a touch of the poet lodged somewhere in her dull brain. If so, in some unknowable way she might see the entire conspiracy, which rested solely on her words, as a kind of artistic creation.

77. MARY

I knew just what I would do with my money. I walked on up north until I come to that carpenter shop with the pretty wooden carriage outside. I ask the carpenter if I could climb in and see what it feels like. *Are your hands clean?* he asks me, and I show him they are. *I guess that would be all right* he says, and he pulls open the door and in I climb. The seats is all red leather trimmed with gold. Perfect to match my footman Jarvis's uniform that I will have. I lean back and it is so comfortable I feel like a rich lady already. When I climb down I tell him not to sell this today, I will be buying it tomorrow. He says, *I doubt you have* *enough money girlie. That costs thirty-five pounds sterling.* I tell him I will have the money tomorrow, guaranteed.

A man is standing nearby, slim and looks like a workman, his face tan, who been talking to the carpenter. I ask him if he works there. He says not no more, not since they finished ordering coffins. I ask him if he wants a job. He says he might. I ask him if he can drive this carriage. *Ain't nothing to that,* he says, *so long as you put a horse up front.* So I say, *Do you want to be my footman? I would pay your room and board and some wages, but we would have to go out of town.* He says sounds good, he ain't got no problem with that, he's been thinking about moving on anyways. So I say, *Good.* He says his name is Reg. *That's too short,* I say. *Well,* he says, *my full name is Reginald Spartacus Anderson.* So I say that's much too long, how about I call you Jarvis? He says call me whatever you want, so long as you don't call me late for dinner. He laughs, and I laugh too. Be good to have a footman who laughs. So I say we got a deal, and I am going up the road now to pick out my horse, you wanna come? He says sure, so we walk up the road to that farm pasture and the silver Gweebarra Number Two is still there among the blacks and the browns. I find the farmer in his barn, whose name is Cash, and tell him I want to buy that silver one tomorrow, and her name will be Silver. The farmer is happy. On the way back I ask the carpenter if he could make me a wooden trunk for my new clothes. He says if I really buy the carriage he will throw in the trunk for free. I don't want him throwing it in it will have nice new dresses and bonnets and shoes in it but he says he will be careful.

Dear No-Denture Diary,

I'm so excited I cant fall asleep, so I figure it's time to say hello to you. Today was the bested day of my whole life ever. I bought a fancy carriage that I will pay for tomorrow and I bought a horse named Silver that will pull the carriage that I will pay for tomorrow and I bought or rather hired a footman that will drive the carriage that I will pay for tomorrow. I was hungry then so I went to Vaarcks bake shop where I have not been for a while and I had me a blueberry tart. Nobody said nothing bad to me. Nobody said nothing at all. I thought, this is the last blueberry tart I will have in New York colony. Then I thought, maybe I will buy a box of them tomorrow to take in the carriage to somewhere. Then I went to Miss Nightingale's dress shop which is for fancy ladies on Broad Way. At first the sales lady said I cant afford anything in the shop but then the owner come out *from the back and said are you Mary Burton and I said yes. Do you have your money she ast and I said tomorrow so she told the sales girl to show me whatever I wanted but I could not take it with me until I paid for it tomorrow. I tried on this yellow dress that fit me perfeckly with long sleeves with lace at the end and more lace at the collar. I ast if it came in other colors and the lady said also in white pink and blue. I told her I would take one of each and also bonnets and petticoats and white stockings and shoes. The sales ladys eyes grew big as a horses. I told them my footman Jarvis would come by to get them tomorrow. Me what growed up in the Belfree Cathlic Orfinage. Whoowee! I didnt say that though. Now I will try again to sleep, cause tomorrow will be another big day.*

The sun was already high up outside the window when I woke up. I dressed quick in my old grey dress and took my box of pencils and dairy from Sister Beatrice and hurried to City Hall, where the Horseman had my money. He gave me 83 pounds instead of a hundred. I asked why and he said the city had some expenses with me. They had to buy my denture from John Hughson, and provide me with clothing and food during the trials, and he himself had given me three pounds. That added up to 17 pounds, he said, so there was 83 left. I didn't care, I will still be rich. He asked when I was leaving town and I said this very day. He thanked me for all I had done. I knew that my real father, that priest in Belfry, Father Burton, would be proud.

From there I hurried up to the pasture where my footman Jarvis was waiting for me. I paid for Silver and the farmer threw in a bridle and reins. Lots of people is throwing things in these days. Jarvis put the bridle on Silver and when he led her to the gate she started dancing and prancing like a girl going home from the orphanage. We walked her down the road to the carpenter where I paid him for the carriage and Jarvis hooked Silver on to it. The trunk the carpenter threw in Jarvis strapped to the back of the carriage with leather straps that was already there to hold the trunks of fancy ladies. Then we was off to Miss Nightingale's to get my dresses. I decided to wear one for our ride out of town so I put on the yellow one. Jarvis packed the others in the trunk and also my Dairy. I left my old dress and shoes in the little changing room and the sales lady asked what I wanted to do with them. *I'll throw them in,* I told her, and I climbed into the carriage outside. But after we rode a few feet I yelled *whoa,* as I used to do with Gweebarra, so Silver stopped when Jarvis pulled on the reins. I flew into the shop like a giant yellow butterfly.

Changed my mind about throwing it in, I said, and I took the grey dress I had been wearing. The reason being I had left in the pocket all the money I had left.

Where to now Miss Mary? my footman said, and I told him to drive us down to the Black Horse Tavern.

My home way from home, he said, which I did not know what he meant but no matter.

Are we going to get some vittles before we leave? he asked. I told him I was too excited to eat but I gave him a sixpence to get himself food while I crossed the street to the print shop. *Thank you mam,* he said. First time I ever was a mam.

In the print shop that smelled even more of ink today than yesterday Mr. Zenger was holding up a large sheet of paper.

Mary, he said. *You're just in time to see your story. Hot off the press. But you don't want to get ink on that pretty yellow dress.*

It didn't look hot but I asked if he could read it to me. He said he was busy with the printing but he would read me the first paragraph. So he did.

Mary Burton, the 16-year-old indentured servant whose court testimony led to the execution of 33 persons, leveled astonishing new charges Wednesday, accusing five prominent white civic leaders of planning a new plot to have Negro slaves burn the city. The men, who included three attorneys and two bankers, were labeled by Miss Burton as "men in ruffles." Judge Daniel Horsmanden seemed bemused, but said he would have no course but to investigate.

Mr. Zenger laid the large sheet of paper on the table. *You write good, with big words,* I told him. *Where is what the Horseman wrote?*

Right there near the bottom, he said. *But be careful of getting ink on your dress. It might never come out.*

It was hard to read leaning over. Mr. Zenger saw this and come and read it to me.

To Awaken the People to a Sense of Danger

You Negroes are treated here with great Humanity and Tenderness. Such worthless, detestable Wretches are many, it may be said most, of your Complexion, that no Kindness can oblige ye; there is such an Untowardness as it should seem, in the very Nature and Temper of ye, that ye grow cruel by too much Indulgence: So much are ye degenerated and debased below the Dignity of Humane Species, even the very Dogs will by their

**Actions express their Gratitude to the Hand
that feeds them, their Thankfulness for
Kindnesses; they will fawn and fondle upon
their Masters; nay, if any one should attempt
to assault them, they will defend them from
Injury to the utmost of their Power. Such is
the Fidelity of these dumb Beasts; but ye, the
Beasts of the People, though ye are clothed
and fed, and provided with all Necessaries
of Life, without Care; in Requital of your
Benefactors, in Return for Blessings ye give
Curses, and would scatter Firebrands, Death
and Destruction around them, destroy their
Estates and Butcher their Persons. Thus
monstrous is your Ingratitude!**

Sounds like the judge don't like Negroes much, I said to Mr. Zenger when he finished.

That would be a fair assumption, he said. *So, Mary, are you leaving the city?*

This very day.

Where will you be going?

I ain't sure yet. Someplace where people won't sneak up behind my back and try to kill or even poison me.

Sounds like a good plan. Good luck to you, Mary Burton. I won't shake your hand because mine is covered with ink.

I said goodbye and left the print shop. There was no black ink ruining my yellow dress, leastways not as far as I could see.

My footman was standing near my horse, drinking beer. He said we need to hurry to catch the last ferry of the day across the North River to Jersey Colony, but I told him I want to swing by the Collect first. I want to see if what everyone has been talking about is true. The footman said it surely is true, he gone over and seen it a few times himself. But I told him I want to see it for myself. So with me in my new finery like a fancy lady he drove over there. And it was true. The body of Caesar was hung up on a tall pole in chains, but his body which used to be black as black had been turned almost white by weeks in the sun. His face and hands and chest, and his arms where his shirt had been ripped off by the wind, and also his feet, were white as mine. A few feet away, hanging in chains on another pole, the face and hands and feet of John Hughson, which used to be all white, had been burned by the sun until they was black, black as barbecue and maybe crispy. Black and white had switched places. Nobody in the streets knew what it meant. Me for sure neither.

Them ugly decaying bodies, each color switched to the other, was the last items I saw before I left New York colony in my fancy carriage, dressed like a fancy lady. Only thing I forgot to bring was a box of blueberry tarts.

78. JOHN PETER ZENGER

In the ensuing months and years, the people of New York remained divided about the truth of Mary Burton's charges – about whether there had been a conspiracy or not, about whether those who had been hanged or burned had been guilty or not. Either way, the episode did not help Daniel Horsmanden's political future, as he had hoped it would. He never became governor.

No one disbelieved, however, that the bodies of the slave and the white man, hanging over the city, had, after several weeks in the sun, exchanged colors, the black slave turning white, the white inn-keeper turning black. The people could not disbelieve, because they could see this phenomenon with their own eyes. Myself among them.

79. NORA

By losing Peggy I became a writer. Not professional, not published, not yet, but maybe some day.

Starting to write stories was a way of passing the time that Peggy and I used to spend frolicking together; a way of avoiding the depression brought on by missing her. Her leaving was like losing a twin sister. My stomach would ache, my hands would ache even when I was at work in the cafe. There was no cure, until I discovered writing. I bought paper and pencils in St. John's and after work I would write, sometimes missing dinner. Or in the mornings before breakfast. At first mostly I wrote about her – about us. Our silly fish fights among the capelin. Just writing about that made me smile. Or wandering through the cemetery high above the sea, looking at the names on the tombstones, some of them already half worn away by the winds, wondering who they had been, making up stories about them, some strangely funny, some strangely sad. Or scaring one another by making the sounds of ghosts as we imagined ghosts might sound. I suspect we were far off on that one. Or trying in the graveyard to discover if she was Margaret or ~~Marguerite.~~ That, I admit, was hard to understand. She was who she was – whomever that was. Names aside, do any of us really know who we are?

At first I was writing true memories, but then I began mixing together truth and made up stories. Who was to say I couldn't, I wasn't showing them to anyone anyway. The first time I did this was when I heard from one of the fishermen that we in Newfoundland killed more baby seals for their white fur than any other place in the world. So I wrote about this wonderful small town where everyone was nice to each other. People helped out those who were sick, and cooked for those who were old and made clothing for those who were poor. Until spring came, and the men went out to the ice floes with big sticks and battered to death the innocent little seal pups to sell for their fur. I didn't tell what the story meant, anyone who read it could figure that out for themselves. At first I called the story *Blood on the Ice*. Then I thought of a title I liked better. I called it *Paradise*.

Came a time then when I didn't just not show the stories to anyone, I decided I had better hide them, so no one would read them by accident or by snooping. That was after I wrote a story called *Two Fathers*. The first father in the story was a fisherman who used to drink a lot, drank more and more until he could not stand up straight in his boat anymore and could no longer provide for his family. A lot of the people in the fishing village had sympathy for the man, because his wife had died many years before in childbirth, and left him with a little girl to raise, and he did not know how to do that. They figured that was an understandable reason, if not a good one, for a man to become a drunk. But the elders remembered that the fellow used to drink long before his wife died. They never told anyone, because they could not explain it. Sometimes things just are, and we don't know the reason. The other father in the story ran a bake shop. He was up at four in the morning baking the bread the fishermen wanted to take with them when they went out to sea before sunrise. He was always tired and always kind. If a fisherman could not pay for his bread this man would give it to him on credit, and let the man pay when he sold his catch. The people of the village thought the man was a saint. What they did not know was that many times, when his wife was out helping people, he would grab his daughter, who was twelve years old, throw her onto a bed and ravish her. He warned her he would kill her if she told anyone. This happened about once every week until the girl was fourteen. Then she decided she would not stand for it any more. She found an old cast iron frying pan in a dump, and she sneaked it home under her dress and hid it under her pillow. She promised herself that if he touched her again, she would smash his skull with the frying pan. For that one I couldn't decide between my first title, *Two Fathers*, or a different title, *The Frying Pan*. I also could not decide how to end it. In the very last scene the father is coming toward his daughter, with late afternoon sunlight dying in the window. As he comes closer she grips the heavy pan under the pillow. But I could not decide who should kill who. I never finished the story. That is the hardest part of being a writer, I think. There are so many different things that could happen, and you alone have to decide. It's not easy. How do you know which ending is right? In stories, is there any such thing as which is right?

Anyway, after I wrote about the two fathers I decided I had better make sure no one would ever read it. I thought a lot about a hiding place and chose the church. I rolled my stories together and went to the church one hot afternoon when no one was about. I picked a pew near the side, where nobody ever sat because it was behind a pole and you could not see the priest. The tops of the benches of the pews all opened up, and inside were Bibles for people to use. In this side pew the Bibles were covered with thick dust. I slipped my stories under the Bibles and closed the seat. I was sure no one would find them.

When I decided to come to New York to visit Peggy, and perhaps make my home here if it seemed agreeable, and packed my trunk and took a carriage to St. John's and boarded the boat, we were miles at sea before I realized I had forgotten to go to the church and retrieve my stories. There was no one in the Village of Carey, or in all of Newfoundland for that matter, whom I trusted enough to excavate the stories from under the dusty Bibles and send them to me without giving in to the temptation of reading them. Having been in New York for three years now, I realize how foolishly I overreacted. So what if they are found? Chances are I will never return to that place, and if I do, perhaps for a funeral or some other family event, what could be done to me? My father could carry out his threat and try to murder me, of course, but he is three years feebler now, and there are lots of iron frying pans about.

On the journey to New York I planned to write another story, or at the least make notes for one. Instead, I was able to compose but a single sentence:

The black water is a sea of ink through which the rudderless boat trembles like a trembling quill in the hand of a writer who dares not write what she wants.

I liked the sentence. It remains alone on a single sheet, in a trunk in my parlor, on top of my recent work.

Upon receiving her joyful letter some weeks ago about her fine job at the Hotel New York and her two beaus, one older but wealthy, the other young and handsome and finely sculpted, I had been ecstatic for her. I felt not a tendril of jealousy, of the pointless emotion of why her and not me. When you share a mind, indeed almost a body, as we did, such thoughts need not be quashed, repressed, because not for a second do they breathe the air. In the closeness of our breasts there was no space for them to take root.

Her letter happened to be the only one to arrive on the New York postal boat that day. I did not have to ring the bell for the other villagers. Reading it in a wash of joy, and with the cafe almost empty in mid-afternoon, I ran to Peggy's house – her former house – to show it to her Aunt Dottie, who loves Peggy almost as much as I do. I read it aloud to her and my joy became hers, I could see it in her flushing face. I think in that very instant the idea was confirmed in my little-used brain that I should sail to New York and visit Peggy. I read the letter again back in the cafe, told the good news to the early drinkers, all of whom know Peggy, of course, and then for a third time in my room, by lantern light, as night darkened the sea. The house was quiet. Out the window I could see the stars, but as I watched they became hidden by cloud cover. It was then that a nebbin of uncertainty began to niggle my brain. Something was wrong with her letter. I could not tell what it was, but a thin veil of fear settled over me. I read it again. Nothing wrong was visible.

Then I realized that what was wrong was not visible. It was something that was missing.

Years ago, when we were about 16 years old, we began going strolling with boys. That's what it was called, *going strolling*, because in the Village of Carey there was nothing else to do.

All the boys, except those who were too shy, wanted to stroll with Peggy, of course, with her beautiful face and lovely shape and flaming red hair. I had my share of strolls, with the shy boys or those whom Peggy had rejected. On the first walk we would stroll up or down the one street in the village, while the grown-ups on their porches nodded approval as we passed. Or not. A week or so later, if the same boy asked us again we would stroll holding hands. On the third stroll we would climb cemetery hill and watch the sun sinking into the sea, and, if we were daring, we might kiss a bit. On the way back from kissing we would hold our hands stiffly at our sides, as if to deny that any such thing had gone on; in our naivete we did not realize that was a sure sign that it had. Peggy and I several times discussed these strolls. Not to gossip about the boys – at least not much – but because we discovered we both had the same problem. When strolling with three or four different boys in the course, of say, a month, we could not remember which childhood stories or new jokes we had already told to which boy. Rather than be insulting, we stuttered into silence. The boys, it turned out, were having the same problem. This led to very quiet and therefore slightly embarrassing strolls. How much easier, we decided, if we each had only one boy companion.

Peggy's problem was resolved when she and Billy Reilly became taken with one another. This prevented other lads from asking her. I took a different approach. So as not to hurt the feelings of the boys when turning them down, I told them a doctor in St. John's had told me I might be suffering from a rare disease. They did not yet know what it was, but in the meantime I should not have any contact with boys. Although working in the cafe was alright. Whether the boys believed me or not was irrelevant. They were happy to save face. I used the time instead to fiddle with silly poetry I was trying to write.

What did these recollections have to do with Peggy's letter? Only this. She had mentioned two simultaneous beaus. Nothing wrong with that; we were older now. But knowing Peggy, she would have recalled our earlier difficulties, and would have joked about them. Peggy was never one to pass up a chance to be funny. At least with me. That was a slim reed on which to hang a sense of trouble, but I did. I became worried about her. I felt that something in her situation in New York was not right. I did not mention this to anyone, not even to her Aunty Dottie, who would have told me I was being absurd. I tried to tell myself that. But some subtle worry-wart place in my brain was making me anxious, was telling me I should go there as soon as possible. Before it was too late.

Too late for what? I had no idea.

I began to hoard my money for passage. I was of age now, my parents could not prevent me from leaving. On the boat my anxiety increased as we neared New York; perhaps that's why I could not write.

My intuition was proven correct within minutes after we docked.

Waiting at the pier were two carriages. When I approached one, a fit young man with curly brown hair and a slightly pocked face hoisted my two bags onto it. I climbed in, holding my petticoats close. The conversation that took place between us shook me to my shoes.

Please take me to Hughson's Tavern.

Why would you want to go there, Miss? It's been closed for weeks.

That can't be. I'm here from Newfoundland to visit my friend. She's staying there.

There's been some trouble here you may not have heard about. Hughson's is closed. The owners have been — well, they died, Miss.

Oh, how awful. I wonder where Peggy went. Then take me to the New York Hotel. That is where she works.

There is no such place, I'm afraid.

My anxiety pressed around my head like ice tongs. Dizzily, I grabbed the open carriage to keep from falling. Was her letter all lies? But why?

Not to put my nose in your business, Ma'am, but might this Peggy you're referring to be a lovely young lady with bright red hair? Peggy Kerry?

Yes! Yes, that's her!

A hint of relief …

Oh, Miss, I'm so sorry. I think I need to take you to City Hall.

City Hall? Why City Hall?

That's where the dungeon is.

That's absurd? There must be some mistake.

A lot of people think so, Ma'am. But that's where Miss Kerry is nonetheless.

His words were chipped into my brain as into a stone at the cemetery. There they remain, and always shall. I am grateful he did not reveal more. I would have swooned entirely.

The man in charge was named Daniel Horsmanden. Visitors were not permitted in the dungeon, he told me. But because I had traveled so far he would make an exception. I sensed he had taken an instant liking to me; I could not say why. He ordered a constable to escort me to Peggy's cell, so I would not be bothered by the other prisoners. The constable opened the door to her cell, then stood away from it.

Silence.

Framed by the door in my blue dress and blue bonnet and white stockings, I was an apparition, she would tell me later.

Silence. Staring.

She was standing in the center of this forlorn cell, her tangled hair more brown than red, pregnant as a horse beneath her wrinkled grey shift, she was … I had no word for it. Nausea made flesh. This I would never tell her.

Who it was told me she would be hanged after the child was born? I don't recall. It might have been the judge. It could have been the constable. Or else the dungeon itself whispering through its stench. I must have fainted on hearing the news, but I do not recall doing so.

Motionless we stood. Motionless and staring. My arms and legs felt wrapped in fishing wire with which we used to repair the nets. The slightest movement would slash my skin.

It was she who took the first small step, her soiled feet bare, her eyes wide, like a blind woman's. I thought she was about to collapse, yet I could not move. With a wrenching effort I broke free of the wire and rushed to her, engulfed her with my arms, embraced her, pressed my lips to her cheek. She had no life. She merely let me. Then she too snapped her bindings and pressed her face, her nose, into my shoulder. Together we began to sob. Our sobs became violent. Knees weakening, we could barely stand. We could only lean against one another.

Our vocal cords had been cut. We could not speak.

My belly was pressing too hard against hers. Against her child. I inched back, touched my fingers to her forehead, her hair. Lightly untangled invisible knots. She kissed me then, on my lips. Whispered one word, softly.

Nora.

New tears rolled down my cheeks. I could not say her name. Just took her hand in mine. She played with my fingers, as if we were children.

Somehow we found our way to the stone bench in her cell, no more than four feet away. We sat together, holding hands. It may have been an hour that we did no speak. Or only a minute. With no daylight visible in the four-walled cell, time did not pass. I was not about to ask her what had happened. She would tell me when she was ready.

She inhaled deeply, seemed to be gathering all her strength with which to speak. She managed four words.

I'm sorry I lied.

My response was as short and as weak as hers. *You had good reason.*

You don't understand, she said. *I was wishing you would die rather than have you see the truth.*

Well, sometimes I'm ornery.

She lifted my hand to her lips, kissed the tips of my fingers one by one.

I became aware of other prisoners, all Negroes, gazing at us from far back, through the open door. The constable saw it as well, closed the door, indicating he would remain outside. Hands on her oversized belly, Peggy breathed deeply again, let it out, once again as if summoning all her strength with which to speak. Still holding my hand. This time she spoke five words, surely the most painful of her life.

Will you keep my baby?

No thought was required. No thought was possible. What's mine is yours, what's yours is mine.

Of course.

She squeezed my hand in silent gratitude.

The constable knocked on the door. He warned that I must leave, that City Hall was locking up.

We'll talk tomorrow, I said.

You'll come tomorrow?
I'll come every day. What do you think?
The judge will let you?
I think he likes me.
So you're the one! Peggy said.
We collapsed into giggles shot with tears. Held each other, hugged.
My best friend was back.

Outside, the young man was waiting by his carriage. He'd had
no other business this afternoon. He carried my luggage from outside
the judge's office. Merchants were locking doors up the street, ending
the work day. When I told the driver I needed a place to stay, he
recommended the Black Horse Tavern. *Best food in town, and a short walk
from here.* I told him to take me there.

With my sleepless nights and lonely agony I shall not try your
patience. The next morning, asking around the hotel for a midwife, I was
directed to a small, neat house not far away, the home of two sisters, free
Negroes. The midwife, Luanne, was tall and thin. Her sister, Roxanne,
a wet nurse, was short and stout. I engaged their services for when they
would be needed.

Give the baby directly to me, not to the mother, Roxanne said. *It's not healthy
the baby switching teats after a week.*

The whole town seemed to know Peggy's sentence.
We'll do what the mother wants.
I'm telling you …
We'll do what the mother wants, I said again.

Before going to City Hall I walked to a bake shop called Vaarck's,
which a waitress at the Black Horse had recommended, and bought a
box of assorted fruit tarts. I gave one to each of the two constables on
duty, left two for the judge, who was not in his office, and took the rest
to Peggy's cell for us to share. I must admit, even amid the dungeon
stench they were far tastier than those we served at Neal's Cafe. If I were
planning to return home I would have to ask for their secret. But it did
not appear I would be returning to Carey any time soon – not if Peggy's
baby lived.

She was more relaxed today, perhaps because I told her of the
midwife and the wet nurse who would be attending her. While she let me
comb her stringy hair she told me all that had transpired to land her in
this hellish place. I don't think she held anything back out of shame or
modesty.

I did not want to become a prostitute, of course, she said, finding a bit of
tart that had dropped from her lips to her lap. *But I was desperate for money.*

And the fact that my clients were coloreds was only circumstance. My room was at Hughson's. That's where the Negro slaves gathered in the evenings to drink and talk. At first I was timid. I imagined what the folks at home would think — Aunt Dottie, and especially you. But once I settled into it, a strange thing happened. I realized that I would rather sleep with these slaves than with rich white men, lawyers and bankers who were bored with their oh-so-proper wives. I have no idea why, but that's how I felt.

You don't know why? I can tell you why. Because of that dead baby you found in the ice. That was your first day here, right?

My first hour. What's that got to do with anything?

I set down her comb and fluffed her hair. It was a big improvement, she looked more like herself again. My red-haired angel. I'd started with a lemon tart, now I sat beside her and stuffed my face with squishy blueberry. Neatness be damned.

Sweetie, listen. The baby was mulatto. Hughson told you the mother must have been a Negro slave, and the father white. That meant the baby was born a slave. What would cause a mother to kill her own infant? You must have asked yourself that. There was only one answer. Because she did not want to raise her son only to see him ripped away from her and sold off somewhere. Or if he was not sent away, she'd watch him spend his life working in the fields from dawn to dusk for all of his days. A life of torture. You'd never thought much about slaves, just as I haven't. We never saw a Negro in Newfoundland. There were none. But through this mother who left her child on the ice to die you understood how terrible the life of a slave must be. So when you were servicing them — I'll use that harsh word — you at least were giving them pleasure. Something for them to live for once a week, or however often they could afford it. It was not charity, you needed the money, but it did have that positive side. I think some part of you understood that, even if in that judge's eyes you were the lowest of the low.

She looked at me, saying nothing. Clearly she had not thought of this before. And perhaps she shouldn't have.

You're going to be a good writer, Nora.

We'll see about that.

No, I won't see ...

I'm sorry ...

I won't see, but I can tell already. You think in ways I don't. Ways most people don't.

Peggy, you didn't set any fires. You didn't urge any fires. Even Mary Burton didn't claim you did, am I right? So why is that bastard killing you? I'll tell you why. Because you fucked Negroes. Jesus! There has to be a way to get this stopped.

Only the governor can grant a pardon.

And?

Horsmanden has to recommend mercy. He won't.

Has the man no conscience? No shame? Shit. I should have poisoned his tarts.

At least I believe in God now

I heard a voice say that. Was it Peggy's voice? How could that be? If she intended to astonish me, she succeeded.

How can you say that, in this place, at this time?

I slipped to my knees and prayed, she said. *Prayed for someone to come and take my baby. And here you are.*

No God brought me. A boat called Labrador brought me. No prayers summoned me. Your strange letter summoned me.

Perhaps God wrote my letter.

Then God is a liar. That I can believe. And Mary Burton is a priest.

You're taking me back to our sandy arguments among the capelin.

That was my intent.

She hugged me, I hugged her, who could discern the difference?

When her time arrives, can't the constables carry her out into the sun, into a secluded courtyard perhaps, with perhaps one miserable tree? No. Her confinement will be in this cell, on a soiled straw mat, with rat shit where two walls meet. The time is now. I pay a constable to fetch Luanne and Roxanne – the birth sisters, I have come to think of them. The mid-wife carries what she needs in a canvas satchel. The wet-nurse carries all she needs in her blouse.

Moans from Peggy, lying inches off the concrete floor. Groans. Cries. I imagine the black prisoners crowding the outside wall of the cell, listening intently. Or with glee. I tell the wet-nurse I will pay her for the week, so long as she remains available. *That's nice,* she says, *but the baby …*

The baby will be fine, I say.

The midwife kneels between Peggy's spread knees, lifts them, inspects. Soon, she says Soon. Leans forward.

Now, push. Push!

I'm pushing! Peggy bleats. *I can feel him. He's stuck. Come on out you rascal! He doesn't know he's free. You're free, dammit! Free! Come on out!*

Push!

The midwife spits a word I do not know. A curse? African? The wet-nurse pushes me aside, drops to the ground, reaches under Peggy's raised knee, muttering, seems to be grabbing something I cannot see, pulls something out, swings it against the concrete wall. *Splat.* The rat falls dead to the floor.

My head spins, I sink to the stone bench, put my head between my knees to keep the blood in my brain, to keep from fainting. Mid-wife and wet-nurse are chattering African words.

Push!

What's wrong? Peggy asks. *What happened?*

Nothing is wrong, the mid-wife says. *You're doing fine. The baby is doing fine. Push!*

They love to drink the newborn wet, the wet-nurse says.

Quiet!

He knew not to come out yet.

He knew nothing. Push. Push. Good, he's coming now. One or two more. Push. Good girl. Here he comes. You have a baby! Let me look. A boy!

None of this am I seeing, just hearing, bent, my head still down. I raise my head slowly, look at Peggy on her mat. Her face is washed in sweat. She is smiling.

A boy, she murmurs. *I knew.*

In the flickering light of the lamp Luanne is cleaning the infant with wet cloths she brought in her satchel. Peggy though smiling looks exhausted. A terrible thought: would it be better to die in childbirth or one week later by the noose? Anxiously I look at Luanne. *She will be fine,* the mid-wife says, and places the mulatto boy on Peggy's creamy breast. I never tasted hers, nor she mine. Despite our fantasies while wrestling among the capelin, we never dared.

James, Peggy murmurs, sounding content as the infant sucks.

The little prince. To me he will be Jamie.

I need fresh air, badly. With mother and child sleeping, Roxanne and Luanne standing guard, I leave the dungeon, climb the stairs, slowly, holding on to the rail. Outside, the relief is almost painful. I walk to the Black Horse, have a cool bath, put on clean clothes, manage a cup of soup for lunch, which is all my tense stomach will accept. As I leave the tavern to return to Peggy I am surprised to find standing right outside the Inn a gleaming coach, polished wood, oak I believe, a slightly swaybacked grey horse waiting to pull it, a man, probably the driver, standing near the horse drinking what smells like beer. A moment later a young girl emerges from a door across the street wearing the brightest yellow dress I have ever seen, with a matching bonnet. She is perhaps fifteen years old, no more than sixteen. Crossing the street, smiling, she speaks briefly to the driver, climbs into the coach with a rustle of petticoats. Who is this girl in yellow, alone, no parents visible, acting as if she owns the coach and the driver both? Is there a story to be written about her? Surely there is – at some future time when my mind reveals to me a satisfying answer, the answer to the question of where she is going, alone in her finery, in the heart of the city, on this sunny afternoon. That is the question that will lend the story its necessary tension. The driver mounts his buckboard, clucks to the horse, which begins to walk lazily up the road, carrying the girl toward what gay rendezvous?

Returning to the stinking dungeon is like having a return ticket to hell. In her cell, as Peggy lies on her mat, awake but heavy lidded, the infant sleeping on her chest, the slight smile on her lips so beatific that surely St. Peter must have made a mistake.

Her expression changes when she sees me. *I'm such a terrible person,* she says.

What are you talking about?

You've been here two, three, four days — I can't even tell in this place — and not once have I asked how Aunt Dottie is doing. Or your parents. Or my father.

My first impulse is to lie. But why lie to someone about to die?

My parents are fine. Dottie is in good health. But your father is driving her to despair. His drinking is worse than ever. He doesn't go out to sea anymore. He drinks day and night, sleeps wherever he happens to fall. In front of the house, in back of the house, even in the road, and has to be moved away so carriages can pass.

How awful for her.

But that gives me an idea.

What?

I'll do it! I'll write to her tonight. I think she still has money hidden away from her teaching days. I'll tell her to sail down here. She can live with me, help with the baby. Your baby — he's almost her grandson. It will give her a new life — and would help me. What do I know about raising a child?

And where did I disappear? What will you tell her?

In the letter? That you birthed a healthy boy — and then you died. Like your mother. The rest is too much to explain in a note. Later, when she's here, I can tell her the truth. I wish she could get here—

She can't get here in time. That's just as well.

Two sharp raps on the door were followed into the room by a cake, in the hands of a constable. The frosting was half chocolate, half white.

One of Vaarck the baker's girls just brought this over, he said. *In celebration of the baby.*

Goodness, news travels quickly here.

Peggy corrected me. *Or gossip.*

Setting the cake on the stone bench I looked about for a knife, but found none. The constable removed one from a sheath at his belt, wiped it across his sleeve, handed it to me. I used it to cut slices for the guard, for Luanne and Roxanne, who were still there — the midwife to make sure Peggy remained stable, the wet-nurse to keep Jamie content. And for Peggy and myself, of course. We held the slices in our hands, broke pieces off with our fingers. The mice and rats would have a midnight supper with the crumbs.

John Vaark is so thoughtful, Peggy said. *Did you meet him when you bought those tarts yesterday?*

No. I was served by a large Negro man. He didn't say a word.

Zion. He has no tongue. But he has a big heart.

If he were in a story, I said, perhaps foolishly, *he would be a metaphor for what is happening here. The unspeakable.*

I don't understand that. No matter. He's a good man. Nora, after I'm … gone, please show the baby to Vaarck. I'm sure he would love that. Zion, too.

Of course.

When it was time to leave for the day, Roxanne insisted on taking little Jamie home with her. *He can't stay in this dungeon at night,* she said. *It's too dirty. With rats, flies. He could die. We keep a clean house. A clean crib. I'll bring him back in the morning.*

Peggy closed her eyes, kissed his forehead as he slept on her chest, reluctantly handed Roxanne the infant.

The sun was still bright outside. Instead of going back to my lonely room I went to Vaarck's Bake Shop, introduced myself, thanked Mr. Vaarck for sending the cake. He was a thin man in work clothes whose face looked worn, perhaps, as Peggy had suggested, from losing his wife recently. We talked a bit, he asked where I was staying. When I told him the Black Horse he offered to walk back with me, which he did. His loneliness was apparent when he asked if we might have supper together. Facing an empty room upstairs, I was glad to oblige. He turned out to have a fine intelligence and an appetite for plain talk. Midway through the meal, a good lamb stew, I confronted him with what Peggy had questioned: How could he hate slavery and still own slaves?

My wife and I started the business ourselves years ago, he said. *She was a fine baker. We discovered early on that we needed help – but we had no money to pay wages. I did not want to use slave labor, but I talked myself into it. These people had already been brought here as slaves. If I didn't purchase them, someone else would – and might treat them badly. I vowed to treat my slaves better than most. Zion was the first. He came very cheap at auction. No one wanted him because he had no speech. Also, they assumed he must be terribly rebellious to have been mutilated. I assume he rebelled against beatings, perhaps. But he's worked out fine. Every few years, as the business grew, I had to add another girl in the kitchen. We have six now. When their work is done for the day they have complete freedom to do whatever they want.*

Except leave, I said.

Yes. Except leave. But I doubt they would. At Vaarck's they have room and board, and perhaps most important, no one is assaulting them. Where would they find a better situation? Maybe I'm a hypocrite. Maybe I'm rationalizing my way to innocence. There's no doubt I'm part of an ugly system. But only the wealthy can forego slaves and survive in business.

Yet they all have them, don't they?

Most do, yes.

He paused to break off a chunk of bread with which to mop up the last of his stew.

Somehow, Nora – may I call you Nora?– I don't think I have convinced you of my rectitude.

I'm in no position to make judgments, I said. *I'll have to think about it.*

Perhaps we could continue this discussion another time.

I would like that.

Before I leave I have a thought. A terrible thought, but it must be faced.

With the baby born, Peggy will be … her sentence will be carried out next Tuesday. That will be an awful day for me. It might be wise for us to comfort one another, not to sit alone.

Perhaps.

Is there no hope of her being spared?

I do not think so, no.

Tears welled up. I could not stop them.

When the exact time is set I will let you know. And will send a carriage for you half an hour before. Will that work?

I nodded, pressing my handkerchief to my face, unable to reply.

In the dungeon the next morning, perhaps for the first time in our lives, Peggy and I had little to say to one another. I suppose I should not have been surprised, with the shadow of the noose hanging over the cell. To end an awkward silence I asked if she wanted to hear my theory about her father. Gazing anxiously at the door, no doubt wondering where Roxanne was with the baby, she told me to go ahead, so I did.

I think your father was afraid of the water, I began. *I think he was afraid he would drown.*

What? He was a fisherman.

I know. People assume he began drinking when your mother died. But he used to drink in excess long before that. Aunt Dottie says so. So does my mother. Lots of the men returned from a day at sea with a few beers in them. But your father imbibed not beer but Irish whiskey before he went out on his boat. Why did he do that? I think you become addicted to drink when you are afraid of something. On land he drank as well, we know that. Why? Because he was afraid someone might discover his weakness. I don't know what caused the fear of drowning in him. Maybe you can be born with that. Maybe something happened to him as a child. But imagine growing up in a place like Carey, where most every boy is expected to become a fisherman, and having this fear in you. He was like a terrified slave – a slave to this weakness within him. When your mother died he was not terribly upset, he was drunk all that day, as Dottie told you. Perhaps she had discovered his secret, and he was afraid she might reveal it. Nor did he grieve over your dead twin. Now she would not be a threat to him as she grew up. And you – he never let you get close, he never showed love for you, he kept you at a distance, for the same reason.

Is there a point to all this?

I think that's what drove you down here. You followed Billy Reilly even after you knew he was living with that widow woman. If you had love from your father you might have been content to stay in Carey, to wait for a better man to come along. But you were desperate for affection, so you came after Billy. All of that led to this situation. It's just a theory – not as clear as the baby in the ice – but I think I may be right.

Is that what writers do, make up theories like that?

Sort of.

Then maybe you should stay in the café.

She did not say those words, but I read them in her face. Or thought I did. And was much disturbed.

She reached deep into her pocket, pulled out a coin, showed it to me.

What's that?

It's not as shiny as it used to be.

A shilling in a cod. That's impossible, of course.

I know. But it's all I have of him.

She dropped it back into her pocket.

What about what your father did to you?

I have no theory. Perhaps our own parents remain a mystery.

She was looking at the door again. Our attention was distracted when Roxanne bustled in, holding little James in a blue blanket. On her face was a great smile.

What is so funny? I asked as she handed the infant to Peggy. She had to have fed him during the night. He seemed none the worse for switching breasts.

Have you heard the talk in the streets? People are saying Judge Horseman is a fool. That there never was a Negro plot. It's in the newspaper. The Burton girl has accused five of the richest men in the city – white men – of being behind the plot. Everyone knows that can't be true. People are saying Mary Burton is a liar – and if she's lying now, maybe she's been lying from the beginning. Men are gathering outside the building, demanding that the remaining slaves in here be freed. Maybe they'll free Peggy as well.

My heart accelerated. Peggy kissed the baby. She did not smile, did not speak.

I'm going up to see, I said, and hurried out of the cell and up the stairs.

Perhaps a dozen men were gathered in the street outside the main entrance. Others were streaming to join them from both directions. I spotted John Vaarck and went and stood beside him. Shouts were being hurled at a second story window.

Mary Burton is a liar!

The conspiracy was in your head, Horsmanden!

Give us back our property!

I asked John to what property they were referring.

Their slaves. There are about one hundred and thirty in the dungeon who have not yet been brought to trial.

Free the innocent! someone shouted,

Another man tossed a small rock at the large vertical window. The window cracked but did not come crashing down. Constables came rushing out of City Hall and moved the men back several feet. A small riot seemed imminent. The window opened and Judge Horsmanden, wearing a fine brown suit, stepped onto a small balcony. He held up his hand for silence. The shouting stopped.

Gentlemen, the judge said. *Some civility, please. There is no need to hurl missiles. You are merely anticipating our imminent deed.*

What in God's name does that mean? someone yelled.

The Common Council has been meeting this morning. In the dungeon below are one-hundred and twenty-four prisoners, slaves, who have been awaiting trial until more evidence was found against them. Since no such evidence has been found, the investigation of this heinous plot has been declared ended. The charges against these prisoners will be dropped. They will be freed, a few at a time, as soon as you sign receipts for them. They must be taken into your charge forthwith, or they will be held in the dungeon until they are.

It's about time, someone yelled.

It's way past time, another cried.

Shouts of approval went up from many of the men. I could not help thinking, What about Peggy? It was not my place to ask. But John Vaarck did.

What about Peggy Kerry?

Right, free Peggy, several men yelled. *Mary Burton lied!*

Horsmanden held up his hand for silence.

Peggy Kerry is a different kettle of fish, he said. *She has been found guilty of a capital crime against King and Country. She was sentenced to be hanged from the neck until dead, one week after the birth of her child. That child, a boy, was delivered yesterday, quite safely, I am happy to report. Therefore her sentence shall be carried out as ordered, at noon by the clock, one week from today.*

Free her! Free her! rose a mass of shouts. *Burton lied! Show this woman mercy!*

Again he raised his hand.

We must follow the law. I have no power to free this woman, or to reduce her sentence. Only the Governor can do that.

He needs your recommendation.

That is correct. But Kerry has been asked many times to confess to her crimes. If she did — if she does — then mercy might be in order. But lacking a confession, it is not.

That's backwards, I whispered to John. *If she says she is guilty she will be shown mercy. If she maintains her innocence she will be killed?*

Horsmanden is desperate for a confession, John whispered back. *He wants to be governor. His chances right now are nil. He's a laughingstock. Many believe he executed mostly innocent people. If he can get Peggy to confess, he'll claim that as proof that Burton was not lying, that all of the hanged and the burned were guilty. Without that his career is over.*

John turned his face back up to the window.

Judge, he shouted. *Can you guarantee that if Kerry confesses, she will be allowed to live?*

Mr. Vaarck, as I have said, that decision will be the Governor's. But I do have certain persuasive powers with him. So I will state publicly now that yes, that is a fair assumption.

Excitedly, I grabbed John's hand. At once, embarrassed, I let it drop.

Peggy can live! I said. My heart was joyous.

If she so chooses, John murmured.

I hurried down to the dungeon with the good news. The walls were bouncing with song and dance. The prisoners had heard they would be freed, were singing what must have been African chants, flinging their arms wide, spinning about. As I threaded my way through, one of them smiling broadly took hold of my arms and whirled me around, my feet coming off the ground, set me down and clapped in rhythm. Roxanne was peering out the cell door, watching. Peggy sat on the stone bench, Jamie in her arms.

You're going to live! I tell her, kissing her cheek, squeezing her shoulder. *All you have to do is confess!*

That's all? Her voice is soft, flat, unemotional.

That's all!

Nora, do you know what I would be confessing to? That I instigated the slaves to burn down the city, to kill the white men, to rape their wives.

So what? It's only words. Words don't matter. You'll be alive to raise little James.

You want to be a writer, and you say that words don't matter?

People will understand why you said them. That they aren't true.

How will people know that? Some mother I would be, with that confession coloring my life.

You have a week, Peggy. Think about it. About the baby. You're not thinking straight right now. Here, let me hold him for awhile. So he gets used to me.

She handed me little Jamie. I meant only what I said, but there could have been a deeper reason. For her to feel in her bones what it would like to give him up. In every word spoken hung the shadow of the noose.

The infant's face, his tiny cocoa hands, pressed against the breast of my dress. Not as inviting, I imagined, as the unfettered nipples of his mother, of the nurse. His eyes were closed and I closed mine, sensed all of him. Was transported by his little breaths to visions, sounds, smells; to Newfoundland. The first silver sword of the dawning sun was stabbing the steeple of the church, sending its shadow down the mountain, bending it across the dirt road, bending it down the cliff to the beach, straining across the sand to the sea. The orange sun at eventide curling into a perfect blazing ball before drowning itself for another day. The cawl of the seabirds for their mates, if that's what they were cawling for. The hum of dragonflies in the wind. The gurgle of baby waves upon the silty sand. The sizzle of bacon on the grill, a moment later its saliva-inducing smell. The howl of the dog in the night. The tickle of Peggy's hair on my skin and the scent it leaves behind. The sheen of the surface of the just-polished bar, in which I can see my face. The stars, so far, so near. Could a child emerging between my own sticky thighs paint greater ecstasies? Perhaps some day I would know.

A foppish presence enters the cell. Daniel Horsmanden.

Peggy Kerry, to put your soul at rest, do you have anything to confess?

My lids fly open, find her lips, read them against the sound of the chanting slaves. Hoping.

Only that I am innocent.

He turns on his heel and leaves without a word.

The next day he asks the same. She says nothing.

And the next.

I ask myself what I would do in her place. I cannot put myself in her place.

Each day is lit only by the flame of his arrival. And snuffed by the silence of her response.

I do not badger her. Not in the days before the noose.

She is down to one last chance. At the foot of the gallows he will ask her to confess. He always does, I've been told. And sometimes prisoners do, to save their skins. And sometimes they are hanged regardless, I've been told.

We hug goodbye, mingling silent tears on sticky cheeks. I leave, and the wet nurse with the child. Peggy stays behind, alone.

✳ ✳ ✳

I dreamed that night we were back on the beach, the sea water salting our skin, wrestling among the capelin.

✳ ✳ ✳

They hanged Peggy Kerry in the rain.

No sun was visible. Gloomy clouds reflected the mood of the city.

An hour before the hanging a light rain began to fall.

Half an hour before the hanging a coach came for me, as John Vaarck had said it would.

To the Little Collect pond? the coachman asked.

What's that?

That's where lots of folks are going this morning. That's where the gallows is.

Take me to the home of John Vaarck. Do you know where that is?

Yes, ma'am.

He met me at the door. Our fingers brushed lightly, perhaps accidentally. We sat on a settee in the parlor. The rain fell harder,

He looked at his watch. I half expected lightning to split the sky, thunder to bellow. But it did not.

He checked his watch again.

A human roar rose, bounced off the clouds, passed over the house like a Bible story, settled over the city.

Perhaps they are cheering because she was spared! I said with some excitement.

More likely they are cheering because she was hanged, John said.

✳ ✳ ✳

Our new house – actually an old house we repaired – came with adjacent slave quarters. We both appreciate the irony.

After Peggy's death, despair kept us captive for six months or more. John, still mourning his wife and Caesar as well, worked as never before to fulfill two of his lifetime dreams. With the city growing rapidly, new homes being built everywhere, he obtained a sizable loan from a bank to expand his business. First he opened a second bake shop on the north side, which replaced door front deliveries. Soaring profits enabled him to fulfill his first life's plan: one by one, beginning with Zion, he set his slaves free, and hired them on as paid employees. None of them left. He slept much better, gained weight he had lost, his sallow aspect brightened. He hoped that freeing his workers would set an example, that other merchants would follow. The bank managers were horrified that he was using part of his loan to free his slaves. They feared that if other merchants felt pressured to follow suit, this would increase everyone's costs and wreck the economy of the city. Thus far, to our knowledge, not a single merchant has.

When Aunt Dottie arrived we cried a lot together. For several days I feared her mind had snapped; she sat long hours without speaking. I felt like doing the same as well; by killing Peggy they had amputated half of me. Little Jamie was my anesthesia, our savior. By some miracle he was a happy child, smiling much of the time. He seemed to have left despair in the womb. With Dottie joining myself and the wet nurse and Jamie, the small house I had rented grew crowded. John bought this rundown place north of the city, which overlooked the river and made Dottie and I feel more at home. Together we fixed it up, painting and plastering and caulking those separations through which the wind blew, and furnished it one room at a time. John named Zion manager of the business. It worked out fine, John going into town just two days a week, to visit each shop and deal with any problems.

If freeing his slaves had been one goal, he now was able to fulfill his other dream: to try his hand at oil painting. He converted one room of the old slave quarters into a painting studio, filled it with tubes of paint, turpentine, canvas and easels. He paints there only in foul weather, however. He much prefers working *en plein air.* (That's French – Peggy would be proud of me.) He's done many canvases of different aspects of the North River: at dawn, at sunset and so forth, and people have begun buying them. He does not charge much, but the fact that people enjoy them gives him much satisfaction.

Dottie and Roxanne (until Jamie was weaned) and I took care of the cooking and cleaning. And of Jamie, of course, though John stopped by often to play with him. Of late I have fixed up the other slave quarters into a writing space. After putting Jamie down for a nap I disappear into that room and into my imagination. When he awakens Dottie explains that mama is working. He has come to accept that. He is three years old now, and runs about the front lawn like the free spirit he is, always under my watchful eye or Dottie's, of course. For his third birthday John bought him a pony – a small piebald, black and white. Right now he can only sit astride it with one of us holding him, but he will grow into it. A story of a boy and a horse unblocked my brain, and I have started writing up a storm. My goal for now is modest – to make each story better than the last. They all go into my treasure trunk, where they will remain until I decide they are good enough.

Just now I am watching through the window as Jamie romps about. It is Sunday, his favorite day, and he knows it is Sunday, because every few minutes he glances toward the dirt road that leads to our house. When he hears the creaking of wooden wheels he scurries up the road a bit – there he goes now – and the cart stops, long dark hands lift him, and he snuggles into his favorite place on earth, the soft upholstered lap of Grandpa Fez, from whom he will hear a story or two, before the day is out, of a different, leafy place far away.

Sometimes while listening to these stories Jamie will point to a treetop and say *Bird! Bird!* I ask him where the bird is, because I do not see it. *Bird!* he says again, pointing. *Big green bird.* Still I see nothing.

The one subject I shall never write about is Jamie's father. A king become a slave. The drama inherent in such a tale is false gold. Who would believe it?

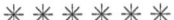

Afterword: The Names and Sentences

Thirty-four persons were executed during the alleged Negro Conspiracy in New York colony in 1741. That compares with 20 executions in the much better known Salem Witch Trials of 1692-1693.

Those convicted in New York, and their fates, are listed below. In the case of slaves with duplicate names, the owners are cited in parentheses.

Hanged and Gibbeted:
Caesar (Vaarck)
John Hughson

Hanged:
Peggy Kerry
Sarah Hughson (the mother)
John Ury
Prince (Auboyneau)
Cato (Cowley)
Othello
Prince (Duane)
Harry
Tony
Cato (alias Toby)
York
Frank
Juan de la Silva
Cato (Shurmur)
Venture
Fortune (Vanderspeigle)
Galloway
Quack
Fortune (Walton)

Burned:
Francis
Albany (Carpenter)
Robin (Chambers)
Cook
Cuffee (Gomez)
Ben (Marshall)
Dr. Harry
Caesar (Peck)
Cuffee (Philipse)
Quack (Roosevelt)
Quash (Rutgers)
Curacoa Dick
Will (Ward)

Acknowledgements

A native of New York City, I did all 16 years of my schooling there, from kindergarten through graduate school, and never once heard of the alleged "Negro Conspiracy" of 1741, or its violent denouement. I did not even know there had been slaves in New York colony; slavery was presented as a southern practice.

Several years ago, a student in a writing workshop I teach in Santa Fe, Sheila M. Stalder, told me of the terrible events of 1741. Also a New Yorker, she had happened to come across papers relating to the "conspiracy" in an old bookshop in California. Intrigued, she began to research those events, and decided to write a non-fiction book about them. But a professor at Harvard, Jill Lepore, beat her to the punch, publishing a historical account called New York Burning: *Liberty, Slavery and Conspiracy in Eighteenth-Century Manhattan.* (Alfred A. Knopf, 2005.)

I suggested that Sheila make use of her research by writing the story as a novel; Lepore's book was accurate history, but lacked the emotional impact that could come from bringing the participants to life in fictional form. Sheila, however, had by then moved on to other projects, and was not interested. Instead she encouraged me to write such a novel, which I was eager to attempt. The result is this book.

Lepore's history served as ground zero for the novel. I am grateful for her solid research into a story that needed to be told. But the lives of the characters, which account for more than two thirds of the novel, emerged solely from my imagination.

Several other publications enriched my work. Prominent among these was The Door of No Return: *The History of Cape Coast Castle and the Atlantic Save Trade*, by William St. Clair (BlueBridge Books, 2007.)

Surprisingly helpful in a vivid way was a children's book called *Bound for America: The Forced Migration of Africans to the New World,* by James Haskins and Kathleen Benson, with illustrations by Floyd Cooper (Harper Collins,1999.) Cooper's full color, full page paintings bring to life the horror of the slave trade in ways that words can only approximate.

No court reporter was present during the trials of those convicted. But Daniel Horsmanden made thorough notes, and wrote a book after the trials, published in 1744. It had the lengthy title: *A Journal of the Proceedings in The Detection of the Conspiracy Formed By Some White People, in Conjunction with Negro and other Slaves, for Burning the City of New-York in America, and Murdering the Inhabitants.*

The journal was not a commercial success, but lives on as a boon to the historical record. Most of it can be found on the Internet.

My depiction of life in a Newfoundland fishing village was given flesh by the book *Canada's Incredible Coasts* (National Geographic Society, 1991) particularly an historical essay on Newfoundland by Tom Melham. The discovery of beaches piled waist-high with living capelin, and the fact this region was horror central to the bludgeoning of baby seals for their fur, added both subtle humor and cruel symbolism to the story.

During the shameful downheaval of the publishing industry in the past two decades, in which once-respected publishers have wallowed in fifty shades of greed, a myriad of small presses has attempted to fill in the high ground. Among these is Combustoica, based in Camarillo, California, which has published my five most recent novels. One of those, *The Origin of Sorrow*, is ever so slowly making its way around the world on the laughter and tears of readers. Now comes *1741*. The events of that year in New York City deserve much wider recognition than they have thus far received. I want to thank Combustoica (okay, it's a strange name, so what?) for dragging a so-called "conspiracy" from a dark corner of American history into necessary light. You're a good man, Nat Gertler.

Books by Robert Mayer

Fiction

Superfolks

The Execution

Midge and Decker

The Grace of Shortstops

Sweet Salt

The Search

I, JFK

The Origin of Sorrow *

The Ferret's Tale *

Danse Macabre *

Confessions of a Rain God *

Eyes *

Non-Fiction

The Dreams of Ada

Notes of a Baseball Dreamer
(First published as *Baseball
And Men's Lives*)

* Available in print and e-book at www.Combustoica.com

www.ingramcontent.com/pod-product-compliance
Lightning Source LLC
Chambersburg PA
CBHW020757250626
47155CB00003B/1110